A cottage set deep in a forest outside a small English village is the back-drop for the beginning of an enchanting love story. Ms. Misencik brings to life the spirit of passion and adventure in every single page of this novel. When Jessica, a ravishing beauty, meets Jacob, an arrogant duke, their tumultuous pairing will take you on a ride throughout England that will have you turning the page almost before you are finished with the previous one. Join them in their journey where a pre-arranged marriage almost certainly cannot survive the onslaught of treacherous deceit, heart-breaking misconceptions, and even murder. This novel will have you excusing yourself from the dinner table early. It is beautifully written with words that become canvas portraits for the reader to see as well as read. This novel has all the potential of being a #1 best-seller; riveting and filled with life. You won't want to miss a single word.

—Darrel Day,
Author of *Abduction* and
Until Death Do We Meet

Gavin —
I'm so glad we've reconnected! Wishing you all the best — Denise

Bound by Honor

By

Denise Misencik

Denise Misencik
2008

PublishAmerica
Baltimore

First printing

ISBN: 1-4137-5910-6
PUBLISHED BY PUBLISHAMERICA, LLLP
www.publishamerica.com
Baltimore

Printed in the United States of America

To my loving, patient husband and daughter, and to all those who urged me onward.

Thank you.

Prologue

"I have no idea how I'm going to do this without you, Father. But I promise you, I'll do my best."

Jessica squared her shoulders and took a deep breath, holding it for a moment to suppress the sobs that were so close to taking control of her body.

The musty smell of damp earth filled her lungs with heaviness. Beside her, the small boy reached for her hand to comfort her. She smiled through the tears that ran silently down her cheeks and gently squeezed his fingers in acknowledgment.

They both knelt down on their knees and sat in silence for several minutes. Finally, Jessica placed the small bunch of wildflowers she'd gathered on the two-day-old grave of her father. "I'll do my best," she repeated.

One sob escaped as she rose and pulled the young boy to her side. Looking down at his worried little face she said, "We'll be fine, sweetling, I'll see to that." But even as she spoke the words she wondered just how she'd make them come true.

As strong as you are, Jesse, you'll need some help eventually. Don't be as stubborn as I've been. Don't turn it away without careful consideration. I love you my darling girl, and although you'll likely be angry with me for what I've done please understand that it's for your own good. Yours and the boy's. I love you, Jess.

Those had been her father's final words. For the two days since his death, she'd heard them repeating over and over in her head until she thought she'd go mad.

"I love you too, Father," she whispered, still no closer to figuring out what he'd meant.

Angry? Why would she be angry? She could never remember even one moment of anger towards her father.

Jessica sighed heavily and turned towards the rocky trail that led down the hill into the woods where their cottage was nestled safely in the trees. As she picked her way slowly down the path she knew so well, she turned and looked back over her shoulder at the burial site she knew her father would have approved of. It was the place where he had watched the sun rise on almost every clear morning. He would rest well there.

The boy trotted along in front of her, looking back now and then as if checking to make sure she was still there.

Jessica quickened her pace and caught up to him, taking him by the hand and turning him to face her. She knelt before him. "Sweetling, I know you've been through some very frightening times recently, and have lost so much. But I promise you, you won't lose me. Never fear for that, hm? We'll be together no matter what."

Chapter 1

"Martin, I'm not sure who the bigger fool is, my father or me, for agreeing to this ridiculous plan. But since I am the one who's soaked to the skin and freezing my tail feathers off, I will have to assume the title will be mine," Jacob said, pulling the collar of his oiled coat tighter around his neck.

Martin snorted and shook his head, sending drops of water scattering.

Jacob smiled crookedly thinking that it was perhaps a good thing that Martin, his roan stallion, couldn't actually tell him what he thought of this mad journey.

The wild beauty of the English countryside was lost on Jacob as they trudged onward. The road, if you could call it that, was muddy and slick; a scar through the green, rolling hills. Luckily, Martin was very sure-footed, allowing Jacob to indulge in his thoughts which were completely occupied with what lay ahead.

He could make no sense of the situation.

Jacob's father, Austen Callaway, the Sixth Duke of Fairdale, was nearing his last days of life. And so, to refuse him even the smallest wish was unthinkable to Jacob. He loved his father very much, but even so he had to admit that this last request had made him wonder over the duke's mental state.

Yet here he was, two days' ride from his home at Fairdale, trying to locate the daughter of his father's recently deceased friend.

On the surface it had sounded like an easy task and Jacob questioned why they couldn't send a messenger to locate the girl.

"You must go, Jacob," his father had said. "Obviously I cannot make the journey. Although the idea of traveling to Wilfordshire after spending nearly four years confined to this bed is wonderful to me, I think we both know it would be impossible. I cannot trust this to anyone else. As you know, James Patrick saved my life twice. I owed him more than I could ever repay. Now he's dead and his greatest fear is that his daughter won't be safe. She's twenty years old, unmarried, and in danger of being snatched up by her maternal grandparents if they find her."

Looking back on that conversation and the hours of arguing that followed, Jacob was still unsure as to how his father convinced him to consider this.

Yet here he was, nearly an hour past Wilfordshire, looking for a young woman that everyone in the town, save the innkeeper, had denied knowing anything about. Even the innkeeper had been tight-lipped but with several extra coins placed next to those that paid for his ale, Jacob had managed to find out that James Patrick had lived in a cottage on a heavily wooded hillside about an hour north of the town.

As if that weren't enough, now another concern had presented itself. The good people of Wilfordshire, although denying the girl's existence, did allude to a young lad that was living at the cottage.

That was all he needed: to find the young woman, raised in who-knows-what manner in the wilds, now potentially living unchaperoned with a young man. And this was the woman his father hoped would be the next Duchess of Fairdale?

Jacob pulled Martin to a halt and dismounted at the base of a narrow trail. He looked up at the darkening sky, the rain poking at his face with sharp fingers

"Well, Martin, I have too many questions and no answers.

The only way I'll be able to solve this will be to find James Patrick's cottage and find out who actually lives there."

Jacob followed the narrow trail for some distance on foot. The path worked its way through thin underbrush beneath a heavy canopy of trees. Although the roof of trees protected him from some of the rain, it also blocked much of the light. Just when he was certain he was completely lost, he spied a small dwelling in the distance.

This had to be the place. Even if it wasn't, Jacob realized that he may be forced to beg the occupants for shelter this night.

When at last he reached the cottage he saw that the area surrounding it was barely cleared. On either side of the building huge trees stood with long limbs reaching out to cover the roof as if protecting the little house.

There was only a narrow opening for the door, and even the windows were long and thin, having to fit between the massive trunks of the trees. It must have been a bloody nuisance for James to build where he did, but Jacob had to admit the house was well-sheltered and almost completely hidden. If it were any darker he would have missed the site completely.

To one side of the small house he saw a make-shift stable; whether or not it actually housed any animals Jacob couldn't tell.

"Hello!" he called out, looking for some sign of life. Only the smoke curling from the chimney gave testimony to the fact that the house was not entirely deserted.

Jacob was about to call out again when the chilling sound of a gun being primed from somewhere behind him made him pause. He held his arms out from his sides, wanting to show whoever had approached him that he had no similar weapon in hand.

"I am unarmed," he said slowly with a calmness he didn't quite feel. The only weapon he did have was secure in his small saddle bag on Martin's back. Testimony once again to his hurried and harried state of mind when he left Fairdale. He silently cursed himself for not having some sort of weapon on his person.

"I mean you no harm, I assure you," Jacob said.

"Who are you?" a low, husky voice came from behind, "and what do you want here?"

"I'm merely a traveler, lost, I'm afraid, and I am seeking shelter for the night," Jacob said evenly. Until he knew who he was dealing with, he decided it was best to leave his true purpose a secret.

The voice, Jacob deduced, was that of a young lad and it was coming from below his own shoulder's level. Who ever it was wouldn't stand a chance if Jacob could get past the gun and engage him in weaponless battle.

Stillness filled the air for several moments. Jacob honed in on the lad's position, determined not to let him make another surprise advance.

He heard the boy move to the right. "If you're truly a traveler," the boy said, "then where are your traveling supplies? Why do you wander here in these heavy woods when there are dozens of roads leading across the countryside that are cleared?"

From the corner of his eye, Jacob could see the young man to his right side. He appeared to be a boy of no more than seventeen or eighteen. His face was smudged with dirt and his eyes were all but covered by the brim of an oversized hat.

Perhaps this was the young man whom the innkeeper had referred to. Jacob berated himself again. He hadn't thought to get the lad's name. Being able to address the boy would certainly have helped his predicament.

The lad glanced back at Martin, a tall, strong-boned animal. Horses of Martin's size and strength were a rarity, and most everyone Jacob met stopped and stared at the fine stallion.

Jacob took advantage of the split second diversion and whirled around, throwing his right arm back and up against the boy's arm. The gun fired as Jacob lunged for the boy, but the shot was directed harmlessly into the air. A startled cry came from the lad as he leapt away from Jacob and turned to run.

Jacob dove and caught the boy by an ankle, sending him tripping over his own feet. The gun spiraled out of reach landing several yards away behind a large rock.

The boy twisted in Jacob's grip and with his free foot he managed to kick Jacob, sending a blinding pain shooting through Jacob's forehead.

Jacob's hands remained tight around the boot, but the boy slipped his foot free. Struggling to his feet he began to run again, this time towards the cottage, splashing through puddles of thick, muddy water.

Jacob leapt to his feet, caught up with the lad just outside the cottage door, and spun him around. Another sharp pain exploded, this time in his leg as the boy's remaining heavy boot connected with Jacob's shin.

"You rotten little son-of-a-whore!" Jacob yelled without relinquishing his hold.

The boy fought even harder, this time bringing his knee up towards Jacob's groin. Jacob stepped quickly aside, the knee then only connecting with a steel-solid thigh.

"Cease your struggles, boy!" Jacob commanded, but to no avail. "I'm not here to cause you any harm!"

Words failed to calm the lad, and in fact seemed to incite him further bringing about a new barrage of kicks and stomps. Jacob side-stepped the kicks and eventually, between the two of them trying to go in opposite directions on the slippery ground, they both fell hard into the mud with Jacob landing on top.

Nose to nose for a moment, the boy quickly recovered, rolled to his side and scrambled to crawl away. Jacob grabbed him by the oversized coat, but the slim lad slipped his arms out of the sleeves and squirmed forward on his belly, heedless of the dirty water he was crawling through.

Jacob heaved himself forward and landed on the lad's back, flattening the boy and forcing the air from his lungs with a *whoosh*. One arm circled around the boy's waist, which Jacob vaguely noted was quite small, and with his other hand he grabbed the boy's wrist, twisting that arm behind his back.

Jacob expected to hear the young lad cry out in pain, for the wrenching hold was by no means gentle. But instead the struggle continued with the boy still trying to crawl out from under Jacob's weight.

Jacob tightened his grip on the boy's wrist and rose to one knee. He slid higher along the lad's back and then dropped his weight once again, effectively pinning the boy to the ground.

"Will…you…stop!" Jacob growled as his captive continued to squirm beneath him.

Jacob rose again to one knee and moved his hand free hand underneath the boy to encircle his chest, hoping to immobilize the lad.

Immobilize the lad, it did.

And Jacob as well.

With a sharp intake of breath, Jacob realized that rather than squeezing the firm, narrow chest of an angry young lad, his right hand was now squeezing the softly curved breast of an angry young *woman*.

Chapter 2

Jacob was too stunned to move for several moments

When at last he did, he moved only enough to take his hand from the young man's—woman's—oh, hell—breast.

She had, at least, quit struggling, and he was able to flip her over onto her back. He quickly straddled her and pinned her down with his weight once again. With one of his large hands he easily held her small wrists over her head, the other he placed on the ground near her head as he leaned in closer to her.

He sat atop her for a moment, waiting to catch his breath. This had to be Jessica Patrick; certainly there were not *two* young women living in a cottage on a remote hillside. Looking into the mud-streaked face of the young woman he wished—*oh how he wished*—that his father could see the proposed next Duchess of Fairdale.

"Would you mind telling me just what the devil you're hoping to accomplish by attacking me like that? You know, I was near to leveling you with my fist, thinking you were a lad in need of a good whipping. However, now that I've seen how you behave as a young woman, I'm not sure the same punishment doesn't warrant some consideration!"

The girl was silent, her chest still heaving from the exertion of the fight.

"I repeat," Jake began, "what—"

"I heard you the first time," she answered, still using what was now an obviously a fake voice.

Jacob was amused, but only slightly. He looked down at the shirt that barely covered her breasts. The front of the garment was open nearly to her navel after their struggle, and the thin cotton shirt beneath was so wet that it gave very little room for modesty.

"I would say, madam, it is futile to continue on with your attempted charade at being a boy. The truth is—er—rather evident."

She lifted her head as far as she could and looked down at her shirt, a sharp gasp escaping her at the sight of her transparent shirt and the dark circles of her cold, hard nipples pressing against it.

Jacob's free hand moved to her shirt front, the action causing a renewal of frenzied squirming from the young woman. "Hold still! I'm only trying to salvage what's left of your modesty."

She finally stopped moving, seeing that her struggles were not only futile, but were in fact opening the front of her shirt even farther. Dark color suffused her face as his green eyes traveled slowly back to hers.

When he slowly pulled together the two halves of her shirt, his knuckles lightly grazed the rounded flesh that rose above the top of the cotton undergarment.

Still she said nothing. She only set her jaw and stared back at him, her sherry-colored eyes narrowed to angry slits. He began to remove the oversized hat which covered all of her hair and most of her forehead, but that earned him a head-butt to his nose. Although it didn't hold much force, it was enough to make him angry all over again.

"That's enough!" he growled, leaping to his feet and dragging her with him. Jacob moved swiftly to a large stump and sat down, pulling her into his lap. He wrapped an arm around her waist, pinning her arms to her sides. His other arm he wrapped under her knees, nearly crushing her long legs in his attempt to keep her still.

"Let go of me, you beast! You have no right—"

"So you do have a woman's voice after all! I'm pleased to hear that. But for now, quiet it so I may tell you who I am and why I'm here. Perhaps then you won't be so eager to scratch my eyes out."

"Don't wager on it!"

With a heavy sigh and a shake of his head, Jacob adjusted himself on the stump but never once loosened his hold. This was even worse than he'd anticipated.

He'd never really considered himself a snob, but he couldn't stop himself from looking at this hoyden with distaste. She was a ruffian, she was filthy, and she smelled of horse dung.

"My name is Jacob Harwood Callaway. I am the son of the Duke of Fairdale, Austen Callaway." When that revelation brought about no response, he continued. "I can only assume," *much to my dismay*, he added silently, "that you are Jessica Patrick. My father and yours were friends, although they hadn't seen each other in years. It seems that your father saved—"

"Yes, I know; I know of the duke. My father spoke of him often, especially during the last few weeks of his life."

"Well if you knew who I was, why did you fight me so?" Jacob asked. He felt the tension draining from her body and so began to loosen his hold.

"I said I knew of your father, I didn't say anything about knowing who *you* were."

Jacob considered this for a moment and realized that she was right; she had no way of knowing who the strange man was that had invaded her privacy. "Might I ask why you are posing as a lad?"

"I would think that was obvious. I live here alone now; it's protected me over the years. Many people think I am a boy since I rarely leave my mountain here. My father felt that if most people thought I was a boy then if anyone came snooping around for a girl, it would throw them off the trail." She knew she was rambling, but sitting in this man's lap was creating some strange feelings in the pit of her belly that she had no idea how to deal with.

"I will grant you that. You had me fooled until I got a close and personal look at you. I assume you wear that heavy coat most of the time, for there are certainly a *handful* of ways that one could easily ascertain your true gender."

Jessica blushed hotly at the memory, hating this oaf who was holding her captive and wondering why when he mentioned it her flesh started tingling where his hand had brushed against her.

"However," Jacob continued, "I do have a letter here from your father proving who I am and why I'm here."

Her eyes widened at his words. A letter from her father?

"If I let you go," Jacob said, "will you promise not to attack me again?"

"Yes. Just let me see the letter," she said eagerly. James had only been dead a few weeks and she missed him terribly. Anything from him, even a letter to someone else, would be a salve to her wounded spirit.

She stood the moment Jacob's arms released her and moved several feet away. While she bent to retrieve her lost boot, he reached into his pocket and produced a small packet.

Jessica snatched the packet and then put her boot on, never taking her wary eyes off of Jacob.

Finally, she opened the packet. Without even reading the document, she knew it was truly her father's letter. The bold handwriting was so familiar, so strong. She actually smiled a little while tears filled her eyes, and Jacob was struck with the thought that beneath the grime, if nothing else, she did have a rather pretty smile.

Jessica read and re-read the letter, and then frantically scanned the enclosed, signed document which was obviously many years old. Her tears of sadness quickly turned to tears of anger.

"No! How could he do this? What exactly does this mean?

Surely not that—can you explain *this*?" She held up the oldest of the papers, a much faded and wrinkled document.

Her father's final words came back to her.

"…and although you'll likely be angry with me for what I've done please understand that it's for your own good…" *NO!*

More to herself she said, "I thought my father was sane until the moment he took his last breath, but this proves he should have been housed with Georgie Three."

"Georgie Three?"

Jessica looked up with exasperation. "Our king, you nit. You are aware that he's quite insane at times?"

Jacob raised his eyebrows. To be sure, he'd never heard their monarch referred to as Georgie Three. "Yes. Of that I'm well aware. But I'm not here to discuss the mental state of King George."

He paused, even more confounded by this young woman, shook his head and continued.

"Believe me, I felt the same way when my father explained this to me," Jacob said morosely.

"But—"

Jacob held up his hand. "Please, just give me a moment and I'll do my best to explain. Um, perhaps you should sit down," he advised, gesturing towards another stump some feet away.

"I'm fine. Just get on with it." Jessica's stomach was turning in knots. Surely this couldn't be—

"Our fathers became acquainted some years ago when—"

"Yes, yes, I know all that. My father saved the duke's life and—"

"Twice."

Jessica looked at him with exasperation. "Twice. Apparently the duke wanted to help us when we were forced to leave Ealing after my mother died, but my father, being the proud, stubborn man that he was wouldn't allow that. The only other thing I know about the duke is that he came to visit my father several times over the past fifteen years but I never actually saw him for myself."

"Mm-hmm." Jacob nodded.

Jessica looked down at the paper in her hand again. "But none of that history could possibly explain what looks like a marriage contract! Will you kindly explain this?" she asked, her voice rising along with her hand holding the papers.

"I'll do my best, Miss Patrick. First let me ask you, do you know who your maternal grandparents are?"

Jessica rolled her eyes. "What in heaven's name has that to do with anything?"

"I'm trying to decide how far back I have to go to explain this to you, so if you'd please just answer my questions we can have this settled shortly. At least the explanation of it."

Jessica decided she really didn't like this pompous oaf who had just set her world spinning. He was much too self-assured, and too damn handsome and she was sure that whatever it was that he was about to explain, it couldn't possibly make her feel any less anxious.

Jessica took a deep breath. "My father only told me that they were harsh people, and that we had to stay away from them because they wanted to take me away from him. Of course I would never have wanted to leave my father so I never fully understood what he was worried about. I just figured if they ever showed up I would simply tell them *no* and that would be that."

Jacob wondered briefly just how much he should tell Jessica about the Atterberrys. The picture she had in her mind surely was not accurate. He decided a condensed version would be best for now.

"Your grandfather and grandmother, the Marquis and Marchioness, were very powerful people a few years back. With their money and connections they could have found a way to take you, their daughter's child, away from your father— a man they considered 'common' and who didn't have much money. Since then, through some— shall we say— rather suspect business dealings, they've lost a great deal of money and most of their power. However, now that your father is no longer here to protect you, it would be easy for them to force you to go with them."

Jessica held up her hand. "First of all, if they are struggling both socially and financially, why would they want to take another person into their home? From what I've gathered they're not the overly kind and generous types. And second, I've lived out here for the past fifteen years without them finding me. Why should I start worrying now?"

Jacob looked at her and it occurred to him that Jessica really had no concept of how eager the Atterberrys would be to try and barter her off. "Miss Patrick, in answer to your first question, you could be used as a trading tool to secure them an agreed-upon sum of money as a bride." Jacob looked her over from head to toe. What he saw before him was not a bride that would fetch a large sum of money, but to the Atterberry's that probably wouldn't much matter. They'd take what they could get.

Jessica's cheeks burned under his perusal. She knew she looked a mess and having this fine stranger staring at her made her acutely aware of how different their worlds must be. She'd never heard of such a thing! Her own grandparents would try to *sell* her? Right then and there she decided that she would be much better off staying just where she was.

"And I suppose that this," she held out the contract, "is any different than what my grandparents would be trying to do?"

Jacob could not stomach being categorized anywhere near the Atterberrys and resented the implication that he and his father were out to do the same. "Not at all. You see, if your grandparents traded you for a sum of money, they would actually gaining something. If you marry into my family, we get nothing but *you*."

Jessica's mouth fell open at the rudeness of his statement. She recovered and ground her teeth together. "And from what I can see," she said slowly, "I wouldn't be gaining much either."

21

Jacob was weary and frustrated. "If we can cease with the insults, I will finish."

Jessica nodded.

"In answer to your second question, how they might find you, well perhaps you would remain lucky for a time. However, now that people know James is dead you can bet that at some point in the near future the Atterberrys will find out. And then, they'll find you. I know you think you're safe but it took only a few coins for the innkeeper to tell me how to find this cottage. Perhaps the people in town were more close-mouthed when your father was alive. Perhaps some of them now feel you shouldn't live up here alone. But the amount of money I had to put down to find you wasn't great. It was certainly nothing more than your grandparents could afford."

Jessica finally sat on the stump. "And so are you telling me that you think this is a good idea? This ridiculous contract?" She looked at the paper again. "It actually says that I am to marry either the duke or one of his sons. We don't even *know* one another. How can you think this is even an option I would consider?"

"Believe me, I am no more excited about this than you. I have no immediate plans to marry."

Now more than ever, looking at this young woman's mud-streaked face in the fading light, he was dreading even taking her to Fairdale, let alone bringing her into the family via marriage.

Then a thought struck him. He should take her, just as she sat there. Surely then even his father would see the futility of this plan.

He sighed. Or should he just leave her here after all, claiming that he couldn't find her? No, he knew better than that. His father would never forgive him if he returned empty-handed, and would merely send someone else to fetch the young woman. "Bloody hell," he muttered in disgust.

Jessica looked up at the tone in Jacob's voice. Although she didn't like the idea of this ridiculous plan any more than he did, the obvious distaste Jacob felt stung her pride.

She let her hands fall to her lap, lifted her chin and looked him over closely from head to toe, not knowing or caring that properly raised young women didn't peruse a strange man, any man, in such a way. But then her experience with men other than her father had been somewhat limited. She'd had very little chance to peruse *any* man.

He was very tall, she noted. Tall and strong. That fact she'd found out the hard way.

Piercing green eyes were set above a well chiseled nose. His mouth had full lips, and for a moment Jessica caught herself wondering how those lips would look if he smiled. She mentally shook herself and remembered that he was the enemy.

She eyed the obviously expensive riding clothes he wore. This man appeared to be everything of which she'd learned to be suspicious.

How could her father do this to her? Expecting her to marry some boorish, mean-tempered, haughty son of a duke?

And then Jacob's words repeated themselves in her head. *I have no immediate plans to marry."*

The old man himself? The contract said she would marry the duke or his son.

Suddenly she envisioned herself bound up in corsets and stiff-necked gowns, wandering through the dusty, dark halls of a dreary old mansion, answering the whims of a sickly old man and—oh, surely she wouldn't be required to share the old man's bed? Oh, no!

Jessica shook the unpleasant thoughts from her head. She finally broke the silence that had stretched uncomfortably between them while they were both lost in their own thoughts.

"I still don't understand how the contract came to be."

"Ah yes, that's the really interesting part. You see, the night James saved my father's life the second time was actually the night before the two of you were leaving Ealing. To show his thanks my father took James to a tavern and they celebrated with several pints of ale.

"Your father told him about the Atterberrys' plan to take you away and how he planned to flee. Understand, Miss Patrick, my father has a heart of gold that rivals that which is in his coffers. He offered you and your father financial aid, shelter at our estate, whatever he wanted. But as you mentioned, James was stubborn and proud."

"Well, if my father wouldn't even take money from the duke, why would offer me in marriage?"

"He didn't, exactly. My father got pretty good and foxed that night. Near the end of the evening, he drew up this contract stating that if anything should happen to your father before you were married, that he would either marry you to one of his sons, or if they were married he would give you his own name. By the look that flashed across your face just now, I assume that last thought is even more distasteful than the idea of marrying me," Jacob said tersely.

Jessica merely raised an eyebrow.

"My father is no lecherous, old monster. He would marry you in name only. You would likely find yourself a very wealthy young widow in a very short time." Jacob's tone took on an edge of anger at her ungratefulness.

"Well, what woman wouldn't want to be a wealthy young widow, and a duchess to boot?" Jessica said sarcastically.

She wouldn't. If she ever married, it would be for love and nothing else.

She stood and faced him, the papers in her hands wrinkled from her angry clutch. "There's no need to look so worried, Mr. Callaway. I have no intentions of coming with you, nor would I even remotely consider marrying you or your aged father."

Jacob met her cold stare and wished he could enjoy the feeling of relief that should have come with her words, but he knew she didn't have a choice in the matter any more than he did. "First of all, it's Lord Callaway, not 'mister.' You might as well get used to addressing people correctly. And as you know, my *aged* father is a duke, to be addressed as 'Your Grace'."

"As you wish, Lord Callaway," she said, her voice dripping with as much sarcasm as the stilted curtsy she dropped.

"And second, you *will* come with me, if only to satisfy my father's—"

"What? His curiosity? I'm not about to become the center of your mission of mercy, m'lord. I'm quite capable of staying right here and taking care of myself."

"I had no intention of making you a mission, *my lady*," he said, matching her earlier sarcasm. "But as much as you loved and respected your father, I also love and respect mine. He is very ill and if this is his last wish, to help the daughter of his friend James Patrick, then I intend to see it fulfilled. You may come with me willingly in the morning taking whatever possessions you wish, or I can forcibly haul you up on my horse and ride us out of here in the darkness," he finished, raising his hands toward the sky which was now almost black.

It was nearly impossible to make out her features, but he saw by the lowering of her shoulders that she was nearly out of fight.

Jessica knew well what it was to love a father dearly. For that she could not, would not, blame this presumptuous bully. Had it been her own father, she would have moved the heavens to give him his final wish.

But this? Marriage to an unknown old man or a snobbish brute?

Jessica turned and walked slowly toward the cottage.

"Come inside, *Lord* Callaway. I've yet to make my decision, but neither of us will be riding or walking out of here tonight. That trail is too dangerous, and there's no moon for light. I assure you I won't attempt to leave in the middle of the night. You can put your horse in the shed off the back of the cottage. I'd just finished cleaning it when you arrived. I hope he won't find it too offensive," she finished dryly.

Well, at least that explained her scent, Jacob mused.

Chapter 3

Jacob stood in the doorway of the crude cottage. He wondered why she had a clean horse stall and tack but no horse to put in there. Now was probably not the time to ask.

He stepped inside, trying to formulate a way to discuss this matter without further arguments. But no answer was forthcoming. He looked around the small dwelling and could see that the interior was not surprisingly different from the exterior, simple but well maintained.

Two curtains hung at right angles in the far corner forming the only hint of a separate room; a bed and small bathing tub were nestled in the makeshift alcove. A large fireplace took up a good portion of the wall to his left, with a small table and three chairs positioned in front of it. The kitchen, if you could call it that, was beyond the table to the right.

With her back to Jacob, Jessica said, "I trust your mount was not offended by his accommodations?"

"I'm sure Martin will rest just fine."

Jessica turned slowly, her eyebrows raised and a tiny smile teased the corner of her mouth. "*Martin*? Your horse's name is *Martin*?"

"It's actually Martinique. He came from France. But I find that Martin is much more informal. It keeps us on a friendlier level."

Jessica rolled her eyes and turned away. "You people of fortune have far too little to do."

Jacob smiled and moved into the cottage, taking a closer look at its furnishings. He was struck by the contrast. For all that the cottage was simple and rough, the furniture within was finely crafted.

"My father did beautiful woodworking, did he not? You seem surprised. Perhaps you thought we lived like barbarians up here in the wilderness?"

Jacob ran his hand over the smoothly finished table. "To be honest, I didn't give any thought to how you lived. Please keep in mind that until recently, I didn't even know you existed. I will admit, however, that this is some of the finest woodwork I have seen. Your father did indeed have a talent. Tell me, is this how you managed to survive? Did he sell his work?"

Jessica threw him a glance as she went to the fireplace and began stoking up the still glowing embers. "Yes, if you must know. His work was well appreciated in the village and beyond. People would come from neighboring towns to purchase it. We had a friend in the village who would sell the work as his to the strangers so no one could trace the crafting to my father." She glanced over her shoulder at him. Somehow in the light of the fire's glow he didn't seem quite so intimidating.

Jessica couldn't help admiring the strong hands that now worked over the back of one of the chairs.

"The chair you're fondling is mine," she said stiffly.

"Yours?"

"Yes, I made that one. And a few other pieces. He taught me well. We didn't have much else to do here during the winters. Woodcrafting is how I intend to support myself now that I'm alone. I'm not as skilled as my father, but someday I hope to come close."

She felt tears burn at the back of her eyes remembering the hours she'd watched her father at his craft and the many more he'd spent teaching her; the smell of the wood as he lovingly carved and polished it, the little wood shavings that were forever on the floor of the cottage

Jessica took a deep breath and stood up, pulling her hat down further over her forehead.

"I'm afraid you won't be very comfortable here tonight, Lord Callaway. My humble furnishings are not, I'm sure, what you're used to in your own fine home," she said, daring him with her eyes to confirm her words.

"I'm certain I'll be just fine."

Jessica was surprised by his acquiescence and so, against her earlier thoughts to make Jacob sleep on the small bed near the fire that had once been hers, she decided to let him have the large bed; the one that had until recently been her father's.

"You may sleep in the bed back there," she said, pointing to the small curtained area. However, first I need to bathe. Thanks to you, I'm covered in more dirt than a buried treasure. I'll fix you something to eat while you fetch water for my bath."

Jacob looked around quickly to see if she was joking. She wasn't.

"Your bath?" Was she truly going to bathe in the same room as a strange man with only a thin curtain separating them? Then another thought hit him that threatened to make him chuckle. Jacob had only hauled his own bath water when he was at his small hunting cottage, and certainly never hauled anyone else's. Between wrestling in the mud and now this, Jessica Patrick was already proving she was full of surprises.

"Yes. Surely you don't expect to be treated as a welcomed guest. After all, I didn't invite you here and I didn't ask you to stay once you arrived. Had you timed your visit earlier you could have ridden back to the village in daylight."

He quickly decided not to tell her that his arrival was late only because he became lost several times.

Jacob sighed. He knew this was hard on Jessica as well. "Where might I find the buckets, and where is your water source?"

Again Jessica was surprised by how easily he gave in. "The buckets are on the porch, and there's a stream to the left of the cottage. Stay on the path; it's well traveled and easy to follow. I won't be coming to look for you if you get lost," she said turning her attention to the carrots and cabbage that were on the counter.

When Jacob returned with the four buckets of water, she told him to pour it directly in the bath tub. "Don't you want to heat it?" he asked in astonishment. He'd felt the water; it was cold!

"No. I'm used to it. I rarely have time to linger in a leisurely bath."

Jacob shook his head, again surprised by this young woman. Jessica was truly unlike any female he'd ever met. He'd noticed her speech, her movements. She was graceful and spoke with proper grammar. Obviously, her father had seen to it that she was tutored in at least some of the social graces. Yet she was hard-headed and out-spoken to the point of being rude. Life with her would never be boring.

Jessica could feel him staring at her back. "Are you going to dump the water or not?" she asked tersely.

Jacob moved to the bath tub with the buckets. As he poured, he noticed several books near the tub on a small table. When the buckets were empty, he reached for a book of poetry with which he was familiar. "You've read this?" he asked, unable to keep the surprise from his voice.

Jessica turned and practically leapt to his side, snatching the book from his hand. The last thing she wanted was for this oaf to know she had a vulnerable, wishfully romantic side. "I would appreciate it if you would not snoop through my things. For someone who is supposedly so well-bred, you certainly are lacking in manners."

Jacob couldn't help but chuckle at her. Jessica was surprised by the warmth and quickness of his laugh, especially since it was for an insult that was directed at him. Some of the tension in her shoulders ebbed away at the sound, allowing her to relax a little for the first time since his arrival.

Jacob's eyes met hers under the brim of her filthy hat and held for a moment.

The sudden pounding of her heart made the blood rush to her cheeks and scalded them with red.

Jessica forced her eyes away from his.

As she moved to the fireplace where the cooking pot hung, Jacob watched her curiously. For a moment he had felt something with her. A recognition. There had been a deep, albeit brief, moment between them and the stirring he'd felt for that moment left him more than a little uneasy.

He shook his head. Momentary connection aside, it was not enough to make him consider having this girl as a wife. She was a dirty, boyish, chit, the complete opposite of every woman he knew.

He chuckled out loud at the split-second vision of Jessica, dressed as she was, strolling through a fancy ball room on his arm.

Jessica whirled around at the sound of his laughter. "And pray tell, what do you find so hilarious, my lord? Do my simple ways amuse you? Do you find it so laughable that a woman might—"

"Do you ever cease?" Jacob interrupted. "My apparently ill-timed chuckle was due to a purely private matter, one that entered my mind of its own accord. I'm sorry that you took it as an offense."

Jessica felt ridiculous. She turned back to her stew. Why did this man make her feel so defensive?

Jacob moved to the table and sat in a chair, unsure of what to do with himself.

At his continued silence Jessica turned around. Again their eyes met. When her stomach began to flutter once more, she pulled down on the brim of her hat and walked quickly toward the bath tub. "The stew needs to cook for a few minutes more. I'll bathe before we eat."

She drew the curtains and then re-opened them; suddenly realizing that he would be in the room with her while she bathed. For the past couple of weeks she'd not had to worry about a man in her house, and before that her father would always take his evening walk when she chose to bathe. "You may take a walk outside if you like."

Jacob leaned back and crossed his ankle up over his knee. "As you pointed out earlier, there is no moon by which to see. I barely made it back from the stream without getting lost. No, I think I'll stay right here." He chuckled inwardly and wondered if she would truly bathe with him in the room.

Jessica saw the smile that played at the corner of his handsome mouth. The rat! He was enjoying this!

"Fine. As you wish," she said, trying to control the shaking in her voice. She would not let him keep her from her bath for it had been two days of hard work, hauling wood and cleaning out the stalls, since her last one. Add to that her recent tumble in the mud and she was not a pretty sight. She disappeared for a moment and then returned with two books. "Here," she said as she tossed them on the table. "This will give you something to do while I'm bathing."

"Thank you," Jacob said, picking up the books. He scanned the covers before dropping them back on the table and then boldly met her gaze.

His raised eyebrow dared her to go and tend to her bath. Certainly he had no interest in the girl, but for some reason he found it very amusing to torment her. She had such—*spunk!*

Jessica felt her cheeks begin to color and turned quickly towards the alcove before he could see his effect on her. With a flip of her wrist she closed the curtains and stomped around the tub to a small stool where she flopped down.

Damn him! Her dirty boots hit the floor with a thud, sending chunks of dried dirt to mix with some spilled water on the floor. She sighed, suddenly too tired to care if the floor was dirty or if there *was* a strange man in the same room with her.

Jessica eyed the tub and then dipped her finger in the water, stifling her intake of breath. She hadn't been totally honest with Lord Callaway. Usually she did warm her water before her bath, but she didn't want to waste any time with that this evening.

Besides, for some reason, it was important to her that his lordship thought she was strong, strong enough to stay here on her own. And if part of that proof came by way of enduring a cold bath, then so be it!

Quickly she finished undressing. She moved the lamp to the small table where the books had been and piled her dirty clothes, including the hat, on the floor.

Now it was Jacob's turn to stifle his own gasp.

Jessica had no way of knowing that the lamp sharply silhouetted her figure against the light curtains that separated her from Jacob.

Jacob tried to look at the books on the table, but as she moved against the light, stretching her arms above her head and releasing what appeared to be amazingly long hair; his gaze was fixed on the wavering shadow.

He watched as she stepped slowly into the tub, and had to smile when she was unable to cover her next intake of breath as she stepped into the water.

Jessica washed quickly, wondering what Jacob was doing. It was so quiet out there; too quiet.

Every drop of water sounded twice as loud tonight, knowing that someone else was there to hear it. With a final quick dunk under the surface to rinse her hair, Jessica rose and reached for her towel, still unaware of the spectacle she was presenting to Jacob.

Try as he might, he was unable to tear his eyes from the curtain. Her form, though softened by the lamp's glow against the curtain, was that of an obviously well-shaped woman. In the silhouette he could see that the breasts he'd accidentally grabbed earlier were of a perfect size above a long, flat midsection. When she turned, Jacob could see that her waist was very slender, leading to lightly flaring hips and long legs.

She bent forward to finish drying and he finally closed his eyes. He could see no more, but he didn't need to. Had his view been unobstructed by the thin curtains, he could not have been more aroused.

Jacob shifted uncomfortably in his chair, embarrassed by his reaction. Good Lord! She was a ruffian; a dirt-streaked hoyden! Even with that obviously alluring figure, how could he possibly be having this reaction to her? He'd been too long without a woman in his arms. That was it.

He shook his head. Surely the shadows had given her figure more voluptuousness than she truly deserved, and her face certainly hadn't been comely. And what good woman would have allowed herself to become so filthy?

Good. Keep talking to yourself! It was working.

He felt his blood slowing and the front of his trousers were once again becoming more comfortable.

But only momentarily.

Chapter 4

When the curtains opened Jacob glanced up, expecting to see simply a cleaner version of the same ragged waif that had disappeared behind them. What he saw instead was a young woman dressed in well-worn but clean trousers. The white cotton blouse she'd donned was slightly too big and hung just a little off one shoulder.

Jacob was too painfully aware that she wore very little, if anything, underneath the blouse. When his eyes were at last able to work their way up past her lovely white throat, he was in for yet another shock.

The dirt had washed away and in its place a breath-taking beauty had emerged. Sherry-colored eyes flecked with amber sparks and framed by thick, dark lashes—*how could he have barely noticed them before?* stared back at him. Her hair, waist-length and thick, hung in a heavy auburn braid to one side.

All composure gone, Jacob merely stared at her with his mouth open. She was surely one of the loveliest creatures he'd ever laid his eyes upon. A warmth began spreading through his veins, again, and this time there was no stopping it.

During her bath he briefly considered posing the idea of being her guardian, of helping her find a proper husband. But not only was he certain his father would not agree to that, he suddenly wasn't so sure that he would be comfortable with it either.

Moreover, if her grandmother caught sight of her, the war would undoubtedly be on once again. Lord and Lady Atterberry would see this lovely young woman as a means to secure wealth through whichever suitor had the greatest purse to offer; no thought would be given to Jessica's happiness or lack thereof.

Looking into her beautiful yet seemingly innocent face just now brought about a surge of protective instinct.

Jessica became uneasy beneath his open perusal and shifted her weight back and forth, looking quickly down to make certain that her blouse had not become unbuttoned in her haste. No man had ever looked at her in such a heated, considering way.

Jessica took a moment, clenching her jaw to stop it from shaking, and then said, "I apologize if my attire offends you. My seamstress and hair dresser were unable to attend me this evening."

Her wit took Jacob by surprise; but his laughter only served to confirm her notion that he was ridiculing her.

She glared in his direction and then moved off to the cooking pot. Stirring the stew roughly, she fought back the tears that threatened to spill. Why should she care what this pompous oaf thought of her? Just because he was the most handsome man she'd ever seen, the kind of man her dreams were made of. Did that truly mean anything?

Yes! It did! He held her future in his hands, more or less. If she truly had to go with him she couldn't bear the thought of being his source of amusement. Oh, she could envision him now at one of his fancy clubs, re-telling this tale to his cronies, laughing at her backward ways. She must find a way to convince him not to take her.

Drawing in a deep breath she turned and took one quick step before falling into his arms.

"Oh! I—I—What are you doing?" she gasped, her body

leaning fully against his as she was still off balance.

He'd been unable to keep from moving closer to her. The clean scent that had wafted his way when she stormed past him, the all-too-enticing derriere that had presented itself when she bent over the cooking pot, the still-surprising revelation that this was no filthy tomboy but indeed a beautiful and desirable woman had been more than he could stand at that moment.

His hands were at her shoulders to steady her, and more, they were holding her firmly against his body. He shuddered with the sudden desire that swept over him. His eyes narrowed with the confusion that seeped into his mind: how could *this* woman have such an effect on him? No woman had ever caused such an immediate and forceful reaction.

He could feel her heart beating against his chest, smell her freshness.

She looked up into that handsome face, her palms flat against a chest that felt as if it were made of armor. The heat from his body, the mysterious scent of man mingled with the smell of leather from his travel; her head was spinning. Any breath she might have had was now caught in her throat. Surely she would burst at any moment. What was happening to her?

A slow smile spread across Jacob's face, softening his features. This time she saw no malice, no denigration; only a hunger that she'd never before seen in a man's eyes.

"We always seem to wind up entangled in each other's arms," he whispered softly against her cheek. He was no longer aware of anything but Jessica. All thoughts of her father's request and his father's plan fled his mind. He knew only the heat that was coursing through his veins, and oh yes, he could feel it coursing through her as she shook against him.

As he stared once again into amber eyes that seemed to burn into his soul, he slowly began to lower his lips to hers. He was powerless to stop himself.

Jessica's eyes were wide with wonder, staring in disbelief at the man so dangerously close to her. He was going to kiss her!

And worse, she suddenly realized that she *wanted* him to kiss her; wanted it desperately. There was a fluttering in her stomach that extended down her thighs. She was grateful that he was holding her, for she would surely collapse if left to her own strength.

His lips were so close. She could feel his breath against her mouth; it was as though she could feel his kiss before they even touched.

Her eyes closed as a ragged breath gently escaped against his lips.

His lower lip brushed over her upper one, feather-light and warm, before brushing over her lower lip as well. A tiny moan escaped her.

Fire met fire as their mouths came fully together and for the briefest of moments Jessica felt she had been swept away from the world she knew. She could feel his heart beating wildly beneath the palm of her hand while his hands pressed her tighter against the length of his body. She came in contact with his hardness and that, being the first time she'd felt such, sent a shock wave through her like nothing she'd felt before. A blaze that started in her center and shot out to her head and toes at the same moment.

Jacob's lips urged hers apart ever so slightly. Warm, wet tongues touched and teased, exploring, seeking, finding. He was sure he'd never tasted anything as intoxicating as her mouth.

Encircling her waist, lifting her to the tips of her toes, he pressed harder against her. The sound that came from deep in his throat was filled with an animal-like intensity. That alone caused Jessica to pause, for never had she heard the sound of such longing. It suddenly frightened her.

Sanity returned in a rush and all the passion she'd felt just a split second before turned into fear, fear of the spiraling headiness that threatened to take her, fear of this man who had so quickly gained control of her emotions.

Pressing her hands against Jacob's chest, she turned her head quickly to one side and tore her lips from his. The sudden separation caught Jacob by surprise and he nearly dropped her as she stumbled backwards.

Jessica spun and landed clumsily on the small bed near the fireplace. Quickly she scooted down the bed and then stood, moving behind it to put some distance between her and Jacob.

Jacob was rudely ripped from his desire-induced trance. What had happened? He knew women well enough to know when one wanted to be kissed, and this one definitely had wanted that. He took a step forward and Jessica mirrored it with a step back.

"Jessica, what is it?" he asked, still breathing heavily.

Common sense was returning to him now, the world was righting itself once again. He should thank her for interrupting what was well on its way to a heated session of love-making, for it had yet to be determined just what role he would play in her life. Certainly if she were to marry his father, he could not be bedding her; she would, in fact, become his step-mother!

He sighed and then smiled over his confusion, suddenly finding the entire situation ironically laughable. Yet above it all, he still wanted her. "Jessica, I would apologize for what just happened, but I find that I'm truly not the least bit sorry."

Jessica looked up with a snap when she heard his laugh and glared at him. Her breathing was still coming in ragged gasps and yet he seemed to be fully recovered.

"Well I *am* sorry," she said. Now more than ever Jessica knew she could not live in the same house as this man. In a matter of an hour he had gained complete control of her senses.

Chapter 5

Her first kiss... it had tilted her world. Inexperienced though she may be, in her heart—and various other parts of her body—she knew that no other man would ever be able to evoke those same deep, immediate, uncontrollable desires.

Oh, Jacob Callaway was dangerous.

She would find a way to stay here if it was the last—

And then it struck her. She looked at the small bed in front of her. Why hadn't she thought of it before? There was her very reason to stay; the one excuse she could use that Lord Callaway couldn't toss aside.

Jessica gathered her wits about her, determined to put behind her what had just occurred. She lifted her chin and crossed her arms in front of her. "I would appreciate it if you would keep your distance from me. It's hardly considered good manners to accost your hostess. You'll recall that you are in *my* home, and I'll not have you groping me at every turn! I'm not the kind of woman you're obviously used to keeping company with!"

Jacob lifted an eyebrow and folded his arms across his chest, copying her stance. "Accost? My dear, *you* fell into my arms. I was merely trying to steady you. What happened after that was—" he raised one hand in the air, "shall we call it an accident?"

She eyed him carefully and took a deep breath. Jacob had positioned himself conveniently next to the cooking pot and she was certain that it was still too soon to pass so close to him. Not only did she not trust him, but she was entirely unsure of herself and her unexpected reaction to this stranger.

Looking back at his relaxed form she said, "Fine. Call it what you like, Lord Callaway. If you choose to see things that way, as an accident, then you are most welcome to do so." She motioned toward the cooking pot. "Dish yourself some stew if you're hungry. I find I've lost my appetite."

Again he raised his eyebrow and smiled. "Dish myself? After you so carefully pointed out that you were my hostess? Tsk. Now whose manners are lacking? Ah well, no matter." Jacob took a wooden bowl from the mantle and did in fact serve himself a bowl of stew, then took a seat at the table.

Jessica walked around the table and leaned back against the kitchen counter, looking around the room as if she were studying it for the first time. She stole occasional glances at her guest, but he appeared to be completely occupied by his meal.

She had no way of knowing that he was warring with his own emotions over the decisions they'd have to face shortly; the most immediate one being simply whether she would accompany him to Fairdale without a fight.

Jacob considered their fathers' plan. He knew in his heart that this wild, beautiful creature standing before him would shrivel and die if she were to marry a—he had to admit it—a sickly, elderly gentleman. The few moments that she'd been in his arms had assured him of a fiery passion that smoldered just beneath the surface.

To marry his father, even for her own safety's sake, would be a senseless tragedy to her womanhood. The duke could not perform in a marriage bed; even the thought of his father and Jessica together in that way made his stomach tie up in knots.

But what was the alternative? Marry her himself? The thought didn't set as sourly as he'd thought it might. But for heaven's sake! He'd only known the woman for a few hours. True, she'd drawn a physical reaction from him, the strength of which he'd never known before. But was that grounds for marriage?

He paused in his eating and considered his sole purpose for a marriage: to continue the ducal lineage. Certainly this woman would make it easy; more, she would make it pleasurable to constantly tend the survival of his family name. Perhaps this physical desire was *just* the reason to consider that option of his father's request.

Jessica cleared her throat. It was time to broach the subject that was between them. She took a deep breath and summoned all her courage. "Lord Callaway, I—"

"Please, call me Jacob."

His interruption caught her by surprise. Damn! Did he have to smile at her like that?

Get a hold of yourself, Jess!

Taking another deep breath she continued. "Very well, Jacob. I want you to know how grateful I am to your father for his seeming interest in my fate. However, I must decline your invitation to come to your estate and join your family. This is my home, crude though it may be. I was raised here and I intend to—"

"Apparently you don't understand, Miss Patrick," he interrupted, setting his spoon down on the table.

"Oh, but I do understand, my lord," she said, her annoyance returning at his continued interruptions. "You surmised, and rightly so, I'll grant you, that someone who lives here in the woods without many comforts would leap at the opportunity you're presenting.

Why, to live in a fine mansion with a service staff and other conveniences would be the dream of almost any young woman, even those better situated than I, and even if it meant marrying someone your father's age. I'll go even further and guess that you're surprised I've shown such a hesitancy to accept this offer."

He tilted his head to one side and gave a small nod. He *was* surprised at her initial refusal of such an offer.

She stared at his unreadable features. So strong was her attraction to Lord Callaway that she had to wait several moments before continuing, unsure that her voice would sound steady even then.

"Therefore, I must formally decline your invitation to—"

Jacob rubbed his hand over his face, "I must repeat, apparently you don't understand, my lady. As I said before, this isn't merely an invitation. It is a direct request from your father to my father that you come to our home and—"

She'd tried reasoning with the buffoon, the handsome buffoon! "And what? Become a child-bride for your father? I think not!" She pounded her fist on the counter top. All thoughts of portraying herself as a well-mannered lady flew out the window as she saw her fate, chained to an old man, or *this* man!

To hell with the Duke's protection. She could take care of herself!

Jacob was certain he'd never seen someone so beautiful and so angry at the same time. He couldn't resist teasing her, just a little. "Who said that you would be marrying my *father*? The pledge my father made said—"

"Yes, that I would marry one of his sons or himself if they weren't—" she stopped as another scenario formed in her mind.

"One of his sons," she whispered again. "Is there a brother that I'm intended for, then?" she asked quickly. "And what's wrong with him? Why would you and your father seek to marry him off to some penniless woman that you don't even know? Is he some kind of dimwit or outcast? Because I promise you I will not be foisted off on some imbecile any easier than I will on some old man or a pompous oaf such as yourself!"

The teasing and laughter left Jacob's features all at once. Jessica was taken aback at the hardness that settled over his face so quickly.

Jacob could easily withstand attacks on his own person, letting them slide off him with no consequence. But he could not abide someone, especially this ill-mannered chit, speaking maliciously of his family.

"My father is not merely some old man; he is a respected duke. Any woman should be honored to marry him, no matter what his age or the circumstances. And my brother is dead. He was murdered the same night as my mother. But no, he was not an outcast and certainly no dimwit. I can assure you, being married to him would not have been your worst fate."

Jessica stood in silence, feeling foolish for letting her anger and weariness make her imagination run wild. "I'm sorry. I didn't—I had no way of—" she fell over her words, not knowing what to say. Suddenly it all seemed too much for her to take.

She lowered her head and rubbed at her temples, trying to stave off the headache that was growing by the second. "What would be my worst fate?" she asked, more of herself. Jessica hadn't expected an answer, and so was dually shocked when Jacob spoke.

"Marrying me."

Jessica's head snapped up, her fingers still at her temples, her mouth hanging open. She snapped her jaw shut and folded her arms across her chest. "Marrying you. What a joke. Is that supposed to make me feel better? Or perhaps that's supposed to be a punishment for my thoughtless—and much regretted— outburst regarding your family?"

Jacob leaned back in the chair and crossed his ankle over his knee. "You ask a lot of questions."

"It's the only way I can get answers, and since we are seriously lacking in those this evening, questions are what you'll have to settle for. So, which is it?"

"It's none of those. Not a punishment or a joke. It's merely an option that is being considered."

"Considered by whom? Certainly not by me." Jessica said with a snort.

"Oh, certainly not," Jacob answered caustically. "And lady, may I point out that it's not a very tempting option for me either. However, I do have certain duties to consider as the next Duke of Fairdale. And so the situation at hand does provide me with some fodder for thought."

She tried to ignore the sting of his words once again. "Duties? Such as?" she asked, intent on keeping her wounded pride hidden.

"Such as producing heirs, keeping the family name alive and well-stocked for generations to come. That would be the only reason I would ever choose to marry." He was still angry at her derogatory, if unintended, remarks about his family. "And you, although lacking in manners and social graces, do not have a face that is too hard to look upon. You appear to be healthy and therefore I assume you could likely produce children every two years or so until I feel we have enough."

Jessica's eyes were wide in amazement. She could not believe what she was hearing. Her mouth opened and closed several times before she could find her voice.

"You—you overbearing, egotistical, pompous ass! For you to think I would even consider marrying you just to become your brood mare is beyond—ugh!" It was as though she was seeing him for the first time, and in a much different way. The attraction she'd felt for the man was now being overshadowed by the revelation of his true nature.

"I would never willingly marry you!" she yelled at his smug countenance. The derogatory smirk on his face was too much for her. She reached behind her back and grabbed the first thing she could find—the left-over cabbage from the stew—and threw it at his head.

Jacob ducked in time and the cabbage missile flew harmlessly past him.

Angry and humiliated at her own childish reaction, she turned away from him and leaned forward on the counter, her face in her palms. Tears were threatening but she did her best to hold them in check.

Jacob looked at the woman before him. He already felt guilty about what he'd said to her. She was no more responsible for this situation than he was, yet he'd allowed her to goad him into saying such hurtful things. He hated to admit it, but it was more than her unknowing slander against his family that had caused his reaction.

The fact that she apparently didn't want him, wouldn't give him a chance, didn't set well with him at all. He could never remember being so flatly refused by any woman.

Jessica could actually feel the heat of Jacob's stare boring holes into her back. She finally turned to face him, knowing now that she would have to use any means necessary to stay here and remove Lord Callaway from her life.

"Lord Callaway, I am spent," she said with a sigh. "I can't discuss this ludicrous situation any more this evening, but I will tell you this. Tomorrow morning you will meet a young man; his name is Ossie, and I assure you that after meeting him you will not only agree that I should stay here, but will likely insist upon it."

"And who is Ossie?" Jacob asked, leaning forward on the table. Was he her lover? Did she think that would truly make a difference? And why the devil did the thought of her having a lover provoke a feeling of—of—annoyance in him?

"He's someone very important in my life and—"

"Miss Patrick, the mere fact that you have a lover will not—"

"A wha—"Jessica's face flooded with color. "He is not—he's—"

Jessica threw up her hands and turned back to look out the window over the counter.

"Lord Callaway," she said quietly, "it will all become crystal clear in the morning. But I fear I am on the very edge of hysteria at the moment. If we don't end this and get some rest, there may be nothing left to discuss tomorrow, for I feel as if I'm about to go mad."

"You're correct about one thing. There will be nothing left to discuss tomorrow. For whether this Ossie person is a lover or not, I cannot imagine anything he could say that would sway my intention to take you to Fairdale."

"Oh, he won't say a word to sway you, m'lord," Jessica said with a sad smile.

Chapter 6

Jacob sat up quickly in the small alcove and looked around, disoriented for just a moment.

For most of the night he'd tossed and turned. Smelling the floral scent of Jessica and knowing that such a beautiful woman was sleeping only a few feet away with nothing but a curtain separating them had been a test of his sensibilities. He half smiled and rubbed his eyes. It had been a long time since he'd shown such restraint.

He needed some fresh air. A brisk morning walk would clear his foggy mind.

"Jessica, are you decent?" he asked, not wanting to surprise her in a state of undress. There was no answer. His heart began to beat faster. "Jessica?"

When there was still no answer, he jumped up and pulled the curtains back. The small cottage was empty.

"Damn her!" he cursed aloud. Certain that she'd snuck out while he slept, Jacob hastily stepped into his trousers and slid his arms into his shirt, grabbing his boots as he hurried towards the door. He silently called her every vile name he could think of and then mentally whipped himself for not hearing her leave.

He'd just reached the door when it was kicked open from outside. Jessica gasped in surprise as she plowed into Jacob, sending the full load of firewood she was carrying scattering all over the floor.

She regained her balance, but not her breath. He stood there, his shirt hanging open to reveal a hard, powerful chest, his trousers left unfastened in his haste. Jessica could not stop her eyes from roaming over his fine form, noting every muscle, the flat, firm stomach, the coarse, dark hair that disappeared down the front of his....

Only when her eyes had traveled below his hips did she realized what she was doing. Hot color scorched her cheeks as she jerked her eyes up to his face. There she found a smile. Not quite mocking, but not quite chagrined at being caught nearly unclothed.

She dropped to her knees and began picking up the scattered wood, anything to avoid meeting his eyes.

"Good morning. I thought you'd left me," Jacob said as he finished dressing. He was not at all displeased by her reaction to him. So, she may not want to marry him, but she could no longer deny that she found him attractive.

Jessica's heart was still beating painfully fast. "I—I told you I wouldn't leave, Lord Callaway. I'm an honest person. You—"

"Here, let me help you," Jacob said as he bent to retrieve some of the wood.

"No!" she nearly shouted as she scooted away from his hand. "I can get it!" Jessica wanted to be no where near the man, wanted no chance of contact. He caused too many unexplained reactions in her body.

"As you wish." He took a step back to allow her plenty of space.

She was a mystery, to be sure. Denying this attraction seemed to be most important to Jessica Patrick, while the women he knew would have purposely dropped that wood just for an excuse to be close to him. Hell, the women he knew would never have considered *carrying* a load of wood.

Suddenly he wanted to make her life easier, wanted to assure her that she would never have to haul another load of wood, never carry her own bath water, never wonder about her next meal. There had to be a harmonious solution to this, somehow.

Jessica finished gathering the wood and went to dump it in a box next to the fireplace. Slowly she turned to face him, hoping beyond hope that he was fully dressed this time.

Thankfully, he was. "I hope you won't be offended with just tea and bread for breakfast," she said, feeling very self-conscious of her surroundings in the light of day.

"Not at all."

"I noticed Martin when I was out, Lord Callaway. I believe he'd like some water. You can take him down-stream from where you retrieved my bath water. You'll find a small pool there." Anything to get him out of sight long enough for her to collect her wits.

"I thought I asked you to call me Jacob."

"You did. But I think, all things considered, that we should not pretend to be on friendly terms. We both know that would be a farce."

Jacob swore softly under his breath. She was going to make this as difficult as possible. He'd hoped to start fresh this morning since they were both rested and had had a chance to think things through.

Jacob ran his fingers through his hair and strode to the door. He stopped and turned before he went out. "We *will* settle this matter when I return. Since I've yet to see the young man you mentioned last night I can only assume he'll not be arriving before we leave, if there even is a young man."

Jessica spread her feet and put her hands on her hips, preparing for another sparring of words. Then she remembered her promise to herself. *I will not let him goad me into another argument. Think of Ossie.*

Jacob was surprised that she didn't have a quick retort and more than just a little suspicious of the smile that touched the corner of her mouth. Seeing her standing there so defiantly made up his mind for him. There would be no further discussion, for that would take them another full day, and likely they would accomplish nothing—again. "No need to stoke up the fire. We shall be on our way shortly. I suggest you use this time to gather whatever possessions you feel it's necessary to take."

He looked around the cottage once again and then pointedly at Jessica. "You'll only need enough clothes for the two-day journey to Fairdale. Once there, we'll see that you're properly outfitted with a suitable wardrobe."

Jacob took his leave then, with Jessica staring after him in disbelief.

The nerve of that man! She was thankful he'd exited so quickly, for she was certain that if he hadn't, she would have found another object to throw at his head.

Instead she paced back and forth. New wardrobe, suitable wardrobe. How dare he! She sat down heavily on the small bed she'd slept in last night, then flopped onto her back.

Be realistic, she told herself. She held up her right arm and looked sadly at the tattered sleeve of the over-sized shirt she wore. If she were to go with him, *which she wasn't,* she certainly could not be roaming around a great estate in her father's grubby hand-me-downs.

She'd owned one gown in her entire life. Her father had bought it for her when she turned sixteen, but that was four years ago and her body had become considerably more curvaceous since then. Although it still fit fairly well, it was obviously the gown of a shorter, less developed *girl.*

The gown was packed away safely in a small trunk that James had made for her. It held the few treasures that were dear to her: the gown, a small wooden horse that James had carved, and a miniature of her mother. Those were the only things she would take with her—if she were leaving.

Which she was not! she reminded herself once again.

Jessica let her arm fall over her eyes. She was still tired. Every time she'd tried to sleep last night she'd dreamt of Jacob.

Sometimes she dreamed of their kiss, and woke with a start to find her heart beating rapidly and her breath coming in short gasps. Other times she dreamed of a fine mansion with her and Jacob standing at the front entry; the picture of a perfect, loving couple. The dreams were wonderful enough to make her consider going with the man and accepting his generous, albeit unromantic, proposal.

But that was all they were. Just dreams.

A short time later, Jacob walked Martin slowly back up the trail to the cottage. He wanted to give Jessica what time he could to let the inevitable sink in.

He stopped short when he heard a man's voice up ahead. From his position, he could see the front door of the cottage. Jessica was standing in the doorway leaning against the frame and just leaving was a small man, bent with age.

Ossie? That was the man she spoke of? She had said 'young man.' Jacob had a great respect for elders and didn't want to laugh aloud, but surely Jessica had to be mad if she thought he would leave her here with that old man. The fellow looked aged enough to be her grandfather, and certainly was not spry enough to protect and care for her.

He leaned against Martin, not at all comfortable with the tight feeling in his gut. Perhaps marriage to his father would not be so foreign to her if this was the kind of man she was used to entertaining.

Jacob clenched his jaw tighter and refused to revisit that option. He'd begun to think more on the option of marrying her himself and somewhere between seeing her struggling with the load of wood and seeing the old man leaving her door, he'd

decided that she would indeed be the next duchess of Fairdale —
his duchess.

"Thank you," Jessica called out to the old man. "I'll see you
soon."

Not if I can help it, Jacob thought, his hands tightening on the
reins.

He waited until Jessica went inside and then walked Martin
back to the small stable area. Jacob was surprised to find two
more horses there.

One was a fine-boned mare, obviously well-bred and strong,
with a glossy red coat. The other was a much older gelding, a bit
shaggy and not as well-bred as the mare, but still a strong horse.

He tied Martin outside the shelter and went to the door of the
cottage, leaning against the frame as he'd seen Jessica do.

Jessica felt Jacob's presence before she heard him. She
turned, wiping her hands on the front of her trousers. "Your
breakfast is ready."

Jacob watched her closely, noting the color that crept into her
cheeks under his perusal. He wondered how she was going to
explain her 'young man' to him. For a moment, he considered
not mentioning that he'd seen Ossie, just to see what sort of story
she'd concoct.

But it was time to quit playing games. They had to get a move
on if they were going to cover any ground today.

"As soon as we finish eating, we'll be leaving," Jacob stated
firmly as he moved to the small table. He placed both hands on
the back of the chair, preparing for an argument.

"I told you last night, and again this morning, I am not going
with you. Nothing has changed since then."

Jacob ran his fingers through his hair and sighed. Jessica
wondered if he realized he did that every time he was frustrated.
A smile touched her mouth as she noted that he'd made that
gesture quite often since his arrival.

"Look, Jessica. I saw Ossie leaving here when I came back
from the stream." Jessica raised an eyebrow and let him

continue. "I'm sure you're quite fond of the old gentleman, and perhaps he is someone who can ease the loneliness brought on by losing your father. But he is not someone you can spend your life with. Why, he's old enough to be—"

Jacob was brought up short by Jessica's wide eyes and sudden outburst of laughter. She took a step forward and braced her hands on the chair opposite where Jacob was standing. As she struggled to catch her breath, Jacob found himself again staring at her. She was even more beautiful when she smiled! And her laugh would have been completely infectious if he wasn't so sure she was laughing at him.

"Might I ask what you find so amusing?" he questioned with annoyance. "Jessica, I'm quite serious about you leaving with me, and Ossie isn't—"

Jessica finally regained control. "That wasn't Ossie you saw leaving here. For heaven's sake, Lord Callaway, Gerald is the village farrier. And yes, he is old enough to be my grandfather. In fact that's the very capacity in which I love him. He was merely returning my horses after putting new shoes on them."

Jacob finally managed a small smile himself, even though it was at his own expense. Oh, the relief he felt!

"I see. Well, I must admit that settles much better than the thought of you and him—never mind. I assume then that we can be on our way without further reference to Ossie, since there appears to be no Ossie?"

"Oh, but there is an Ossie," she said, sobering instantly.

The smile left Jacob's face as his frustration returned. He was about to tell Jessica that he'd had enough of her games when a sound from the far corner of the cottage drew his attention.

Jacob turned and saw a small boy playing in the corner, stacking the wooden blocks he'd noticed there the night before. He stared at the boy for a moment, and then looked back at Jessica. "*Who* is *that*?"

Jessica folded her arms and braced herself for an explosion. "*That* is Ossie. And he is the reason that I can't possibly accompany you."

Jacob's mouth dropped open as he returned his stare to the boy.

Oh, God! She had a son! But the letter from her father had said nothing of a child. Well, of course not! Surely her father had thought if he'd mentioned the boy, the arrangement may not be carried out.

The child looked up at Jacob with big eyes and a shy smile. He stared for only a moment then returned his attention to his blocks.

Jacob turned once again to Jessica. A thousand thoughts were pummeling his brain at once, each screaming to be heard. Finally, one broke free. "But your father implied you had never been married. If you had been, there would be no need for—"

"I have never been married, sir," she said with a frown.

Jacob groaned and looked toward the ceiling as the full impact of her words hit him. It was worse than he'd thought. "Wonderful. I guess it's no small surprise that your father didn't mention your illegitimate son. Surely he'd anticipated what kind of consequences that revelation would bring!"

Jacob heard his voice rising but was unable to stop it. "Just what did he expect? That my father and I would happily accept you and your bastard son into our family? It was bad enough when it was just you, but this—"

Jacob immediately regretted his words. He knew they'd cut through her like a saber; the mixture of pain and anger on her face said more than any angry reply could have.

He looked at Ossie, but that did nothing to ease his guilt. The child had stopped playing at the sound of the raised voice and was now looking at Jacob with fear and confusion.

Jessica went to the boy and picked him up. He clung to her neck, never taking his eyes off Jacob. She was shaking with anger. Her initial intention had been to explain about Ossie. But after his outburst Jessica was determined that Jacob would get nothing more from her.

The hatred that flowed from her eyes was enough to drown Jacob. He felt cruel and petty, but for the life of him he could not explain his reaction to seeing her son. Was it because she obviously had experience with men — or at least one man — and yet had set him off so firmly? He preferred to think his ego was not that overblown.

"Jessica, I'm sorry. My outburst was—"

"Do not even attempt to apologize, Lord Callaway. No words can compensate for your rudeness and cruelty. Just get out. As you can now see, it is quite impossible for me to go with you, just as I said it would be."

Jacob sat down in the chair while Jessica returned to the corner with Ossie. He watched as she sat on the floor with him for a moment, stroking his head and reassuring the boy that the 'loud man' wouldn't hurt him.

When she stood, she walked to where Jacob sat and stood before him. Her chest was heaving with unspent anger. "I meant what I said. Get the hell out of my house and leave Ossie and me in peace. I will not have you frightening him any more."

Jacob looked past her at the little boy. His guilt was nearly overwhelming. He liked children, truly he did. Although he'd not had much experience with them, the ones he'd spent any time with had proven enjoyable. He was also looking forward to having many of his own — someday.

Jacob took a deep breath and rubbed his forehead, not making any move to leave. This had to be addressed. He asked himself, did Ossie's existence really change things all that much? Jacob knew his father well enough to know that he would say, "Nothing's changed. Bring the boy along." His father's loyalty to James Patrick was steadfast and certainly it wasn't the boy's fault that he was born without a father's name.

Ossie seemed to be past any fear he'd felt for that brief moment. He was once again playing quietly with the wooden blocks. Jessica, however, was still standing before Jacob, the anger within her mounting by the second.

Jacob sighed again. "Jessica, I would like you to explain this situation to me. I find it—"

"I have nothing to say to you," Jessica said in a heated growl, not willing to discuss anything further with this beast. He had wounded her deeply. She'd been ready to explain everything to him and let him go on his way amicably. But not now.

Now she just wanted him to leave.

"Jessica, this doesn't really change things all that much." He held up his hand to halt her protest. "I know my outburst was uncalled for and inexcusable. Again I apologize, from my heart."

"As if you had a heart!" she fired.

Jacob bowed his head. He deserved that. "You must try to understand I was—still am—shocked to find that you have a child who's, what, about three years old? Especially at your young age." He tried not to let the fact that she would have only been seventeen when she'd conceived the lad affect him overmuch.

Against her will, Jessica acknowledged that he did seem sincere in his apology. And it was reasonable to assume that he would be surprised, especially since he'd first thought Ossie was an old man. If he would just leave them be! "Fine. I accept your apology," she lied. "Now, leave."

"No. I need some questions answered first."

"Why? It's obvious you no longer approve of me, if you ever truly did. I'm actually relieved that you no longer wish to consider me for the Duchess of Fairdale. As you said, it was bad enough when it was just me. But now, oh, you were quite right in your implication, sir! We would only bring shame upon your fine family name. Why, you should get out of here as quickly as possible before some of our wretched commonness rubs off on you!" she finished sarcastically.

Jacob remained still, letting her vent her anger. "I must have some answers, Jessica. I cannot leave things as they are."

Jessica stood her ground. "If I answer your questions, will

you go?"

"Yes."

She narrowed her eyes, not believing the suddenness of his answer. "What do you want to know?"

Ossie walked up behind Jessica and wrapped his arms around her leg. She tenderly stroked his head and stared at Jacob, almost daring him to say anything untoward again.

"First, where is the boy's father?"

Jessica thought about her answer before giving it. She could make this all very easy, but was not inclined to do so. The less this beast knew about her situation, the better. "I don't know," she finally answered.

"You don't know?"

She shook her head.

Another thought leapt into Jacob's mind. Had the boy's father abandoned them? He was surprised at the surge of anger he suddenly felt.

His immediate inclination was to track down and kill the brute that had taken her innocence and then left her to manage on her own.

"Who is he?" Jacob asked with more anger than he'd intended. Ossie shrunk back a little, and Jacob immediately forced himself to lower his voice. "I'm sorry. Who is Ossie's father?"

Jessica knelt down by Ossie's side. "Sweetling, will you go out and bring your travel sack in from the shed? I think Gerald left it out there. Take your time. Here," she reached up and took Jacob's untouched toast from the table. "Feed the little squirrel family while you're out there."

Ossie smiled and ran outside, obviously glad to get away from Jacob which did nothing to ease Jacob's feelings of guilt.

"Well, who is the boy's father?"

Again, Jessica pondered her answer carefully before speaking. Whatever she said could drastically alter the outcome of this confrontation. She decided on the option that would send this pompous ass on his way. It was the truth, but definitely misleading.

"I don't know who his father is."

"You—Jessica, don't joke—"

"I'm not joking, m'lord. I honestly have no idea who Ossie's father is."

Jacob sat in silence. He would have been willing to wager that nothing else could have shocked him this day. But she had managed to do just that.

Chapter 7

Jacob looked over his shoulder once again to assure himself that Jessica was actually following him on her mare. Ossie was bundled up in front of her in her large coat, falling asleep to the gentle rhythm of the horse's walk.

What had finally convinced her to come with him? He was sure he'd never know.

Jessica met Jacob's look as he turned in his saddle. She held it for as long as she could, and then dropped her eyes to the ground in front of her.

When Ossie had returned to the cottage with his travel sack, Jessica made it clear to Jacob that she wanted no further discussion of the boy's father. But Jacob refused to drop the subject.

It was plain to see that Lord Callaway was not going to be put off in spite of an illegitimate child. Her plan was on the verge of failing. If that happened, Ossie would be the one who might get hurt.

Foreseeing that, she made a change in her original decision. She had to give Jacob credit. He'd been as relentless in his decision as she'd been in hers.

In that brief moment of decision Jessica realized that the only way to solve this dilemma was to go with Jacob and confront the elderly Duke face to face. Her own father had spoken of the Duke so often that she felt she almost knew him. Surely he would be more reasonable than his imperious son.

Perhaps she could convince the Duke that his mission was unnecessary, that she could take care of herself and Ossie without their help. With the Duke she would be completely honest and hope that he would see the situation as she did. It was worth a try.

And, at the very least, Ossie would have an adventure to remember. The little boy's face had split in a wide grin when Jessica turned to him and said, "Don't bother unpacking your sack, sweetling. We're going on a journey with Lord Callaway."

The look of surprise on Jacob's face when she'd conceded was almost worth the arguing she'd had to put up with.

Before she lost her nerve, Jessica had quickly gathered up the few items that were most precious to her, along with some clothing for Ossie and a few toys. She truly wasn't planning on staying at Fairdale for any longer than necessary, but to avoid further questioning from Jacob she knew she had to pack a few possessions to seem credible.

She'd saddled her mare and loaded the old gelding with their possessions and had them on the trail within fifteen minutes.

After several hours in the saddle with Ossie, Jessica's arms were growing tired. Ossie had fallen asleep against her, and it was a struggle to hold his weight. She looked down at the sweet, peaceful face and placed a kiss on his forehead.

Oh, how she loved this child. She drew strength from the need to protect Ossie at all costs.

Jacob was moved by the tenderness Jessica showed the little boy. He remained turned in his saddle watching her for several more minutes despite the fact that she was obviously uncomfortable beneath his stare.

He imagined how she would look bestowing such love on their own children—*their own children?*

He shook his head to clear it.

Get a hold of yourself, old boy! She has an illegitimate son...she changes her mind as easily as she changes her clothes...she—

Changes her clothes. Unbidden, the memory of Jessica dressing behind that thin curtain came rushing into his thoughts. The lamplight enhancing her silhouette; the heavy waves of her hair, her sweet smell, her searching kiss....

Damn! He needed something to concentrate on besides the woman who was following behind him.

Jacob brought Martin to a halt.

When Jessica had ridden up even with him, he reached out to her.

"Let me have the boy."

"No. I'm fine."

"You are not fine. You look as though you're about to fall off that horse if you don't drop him first."

Jessica couldn't argue. The five hours they'd spent traveling were beginning to take their toll. Her arms were cramping from trying to hold the reins and make Ossie comfortable at the same time. She reluctantly handed the child over to Jacob, hating to give in on even this small matter.

Ossie woke only briefly during the transfer. He looked up at Jacob and smiled, then snuggled against Jacob's chest and went soundly back to sleep.

For the second time in as many days, Jacob was experiencing a flood of new emotions.

The complete trust in Ossie's eyes melted Jacob's heart and brought forth a rush of protective feelings. Jacob realized with relief that Ossie had forgiven him for his outburst during their unexpected meeting that morning.

It was hopeless; Jacob knew that now. Not only could he no longer deny his rapidly growing admiration for Jessica, but Ossie was on his way to winning his heart as well.

"We'll reach the inn where we'll be spending the night in about two hours," Jacob commented, trying to focus on something other than the woman riding at his side.

"Oh, so you don't plan on making us ride straight through to your estate? How generous," Jessica said sarcastically. Her sore muscles were making her testy.

Jacob clenched his jaw to keep from making an equally sarcastic remark. Damn but this woman could make a mess of his emotions! One minute he was silently admiring her and the next he wanted to turn her across his knee and spank her until her sarcasm was but a distant memory.

"Ride straight through? No, of course not. I wouldn't do that to the child," he answered tersely.

They rode in silence for several minutes. "Lord Callaway, you cannot expect Ossie to make another day's ride like this tomorrow. He's just a child, he's—"

"I don't expect that at all, Jesse." That he'd used her father's favorite shortened form of her name didn't sit well with Jessica. It seemed much too comfortable.

"My coach is waiting at the inn. We'll be traveling the rest of the way in that. I assure you, you'll be quite comfortable. The horses will follow along behind."

"You had your coach sent? You seem to have been quite certain that I would be accompanying you."

"My lady, there was never a doubt in my mind," he lied.

She had to admit that it was kind of Jacob to have considered her comfort, for he hadn't known about Ossie when he'd made the arrangements. She felt herself beginning to soften; oh, this wouldn't do at all.

Jessica reined her mare in behind Jacob.

Oh, it was going to be a gut-wrenching ride in that coach tomorrow. Riding in an enclosed conveyance with little to distract her except the man she was trying desperately to hate was not going to make for a pleasant journey. Thank heavens Ossie would with them!

Jacob turned in his saddle to find Jessica still staring at him. The blush that crept up her cheeks brought a smile to his handsome face.

"Jessica, exactly how old is Ossie?" He knew he had to

choose his questions carefully.

"He's three and a half." Well, so much for her plan of avoiding conversation.

"He seems to be very well-mannered. You've done a fine job raising him thus far."

"I intend to continue doing so."

He ignored the hard edge to her words. "He's very quiet. Did I really frighten him so much?"

As much as she would have liked to let Jacob feel guilty for Ossie's silence, she knew she couldn't allow her resentment to carry that far.

"No. As you can see, he's no longer afraid of you," she said grudgingly. She'd seen how Ossie had smiled up at Jacob. She was thankful that he was no longer frightened of Jacob but it had piqued her that Ossie seemed to be growing fond of the big buffoon.

She paused for a moment, trying to decide just how much she should tell him. "Ossie doesn't speak."

"He's mute, then?"

"No. He spoke brilliantly until a few months ago."

At her short answer Jacob let his exasperation show with a sigh. "What happened?" Trying to get answers from this woman was nearly impossible!

Jessica waited a moment then quietly said, "He suffered through an extremely terrifying experience. He hasn't said a word since."

"But what—"

"I don't wish to talk about it when he's within earshot. Even the mention of it brings on nightmares for days. Just leave it alone." Jessica pulled her cloak tighter around her to keep the rain from running down her neck.

Jacob was frustrated but he was learning rapidly that the stubborn set of Jessica's jaw meant there was no room for further discussion on the matter. Besides, the last thing he wanted to do was upset Ossie again.

When they finally reached the inn, Jessica nearly fell from her horse in cold exhaustion. It had been a very long time since she'd ridden further than the small village of Wilfordshire, and even that trip was made only rarely.

The door to the inn opened revealing a warm and inviting interior with a huge fire blazing in the hearth across the main room.

A squat little woman came out into the evening's downpour, her apron held over her head to protect her. "Eve'nin' m'lord! I was beginnin' t' think ye weren't goin' t' make it t'day."

"We got off to a late start." Jacob answered without looking at Jessica as he carefully dismounted. Ossie stirred and turned in Jacob's arms, rubbing his eyes as he came fully awake. Quickly he looked around, and upon seeing Jessica, smiled and waved.

"Aw! I didn' know ye'd be bringin' a wee one wit' cha'," the little woman said with a smile.

"Neither did I," Jacob said pointedly without looking at Jessica.

" 'Ere, come inside. I've got lamb and bread left over from supper, still warm!"

At the mention of food, Ossie squirmed to get down and happily followed the little innkeeper inside. Jessica started after him, but Jacob reached out and stopped her.

Jessica looked down at the hand on her arm and then up at Jacob. "I would like to get out of this rain and join Ossie for some food. Or are you intent on starving me? If this is how you intend to take care of me, as you put it, then I assure you I can take much better care of myself."

Jacob squeezed her arm slightly. "Why must you always be so contrary? I do not plan on starving you. You'll be fed soon enough. I'm simply reminding you that we are no where near finished with our discussion about Ossie, and a number of other things."

"And I say that we are quite finished, Lord Callaway. I will speak to your father when we arrive. Since it was the duke, not you, that my father was so fond of I shall save my answers for him. I have faith that he will be a much more reasonable man than you."

They were standing too close; Jessica could feel the warmth from his body warding off the damp chill that surrounded them. Her breathing was becoming heavier and her knees began to weaken. That his mere nearness could do this to her was frightening! She tried to back away but Jacob held fast to her arm.

Even after seven hours in the saddle, her hair wet and clinging to her face he thought she was the most beautiful woman he'd ever seen.

His gaze lowered to the wet shirt that was molded so snugly to her bosom and immediately he felt his desire heighten. With an effort he forced his eyes to return to her face inhaling deeply of her unique scent as he did so.

He raised his fingers to her chin, intending only to force her to look at him, to acknowledge the attraction that was so strong between them. Jacob leaned into her, powerless to stop the small distance between them from closing.

The shudder that swept through her body when she recognized the force of his desire shook her to her soul. When she gasped lightly at the tenderness of his touch and closed her eyes, he forgot the questions he'd been about to ask.

He lowered his mouth to hers, capturing her lips before they had a chance to escape.

Against her will, Jessica's fingers moved to the curls at the nape of his neck. For nearly seven hours she'd studied his back and had, without wanting to, wondered what it would be like to weave her fingers through that thick mass of hair, to have those steel bands that he called arms wrap around her again, to feel his lips against hers just one more time.

Jacob pulled her closer and raised her to her toes. Her body leaned against the full length of him; nothing was left to her imagination, or his. His hand moved to the back of her sodden hair, holding her captive while his lips scorched hers with such a heat.

Stop, stop! a voice screamed in her head. Are you mad? Oh, yes, she was certain that she'd gone quite mad for she was completely without the strength to pull away from him!

His lips parted hers, gently at first and then with a possessive fervor that consumed all rationale. His tongue traced the inside of her mouth, drawing a soft moan from the depths of her soul.

Jessica's hands clawed at Jacob's shoulders wanting to be closer, needing to quench the fire that was burning inside her despite the rain that poured down upon them.

Jacob released her lips slowly, wanting to look into her eyes, daring her to deny what was happening between them. What he saw there was no denial, but a tearful fear of something unknown. What was she afraid of?

It was only the innkeeper's ill-timed return that kept him from getting his answer.

"Ahem. *Ahem*! I'm sorry to interrupt, but ye're supper will be gettin' cold, and if I might be so motherish, ye'll both be catchin' yer deaths if ye continue on out here in this rain!" The little innkeeper chuckled and shook her head then she walked back inside.

Jessica tore herself from Jacob's embrace. She looked at Jacob only to find he was having as much difficulty catching his breath as she was.

At that moment she loathed herself for giving in to her pure physical desire. She loathed him even more for what he was, who he was, and how he made her body react....

Jessica no longer trusted her own common sense. It grated on her pride to do so, but she implored Jacob for help. Left to her own devices, she was not certain that she could stave off another assault on her senses.

"Stay away from me, Jacob. Please!" Jessica said in a hoarse whisper, her eyes pleading with his. "I can't— "She choked on a sob and then touched his arm as she turned and walked quickly into the inn.

Jacob had to wait for several minutes to let his desire reach a manageable level. He'd seen the plea in her eyes, heard it in her voice. But why? Damn it, why? Was the prospect of a life with him really so unthinkable? He could not fathom her resistance when their attraction was so irrefutable.

When Jacob finally entered the dining room of the inn he found it empty. As he stood in the doorway a young man approached him. "I'll be takin' yer mounts out back now, sir. D'ye 'ave everthing ye'll be needin' from them?"

Jacob looked around for Jessica. "Where is the young lady that I arrived with?"

"Me mum took 'er and the lad up t' their rooms, as the lady requested. They'll be 'avin' their supper up there. Now, about yer 'orses—"

"Just bring in the pack from the white gelding and take it to the lady's room. My clothes are already in my room from when I lodged two days ago," Jacob answered, dismissing the young man.

"Right, m'lord."

Jacob found a warm mug of spiced cider and a plate of steaming lamb and fresh bread waiting near the fire. He removed his soaked traveling cape and hung it over the back of a chair. The steam that rose from it caught and held his attention.

He sat and leaned back in another chair, stretching his long legs out in front of him, and sipped on the hot brew, ignoring the fare before him.

Until yesterday he'd been sure of himself and of the life he led. And now, one day later, he'd met a woman who not only frustrated him beyond measure but also drove him mad with desire as no other woman had. His thoughts were unpredictable where she was concerned.

Perhaps he should keep his distance from her as she'd asked, give himself some time to understand these new emotions, time to figure out if these were in fact true emotions or merely novel passions born of meeting this unusual woman—and her son.

He sighed heavily and rubbed his eyes. Tomorrow would be soon enough to sort out his thoughts. Now what he needed more than anything was a good night's sleep.

Chapter 8

A gentle tapping on her shoulder woke Jessica from her nap. She was groggy from the past two restless nights and it took several moments for her to remember that they were traveling to Fairdale. Ossie crawled into her lap and cuddled into a ball.

Jessica put her arms around the small boy and rested her chin on his head. She had no idea how long she'd slept or how far they were from their destination. She hoped they would be arriving soon, for she needed to stretch her sore legs. After yesterday's long ride, sitting in a coach should have been a relief. But even now she could feel her aching muscles longing to stretch and move.

The thought of arriving at Fairdale brought with it a rush of emotions, none of which were pleasant.

When she and Ossie awoke at the inn this morning, the chamber maid informed them that Lord Callaway had left in the dark hours of the morning.

Jessica's initial assumption was that he'd thought better of his plans to bring her to Fairdale and had left her to return to her small cottage with Ossie without so much as a word of farewell. How dare he treat her this way!

Her indignation was about to explode when the innkeeper informed her that she and Ossie were to continue to Fairdale with "'is lordship's fine coach and driver."

Jessica had questioned both the innkeeper and Giles, Lord

Callaway's driver, as to why Jacob had left so suddenly. But neither could, or would, tell her anything.

Now, as they swayed along in the coach, she felt her anger returning once again, but she was having a difficult time deciding where to aim that anger.

She hated the sense of disappointment she'd felt when she thought Jacob had abandoned them, and for that she was angry at him.

But more, she hated the sense of relief she'd felt when the innkeeper had explained that she was still to go to Fairdale as planned, and for that she was angry at herself. She'd known this man for only two days and already he was making her think and feel like a fool!

Ossie stirred in her lap and sat up. He pulled the curtains back and pointed out the window.

No longer were they on a muddied road in the middle of nowhere. At some point they had turned on to a cobbled drive, lined on each side by majestic trees.

The coach made a sweeping turn and as they came around the bend Jessica couldn't stop her shocked intake of breath. Up ahead was a house—no, a mansion; oh hell—it was a building that appeared to be bigger than the entire village they'd left behind all those hours ago.

A light shone from every window, and of those there were many.

Ossie, too, was caught up in the dreamlike vision before him. Jessica held Ossie closer to her, as if his little body was the only thing that could remind her that this wasn't a dream.

The coach rolled to a stop before a pair of tall white doors. Great pillars held a wide roof over the steps and between each of the pillars to the sides of the massive steps were thick green bushes which effectively protected the entrance to the monstrous dwelling.

Within seconds, the doors opened and two men appeared, greeting Giles as he opened the door to the interior of the coach.

Giles handed Jessica down and then reached for Ossie. As he set Ossie on the steps he turned to one of the men who were unloading Jessica's small box of possessions. "How goes it in there?" he asked, jerking his head towards the house.

The smartly dressed valet glanced at Jessica and then back to Giles. At Giles' nod, he answered, "Not well. He'll be lucky to make it through the night. Or perhaps he'd be luckier not to." The valet handed Jessica's box to a young man. "Take this to the yellow suite and tell Lord Callaway and Mrs. Holmes that our guests have arrived."

The boy nodded quickly and disappeared inside.

By the time Jessica and Ossie reached the doors, a round little woman appeared and hurried them all inside. Jessica was at a loss, in complete awe of the entryway and the beautiful furnishings and decor it held. She wondered how she would ever make it through this house to her room with so much to take in.

She wanted to drink in everything with her eyes, create memories to last for a very long time after she left this place; for leaving was still foremost on her mind.

Giles made a low sound behind her and Jessica realized that she was still blocking the doorway. "Oh, excuse me. It's just that I've never, I mean it's all so...." she stumbled over her words and then felt her cheeks grow warm with embarrassment.

"Aw, lassie. Don't ye worry none," a cheery voice said. "Come inside and let me take yer things. I'm Mrs. Holmes. I'm the head housekeeper here, and if there's anything ye need at any time, I'm the one to get it for ye." The woman puffed up her small frame with all the importance she could muster.

"Thank you. I'm Jessica and this is Ossie." Jessica finally managed to say.

"Ah yes, Lady Patrick. I've been told all about you and the young master here," she said with a wink towards Ossie. "Lord Callaway's been expecting ye. Just starting to worry a bit with that weather a-brewin' out there. Poor dear, he's got so much on

71

his mind. I'm just glad that ye've arrived safe and sound."

Jessica was amused to hear Lord Callaway referred to as a "poor dear." Those words would have never entered her mind when trying to describe the man.

Mrs. Holmes helped Jessica off with her heavy traveling cloak and tried to take Ossie's from him as well, but the boy moved quickly behind Jessica's legs.

"I'm sorry, Mrs. Holmes. Ossie has very few possessions of his own, and he rather prefers to keep them close at hand."

Mrs. Holmes bent over to put her face close to Ossie's. "And a right smart lad ye are fer that! But I tell ye what, if ye decides ye'd like me to take care of that fine coat fer ye, just let me know."

"Oh," Jessica said, "I should tell you, he doesn't speak."

"Yes, that's what Lord Callaway said. It looks like Ossie and I will just have to find our own way to communicate with each other, isn't that so?"

Ossie grinned up at Mrs. Holmes and then, to Jessica's surprise, he took off his little coat and handed it to the housekeeper.

Mrs. Holmes straightened and winked at Jessica. "Looks like we're already communicatin'! I'll take real fine care of this."

"Thank you." She looked around the great entryway and her eyes followed a polished balustrade up a wide curving staircase. "Mrs. Holmes, is Lord Callaway—is he—what I mean is he left in such a hurry and I—"

"Ah, and I can see no one bothered to tell ye what happened. Men can be such inconsiderate oafs," Mrs. Holmes said matter-of-factly.

Jessica had to smile. "I don't mean to pry but perhaps now is not the best time for us to be here."

"On the contrary, my dear. Ye see His Grace took a drastic turn for the worse yesterday. We sent a messenger to fetch Lord Callaway from the inn. It won't be long now." Mrs. Holmes' eyes filled with tears. It was obvious she truly cared about her employer. "It was very important to the duke that he meet you. I believe that's what's keeping him alive."

Jessica shook her head. "Oh, but I don't even know him. Surely it's not—"

Mrs. Holmes held up her hand. "My dear, I'm just the housekeeper. I run this house from top to bottom, but when it comes to the personal tides that flow here, I sail clear. All I know is that Lord Callaway wanted to be informed the second you arrived. I'll take you to him."

"That won't be necessary, Mrs. Holmes." Jacob's voice boomed down from the top of the stairs. Both Jessica and Ossie jumped at the sound. "Johnny informed me of their arrival."

"Shall I show them to their rooms now, my lord?"

"No. I'll show them later. My father wants to see them first. Please come with me," Jacob said as he held out his hand from the top stair.

Jessica took Ossie's hand and led him toward the stairs. She glanced down, expecting to find a fearful look on the boy's face. But instead she was surprised to find a huge grin and twinkling eyes. Her eyes followed Ossie's to Jacob, who was smiling warmly at Ossie.

Jessica shook her head. There was no accounting for a child's taste!

At the top of the stairs Jessica stopped and looked up at Jacob. Her memory hadn't exaggerated his fine looks in the hours during their separation; but now he looked haggard and worn. His eyes were red-rimmed, attesting to his lack of sleep.

"Hello, Ossie. I trust you had a pleasant journey?"

Ossie looked up at Jacob and nodded. The boy's eyes caught sight of a full suit of armor standing further down the hall. He looked up at Jacob with a question in his eyes and pointed down the hall.

"By all means, Ossie. Have a look at it." The boy skipped off, leaving Jessica alone with Jacob.

Jacob's eyes swept over Jessica, his heated gaze immediately taking the chill from her bones. "You're wearing a dress?" he asked with a raised eyebrow.

Jessica felt her face burn. For some reason she felt it necessary to don her only dress that morning. It was too tight across the bosom and a few inches too short, but it was the only one she had. "Does that surprise—or offend you, my lord? After all, I am a woman. Or had you forgotten?"

Jacob folded his arms across his broad chest. "Oh no, my dear. I've hardly forgotten. In fact it was the vision of you in that wet, transparent shirt and those clinging trousers that kept me awake on my journey here last night."

"Oh! You are despicable! How dare you—"

"What? Speak the truth? Come now, Jesse. It's not even been twenty-four hours since we last kissed. And wet clothes or not, I could hardly forget that you are all woman. As for your dress, I find that it suits you very nicely. However, you can hardly blame me for being surprised since until now I've only seen you in britches and your father's shirts. And of course you'll recall that you tried to pass yourself off as a boy when—"

"Of course I recall!" Jessica said through clenched teeth.

"That's something else I would like to have further explained to me. But not now. My father is anxious to meet you."

Jacob crooked his elbow and held in out for Jessica to take. She looked at his arm as if it were a snake poised to bite, for she knew the jolt that would course through her body if she were to touch him. Instead, she made a show of reaching to gather her skirts and step around him.

Jacob chuckled. "Oh really, my lady. I will hardly bite you if you take my arm. At least not here, in the presence of the boy. And your dress is already on the short side. If you gather it up much further I may have no recourse but to openly admire the length of leg you present me. Of course if you're afraid...."

Jessica dropped the folds of material immediately and roughly grabbed Jacob's arm. He lightly placed his hand over hers to hold it there.

She was not surprised at the surge of heat that coursed through her body at his touch. The silence as they stared at one another was deafening.

"I acquiesce only to keep you from further insulting my poor manner of dress," Jessica said tightly as they began walking down the hall.

Jacob stopped and turned her to face him, a hand on each arm, his eyes looking deeply into hers. He'd heard the faint tone of pain in her voice and suddenly realized how she must feel, coming to a new home, an admittedly grand home, and feeling so very out of place. "Jessica, I was only jesting with you. I never meant to hurt your feelings. If I did, I humbly apologize."

Oh, why did he have to sound so sincere? Jessica had known he was teasing her, but her retort was the only thing she could think of to give her a safe way to escape the mesmerizing spell he so easily cast. And now he was being so damn courteous.

She backed away from Jacob without answering him and turned her attention towards Ossie. "Come, Ossie. We are going to meet a very important man. He is a duke, and as such you must show him great respect. Remember to bow when you meet him."

Ossie nodded and offered Jessica a practice bow. "That's fine!" she said as she knelt in front of the boy. "There's one more thing, sweetling. The duke is very tired right now, so he's lying in his bed. But you're not to worry about that, all right?"

Jessica rose and turned back to Jacob as Ossie skipped ahead of them, stopping on his way to inspect a statue. "Shall we?"

Jacob nodded. "Why did you tell Ossie that my father was only tired? I've come to terms with the fact that he won't be with us much longer. Don't you think it will difficult for him to understand why Father is suddenly gone?"

"Perhaps a little," Jessica answered as they moved toward a set of double doors at the end of the well-lit hall. "But Ossie has been frightened of sickness and death ever since he—"Jessica stopped short. "—ever since he watched my father fall ill and die," she finished rapidly.

"I see. You should brace yourself too. I'm afraid he doesn't look very well just now."

Chapter 9

Jacob opened the double doors. The room was dark compared to the bright hall. The only sources of light came from the large fireplace and one lamp sitting on the table next to the bed.

Jessica's eyes strained to find a figure in the ornately carved bed. At last she was able to make out the duke. His thin body barely made a wrinkle in the quilts; his hair and skin were so white that they nearly blended into the silk cases on the pillows.

At last the duke opened his eyes. They were like two shocking green emeralds that had been cast into a drift of snow. His eyes—so like Jacob's—had an edge that told Jessica this man was still sharp.

For that she was grateful, since she still planned on trying to reason with the Duke of Fairdale and negotiate her return to her own home.

"Father, may I present—"

The duke raised a frail hand and spoke with a raspy voice. "No need for introductions. Young lady, you are the image of your mother. Please come closer."

Jessica took a tentative step towards the bed, Ossie clutching her hand at her side. The closer she went, the more life she could see in his features. How tragic that his body was apparently giving up the fight when his spirit was still so strong.

"I'm very pleased to meet you, Your Grace. My father spoke very highly of you. I hope you're not offended when I say I feel as though I know you."

"Not at all, dear. I hope you understand why you were brought here. It was not to purposely disrupt your life. Truth be told, this is more my fault than your father's, so if you are feeling any anger towards him, please let it go. He thought that contract was made in jest, but I was serious. He didn't ask to have it fulfilled. I'm the one urging that. I'm sure James didn't expect to fall ill; none of us do."

Austen took a ragged breath and Jessica and Jacob both rushed forward to help him sit more upright. He feebly brushed them aside. "I'm fine. Really. But I must say I find it hopeful that the two of you can work as a team!" he said with a little laugh.

Jessica and Jacob both straightened and Jessica took a side-step away.

"Now as I was saying," Austen continued, "your father had only your safety and best interests at heart. As you know, he feared that your maternal grandfather, the marquis, would set out to find you if they heard of his death. Actually, it is the marchioness that you must be wary of. As I understand it, she is still intent on getting her hands on you."

"But Your Grace, I have no desire to find them, let alone go to live with them."

"Your desires would mean little to them. I'm not usually one to speak disparagingly of others, but I can tell you that Hayden Atterberry and his wife should be avoided. Without your father, they can and will attempt to sway you to their side."

"But why would they even want me?"

Austen eyed Jessica closely, looking for any false modesty. There was none. "My dear girl, have you any idea how comely you are? Why, the Atterberrys could marry you off to any number of extremely wealthy suitors. Whoever would offer them the best financial reward would become your husband, despite age, looks, or manners."

"But I have no interest in marrying—anyone—at this time." She shot a quick look at Jacob which was not lost on Austen.

He chuckled hoarsely. "Am I to understand, Jake, that you took it upon yourself to propose the marriage and our fair Lady Patrick has flatly refused you?"

Jacob colored slightly. "I fail to see what you find so amusing, Father, since it was your idea that she marry into the family. And by the way, she refused to marry you as well," he finished with a half-mocking bow.

"Well, I can't blame her for that," Austen said with a smile.

Jessica glared at Jacob. Could he not go one hour without reminding her that he only wanted to marry her out of a sense of commitment and duty? Her pride would not stand much more of this.

For a few brief seconds she had entertained the idea of being the lady of this house, the next Duchess of Fairdale. But the thought of being tied to this inconsiderate oaf effectively drove those thoughts from her mind.

It was time to set things straight.

Ossie had been standing quietly behind Jessica, watching the duke without being noticed. Jessica reached for Ossie's hand and pulled him gently around in front of her.

"Your Grace, there is one very good and simple reason why I won't be marrying into this family."

Austen raised his head a little and noticed the boy for the first time. "And who have we here?"

"This is Ossie."

"Ossie?"

"Yes," Jacob offered. "It appears James failed to mention that his daughter had a child of her own. Ossie is Jessica's son." He folded his arms in front of him and waited to see his father's reaction, though he knew what it would be.

His father, as he had, would see this as a minor hurdle after the initial shock wore off.

Austen narrowed his eyes and looked closely at the little boy. To Jessica's surprise, Ossie showed no fear of this man. In fact, he walked right up to the duke's bed and stood very near the elderly gentleman.

Jessica took a deep breath, preparing herself for a heated confrontation with Jacob. She kept her eyes on the duke. "Actually, Your Grace, Ossie is—"

"Oh my," Austen whispered. "Oh—my—God."

"Father, are you all right?" Jacob hadn't expected his father to take the news so poorly.

Austen reached out and took the boy's hand. Without looking away from Ossie's face he said, "Jake, I wish to speak with Jessica and the boy alone. Would you excuse us?"

Jessica tossed a worried glance at Jacob. "It's not really necessary for your son to leave; he will find—"

Austen looked at Jacob. "Please, son. I need a moment."

Jacob looked warily at Jessica and then nodded to his father. "As you wish."

Jacob didn't like being dismissed, but he could hardly refuse his father's wishes for privacy. What the devil could this be about? His father's face hadn't held this much color in weeks.

He turned back to Jessica. "My rooms are the next set of doors down the hall. Please let me know when your meeting is adjourned," he said with barely hidden annoyance.

Jessica watched as he left the room, closing the doors behind him. She turned back to Austen, more confused than ever.

To her dismay, Jessica saw that Ossie had climbed up onto the bed and was now reaching to touch the duke's face. "Ossie! No! You mustn't bother—"

"Please, Jessica, let him be," Austen directed softly.

Jessica watched in amazement as Ossie tenderly touched the old duke's face and hair. He cupped his small hand and laid it upon Austen's cheek. For several minutes the two stared at each other in silence, until at last a tear slipped from the duke's eye. Ossie gently brushed it aside and flashed one of his infectious smiles at the duke.

Austen smiled in return and nodded ever so slightly. It was as if the two, young and vital, old and weak, were communicating on a private level.

Ossie looked across the shadowy room and spied the huge tapestry that hung on the wall. He pointed at it and at Austen's nod slipped off the bed, giving the duke's hand one last squeeze, and went closer to study finely crafted piece.

Jessica still stood in awe of what she'd just witnessed. Something magical had just happened here. Now that Ossie was gone, some of the color had once again faded from the duke's face, but his eyes still shown brightly.

"Your Grace, I—"

"Jessica, why did you tell Jacob that boy is your son when in fact he isn't?"

Jessica's mouth dropped open and she stammered for a moment before finding her words. "I—I—what I—" She took a deep breath and began again. "Actually I didn't tell him that. Jacob assumed Ossie was mine from the start. And then he made me so angry with his rude remarks and misbegotten ideas that I didn't feel like disabusing him of the notion."

Austen smiled. "Yes, Jacob will occasionally make a fire out of an ember. But he usually comes right before too long."

"I had planned to tell you immediately, Your Grace, and explain to you that I am merely the boy's guardian. As such, I could never leave him behind. More than that, I love him as if he was my own son. I would not expect your family to take us both in, but you see, in our own way, we are family. I would rather live in my cottage with Ossie than in your grand home without him."

Jessica feared that she sounded ungrateful, but Austen paid no attention to her last statement. "You're his guardian, you say? But why? Where is his mother, Jessica?" Austen asked, his voice raising a notch.

Jessica worried at the duke's sudden reaction and wanted to calm him quickly. "She's dead," Jessica blurted out. "She died a few months ago. A terrible sickness took hold of our village and unfortunately we lost many good people. My father was one of them. We'd felt since we lived so far out from the village that we'd be relatively safe, but you knew Father; he couldn't stop himself from seeing to others. I guess he eventually had too much exposure and he took ill himself. I suppose I'm just very lucky that I was spared."

Jessica looked towards Ossie to be certain he was out of earshot. "As for Ossie's mother, I was her closest friend and when she realized she was not going to make it through, she asked me to take care of Ossie. I have no idea who his father is. As close as we were, she would never tell me. It was to protect both the father and Ossie, I suppose. Evidently he was a well-respected man, perhaps even married...I don't know."

Austen closed his eyes. "No, no, no," he said whispered in a barely audible voice.

Jessica was silent for several moments, then, "Your Grace, may I ask how you knew Ossie wasn't my son?"

Austen opened his eyes and looked across the room at the boy. "Because he's my son, Jessica," he said quietly.

At Jessica's sharp intake of breath he refocused on her. "But that can't be," she whispered. "With all due respect, sir, you must be mistaken." Jessica was beginning to wonder if her initial assessment of the duke's wits had been wrong. But his next words took her breath away again.

"Lizette," he whispered. "My poor, darling Lizette."

Jessica felt her knees growing weak; she took several steps backwards before finding a chair to brace herself against. How did he know her friend's name? "Your Grace, I don't—"

"Bring that chair closer, girl." Jessica did as she was told and sat forward to hear Austen's whispered words. "I don't want to upset the boy so I ask that you don't tell him, or anyone, of this until the time is right. You'll know when that is. I can see that you're very devoted to him and for that I shall be eternally grateful."

"I told you, I love him as if he were my own. But please, you must tell me how—"

Austen held up a bony hand. "On occasion I went to Wilfordshire to meet with your father. James was a fine man and I still wanted to help him if there was any way I could. As you know, he was stubborn in his refusal. I see he passed that trait along to you, my dear."

Jessica's cheeks colored but she held her silence. Austen continued. "When I would come to visit I always stayed at the inn. On my third visit to your father, I met Lizette. She was such a beautiful girl, even despite that ragged scar on her face." Austen drifted away for a moment, remembering his darling. "I never understood how other men didn't find her beauty as alluring. I suppose it was to my advantage, though, for if she'd had suitors, she likely wouldn't have had the time for me. She was kind and doting to this old man, and so very honest. Mind you, I was in much better shape than I am now," he said with a sad smile.

Jessica leaned back in her chair, still unable to fully grasp what the duke was telling her. "So *you* were her special love? The only things she would tell me about you were that you were the kindest man in the world, very handsome, and very prominent. She never even told me your name, only that she called you Ossie and thus named her son after you."

"My given name is Austen; she called me Ossie in jest."

Jessica sighed and rubbed her temples. "Of course. But I still don't—when he was born—you've never seen—"

"I don't know what Jacob has told you of my illness, but I've been confined to my bed for a little over three and a half years now. Before that time, I saw Lizette monthly. I even purchased some properties near your village so I would have an excuse to travel there.

Lizette and I were together for several years. After the first six months, I asked her to marry me. She refused, but I asked her every time I visited. She always turned me down, citing our different backgrounds and social statuses as the reason.

No matter how persuasive I tried to be or what steps I

offered to take—I even offered to leave Fairdale and move into a modest cottage there—she simply said she was scared to risk upsetting our relationship with any kind of change. Personally, I believe that damned scar had her convinced that she wasn't good enough or lovely enough to be my wife. What a misconception that was! She was the one true love of my life."

Austen weakly pounded his fist against the quilts. Jessica had so many questions drumming at her she that didn't know which to ask first. Finally she settled on one. "What happened when you found out she was with child?"

"Ah, well, unfortunately I had taken to my bed by the time she realized her condition. She became pregnant on our last visit together. Lizette was going to wait and tell me in person upon my next visit, but alas, I was never to leave this bed again. I sent word telling her of my condition and again begged her to come and live with me as my wife.

"She sent me a long letter in return. I still have it folded away in my journals," he motioned weakly to a row of leather bound books on a shelf above his desk. "Lizette told me once again that she couldn't marry me, even though she loved me more than almost anything.

"It was that 'almost anything' that she explained in the following pages. She told me she was with child but she begged me—upon my love for her—to let her have the child and stay where she was. She was happy with her life and she knew that after the initial shock was over that the people would accept her child too. She would accept no money from me for herself. However, I did manage to get her to accept a small stipend for the care of the child. The only gift she would accept from me was the mare I sent her from my stable. I knew she loved to ride so I sent the horse and paid for its boarding and care for many years in advance."

"And a fine horse it is. I have the mare now, too. I'll be happy to give it back—"

"Absolutely not! It is yours now, and then to be Austen's—

er—Ossie's."

"Thank you," Jessica said. "But if you've never seen Ossie how did you know he was your son and not mine? And how could you not know of her death? Surely someone had to know of your relationship that could have told you. And weren't you curious about your child?" Jessica knew her voice was rising, but was unable to stop it.

"The only other person who knew of our relationship was Giles. After all, he drove me to the village for many of my last visits. Riding a horse had become too tiring. But obviously he had no way of knowing of her death. Since I had agreed not to interfere with her or the child, Giles had absolutely no reason to go to Wilfordshire.

As for the child, of course I wanted to see him. But Lizette had never asked anything of me before that time. All she wanted was to live in peace and simplicity with her child.

She feared bringing the child to see me in case Jacob would try to take the babe and raise it here. I assured her that Jake would never do that, but she said she'd lost too much in her life to chance it. She pointed out that after I am gone, Jacob will have complete control of the estate and could very easily go after her child which would be, of course, his half-sibling."

He paused, closing his eyes at the memories.

"Again, I assured her that Jacob would never do that, but she begged me for this one thing. In the end, I reluctantly gave in. How could I not? We corresponded only twice more after that: once when she told be of the boy's birth and to declare her undying love and gratitude to me, and the last time to beg no further contact. She didn't want to leave a trail to follow should anyone get wind of our situation. She was always so concerned about sullying my reputation. Pah! As if I cared!

So, until today, Jessica, I had never set eyes upon my child. But look at him! He has his mother's eyes, but other than that, he is the exact image of Jacob at that age. I would have recognized this child anywhere."

Austen stared at the child, his eyes sparkling with tears. Then he turned and reached for Jessica's hand.

"I thank you for allowing an old man to see his last wish come true. I can die in peace now." He smiled weakly. "One last thing, and then I must rest. Why doesn't he speak?"

Jessica looked at Ossie to be certain he still couldn't hear her. She leaned closer to the duke and whispered, "Lizette died in her sleep in the middle of the night. Through a miscommunication, it was three days before anyone came to look for her at her cottage. Ossie had been locked in there with her for the entire time and was hysterical with fear by the time help arrived. The boy slept for a day and a half after that and when he woke, he was silent. He hasn't said a word since."

Austen looked at the boy and then begged Jessica, "Please take care of him."

"I shall. But not—"

"Don't make any hasty decisions about leaving here. You just might find that you and Jacob are well suited for each other, and it would be a much easier life for you and the boy if you stayed here rather than returning to your own home. Ossie belongs here, Jessica. It's his right to be raised in his familial home. Things will work out with Jacob. You'll see."

"I have my doubts about that." She was quiet for a moment, afraid to ask her last question, but needing to know. "Are you going to tell him about Ossie?"

"I intend to. Expect an uproar, my dear. But I promise you we will all work something out. I wouldn't dream of taking Ossie away from you, not when you're both so attached to each other. Now, Jessica, I must rest. I thank you from the depths of my soul. You have given me peace," he finished with a smile.

He squeezed Jessica's hand then and closed his eyes, his breath catching in a small sob.

Ossie came around the edge of the bed and tugged on Jessica's skirt. He folded his hands and leaned his face on them, closing his eyes momentarily.

Jessica smiled. Ossie was telling her that the duke had fallen asleep and they should leave. She leaned forward and kissed Austen lightly on the forehead then turned to take Ossie's hand.

As they started toward the door, Jessica looked up to find Jacob standing at the entrance to the room. How long had he been there? How much had he heard?

Jessica's heart began pounding against her ribs. Would he take Ossie away from her? Would the duke tell Jacob about Ossie? And if he didn't, would she have the courage to tell Jacob that Ossie was his brother?

A stony feeling settled in her stomach. The way things stood between her and Jacob at the present, she had a very real fear that he would take Ossie from her. After all, once the duke passed on, Jacob could easily dismiss her and keep his little brother at Fairdale. His power, his money, and the law would be on his side.

Jessica held her finger to her lips and nodded towards the bed to keep Jacob from speaking to her. Before she could war another confrontation with Lord Callaway, Jessica knew she must gather her wits and prepare for the battle.

She bent and gathered Ossie into her arms. When she stood, she once again met Jacob's cold gaze. It was obvious that he was still stewing over being dismissed by his father. But rather than being angry with the duke, Jacob unquestionably held Jessica responsible.

Only when he looked into Ossie's sleepy eyes did his features soften. Clearly the little boy had already found a place in Jacob's heart.

No, this would not do. She could not let Jacob take Ossie away from her. There was only one way to assure that she would be able to stay with Ossie.

The sudden realization of her decision washed a wave of panic over Jessica. Without a word she hustled out the door and down the hall to where Mrs. Holmes was waiting outside their rooms.

Jessica didn't need to look back to know that Jacob's stare had followed them the entire way.

Chapter 10

Several hours later, Jacob knocked on her door.

Jessica had let him into her rooms and then closed the door to Ossie's smaller adjoining bedroom. She turned to find Jacob sitting on the small love seat in front of the fire, leaning forward with his elbows on his knees.

He looked so fragile at that moment, she thought. His eyes were red-rimmed and puffy. Seeing this vulnerable side of Jacob confused her even more. She found herself wanting to wrap her arms around him in comfort, but that was impossible.

Jacob looked up at her, placing his chin on his fists. His eyes swept over her, but this time there was no heat, no passion. Just an obvious weariness. "Are you planning on leaving us this night?"

"No. Why?" Jessica asked.

"Well, it's three o'clock in the morning and you are still in your traveling clothes."

In truth, Jessica had been pacing her room since Ossie fell asleep. Over and over in her mind she tried to come up with another way to solve her dilemma. She had come up with two solutions, but only one would guarantee her remaining with Ossie.

Jessica resumed her slow pacing before the fire. "Oh that, well I wasn't at all tired and I was very worried about your father, so I—"

"Yes, apparently you and my father had quite a conversation."

Jessica froze. Her heart leapt into her throat. Had the duke told him about Lizette and Ossie yet?

"We did. He's a fine man, Lord Callaway. I felt immediately at ease with him. Too comfortable, in fact. I fear I may not have paid him the homage due to a duke. I apologize if I offended him."

Jacob snorted. "Hardly." He looked up at Jessica and leaned back in his chair, his hands moving to rub his eyes. "In fact, you quite won him over."

"Did I?" Jessica asked, still trying to gauge his mood. She had to let Jacob do the talking in order to find out what he knew.

"Mm-hmm. He spoke very highly of you, Lady Jessica. It was as if you two were old and dear friends. Of course that isn't possible, is it?"

"N-no. Of course not." She moved behind a large wing chair and stood behind it, gripping the back for strength. So Austen had awakened and spoke to Jacob. What did he tell him?

"I'm curious, what did you two have to discuss? You were in there for quite some time," Jacob asked casually.

"I prefer to keep the content of our conversation private. Certainly you can understand—"

"No, actually, Jessica I don't understand. But it appears that will be one of the many things I'll never understand."

"What do you mean?" she asked. This is it, she thought. He knows.

Jacob leaned forward on his knees again and rubbed his face, then ran his fingers through his hair. "Please sit down. I know you must be exhausted and there's really no need to be so nervous."

Jessica walked around the front of the chair and sat poised on the edge, her hands clenched together in her lap. Her inclination was to argue that she was not nervous, but in fact, she was.

He knows. Why didn't he just get this over with?

"As I said, you made quite an impression on Father. He spoke very highly of you and again strongly urged me to marry you. I reminded him that you had flatly refused me once already but he was of the opinion that I should ask you again, Jessica. It seemed extremely important to him." Jacob paused and stared hard at her.

Jessica had to look away from his bold gaze. Even at this most anxious of moments, he still had the ability to make her feel weak with longing. She stared hard at her gown, plucking the worn fabric at her knees.

"Do you know why that was so important to him?" he asked.

"I suppose to honor my father's bizarre request for help. They seemed to have quite a bond between them," she said uncertainly, not wanting to offer any more information than was necessary.

"That's part of it, I'm sure. However, there's more to it now and it has nothing to do with that farce of an agreement, but more to do with you yourself. He was insistent that I take care of you—and your son."

Your son? The duke hadn't told him yet!

In all honesty, she had to admit that the thought of living in this grand home—with Jacob—was becoming less and less distasteful by the moment. And in truth, marrying Jacob was the only way she could be sure she'd be able to stay with Ossie. She'd turned the idea over and over in her mind. Any other option and she'd run the risk of losing the boy.

"Yes, Lord Callaway, your father was quite insistent with me as well. He made some very relevant points and I find that I simply could not refuse such a kind man who has only my best interests at heart. So, if your offer of marriage is still open, I will accept."

Jacob's mouth dropped open. This was not the direction he'd anticipated this conversation to take. "You will accept?" he repeated.

This woman never ceased to baffle him. Each time he

prepared himself for a hard-fought battle, she turned the tables on him and handed him the victory. Yet it was a wary victory at best.

And now, what was this feeling creeping over him? Could he actually be happy that she'd finally accepted? Well, if that was the case, he knew he must keep it to himself. She had given in far too easily.

Jessica grew uneasy under his baffled expression, and then irritated. "Yes, I will accept," she snapped. "Or have you now changed *your* mind?"

"No, no. I haven't changed my mind," he said, leaning on the arm of the chair. "But I am curious as to what changed yours. That must have been quite a conversation you had with my father."

It was, Jessica thought to herself. Now, if she could just get Jacob to marry her before Austen told him the entire tale! Once married, she doubted Jacob would throw her out upon learning who Ossie was. But until then, he may choose to send her on her way and ignore his father's wishes, since there was now another Fairdale heir.

"Your father made me understand how important this was both to him and to my own father. And also for Ossie's sake."

"Yes, the boy managed to win my father's approval as well. To be honest, I wondered if he might still insist on our marriage. I knew my father wouldn't judge you too harshly for having an illegitimate son, but I didn't expect him to become such a champion of you and the boy in this short amount of time. He seems more insistent than ever that we marry and provide for the boy as well as heirs of our own."

Jessica was growing ever more irritated at his constant reminders that it was his father's wish, not his, that would bring about this marriage. Suddenly she was very unsure about her plan, and her alternate thought of leaving in the morning was looking much better, despite what she'd learned about Ossie.

She stood and took several steps forward until she was

standing directly in front of Jacob, forcing him to look up at her.

She put her hands on her hips and said, "Listen to me well, Lord Callaway. If you are going to continue reminding me at every turn that Ossie is an illegitimate child, and as such he and I should both be ashamed, then I will have to rescind my acceptance. I will go and tell your father first thing in the morning that we simply cannot find a way to work this out. And then we will leave. Now, if you will excuse me, I find I'm suddenly very tired."

Jacob didn't move to rise. Instead he sighed deeply and rubbed his furrowed brow.

"That's not possible, Jessica."

"Of course it's possible. Leaving in the morning was what I had intended all along until I spoke with your father. In the morning I will simply—"

"It's not going to be possible for you to tell my father anything in the morning. He died two hours ago, Jesse."

Jessica's heart stopped for a moment and then she dropped to her knees. "No!" she whispered. "But you didn't say a word! Why didn't you—"

"I've been with him for the past couple of hours, just holding his hand and asking him questions that will never be answered. I had to come to terms with his passing, with my loss. It's still hard for me to accept that he's gone, even though I thought I'd be prepared for this after his long illness.

One minute he was whispering something to me, and then the next he asked me to go to the library and get the family Bible. I had a hell of a time locating it, but he was so insistent. When I returned, he was taking his last breaths."

Jessica could not stop herself from leaning forward and taking Jacob's hands. "Oh, Jacob," she said, his name sounding unfamiliar to her lips. "I can honestly say that I know how you feel. No matter how sick your father became, you could never prepare yourself for the moment he's actually gone."

Jacob closed his eyes as a tear trickled slowly down his

cheek. Jessica rose on her knees and put her hand behind his head. Gently, she pulled him forward until his forehead rested on her shoulder.

Jacob spread his knees and pulled Jessica between them, slipping his arms around her waist and holding on as if she were a life-line. One sob escaped his lips and in that moment Jessica knew that she cared for this man more than she'd realized, and a great deal more than she wanted to.

They stayed that way for several minutes. Jacob's thoughts ran rampant until his head was spinning. He took a deep breath and inhaled the scent of Jessica which was now becoming familiar. Pulling his head back, he placed a chaste kiss on her cheek in thanks for her comfort.

At last Jacob sat back in his chair. "I apologize for my behavior, Jessica. It doesn't speak well of the seventh Duke of Fairdale to be wailing like an infant in the arms of—of his fiancée," he finished with a half- smile.

Jessica returned the smile and said softly, "My lord—I mean, Your Grace, I can most definitely assure you that your quiet grief can in no way compare to the wailing of an infant."

"I suppose you would know that better than I," he said with a nod of his head toward Ossie's door.

Jessica was still unwilling to move, unwilling to break the fragile spell of peace that hung over them at this saddest of moments.

Jacob continued. "I suppose I should wake Mrs. Holmes. She'll have many preparations to make." He took her hands then and helped Jessica to her feet as he rose from the chair. For a moment he just stood there and looked at her.

"Perhaps I am beginning to understand what my father saw in you. You have a kindness that soothes the soul. Father said, in nearly his last words, that you could be trusted beyond doubt. And honesty is the most important quality I must have in a wife, Jessica. He reminded me of that."

"Your father said that?" Jessica asked, her face reddening at the thought that she was, even now, deceiving her soon-to-be husband.

"Yes."

"Wh—what else did he say?"

"Just that he could rest in peace if he knew I would take care of you and the boy. When I assured him that I would, he told me he loved me dearly and then he smiled and murmured a word I couldn't make out—lis—liz—I don't know what it was. Then he closed his eyes and passed."

Now it was Jessica's turn for tears. Without thinking, she leaned her head forward and buried her face against Jacob's chest. But her tears were not only born of the loss of a great man; they were born of guilt.

She knew she should tell Jacob about Ossie, but she couldn't. Not yet. Not until she was secured to Jacob and certain that he wouldn't take Ossie from her.

Jacob squeezed her close and then set her back. "Ssh, don't cry anymore. Father is now in peace. Jessica, I fully intend to make good on my promise to my father. A few minutes ago you were about to rescind your acceptance of my proposal, but may I assume now that you will accept me?"

Jessica nodded slowly, unable to speak for fear of dissolving into tears again.

"I'm sorry, Jesse," he continued. "I'm sure that in your dreams you never expected to have marriage proposed to you in such a business-like manner. If circumstances were different," he paused and wiped a tear from her cheek, "—but they're not. Father's funeral will be in a few days. If you have no objections, I will have the bishop marry us in a short, private ceremony after the services. I'll send word to him to secure a special license. He is a dear friend of my father's and I know he will understand our rushed circumstances and keep our business private."

Jessica managed to find her voice at last. "Whatever you think is best. I know your father wanted this taken care of expeditiously."

And for her purposes, the sooner the better. If Jacob read his father's journals, he would know everything. Jessica prayed that the agreement would be carried out before Jacob would find the time to read them.

Chapter 11

It was two days before Jessica had a chance to speak with Jacob again. After the quiet passing of the old duke, the influx of attorneys and bankers who stormed the house was a noisy intrusion.

She'd seen him briefly, across the great hall, talking to a short bald gentleman who was very emphatic about the papers he held. Jacob's eyes had met Jessica's for a moment and they shared a quick smile before the little man demanded Jacob's attention again.

Jacob needed some time away from the facts and figures those men had brought with them and sought out Jessica.

Several times over the past few days he'd thought about their last conversation in her rooms. There had been a quiet truce between two people who understood one another's loss. With the arguing absent, Jacob admitted, he found he truly cared for her and was grateful for her understanding that night.

He found her alone in the library and stood quietly in the doorway, watching the expressions that crossed her face as she read.

Suddenly she looked up at him.

"Oh! I'm sorry, I didn't hear you come in. How are you faring?" Jessica did her best to gather her wits, knowing well that she sounded like an excited child who'd just happened upon her best friend. Worry aside, and against her will, she found that she'd missed his company.

"I'm well, thank you, considering that I've been locked in the study with those less-than-personable bores for the last two days." He walked into the room and took the book she'd been reading from her hand.

"Shakespeare? I didn't know you enjoyed his work." He put the book on the desk and sat on the corner very close to her chair. "Of course, there are a great many things I don't know about you. Odd, isn't it, considering you'll be my wife by tomorrow evening?"

Jessica looked down at her hands. "I suppose so. One consolation we might enjoy is that marriages have been arranged for hundreds of years, although I doubt many of them started out quite like this one, with two fathers foxed in a pub." Jessica looked up and smiled. "A good many of those marriages are successful. Of course, my mother's arranged marriage to that other man would have been a disaster since she so loved my father."

"Some of them work; some of them don't, just as marriages of choice sometimes don't turn out as planned."

Jessica cleared her throat. "Well, hopefully when two people are considerate of each other's feelings and dedicated to a single cause, they will be able to live amicably under the same roof. Especially when that roof is large enough to cover an entire village."

Jacob smiled at her reference to the mansion. "If you are referring to us, my lady, I believe it's safe to say that we could go for weeks in this house without encountering one another, should that be our aspiration. But I would hope our situation would be otherwise."

His eyes held a smoldering heat as her gaze locked with his.

Jessica felt her cheeks color, but smiled and returned his gaze without faltering. "I would hope that too, Your Grace," she said in barely more than a whisper.

Jacob stood and held his hand out to Jessica. She took it and rose from her chair, the heat of his fingers shooting flames up her arms to the back of her neck. Her heart beat faster as she anticipated the next step; she would be in his arms, pressing her lips to his....

A bird's song drifted in through the open window, drawing Jacob's attention to the gloriously sun drenched day.

"Where's Ossie?" he asked, amused by the disappointed look that crossed her face. She'd been expecting him to kiss her. He knew that. And the fact that she'd wanted it was very pleasing to him.

"He's playing with the gardener's children. It's been ages since I've seen him this happy," Jessica answered, disappointed that Jacob hadn't kissed her, but glad that he was interested in Ossie. "Would you like me to call him in?"

"No. Actually I was just thinking we should take a ride together. I can show you some of the property in Fairdale's boundaries. The sun is shining, it's warm outside, and frankly, I need to get away from those vultures my father had hired as lawyers. They can manage without me for a while. Would you care to join me?"

A feeling of elation swept over Jessica. "I would like that very much." She looked down at her clothes. "As you can see, I'm dressed for the occasion, as usual."

Jacob dropped her hand and crossed his arms over his chest, a thoughtful look on his face. "I'll have to admit, I'm growing rather fond of your attire. Perhaps you'll set a new fashion trend in London. After all, you will be the Duchess of Fairdale. Everyone will be looking to you for your style. I can see it now—"

Jessica paled. "They will? But I—I"

At Jacob's chuckle Jessica relaxed again, realizing he was teasing her. "As far as I'm concerned, Jessica, we need rarely go to the city. I do have a townhouse there, and at times I'm force to tend to business in London. On those occasions, you may accompany me if you like, although you will probably choose to dress in a more current fashion while there." He reached out and touched the collar of her shirt, his thumb purposely brushing a feather-light trail along her collarbone. "But when we're alone here at Fairdale, you may wear whatever you like."

The warmth in his voice was still wrapped tightly around Jessica as they rode to a small hill on the east side of the property. Removing the smile from her face just now would have been an impossible task.

Jacob reigned in next to a large tree and swept his hand in front of him. "All of this belongs to me now. You know, as a boy I used to think Fairdale was the whole world."

"I can see why!"

He smiled. "As I grew older, I lost touch with that wonder. Now that I have to take responsibility for it all, I'm seeing it through a child's eyes again. I have several other properties, most of which I've secured on my own, but none of them possess the spirit and grandeur of Fairdale. I'll take you and Ossie to the other properties, but I'm certain you'll agree that nothing can compare."

Jacob dismounted and helped Jessica from her mare. They walked several yards to the edge of a grassy knoll. A large cherry tree stood to their left, dropping blossoms on them in the breeze like silky, pink snow.

"It truly is beautiful here, Jacob. If there was a castle I would think I was lost in a fairy tale," Jessica said with a sigh.

"There was a small castle here. It was built hundreds of years ago and fell mostly to disrepair. But the main part of the house was built on the foundation. My family has owned this land for generations, but it was only when my own grandfather became the Fifth Duke of Fairdale that he cleared away the rubble and built the home that now stands.

"You'll notice that the stables are made of stone throughout. That's the original stable that was built here. The only other original dwelling is a small cottage just to the other side of those trees." Jacob pointed to the distance. "My father called it a hunting cottage, but I can't remember him ever hunting. It's been patched and repaired to the point of almost being completely rebuilt, but I like the solitude of it."

From their position Jessica could see the fine mansion and the large stables in the distance. A sizable wooded area covered a good portion of the west side of the property and a small lake sparkled in the sunlight just to the left of that.

Jacob followed her gaze. "Ossie will learn to swim in that lake, as I did."

"He'll like that. He's such a wonderful child, Jacob." Her conscience was crying out to her, *tell him, tell him he's Ossie's brother!* But she couldn't, not until she was sure of her place in his life. She didn't know him well enough to guess how he might react to such news.

"You don't have to tell me that, Jesse. I've come to care for that little lad a great deal. I'll admit, I'm surprised by the strength of emotions that have overcome me in the past week. And not just where Ossie is concerned."

A warm, wonderful heat crept over Jessica as she took in Jacob's meaning.

"I want Ossie to feel as if he belongs here, Jesse, because he does."

Jessica caught her breath. Belongs? "What—what do you mean?"

"I mean that he belongs here, just as the children we'll have together will belong here. My first son—our first son, will inherit my titles, but Ossie will be loved and respected always. I'll see to that. I still have some questions about Ossie, though, that I would like answered at some point."

Tears sprang to her eyes. Oh, how could she not trust this man with her secret? She had to bite her lip to keep from blurting out everything. It was the only way she could avoid telling—

Well, not the only way. There was one other way, decidedly more pleasurable than biting her lip.

She'd been aching to be in his arms again since she arrived.

Would he treat her any differently now that their intentions were clear? Would any of the passion have died, knowing that she would be his wife?

Jessica turned to face this man she had agreed to marry. Warmth filled her heart and several other places in her body.

Their faces were only a few inches apart, and if she tilted her head just slightly....

Jacob looked down into her eyes. In any normal circumstance, being alone out here before their marriage would have been inappropriate. But there was absolutely nothing normal about their circumstances. And besides, it wasn't as if she were a frightened maiden. She had a child; she'd had another man. He rapidly pushed that thought aside. Above all, he could tell that she wanted him, now.

And he wanted her.

Jacob pulled her close and captured her lips. His fingers gripped her shoulders and then slid down her back as her hands reach up around his neck.

This kiss was unlike their others. It was slow, provocative, searching...gentle. It was questions and worries, it was answers and peace.

It was a learning experience for both of them, and as the moments passed, they were learning without a doubt that the passion they'd felt in their previous encounters was not a fluke, nor was it something that could be denied.

Slowly, they lowered to the ground, mindless of the dampness of the grass that soaked into their knees, their hips, their shoulders. The silky petals that dropped, the birds' song, all of that faded away as they rose on a wave of passion.

With agile fingers, Jacob loosened the braid which held Jessica's hair and let the auburn waves flow over her shoulder and shine in the spring sun. His hand wound through the mass of silk until it brushed against her breast, and then with a sudden urgency, he longed to feel her flesh against his.

Jessica understood the need as her fingers flew to his

shirtfront, fumbling with the buttons there as she was completely naïve to undressing a man. Giving way to the fire inside, she grasped each side and tore the shirt open, sending buttons flying.

Taking only enough time away from their kiss to look into her eyes and smile with his surprise at her boldness, Jacob reclaimed her lips as he freed her breasts from her shirt. Again he blessed the convenience of her unconventional attire.

Gently, he caressed each proud nipple as they vied for attention. With the utmost tenderness, he pulled away from their kiss and captured each bud in his mouth in turn, swirling his tongue around them until they ached with sensitivity.

He inhaled the warm floral scent from the valley between her breasts, trailing his tongue over her skin before seeking her mouth once again.

"Ahhh…" Jessica breathed out slowly just before their lips met. She was lost. And to think she was certain that her first kiss would be the most shocking feeling she'd ever known!

Jessica felt a fluttering begin deep within her. It turned to a gentle ache, one that could not be soothed from outside, yet she had no firm idea what to do about it.

Instinctively, she slipped her leg over Jacob's hip and rolled to her back, pulling him over on top of her. Once there, she wrapped her other leg around his thigh, pulling his pelvis tight against hers. The swelling of his passion only ignited her desire more, making her arch against him in need. She had no idea what she was doing; she only knew if felt right. Her body was leading her places her mind would have never allowed her to go.

Jacob's world rocked as he felt the heat of her desire searing him through their clothing. He was both surprised and pleased by her uninhibited passion, and quickly dismissed the questions that approached his mind about her previous lover.

He ground his swollen desire into her beckoning heat, unsure now if he'd even be able to get unclothed before surrendering to the release that was so near.

Heart pounding, blood racing, he reached to the ties at the front of Jessica's trousers. His fingers had just slipped inside, just felt the warm smoothness of her naked hip when from a distance he heard his horse nicker.

Ignore it, he told himself, but reason washed over him like a bucket of cold water.

Martin wouldn't start nickering for no good reason. Someone must be approaching.

With something akin to a growl, Jacob lifted himself to his knees and looked beneath his horse's belly.

"By God, but he better have a damn good reason for this!" Jacob thundered.

Jessica found her self disoriented when Jacob had pulled away, but now she sat up quickly and peered over Jacob's shoulder. Giles was just coming up the trail towards them, at a very leisurely pace and whistling a tune that carried to them on the breeze.

It took Jessica a moment to clear her head of the passion-induced haze, feeling as if her mind and body were detached from one another. Jacob turned and pressed a kiss to her forehead.

"I'll go see what he wants, but perhaps you'd better right your clothes before you stand up," he said with a wicked grin.

Jessica looked down and let out a small gasp. Her shirt was barely hanging on her shoulders and her breasts were jutting proudly upward, their sensitive nipples still taut with expectancy.

"Oh!" she gathered her shirt around her and scrambled quickly behind the old tree, kneeling and leaning against it for support. She finished buttoning her shirt and then raised her hands to her face.

How could she have been so stupid! Her last conscious thought had been to make sure they'd stopped in time, and yet she'd very nearly ruined everything by giving into her passion.

Of course Jacob had been kind and said all the right things just before they'd kissed, but oh how that would have changed if he'd discovered her virginity before they were married!

She let out a little laugh. Most women would be devastated if their husbands-to-be found out they *weren't* virgins, and she was worried Jacob might find out she *was*.

Jacob appeared around the side of the tree, startling her. He knelt beside her and took her hand.

"I'm so sorry for the interruption, more than you can imagine."

Jessica smiled at him. "Oh, I believe I can well imagine."

"It seems the vultures are ready to leave for London. Apparently we've been out here longer than I thought. They waited as long as they could and then sent Giles to find me. There are a few transfer documents I have to sign. Knowing Giles, I'm sure he took his sweet time in finding us. Unfortunately, it wasn't long enough."

Jessica breathed a sigh of relief. "Actually, I should thank him."

"Why?"

"Because, if he'd been any later, you would have compromised my virtue before our wedding," she began to tease. The words were out before she could stop them.

Fool! She chastised herself. Just seconds before she'd warned herself about this!

Jacob just stared at her for a moment, then began laughing. "Well, you'd have a lot of explaining to do about Ossie if *I* were the one to compromise your virtue!"

Jessica laughed with him, but felt none of the mirth.

Keep this up, she scolded herself, *and you'll have the whole story told before dinner!*

Chapter 12

Jessica attended Austen's funeral the next morning, but was truly there only in the physical sense. Her nerves were strung taut. Every eye in the chapel was on her, the unknown newcomer sitting in the front pew with the new Duke of Fairdale, instead of on the bishop who was paying last respects.

Jacob had been sullen and distant that morning, to the point of Jessica wondering if he'd spent last night reading his father's journals and discovering the truth about Ossie. There had been no chance for her to be alone with him and so she had to sit here, agonizing, wondering over her fate.

With the exception of meeting the coach and guiding her to her seat, Jacob had all but ignored her. There was none of the warmth, the laughter, the heat from the day before.

She couldn't know that he hadn't slept most of the night.

Sadness over his father and the overwhelming realization of what he was about to do had kept sleep far from him until just before dawn broke. In his tired state, his mind had worked double-speed, wondering about Ossie's father, who he was, had there been any others?

Jacob was no prude, but neither did he want a promiscuous woman as his duchess. There could never be a question as to the father of his heirs.

As he turned to look at her now, he just couldn't image that. Certainly he'd never been so wrong in a person's moral character as to misjudge her so completely. He sighed. His tired mind was pulling pranks on him. Jessica was a good woman. He was sure of it.

Doubts be damned.

He stared for several more moments, making her painfully uncomfortable, and then returned his gaze to Bishop Clark.

She pulled her cloak tighter around her, thankful again for the cold temperature in the chapel, for all she'd had to wear was her tattered travel dress. Everything had happened so quickly that no one thought on what she was to wear to the funeral.

Or her wedding.

She and Jacob were to be married in the library directly after the funeral. Not exactly the kind of wedding she'd envisioned as a young girl, but then even in her wildest dreams— or nightmares—she could have never imagined any of this.

Bless Mrs. Holmes.

When Jessica returned to her rooms it was to find a lovely dark gray gown hanging in the dressing room.

"Oh," she said in a whisper. Jessica walked to the dress and put her hand out. She was afraid to touch it for fear that it might disappear. This was the finest gown she had ever seen.

"Ye can touch it, dear. It's yers now."

Jessica jumped at the sound of Mrs. Holmes' voice. "I have never seen anything quite so lovely. Where did it come from?"

"His lordship—er—excuse me, I mean His Grace made it possible. I was wantin' ye ta have a nice gown for this day, even though it's obviously not turnin' out like the bridal dreams of any young woman I've ever known."

So Jacob had arranged for this. She immediately felt guilty about her thoughts in the chapel.

One minute she was certain he was the cruelest, most unfeeling boar on the face of the earth, and then the next she was shocked to find some kind gesture that he'd made.

Mrs. Holmes continued to prattle on. "I was afraid to ask 'im for the only gowns I knew of that would fit ye and do yer lovely figure honor. Thank heavens 'e was the one to suggest it."

"Afraid to ask him what?"

Mrs. Holmes removed the gown from the hook and spread it out on the bed. "This gown, and the two others which are hangin' in the wardrobe, belonged to the duke's mother. She wasn't a very nice person, that one. When she left here, she didn't bother taking any of her finery, just went to town and outfitted herself with an entire new wardrobe. Mostly to spite 'er husband's my opinion."

"She actually left all her clothes here? Gowns of this quality?"

"Yes, she was a wicked thing. Tossing aside her belongings only to replace them with more expensive things was actually one of her less cruel deeds. Spending the duke's money was one of the few things that made that woman happy. But here I am gossiping like a back-kitchen maid. Ye don't need to be thinkin' on the likes o' her on this day. I would warn ye though. Don't even mention the former duchess to His Grace."

"But I'll have to thank him for the gowns."

"And that ye should. Just don't mention that ye know where they came from or ask any questions about his mother. It's a mighty sore subject in this household. I'm sure e'll tell ye all about it sometime. But today he's suffering enough misery, so leave it be."

"Whatever you say. You know him much better than I."

The gown fit Jessica almost perfectly. Although it was slightly too big through the waist, the rest looked as if it had been made just for her. It was of a simple style, one that wasn't dated by the fact that the gown was many years old.

"The other two gowns are of cheerier colors. I figured this one would be best for today. Ye won't be wantin' people t' think ye had a lack of respect fer the deceased. But then, I just couldn't see ye marryin' in a black dress neither. So, this shade of gray should do the trick."

She sat before the mirror while Mrs. Holmes restyled her

hair into something less severe than the bun at the nape of her neck. Jessica rarely wore her hair in anything other than a long braid wrapped around her head and seeing herself being transformed into a lovely, stylish lady right before her own eyes was a bit unnerving.

"Do you think this is really appropriate? It seems so, so formal."

Mrs. Holmes chuckled. "Ah, lass. It is so refreshin' to see such a lovely young woman who is truly unaware of her charms."

Jessica blushed profusely but decided not to question Mrs. Holmes' judgment any further. She honestly didn't know what was in style and what wasn't.

At last Jessica stood at the top of the stairs. Her feet refused to move for the moment so she just stood there, staring down the long curving staircase.

From the large parlor just off the main entry she could hear the voices of at least a dozen people, maybe more. Who were they? Jacob had said no one but the bishop and two witnesses would attend their wedding, and that had been just fine with her. The fluttering in her stomach increased ten-fold.

She took a deep breath and started down the stairs, her hand sliding along the polished balustrade for balance. The shoes that went with her gown had a small heel on them and Jessica had rarely worn anything but flat boots. Don't fall, she sent a silent plea to herself.

At the bottom of the stairs she paused again to collect her thoughts. From the parlor a striking woman, only a few years older than Jessica, made her way out the doors and crossed the entry hall with a grace that made her appear to float.

The woman's jet black hair framed an ivory face that looked as if it was formed from porcelain, and her blue eyes rivaled that of any spring sky. Her very presence was a compelling force.

She stopped just a few feet from Jessica. "At last I can see the woman who has aroused everyone's curiosity so. You kept yourself quite hidden at the funeral service and Jacob was positively *protective* of you."

Oh, where was Jacob's protection now?

Jessica could manage only a small smile for this intimidating woman. What should she do? Did she curtsy? Was this woman someone of importance?

"I'm Baroness Von Kraus," the woman said at last, her eyes sweeping over Jessica's appearance. With satisfaction she saw the look of nervousness that settled over Jessica's features.

She also noted in a quick glance that Jessica's dress was just slightly too big which indicated it was either not made for her, or she had a very poor seamstress. Either way it meant this young woman who had appeared at England's most eligible bachelor's side, at a family funeral nonetheless, was not from an affluent family.

Jessica's silence caught the baroness by surprise. "Do you speak English, dear?" she asked with a touch of sarcasm.

"I assure you she does," Jacob's voice boomed from the doorway.

The baroness turned and followed Jessica's grateful glance towards Jacob. "Can she not speak for herself, Jacob?" she asked caustically as Jacob crossed the entry.

"Of course she can, Lillian. However, if you presented yourself in your usual uh, forthright manner, I would wager that Jessica hasn't had the opportunity to get a word in."

Lillian's cheeks showed just a spot of color as she turned back to Jessica, her painted smile still in place.

"Well, that's not true now is it?"

Again Jacob came to Jessica's rescue. "Lady Jessica Patrick, may I present Baroness Lillian Von Kraus, one of London's most—er—accommodating hostesses." Jacob took delight in subtly reminding Lillian that he'd not forgotten her unwanted advances toward him when last they'd met. "The baroness is *currently* married to Baron Kurt Von Kraus, a fine man who recently moved to London from Salzburg."

Jessica saw the pale cheeks of the baroness color even deeper and had to fight to keep from smiling at Jacob. Obviously the words he'd spoken held more of a sting than the baroness cared to admit. "It's a pleasure to make your acquaintance."

"Ah, so you can speak," the baroness said sharply, folding her arms in front of her and raising her chin a notch.

"I can, and quite well too, should I feel the need." Jessica gained strength from Jacob's lack of deference to the woman. Apparently this was not someone she absolutely had to impress.

Baroness Von Kraus's eyes narrowed. Jacob turned to Jessica.

"If you're ready my dear, I believe the bishop is awaiting us in the library."

"The bishop?" Lillian asked. "Now that the service is over, what need have you of the bishop?"

"If you must know, Lillian, we need to carry out some of my father's final wishes. Now if you'll excuse us."

"Final wishes? I assume you mean from his will? Ah, then are you a distant relative, my dear?"

Jacob took Jessica's arm and steered her past the baroness. "Oh, not as distant as all that," was the only answer he gave.

As the library door closed behind them, Jessica gave out a sigh and rubbed her forehead. Would it always be this way? Would she always feel inferior and witless in the company of Jacob's acquaintances?

Jacob sensed her uneasiness. "You handled yourself well with Lillian."

Jessica looked up at him. Was he teasing her? "Did I?" she asked warily.

He smiled down at her, feeling protective and suddenly wanting to kick himself for all the doubts he'd had this morning.

"Yes, you did. Jesse, at the risk of sounding more self-important than usual, let me remind you that you are about to become the Duchess of Fairdale. As such, you need defer to no one but the royal family, and need show like respect only to other ducal families. However, you'll likely make more friendly acquaintances if you are at least pleasant to the majority of people you meet." His smile broadened. "Unlike the husband you'll have in a few minutes, who manages to offend most of the fine aristocracy."

In a few minutes, he'd said. Was this really happening? She turned away from Jacob. "And will it damage your reputation greatly if your wife becomes a recluse and is never seen at social functions?"

Jacob's laugh caught her off guard and she turned to face him when he answered. "My reputation has suffered worse than that. In all honesty, if you do become a recluse, most people will say I married of my own kind, for I am not a regular attendee at most societal functions."

He paused for a moment. The time had come. "Jessica? Shall we finalize this arrangement?"

Jacob could have kicked himself for those words. The smile that had begun to form on her lips dropped out of sight. How could he be so thoughtless? For all of her attempts to show a stiff backbone, he knew this had to be the death of any romantic fantasies she'd had of her wedding day.

He cleared his throat uneasily. "My lady, I do humbly apologize for my seeming lack of concern. You will find, I'm sure, that I lack experience with many of the tender amenities that more 'socialized' gentlemen are well acquainted with. In no way do I wish to demean your wedding day."

The smile, hesitant though it was, returned to Jessica's face. "Well, perhaps, then, we can fumble through our public appearances and social inadequacies together." She felt her cheeks grow warm under his concerned look.

Jessica looked down and smoothed the fabric of her gown. "Oh, before I forget, I want to thank you for—for providing this gown for me." Her widening smile belied her true feelings.

Her smile held him captive. He had the strongest urge to kiss her and he just might have if the bishop hadn't cleared his throat.

"Shall we proceed?"

Jacob shook off the spell Jessica's smile had cast and nodded at the bishop. "The marriage documents are in my father's study. I'll be back in a moment."

Jessica was alone with the kind-faced bishop. He smiled at her as he crossed the room to her side. "My dear, the fear is verily flowing from you." He took her hand between his soft, wrinkled ones. "I realized you don't know me, but I ask that you trust me."

"Oh, sir, I couldn't do otherwise," Jessica replied.

"Good. Then trust when I say that you are about to marry a fine man. Jacob told me of the circumstances of your—uh—swift betrothal and I would think something amiss if you weren't a little frightened of what your future holds. But I can assure you, never have finer men walked this earth than the Callaways. Austen was a dear friend and Jacob is as close to a son as I will ever have. You will definitely have your differences, for Jacob can be a stubborn man. Often you will think your problems insurmountable. He is, however, sweet as a babe on the inside. Jacob's hard exterior is merely a protective wall he erected to defend against the kind of pain he saw his father go through with his mother."

That was the second time Jessica had heard ill of the former duchess. She had to ask. "Can you tell me anything of his mother? Perhaps I would better know how to—"

"No, my dear. That is for Jacob to tell. Just remember to keep faith in him. You will not find a more honorable and kind man."

The door to the library opened and Jacob entered, followed by Giles and Mrs. Holmes. "Shall we?"

The bishop released Jessica's hand after a small squeeze and went to stand beside Jacob.

Jessica was suddenly rooted to the spot, the bishop's words echoing in her mind. Honorable, kind. And here she was about to wed Jacob under false pretenses. In a daze, she walked slowly to join the two men and bent to stiffly sign her name on the marriage certificate.

The bishop began speaking as she stood silently beside Jacob. Jessica heard very few of the bishop's words, so loud was the voice in her own head.

She had to stop this farce; Jacob deserved to know the truth. Tell him, tell him! the voice cried out. "I will, I will!" she answered. Suddenly she realized, her cheeks flaming scarlet, that she'd spoken those last words out loud and apparently at just the right moment.

Both Jacob and the bishop were looking at her with half-smiles. The bishop continued. "And so with the consent of both parties, the emphatic consent, I might add," he said with a chuckle, "I now pronounce you legally wed."

Both Jessica and Jacob looked quickly at the bishop at those last words. The bishop merely smiled and shrugged his shoulders as if he knew something the two of them did not.

When neither of them moved the bishop stepped aside and walked to the door, Giles and Mrs. Holmes leaving in front of him. Bishop Clark turned back for a moment. "Jacob, may I suggest that you kiss your wife?"

With that he quietly left the library.

For the first time in his life, Jacob was actually nervous about kissing a woman. He didn't know if that should make him happy or angry, but he decided not to dwell on it for now and took Jessica tenderly into his arms.

He stopped when her face was mere inches from his and waited until she opened her eyes.

When she did, Jacob couldn't help but smile. By God, being married to this woman might not be so bad after all. And judging from her emphatic response to their vows, perhaps she had come to terms with their attraction as well.

He placed his fingers gently under her chin. "I must admit I was surprised, but pleased, at your eager affirmation of our vows." Jacob kissed her then, before she had a chance to explain.

Suddenly, all the tension of the past days evaporated as she realized that she was now married to Jacob and there was no turning back. Every nerve ending in her body was ignited; the denial that had been at her lips was forgotten.

The heat that swept through Jessica at his kiss transformed her into a molten being, her body melting against his to form a perfect fit.

Her arms crept around his shoulders, her hand gently cupped against the back of his head.

She pressed her body tighter against his, needing to feel his strong body and the powerful hardness that kept their hips from fully meeting; needing to know that the passion they'd shared yesterday was not merely an accidental thing of the past.

Her unrestrained passion caught Jacob by surprise—again—but this time it didn't cause him to worry. The engulfing onslaught of his need drove all thoughts from his head save one: He had to have her—*now*.

With one arm, he encircled her waist even tighter while he bent and cleared the desk with a swipe of his other arm.

Jessica was barely aware that she was lying back on the smooth, cool wood of the desk top. Her thighs were on fire now that Jacob had lifted her skirts and found her silken skin. A moan started in her throat, matching the one that came from Jacob.

Of their own volition, Jessica's legs came apart and wrapped around Jacob's hips, pulling him forward until once again she could feel his hardness between her legs.

A fluttering, throbbing began to pulsate through out her body, especially where their passion points met, as Jacob moved his free hand to encompass her breast. Briefly, he thought of the first time he'd accidentally felt her breast and smiled into the kisses he was still raining upon Jessica's lips.

A moment later, he tore his mouth from hers and dropped his lips to the breast he'd finally exposed. Her nipple eagerly met his mouth and it was with a sharp intake of breath that she felt his teeth softly tease her to a higher arousal.

Jessica arched her back further, lifting her breast higher, willing him to take it deeper. Her hands grasped the sides of his head while her own head moved slowly from side to side.

Through their passion, neither of them heard the quick knock on the library door just before it opened.

"I say old boy, I saw the bishop leave and—oh ho!"

Jessica let out a cry as Jacob quickly swept her off the desk and behind him to shield her nakedness from the intruder.

"Malcom! What the devil are you doing in here?" Jacob's voice thundered.

Malcom doubled over in laughter at the door. "So sorry, Jake. I thought you were ensconced in here with the bishop and when I saw him leave, well—" The man broke into more gales of laughter.

Jessica stood behind Jacob, embarrassed nearly to tears at being caught in such a compromising situation.

"Malcom, you have exactly half a second to get the hell out of here!" Jacob exploded.

The man made no move to leave. "What? Aren't you going to introduce me to your little pet there? And to think the buzz was that the young woman at your side was a relative. Ha! From what I just saw she's certainly no relative!" Malcom strained to see around Jacob.

To Malcom's surprise, Jacob's face clouded in a stormy rage. He'd never seen his friend look so dangerous, especially over some good natured ribbing about a wench.

"As a matter of fact, Malcom, she is a relative. Now leave us before I remove that smile from your face—permanently."

From her position behind Jacob, Jessica cringed and prayed the man would just leave. She called on all her inner strength to help her endure this humiliation. How would she survive this?

Then suddenly she recalled one of her father's most helpful lessons: laugh your cares away, Jessica, he'd said. Laughter lightens even the darkest despair.

In truth, the situation was amusing. Obviously all common

sense had abandoned them both. It was deserving that they pay for their foolishness with a little humility.

When Malcom made no move to leave, Jacob ran his fingers through his hair in exasperation. "Malcom, if you'll just return to the parlor I shall join you and the rest of the guests shortly. You will receive a full explanation then."

Malcom knew when not to push Jacob any further, and now was that time. He truly did value their friendship and so did not want to chance ruining it over something he didn't even understand.

"As you wish, Jake. I shall impatiently await your arrival, and that of your relative's, in the parlor."

Chapter 13

Jacob turned to Jessica and found her back to him, her shoulders shaking softly. He gently turned her toward him and pulled her head to his chest without looking down at her. It surprised him how much it made him ache to see her cry.

A small sound escaped her as she leaned against him, and Jacob finally chanced a look at her. But to his amazement he found not tears but mirth settled on her face.

"What the—"

The puzzled frown on Jacob's face brought forth more laughter from Jessica.

"Well, I do wish you would tell me what you find so amusing, my dear."

Jessica finally caught her breath. "Oh, Jacob," she managed between giggles, placing her hand on his chest. "It's just something my father told me about making the best of the worst situation. Look at this honestly. Had it been you walking in on your friend Malcom in this—this situation, wouldn't you have found the circumstances worth a good laugh?"

Jacob straightened and folded his arms in front of his chest, a smile teasing the corner of his mouth. "Well, yes, but—"

"And further more, until now we've managed, albeit barely, to keep a lid on our—er—attraction to each other...."

"Not by my choice," Jacob interrupted.

Jessica tilted her head and gave him a 'for shame' look.

"Regardless, we've been wed less than ten minutes. We have, presumably, our entire lives ahead of us to spend frolicking like rabbits yet we lost our heads and very nearly consummated our marriage right here on your father's desk."

Jessica's cheeks colored when she realized the boldness of her words but Jacob's sudden smile eased the sting.

"You're right. I apologize for my eagerness."

"No apology is necessary," she whispered, gazing into his eyes. "I just have to wonder if there will ever come a time when we're not interrupted at the most crucial of moments."

"I assure you, that time will come." He reached down and took her hands, noticing as he did so that she had managed to straighten the front of her dress only a little. "However," he said, "if you don't fully fasten the front of your dress, I may forget my manners once again."

"Oh!" Jessica looked down and then turned partially away from Jacob to do as he suggested while he straightened his trousers and smoothed his shirt.

Neither could say what had happened to the pensive distance that had plagued them just that morning or why it had suddenly disappeared. But something had transpired when they'd committed themselves to one another.

The fear was gone. A sort of happiness had settled over them, an easiness they both knew they could easily accept. For now, they didn't question it.

Only the guilt of her deception kept Jessica from allowing this to become a day of happiness after the sadness of the funeral.

Jacob held his arm out to her once again. He noticed that the laughter had left her eyes and wondered what had brought back her thoughtful silence.

Jessica saw his inquisitive look and smiled sadly. She didn't want Jacob to grow suspicious and now was not the time for her confession. "I was just wishing your father could have been here to see us wed. I know he would have been happy." It was only a half-lie. She truly did wish Austen could have seen them wed.

Jessica's grip on Jacob's arm tightened as they entered the parlor full of people.

The room fell silent as they entered where only moments before there had been conversation in abundance.

All eyes turned to Jessica. Never had she felt more self-conscious. Her eyes met those of Malcom and the amusement she saw there quickly made her look away. What had he told these people?

Her next eye contact was with Baroness Von Kraus. The cold stare of that woman did nothing to ease her nervousness either.

"Lords and Ladies, friends, I thank you all for joining me on this solemn occasion. I ask that you do as my father would have wished and honor the life of that vibrant, charming man whom we all respected. Let there be no more sadness on this day. Let this be a celebration of his life and accomplishments."

Several of the guests smiled and nodded toward Jacob, for they knew Austen would not have stood for tears and wailing. But within seconds all eyes were trained once again on Jessica.

Malcom stepped forward and raised his glass of sherry. "To the Sixth Duke of Fairdale, may he rest in peace. And to the Seventh Duke of Fairdale may he live long and prosper, and not forget his rowdy friends now that he holds such a title."

"Here, here," several voices chimed in with chortles dispersed throughout the room.

"And perhaps," Malcom continued, "you would now like to introduce us to your long-lost relative there at your side?"

Jacob nodded to Malcom. "Certainly. But she is not a long lost relative. In fact she is quite a recent relative. May I introduce to you Jessica, my wife, the Duchess of Fairdale."

"Your *wife!*" several voices exclaimed in unison.

"My wife," Jacob said again, enjoying the shock that was apparent on every face in the room.

A long silence followed, and then suddenly the room erupted with questions.

"When did you marry?"

"Why hadn't we heard of your engagement?"

"Who *is* she?"

"Where did she come from?"

Jessica began to step backwards from the crowd that was closing in around them, but Jacob's firm hand at her waist kept her where she was. He leaned near her ear and whispered, "Remember what I told you earlier. You need defer to no one in this room. Don't let them intimidate you, Jesse. I'll do most of the talking, if you like, and I won't leave your side."

Jessica nodded. She gained strength from his words and the comforting support of his arm. After taking a deep breath, she forced a smile to her face and greeted Jacob's guests—her guests.

True to his word, Jacob remained dutifully by her side, fielding the questions that were thrown from all directions. Jessica had only to smile and make small talk.

After the initial shock wore off, she found that most of the people in attendance were very pleasant. The respect they showed her, she knew, came only from the fact that she was Jacob's wife. But for now that was enough.

Still, a few of the women in the room refused to approach her and were huddled in a corner sending icy glares her way.

Jacob finally led Jessica to the back of the room where a large buffet of food had been artfully arranged.

"Are you hungry?" he asked.

"I could not eat one bite of that lovely array of food. I fear my stomach has not received the message that there is nothing to worry about."

"You're doing splendidly, Jesse. I'm sure you heard the numerous offers we received to hold receptions for us. I suppose we'll have to accept some of them. As I expected, you have charmed everyone here. They are eager to do your bidding. I suppose this is only a portent of how you'll work me over for all that you desire," he teased with a tender smile.

Lord, but this felt good. Jacob had never imagined that he would find happiness and marriage with the same person. And so suddenly, too. Leave it to his father to find just the right woman.

A few hours ago he was dreading the remainder of this day: the wedding, the introductions, the questions. But now, hell, he was actually enjoying the uproar his announcement had caused.

"I'm afraid I haven't won over everyone," Jessica said. "There appears to be a group, or more like a pack of women, there in the corner, who look like hungry wolves ready to eat me alive."

Jacob followed her glance. "Ah yes. Well, you've already met the baroness. And there with her are two mothers who had their sights set on me for a son-in-law. The other is a widow who all but proposed to me herself. None of them are worth your worry, Jesse."

Jessica sighed. "If you say so. Jacob, how much longer will this last? I'm sorry, but I'm suddenly very tired."

Part of that was truth. But she also felt as though she needed to be alone, to gather her thoughts and figure out what, and how, she was going to tell Jacob about Ossie.

"You may leave now, if you wish. Why don't you go find Ossie?"

"Oh, Ossie! Jacob, what will you tell people about—" She stopped short, not sure even what she would tell Jacob about Ossie.

"Never mind that. I'll handle everything."

Her grateful but somewhat sad smile was thanks enough for Jacob. For now.

He escorted her to the door and kissed her gently on the cheek beneath the stares of every one of the room's occupants. With a gentle pat to her backside he whispered, "I'll find you later and perhaps we can finish our...conversation that was so rudely interrupted earlier in the library."

The blush that scarred her cheeks left no doubt to anyone

that Jacob had made some rakish remark to his new bride.

"I'll look forward to that conversation, Your Grace." Jessica flashed him a heartfelt, brilliant smile and turned and left the room without making any further eye contact.

She paused outside the parlor door and leaned back against the wall, content for now to press her flaming cheek against a cool marble pillar and revel in the fact that she was, for the moment, not under anyone's watchful stare.

Just as she was about to make her way upstairs she heard the unmistakably caustic voice of Baroness Von Kraus on the other side of the door.

"So you've taken a wife, have you? And what does Marga think of all this?" the baroness asked.

Who was Marga? Jessica wondered. She hated the fact that she was eavesdropping, but try as she might her feet would not move her away from her position behind the door.

"I fail to see what business that is of yours, Lillian," Jacob answered gruffly.

"Oh, but you know that Marga and I are dear friends. I'm certain she'll be quite upset about all this. She thinks you to be in love with her, you know."

"No. I didn't know. I have never given her any reason to think such a thing. Marga and I had an understanding, no commitments, no promises."

"Still, you've been with her for such a long time. Surely you can't be thick enough to think she doesn't have very strong feelings for you."

"Whatever feelings Marga has are of her own doing. I made my position very clear to her from the beginning."

"Not according to her. No, no. She will be quite devastated when I tell her," Lillian said.

"Then perhaps you should let me do the telling," Jacob replied quietly.

"What? And not tell my dearest of friends that the man she has devoted herself to has taken a young nobody to wife instead of her?"

Even from her position behind the door, Jessica could feel Jacob's anger building.

His voice took on a dangerous timbre. "First of all, baroness, if you are such a true and dear friend to Marga, why did you so pathetically try to seduce me when last I came to visit your husband? Or had you conveniently forgotten that I readily turned away your distasteful offer? I think you are in no position to scorn me for doing something that would hurt Marga's feelings."

"Oh!" the baroness breathed out in rage.

"And second, my wife is not a 'nobody.' Even if she was, it would be no concern of yours. Jessica has more decorum in her little finger than most of you so-called ladies in this room have in your entire bodies. But that aside, she just happens to be the granddaughter of Hayden Atterberry, the Marquis of Brentley. I daresay not even you would consider a marquis a nobody."

Jessica was stunned to hear Jacob admit that. She had been under the impression that they would be keeping news of her reappearance away from the marquis and his wife for as long as possible.

"But—but that's impossible!" Lillian sputtered. "Everyone knows that the Atterberry's daughter died years ago! How could—"

"Not before she had a beautiful daughter who happens to now be my wife. She is beautiful, isn't she, Lillian?" Jacob asked thoughtfully.

Jessica felt a warmth spread throughout her at Jacob's defense and kind words.

"In fact," Jacob continued, "I would appreciate it, no, more than that, I *insist* that you show Jessica only the deepest respect from now on. If you don't, I may find it necessary to speak to your husband about *your* lack of respect—and your lack of restraint. I doubt you would want that to happen, hmm? It wouldn't suit you to find your freedoms and your purse strings tightened, now would it?"

"You—are—despicable, Jacob," the baroness growled.

"Yes, I am. And I'm also very serious. Now, if you'll excuse me, I find that I have yet to greet the baron. I do so enjoy talking to your husband."

Jessica heard Jacob's footsteps carry him away and took the opportunity to race upstairs before she was caught listening in on the conversation.

When she reached her bedroom she closed the door firmly behind her and leaned against it, her heart beating rapidly. A maelstrom of emotions swept over her: happiness at Jacob's defense of her, curiosity at the heretofore unmentioned Marga, and last but ever-present, fear at how she was going to explain Ossie's true identity to Jacob and his reaction to that truth.

She rubbed her forehead and walked to the door adjoining with Ossie's room. He wasn't there. Mrs. Holmes must still have him, she thought wearily.

As she turned back to her own room, she found she could not resist the pull of the great, soft bed. Jessica slipped her shoes off and crawled up on it, fully dressed, and laid her head on the feather pillow. She was asleep within moments.

Chapter 14

Outside, darkness had replaced the late afternoon glow. Jessica sat up, disoriented for a moment. How long had she been asleep?

She rubbed the slumber from her eyes and swung her legs off the bed. A soft light filled the room from the single low-burning lamp on the bedside table.

Jessica stood and made her way to the basin near the dressing table and splashed some cool water on her face to further chase away the remnants of sleep.

A huge vase of roses had been placed near the towels at the basin. Their scent drifted up to her and she couldn't resist burying her face in the fragrant, silky petals. The note which was propped up against the vase said simply, "Your Husband."

Husband. Dear God. So it hadn't been a dream. She really had married Jacob Austen Callaway.

She glanced up at the beautiful grandfather clock which stood near the door and was astonished to find that it read eleven o'clock. It couldn't be! That clock had to be wrong. Had she really been sleeping for all those hours?

She tip-toed quietly crossed her room and stepped inside Ossie's small bedroom. He was there, sleeping the sound, peaceful sleep of a child, a small stuffed bear curled in his arms.

Jessica closed the door between their rooms. She looked down at the beautiful gown she'd worn for her wedding and saw that it was terribly wrinkled. No amount of smoothing with her hands would make a difference.

"Oh, I hope I haven't ruined it," she whispered to herself. Having never owned a gown of such fine material, she had no idea how much abuse it could take. Without a second thought she took it off, replacing it with her comfortable trousers and cotton shirt that she had trimmed down to fit.

The gown was lovely, but this was more like it!

She entered the hall and let her bare feet carry her lightly down the stairs. She'd neither seen nor heard any other signs of life upstairs and so felt an unrestrained freedom to explore the mansion without running into anyone.

A softly burning lamp was sitting on a marble table in the entryway. Jessica picked it up and carried it with her, turning up the flame as she went. The library door was ajar and the light from a softly burning fire shown through. She ducked in there first just to make sure no one was about.

The glow from her lamp illuminated the large desk at the back of the back of the room, along with the papers and pens that were scattered on the floor around it.

Jessica felt that warm sensation spread through her body once again as she recalled just why all the papers were on the floor.

She walked to the desk and placed her hand on it. The top of the desk was smooth and cool to her touch, just as she remembered it feeling against her shoulders when Jacob had laid her back against it.

It suddenly occurred to her that Jacob had not come to continue their 'conversation', as he'd put it, when their guests left. A flicker of disappointment crept through her which she tried to ignore.

But the disappointment began to turn to annoyance as she recalled that this was, after all, her wedding night. All of her other dreams for her wedding were now lost, must her wedding night suffer the same consequences? And where was her husband at eleven o'clock at night?

The name Marga drifted into her mind, but she quickly pushed those budding thoughts aside. She refused to become a jealous, suspicious wife on her very first night, especially since she didn't even know for certain whom Marga was.

She set the lamp on the desk and bent to pick up the scattered papers. The last one she retrieved was the marriage certificate.

Her fingers lightly caressed the dried ink that was their signatures.

Married. To a duke. She was a duchess.

Her head began to swim as she stood. She reached for the edge of the desk and had to hold on for several moments. The full impact of what had transpired this day hit her all at once.

She had married a man she'd wanted to despise.

She had married a man who was part of a society that had cast out her father; a society that was all she didn't want to be a part of.

She had married a man on false pretenses.

But she'd done it for Ossie!

Jessica reminded herself of that over and over, and wondered dully why it was so hard to convince herself that she'd done it only for Ossie.

She couldn't possibly have wanted to marry Jacob, could she?

"No, no!" she whispered out loud. "*I didn't* want to!"

"Really? The last time I saw you at this desk it appeared that you did want to, and very urgently."

Jessica's sharp intake of breath was loud in the silent room as she spun towards the voice that had broken into her private battle.

"What are *you* doing in here?" she asked Malcom.

He was leaning against the door frame, that silly little smile still on his face as it was the last time she'd seen him.

"I've come to refill my snifter. It would appear that Jake and I have drained the parlor of all its liquor. I was hoping that I might find another bottle of brandy in here."

Malcom pushed away from the door and sauntered unsteadily across the room to a small roll-top cottageet. After clumsily fumbling with the latch, he finally managed to slide the lid back.

"Aha! I knew the ol' boy kept a bottle in here," he muttered, more to himself than Jessica.

Jessica folded her arms in front of her. "Do you always make yourself so free in Jacob's home?" she asked.

Malcom turned toward her then took a step forward to balance himself. Jessica put her hand to her mouth to cover her smile. Her annoyance at his opening remark was fading in the light of his drunken antics.

"As a matter of fact, Duchess, I do take many freedoms in Jacob's home," he said while making an awkward bow. With a flourish he rose and then stumbled backwards, landing soundly in a wing-back chair. A smile split his face. "Ah, there's the seat I was looking for. Now, what were we talking about? Ah, yes. My freedoms. Jake and I have been friends for many years, probably about as many as you've been alive. How old are you, any way?"

Malcom was taking a good look at Jessica. Her hair was flowing softly about her waist, a few shorter pieces curling around her face like a soft frame.

Then it hit him: she was wearing men's trousers and a shirt. And she was bare footed!

"I say! Are you aware of how you're dressed?" he asked incredulously. He'd never seen a woman attired in this manner.

Jessica tossed her head back and laughed out loud. It was the first real humor she'd felt in what seemed like ages. She sat up on the top of the desk, crossing her legs and leaning back on the palms of her hands.

"I am aware, Malcom. And believe it or not, I did it intentionally," she finished with a whisper, laughing again at the shocked expression that settled on his face.

"You are quite unlike any woman I've ever met. Is it true, then, that you were raised in the woods? In a cottage?"

Jessica giggled. "It's true," she said, tilting her head to one side and sweeping her massive auburn waves over one shoulder.

She had no way of knowing that her position was extremely un-ladylike, and extremely enticing. No one had ever taught her that ladies didn't prop themselves up on desk tops while carrying on conversations with gentlemen, especially gentlemen they hardly knew.

But something in the way Malcom's expression was changing told her all was not right. His eyes had been lingering on her shirt and just below the waist ties of her trousers for a little too long now.

She looked down at her clothes. "Does my attire offend you so much, then?" she asked self-consciously.

Malcom enjoyed a last glance at the way the buttons strained just slightly across her breasts before he dragged his eyes back to her face with a concerted effort. "What? Oh, no, no. I quite appreciate your—attire. As a matter of fact, I wish that more women dressed this way, but I suppose that will never happen."

He chuckled then and leaned his head back. Wisely, he trained his eyes on the ceiling for a moment lest he forget this alluring creature was his best friend's newly acquired wife.

When he finally looked at her again he forced his eyes to remain locked with hers.

"So tell me," he began, looking for safe conversation, "how do you suppose you will enjoy being a duchess?"

Jessica relaxed once again. "I really don't know. It's a lot to absorb in one day. I suppose I should learn to be a wife first, since that too is something new."

"I have no doubt but that will come easy to you." Malcom laughed before continuing. "Jacob will see to it that you learn all the wifely duties as quickly as possible. I fear I interrupted your first lesson today. But then, that really wasn't your first lesson, was it?"

"What do you mean?" she asked warily.

"Well, I mean it's not as if you were an innocent bride tossed into the lair of the lord, now is it? You do have a child, so you must know something about the, uh, so-called wifely duties."

Jessica felt a knot begin to form in her stomach. What had he told everyone? It was one thing for Jacob to think she had allowed herself to become an unwed mother, but for others to think that? And surely none of them would believe the truth if they already thought she was a promiscuous woman.

Oh, how could Jacob do this to her? She forced herself to remain calm. "And what else did Jacob tell you about me?" she said, forcing a smile to her face. She leaned forward placing her elbows on her thighs and resting her chin on her fisted hands.

She was vaguely aware that she was, for the first time in her life, actively flirting with a man. Any guilt she might have felt about the man being someone other than her new husband was buried beneath the anger that was building at Jacob's apparent lack of concern over her reputation.

Malcom leaned forward on his knees as well. "Oh, he told us this and that." Suddenly, he let out a loud guffaw and slapped his thigh. "I wish I could have been watching when Jake was wrestling with you and caught a handful of your—uh, your— well, when he realized you were a woman and not an obnoxious boy. Oh ho! What a tale he told!"

He took several deep breaths before continuing. "Even now, in this attire, I can scarcely begin to believe he ever mistook you for a lad. All in all, Duchess, you clean up very nicely. You looked lovely today. I must admit I was surprised when Jake lingered with us in the parlor instead of chasing your swishing skirts upstairs. Had it been me, I assure you I would have found an excuse to be eagerly away from that crowd of busybodies and ensconced with my new wife in a great feather bed," Malcom said with a lascivious grin, the liquor giving him a loose tongue.

Jessica forced herself to appear calm. "Well, apparently he

didn't find the need quite as urgent as you would have. Does that say something about my choice in husbands, Malcom? Should I instead have chosen—you, perhaps?" she asked sarcastically, a humorless smile painted on her lips.

Not that she had a choice, she reminded herself sourly. She leaned back on one palm while her other hand twirled a lock of hair between her fingers.

Malcom continued chuckling in his chair, unaware that her choice of words were tinged with anger and not just a wry sense of humor. He was truly enamored of the new duchess. "Had the opportunity risen, Duchess, I'm certain you could have snared me even easier than you snared Jake. And I can almost certainly guarantee you that I would be easier to get along with than my good friend."

"Really? Well isn't that just my poor luck-of-the-draw. Perhaps I did indeed miss out on some things by being reared so far from what you would call civilization. I never realized men as tractable as you existed. Should I be very disappointed, then?" she finished with another teasing smile.

"Oh, not too disappointed. Jake's a good man, if hard to read some times. But can you just imagine the look on his face if I were to tell him you've decided you'd rather have me than him? I assure you it would be a first. I've lost more dalliances to Jacob than I can count, though it's through no fault of his own. It's just that damn pretty face of his."

Yes, Jacob was handsome, Jessica admitted. But now was not the time to focus on her husband's finer qualities! "Perhaps it's time you turned the tables?" she said with a little laugh.

Was she being too brazen? With her lack of experience she could only assume that she was, but she was still testing the waters of flirtation. Malcom, in his state of inebriation, would give her some answers if she could keep him talking.

Malcom laughed heartily. "Jacob wasn't exaggerating when he said you were an oddity."

The smile fell from Jessica's face and her hand stopped its

distracted twirling. "*An oddity?*" she repeated his words coldly.

"Yes. Oh, he meant that in the most flattering way. He said you were unlike any other woman we've ever met, and he was right. Tell me though, you're a pretty little thing, Duchess. Why weren't you already married? And the boy's father, what of him?"

"Ah well, the story of the boy's father is one I've yet to share with Jacob. I think it's only fair that I speak to him first." *Guilt, guilt, guilt.* "And as for not being married, well, with so many young men to choose from in that highly populated area in which I was raised, I just found it simply too hard to choose just one."

Malcom looked at her for a moment before realizing she was being sarcastic.

"Ha! Duchess, I am honored to be the one spending your wedding night with you." Malcom raised his glass in a drunken toast, chortling into his drink.

The reminder of that fact, even in jest, didn't sit well with Jessica. It took all her reserve to force the smile back to her lips.

"Well, since my husband seems to think there are better things to do than tend to his bride, I am grateful for your devoted attention. So tell me, Malcom, does Jacob spend most of his time here, at the estate?" she asked.

Her ire was building. If she wasn't careful, Jessica knew she'd end up storming out of this room in search of her husband, and in her current mood, that would only mean trouble.

"He's here as much as possible. Jacob's not really one to attend the balls and parties that seem to attract so many of our crowd, myself included. Of course, now that he has a duchess to show off, I'm certain you'll both be attending at least the next few galas."

"How exciting," she said without enthusiasm. "I'm certain I'll enjoy meeting all of his friends. But from what I gathered, not every one will be happy to meet me."

"What do you mean?"

"Oh, his past—and current—love interests." Jessica was waiting, hoping that Malcom would deny the latter part of her statement.

Not so. "Ha! You're right about that," he slurred with a chuckle. He leaned his head against the back of the chair. More to himself he said, "She's going to be downright apoplectic. Poor Marga. Ha! I can't wait to see...."

Jessica felt as if the top of her head would burst. Never had she felt such immediate anger. So Marga was, as she'd deduced, his current mistress. The fact that she so overwhelmingly ached to throttle the unknown woman only intensified her frustration. Until now, this feeling of—it could only be jealousy—had been unfamiliar to her. But thanks to her rogue of a husband, she not only was experiencing it but was very nearly drowning in the vile emotion.

That beast! Did he truly intend to sequester her away here in the country while continuing to flaunt his mistress in town? Was this how her life was going to be spent? Acting as a hidden brood mare for the Duke of Fairdale?

"What a sorry sight!" a voice interrupted from the doorway. Jacob leaned against the door frame. "I come in search of drink and find that my best friend and my young bride are engaged in what appears to be a very serious conversation."

He could see that Malcom was enjoying himself, slumped down in a large chair with a drunken grin on his face. But Jacob was already too familiar with the look of outrage on Jessica's face. What the devil had Malcom said to her?

Jessica narrowed her eyes but forced the humorless smile back to her face.

"Oh, indeed, we were very serious, *husband*."

Jacob's eyes swept over Jessica's casual clothing and then to the all-too-appreciative look on Malcom's face. He did not enjoy the possessive feeling that washed over him at Malcom's obvious admiration of his wife, a woman he had at one point thought he would only need for the purpose of bearing heirs.

Jacob looked back at his wife and said with a distinctively stern voice, "Jessica, perhaps you should remove yourself from the desk and find a chair in which to sit. It would be more appropriate."

"Oh, it would? I fear I am just so remiss in the social graces, having been raised so crudely in the wilds and all," she said caustically. Jessica enjoyed the obvious discomfort that Jacob was trying to hide. She had no desire to confront him with Malcom in the room, but neither did she want to make the rest of this night any easier for Jacob.

She straightened out her legs and languidly slid off the desk, pushing Jacob's patience further toward the point of breaking. "I'm so sorry to have offended you, Jacob. But Malcom just put me so at ease." She flashed Malcom a beaming smile that rivaled that of the rising sun.

Jacob's eyes darted to Malcom who was beginning to sense some of his friend's tension. Malcom sat more upright, the smile fading somewhat from his face.

"Is that so?" Jacob asked.

"Why, yes. He's been a great comfort to me in my solitude. In fact, he even offered to spend my wedding night with me since my husband was no where to be found."

Malcom struggled to stand up, but failed. "Now wait a minute, I—"

"You were ever so sweet, Malcom, to keep me entertained." Jessica moved to Malcom's side and placed a gentle hand on his arm. She looked directly at Jacob then, not missing the color that was rising in his face. "But I suddenly find that I am no longer in the mood—for *anything*. Good night, gentlemen."

She tried to brush past Jacob but he grabbed her arm and stopped her short. "I believe I shall join you, madam. Apparently, we have a few matters to discuss."

Jessica yanked her arm from his grasp. "To discuss? Oh, I think we are far beyond having any *conversation* this evening, Your Grace."

Jacob was in no condition to do battle with his wife. Several shared bottles of brandy had seen to that. He bowed and held out his arm. "As you wish. We will settle matters in the light of the morning. Make no mistake about that."

Jessica turned and stormed through the door. Just as she began to climb the stairs, she heard Jacob's voice boom, "And just what the hell did you say to my wife?"

She felt the tiniest bit sorry for having put Malcom in the middle of their argument, but she knew Jacob wouldn't harm his friend for no real reason. Jessica couldn't stop the little smile of satisfaction from touching her mouth as made her way up the stairs.

Apparently her husband wasn't immune to new emotions, either.

Chapter 15

Jessica hated the fact that she held her breath every time footsteps sounded in the hall outside her bedroom, or passed the library, or anywhere else she might be spending her time.

The truth of the matter was that she wasn't even really that angry with Jacob anymore.

A large part of her anger was directed at herself. Ossie's true identity was still no closer to being revealed, and for that she had only herself to blame. Accusing Jacob of intentionally not telling her about Marga would be a hard stand to take, considering the secret she was keeping from him.

And as for Marga, Jessica hadn't really expected that Jacob would have had no mistresses. Their marriage was so sudden and unplanned that he would not have had time to break off his situation with Marga—yet.

"Well, sitting here brooding about it will accomplish nothing," she said aloud. In fact, it was making matters worse. Jacob was obviously not making any effort to seek her out, but there was no need for her to waste even another minute.

Jessica looked out the window of her bedroom. The sky was still swollen with fat, dark clouds but the incessant rain had finally stopped. As if it had a voice of its own, the outdoors beckoned her.

What she needed was a brisk ride.

Some time with her horse and the elements might help clear

her head.

Giles was in the stable brushing down a young colt when she found him.

"Ah, good morning! I was beginnin' to wonder if ye'd left us!"

"Would that I could," Jessica said, though the retort was more from habit than a sincere feeling.

"Now, now. Has it really been that horrible here?"

Jessica smiled at the old gentleman. "No. I guess it could be worse."

"Sure it could," he said, rubbing his stubbled chin. "That fine boy o' yers was down here yesterday. It won't be long before we won't be able to keep him out of the saddle."

Jessica looked at Giles carefully. She knew he'd been with Austen for many years. Was it possible that he knew the truth about Ossie?

Giles began walking toward the stalls where her two horses were being kept. "Yep, he's goin' to be a natural horseman, he is."

Jessica fell in beside him. "Ossie? But how can you tell?"

"Ah, just they way he sits a saddle."

"Sits a—but he can't ride on his own yet. What do you mean—"

"Jacob, I mean the duke, I still can't get used to that. I've been calling him by his given name for so many—"

"Yes, yes Giles, but what has that to do with—"

"The duke took him riding."

"Jacob? But when? He's been locked in the library with those lawyers and—and whoever else for—"

"The duke—ah, heck, d'ya mind if I still refer to him as Jake? It's an awful hard habit to break."

"Of course not. And please, call me Jessica. But Giles, I must know—"

Giles chuckled. "I'm sorry Jessica. I'm just havin' a wee bit of fun wit' ye. I don't get too many visitors down 'ere and the ponies rarely laugh at my foolery. About the young lad, ye see Jake goes for a ride every afternoon, almost without fail. Rain or shine. 'Course this morn—"

"And he's been taking Ossie with him?"

"Aye. I guess he didn't think you'd object."

"Well, I don't, but Ossie's still so young and—" she let her words drift off as she looked back at the mansion.

"Never ye worry, Jessica. Ossie is safe as can be when 'e's with Jake. Never have there been finer horsemen than the Callaways. It runs in their blood. You'll see what I mean by how quickly young Ossie catches on."

Jessica's head whipped around. Giles soft eyes met and held hers. He just nodded slowly and smiled.

Hot color rose in Jessica's cheeks as the full impact of Giles' words hit her. He knew. He knew everything.

Tears began to form in Jessica's eyes as fear gripped her chest. If he told Jacob before she had a chance, oh, that just couldn't happen!

"Now, lass. Don't ye be upset. 'Tis not my secret to tell. I only hope that you will tell him soon. Both he and the boy have a right to know."

The relief his words caused was overwhelming. She sat on a bench near the wall and was finally able to breathe.

"I will. I will tell him. But I have to find the right time. Hell, I have to find any time at all. I've hardly seen the pompous ass since we were—since I arrived." She blushed again, remembering that Giles had come upon them on the grassy hill.

Giles chuckled at her coarse words. "I'm sorry, Giles. I shouldn't have said that about Jacob."

"Ah, lass. I assure you I've used worse to describe him at times. If it makes ye feel better, go ahead."

Jessica sighed again in relief. "Giles, do you know—everything?"

The old stable master pulled up a small stool and sat in front of her, picking up a piece of straw and placing it between his teeth. "I know all I need to know," he said vaguely.

"Which is?"

Giles hesitated. He wasn't used to discussing family secrets. "I know that Ossie is the old duke's son. I know that Lizette was his mama, and that Jacob doesn't know about either of them—yet."

"And how did you come to know all this? How could you know Ossie wasn't my son?"

"I didn't, right off. But something about that boy was all too familiar. He's the image of Jacob at that age." Giles leaned back a little and chuckled. "In fact, for a brief time, I wondered if perhaps Ossie was the product of one of Jacob's, uh, extended visits to the north. But I dismissed that idea when it became obvious that you two didn't know each other before this whole situation arose. So then I thought the boy's looks were just coincidental. It wasn't until I tended to your mare the morning we left the inn that I knew for a fact what was what."

"My mare?"

"Aye. I went with the duke when he delivered the horse to Lizette. Putting' one and one together, well I guess if Lizette trusted you to raise her boy, she'd trust ye with her horse," he chuckled.

"And you recognized the mare after so many years?" Jessica asked in disbelief.

"Lass, come with me." They rose and walked to the large, comfortable stall where her mare was nickering a greeting. "This was not just any horse that he gave to Lizette. It's one of our own fine stock, bred and born right here at Fairdale. Looky here."

Giles opened the stall door and knelt by the mare's front feet. He pointed at a white patch on her underbelly. "Ye see that?"

"Yes. It's in the shape of a heart. Lizette told me that her beloved had given her this horse especially because of that marking, because it was a symbol of their love."

"That may be. But it's also a symbol of Titan, one of our finest stallions. He throws that mark on every foal he sires. Never missed one yet. It's very distinct; always somewhere on their bellies. I've never seen any horse with that marking that wasn't from Titan."

Jessica sat back in the thick straw and let her breath out slowly. "And if Jacob happens to see her marking, well, he's by no means an idiot. It will only be a matter of time until he puts it all together."

"I suggest ye tell him before he finds out on his own, lassie. It'll come off much better." Giles reached up and ran his hand down the horse's leg. "She is a beauty. And now she's yers. A bit curious how she's come full circle and ended up here with you, eh? Say, what'd the duke's lady name her?"

Jessica leaned her head back on the wall and began laughing. She couldn't help herself, it was just too ironic.

"Duchess."

Chapter 16

Jacob warmed his hands in front of the roaring fire. The building storm outside had caught him off guard. Thankfully, he'd been near his father's old hunting cottage when the real fury hit.

He looked around the cottage and smiled sadly. His father had never once come here to hunt anything. It was merely his refuge.

And now it was Jacob's. Oddly, it reminded him of the cottage where he'd found Jessica. She would love this place, of that he was sure.

Jessica. His wife.

Jacob sat on the floor and leaned back against the old couch, stretching his long legs out towards the fire's heat.

Wife. There it was again. That word that kept sneaking into his thoughts, a word that he was having so much trouble turning away.

Time to face it, ol' boy. Jacob took a deep breath and closed his eyes.

Jessica's image floated through his mind. What a mess he'd made of things. "I guess pride truly does goeth before the fall," he whispered softly.

Inwardly he cringed, realizing that it had been two days since his wedding and he'd yet to even kiss his wife after their initial heated moments following the ceremony. Still, all those hours later, and with a cold storm brewing outside, the thought of those moments warmed him and stirred a need deep inside.

And this he denied himself because he was too proud to admit that he was having serious feelings for the woman? Feelings he never thought he could have, feelings he didn't want to have.

Malcom had laughed right in his face after Jessica had left them that night in the library; told him he never thought he'd live to see the day when Jacob Callaway would be *in love*.

"I'm *not* in love, you drunk bastard. Apparently the drink is affecting you more than usual this evening," Jacob had roared.

That statement had only served to bring another loud guffaw from Malcom. "You protest overmuch, my friend. Even while you were relating the events of your unconventional meeting, how boyish and rough she appeared, anyone could see that you are now more than just smitten with your new bride. Face it: You respect her, you admire her, it's beyond obvious that you desire her, and you quite possibly are in love with her."

Those words rang over and over in Jacob's mind. And the fact that they stung so much, even coming from Malcom who knew him better than anyone, made him realized that there was in fact a great deal of truth to them.

I could love her.

Where had that thought come from?

I could love her.

Again. But this time not so hard to swallow.

I could love her.

A smile crossed his features. So, admitting that much hadn't killed him.

Now, he just had to find his wife and start building a foundation that wouldn't be blown apart each time they had a difference of opinion.

Jacob was about to doze off, a new kind of peace and expectancy lying over him like a soft blanket, when a noise from outside wrenched him back to awareness.

There it was again, definitely the sound of a horse blowing

outside.

Who would be out in this downpour? Immediately he was on his feet, crossing the floor and swinging the door open.

Seeing Jessica on her mare in the downpour was as much a surprise to him as it was for her to see Jacob standing in the doorway of the nearest shelter she could find in the storm.

Jessica sucked in her breath.

"What the devil—?" Jacob asked loudly.

Jessica felt her breath leave her. It had been two days since they'd married. Yet between their stubborn argument and the legal matters of the estate, they'd barely said a full, *civil* sentence to one another as husband and wife

His wet shirt, partially unbuttoned, clung to his chest and the waist of his loosened trousers hung low across his hips. Soaked curls were plastered to his forehead giving him a deceivingly boyish look.

Damn! Why must he be so bloody handsome?

"Madam, is it your wish to catch your death in the rain?" he shouted over the rain and wind.

A small portion of common sense returned to her. "What? Oh—no, it's just that I—we lost our direction and I thought perhaps—but I'm sorry to have disturbed you. I thought the cottage was deserted. We'll be on—"

In a flash he was by her side, yanking the reins from her hands. "You'll do no such thing. I'll not be cursed with a sick—or dead—wife after less than a week of marriage. That one I'd never live down." He grabbed her around the waist and pulled her off the mare. For a moment he held her close to him, amazed at the sudden heat that ignited between their cold, wet bodies.

Slowly he slid her down the length of his front, savoring not only the heat, but the look of shock he saw in Jessica's eyes.

Jacob held her tight to him, enjoying the breathlessness that had settled over Jessica so quickly. He smiled just slightly, letting her know that her response to his nearness had not gone unnoticed.

Even though they were getting soaked, he was loathe to let go of her just yet. "Would you mind telling me what you're doing out here, alone, in this storm? I'll flog Giles to within an inch of his life for this."

Jessica's eyes suddenly cleared. "No! Oh, no! It's all my doing, Jacob. I insisted on going out alone and if anyone should be flogged, it should be me. I told him I'd only be gone briefly...I just got a little lost and then the storm hit and well... here I am."

"Hmm. Well, I would never really flog old Giles, but you on the other hand might still warrant a good spanking."

At her look of surprise, Jacob laughed out loud.

"Get yourself inside while I put your horse under the shelter with Martin."

As Jessica turned and went inside, Jacob stared after her for a moment in the rain. He couldn't believe his luck. This was just what he needed. Time alone with her, no interruptions, in a setting in which she would be comfortable.

Take it slow and don't let your pride stick you again as it has in the past, he warned himself.

The fire was just beginning to offer some heat to the room and it beckoned Jessica with its crackling flames. She reached her hands out and rubbed them together, trying to get some feeling back in them.

Jacob's half-dressed appearance as he lifted her from her mount seeped back into her mind. Color warmed her cheeks as she recalled the way their bodies molded to one another when he lifted from her horse. The twinge it caused in her stomach left her wondering if being alone with him was a good idea. And yet the fact that she really didn't have a choice in the matter didn't leave her feeling quite as despondent as it should have.

She surveyed her surroundings, trying to guide her thoughts in a different direction.

The small cottage was not unlike her own home had been. A table stood near the single window with three chairs pushed up to it. Next to her, in front of the fire, a small sofa was angled beside a large stuffed chair. A thick rug covered the wood floor in front of the fire place, its edges darkened from the heat of many fires.

In one corner a bed stood alone, large and out of place in the cottage, but very comfortable looking nonetheless. Errant thoughts of what it might be like to—

She tore her eyes away from the bed, determined to keep the hot flush from further staining her cheeks.

The door to the cottage slammed shut and although the noise made her jump, Jessica didn't dare turn around. Behind her she heard Jacob moving about and could visualize him removing his boots and shaking the water from his hair. She hated the fact that their last conversation had been so full of anger for she had absolutely no idea what to say to him or how to act.

A moment later he was by her side, sharing in the fire's warmth. Jessica was unsure now if it was the cold or Jacob's powerful presence that was causing her to continue shivering.

"Why don't you take your boots off?" Jacob suggested.

She nodded and sat on the edge of the sofa, trying to pull the wet boot from her foot. With her numb fingers she was having little success.

Jacob watched her struggle for a moment and then lowered himself to one knee. "Let me do that." His hand remained on her delicate ankles for longer than necessary after removing each wool sock.

He set the boots by the fire carefully draping the socks over them to dry and then rose, helping her to her feet at the same time. "Stand near the fire. You're still shaking." She did as he suggested, still too cold to even consider doing otherwise.

Jessica's shivering was not lessening and the fact that she could feel Jacob's eyes on her did nothing to dissipate her uneasiness. She tried to pull her soaking cloak tighter around her shoulders but succeeded only in making more cold water run down the front of her blouse and drip on the floor at her now bare feet.

"Come Jesse, take that soaking rag off. You'll never get dry if you don't."

Try as she might, Jessica could not make her frozen fingers work the knot at her throat any easier than she'd been able to remove her boot.

"Perhaps I might be of assistance again?"

Without waiting for an answer he moved behind her, standing so close that she could once again feel his heat. His hands brushed across her shoulders, lingering for a moment before he deftly untied the strings at her throat.

Ever so lightly, he allowed his fingers to graze the delicate skin of her neck, taking pleasure in the smoothness he found there, before removing the cloak from her shoulders.

Jacob inhaled deeply of her fresh, clean scent, more noticeable because her clothes and skin were wet. "Apparently, your cloak did you about as much good as mine against nature's onslaught," he said softly, his breath warm against her ear, smiling as he saw the shiver it caused her. He took the cloak and hung it on the far end of the mantle.

Jessica was still unable to speak. She longed for the heat that he took with him when he moved away, but not because she was cold. His nearness had rendered her unable to think rationally. She knew any words that escaped her mouth would come out sounding ridiculous.

Jacob turned, leaning against the mantle, and looked her over from bottom to top. His own breath caught in his throat now as his eyes drank in the clinging trousers and nearly transparent blouse. She couldn't know what sort of picture she presented, for she stood there before him, arms stretched toward the fire, completely unashamed and unaware of her tempting appearance.

For the first time he considered it a bonus that she had been reared casually in the country. There was no abundance of lace, frills, and corsets to block from his view the perfection that was her body.

At last his eyes came to rest on her face, and finally a frown crossed his brow. Her lovely features were all but hidden by that damn hat she insisted on wearing.

It too was soaked and drooping low across her forehead, little droplets of water falling now and then from the bent brim. In an instant he was standing before her, and in another he had the offensive hat torn from her head and thrown into the fire.

Jessica heard the hissing of the flames as they protested their water-logged fuel before she even realized what had happened.

"Oh! My hat! Why—"

"Because it was the ugliest damn thing I'd ever seen! Really Jessica, if you are so fond of hats and bonnets, I can buy you dozens."

"But that was—" she paused for a moment, watching the flames devour the worn fabric and then began chuckling, the tension beginning to leave her at last. "That was, truly, the ugliest damn hat ever."

Jacob was both surprised and enchanted by her laughter. The sound was intoxicating and he found himself drawn towards this woman who stood before him; this woman who was unbelievably attractive, even in wet, male attire, this woman who was, by God, his wife!

The walls that had separated them came crashing down. With no need for spoken apologies or explanations, a happiness filled them both as they relaxed and enjoyed what was rightfully theirs.

He placed his hands gently at her shoulders which were still shaking lightly in mirth. Seductively, he ran his hands down her arms and finally folded her icy fingers into his warm hands. He kissed her fingertips softly.

His smile widened and a twinkle brightened his eyes. "You are a duchess now, Jessica. If silly bonnets are to be your whimsy, then they shall be yours in abundance." Jacob moved his hands gently upward until they once again felt the softness of her neck, his thumbs caressing the pulse point at her throat.

"And suppose, sir, that it is not fanciful bonnets that I require to satisfy my whimsy?"

Her smile became warmer as she relaxed against his hard body. Immediately she felt the heat rush through her, inflaming her senses. Her fingertips delicately explored his male nipples beneath his damp shirt bringing forth a smile and a tiny groan. His body was a wonder to her, and she intended to fully explore it.

It was a gratifying feeling to know that everything she did, and wanted to do, was the most natural thing to occur between a man and his wife. Giving in to her desires was a heady tonic, increasing her boldness.

Without hesitation she moved her hands up to his shoulders.

She wanted him. She admitted that now and would no longer fight it.

Jessica arched her back slightly and pressed her hips against his, feeling the unmistakable hardness that was his desire. His sharp intake of breath gave her courage to explore her power.

Jacob's large hands found their way slowly down her front, his thumbs pausing to make small, swirling patterns on her already taut nipples, then continuing down to her waist and around to her bottom.

"Hmmm." He pulled her even tighter against his pulsing hardness. "Then I only hope that I will be able to satisfy whatever it is you desire, now and always."

He looked deeply into her eyes, seeing the passion there, and realized with a flood of emotion that he meant every word he'd said.

Now and always.

His hand slid up her back to the knot of hair at her neck and pulled the few remaining pins free.

Glorious waves of auburn spilled to her waist. His fingers wound themselves through the mass as he slowly lowered his lips to hers. "And just what do you suppose, Madam Duchess, your desire will be?" he whispered softly against her mouth.

His fingers tightened in her hair, forcing her to meet his eyes. "You," she whispered, "just you."

Her words were his undoing. With a muffled groan he covered her mouth with his, seeking, finding, teasing until she responded in kind.

He tore his lips from hers and gently pulled her head back, baring her throat to his heated kisses. Her knees went weak and as they began to buckle, Jacob lifted her and carried her to the bed in the corner.

Jacob set her to the ground and quickly peeled away the remainder of her wet clothes. Amazingly, Jessica felt no shyness standing nude in front of him. He paused for a moment, gazing in wonder at her beautiful body.

Her long, lightly muscled legs, the flat, firm stomach, and the perfect roundness of her breasts made a complete package that he had rarely seen, let alone dared to hope for in a wife.

Jacob's perusal warmed Jessica's body. She stepped forward and unbuttoned his shirt, her fingers now able to move having found such a heat and a delightful mission. She slowly dragged his shirt down his arms, leaning in to place a tentative but lingering kiss on his muscled chest. She tossed the shirt to the chair near the fire and reached up to his mouth, capturing his lips in a slow and seductive kiss.

The cords of muscles in his back were a wonder to her as she felt her way down to the small of his back. Her finger tips trailed lightly around his waist, pausing only momentarily on his taut stomach before dropping to already loosened ties at his trousers.

Boldly, she pushed his pants down over his hips. They both drew sharp breaths when his heat came into sudden contact with her downy softness.

She gently caressed his hip and then timidly moved her hand between them to the satiny, smooth firmness that pulsed between them, watching as her fingers closed around it.

Her fingers touched, hesitantly, testing, seeking the most

sensitive spots. This was all new to her, and her unabashed undertaking was done mostly out of passion, but partly out of curiosity. She ran her thumb over the smooth head, and then pulled her eyes away and up to meet his.

Jacob moaned from deep within his soul and his eyes melted into hers. His throat felt tight with emotion that mirrored hers.

Never had he thought he would find a woman that he could not only lust after, but also trust with his heart. Looking into her eyes, he was certain he'd found just that.

He stepped completely out of his trousers and lifted Jessica once again, laying her back on the soft bed. His long body stretched out next to hers as he let his hands wander where they would.

"You are so beautiful, Jesse," he whispered hoarsely, taking the taut bud from her breast into his mouth and praying he would have the strength to hold on long enough to bring her to ecstasy.

"Oh, Jacob, I want—I need—oh—" she whispered just before his lips covered hers again.

Jacob drew his fingers over the curls at her nether region and when he found the hot moistness eagerly awaiting him, he knew he could wait no longer.

He moved his body over hers and nudged her legs wider apart with his knee. Their eyes met again, and held. Jacob's hips lowered and the head of his shaft touched her quivering heat, gently pulsing against the slick softness.

Jessica inhaled deeply, then raised her hips to him, silently beckoning him to take her.

Restraint gone, he claimed what was his. He called out her name as he drove deep in a single thrust.

"Jessica!" he breathed as he entered her. There was warmth and a velvety softness and—a barrier? What the—?

It was too late for questions, for he'd broken through what he knew to be her maidenhead.

He raised his head and stared at Jessica whose eyes were also wide open in shock.

Her shock was not because of the momentary pain of his entry, but because in the heat of their passion she'd completely forgotten to tell him that Ossie was not her child; that she was — had been — a virgin.

"Oh my God!" they said in unison.

Dozens of questions exploded in Jacob's brain. He couldn't believe this. With no regard to Jessica's comfort, he pulled quickly out of her, causing her to wince in more pain than she had upon his entry.

He looked down at the sheets, just to be certain he wasn't mistaken. But there it was, her virgin's blood spotting the clean white linens, testimony to what he'd felt.

It was as if the cold rain from outside washed over them; all joy was gone.

When he drew his eyes back to her face he saw tears slipping down her cheeks. She was biting her lower lip to try and stop its quivering, but to no avail. A shuddering sob escaped her and she raised her hands to cover her face.

"A virgin! But you…Ossie… how the *hell?*"

Jessica took a deep breath and sat up, finally daring to look at Jacob. She reached one hand out to touch his chest, the other found the coverlet and clutched it to her breast. "I'm so sorry, Jacob. Please, let me explain," she whispered.

Jacob exploded. "Explain! Oh, this ought to be good! Another bushel of lies? What the hell is this? What kind of demented game are you playing with people's lives, Jessica? As a new husband, I should be thrilled to find my wife a virgin, but you lied! About something you *should* have been proud of! You come to us as an unwed mother towing a bastard child at her heels, a thing most good families would *not* overlook, I might add."

"Yes, Jacob, I know, but—" she faltered, her voice catching on a sob.

He leaned forward on his knees, forcing Jessica back to the

pillows. "I actually felt sorry for you!" he growled. "I admired how you were living on your own, *with your child!* Do you realized that I didn't even press you for the facts about *your child's* father before I wed you? Do you know why?"

"Jacob, I— "

"I'll tell you why! Because it was my father's wish that I marry you and protect you both, no matter what the circumstances. Ha! He assured me you were a good and honest woman. I must wonder now if that letter my father received was in fact from James Patrick, or if this was some cruel scheme you thought up yourself." He grabbed her wrist, pulling her hand away from his chest. "By God, it makes sense now. When your father died *you* sent this letter. James had never asked my father for help and yet suddenly we receive this heartfelt request. I should have known. Father should have known. But why the child? Was he just there to add sympathy to the ploy?"

Jessica fought her sobs to no avail finding hard to even breathe in the face of his fury.

Jacob ran his hand through his hair. "You played the bereaved daughter so well. All of it a lie. What planning had to go into this scheme. If I wasn't so thoroughly disgusted by you at this moment I might even see the genius in your plan to marry into a wealthy, ducal family."

"No, Jacob. That letter was from my father! I swear! I knew nothing about—"

"Are you even truly James Patrick's daughter?" He paused in his angry tirade and stared at her with narrow eyes. His voice came low and growling. "I warn you, if you're not Jessica Patrick I can have this marriage annulled before you can blink an eye, even though we have consummated this farce. Was it worth giving up your virginity for? This plan of yours?"

"There was no plan! Jacob, I *am* Jessica Patrick. I am James' daughter. I swear I knew nothing about this until the day you arrived at my door. Ossie is—"

She paused. Right now she knew he doubted every word

that came from her mouth and he looked angry enough to explode. If she tried to explain that Ossie was his half-brother she feared he would think it was a lie and very likely toss her out the door.

Jacob snorted derisively. "What? Having problems coming up with your next lie? Ossie. That poor lad. I can see why you chose a mute child, so he couldn't foil your plan with an innocent slip of the tongue. He has no idea who he's tangled up with, does he? I suggest you take him back to his true parents. Or are they in on this too? Ah, God."

Jacob's head was spinning. So many possible scenarios played out in his mind, but only one truth stood out.

The woman on the bed, his wife, had lied her way into his family; had lied about everything. Was their passion, those moments he'd felt pure connection, were they a lie too? That thought hurt almost more than the rest of the deceit.

Jacob rose and quickly gathered his clothes. "Well, one thing's for certain. Whoever tutored you in the art of feigning passion deserves accolades. You duped me more than once. But never again."

"Jacob, please just give me a moment to—"

"What, Jessica? Give you a moment to quickly think up another web of lies? I don't think so."

Jacob had his shirt and trousers on and was stepping into his boots. "I must say, I'm glad my father didn't live to see this great deceit. He truly liked you, Jessica, and it would have hurt him deeply to see what kind of thieving whore you really are!"

Jessica gasped. "A whore? Jacob you can't possibly—you know I was a virgin until just now! And I would never steal from your family! You have no right—"

"I—have—every—right!" Jacob thundered as he kicked her clothes toward the bed. "A whore can fulfill desires in many ways, Jessica. A whore is someone one who falls to her back for money or some other compensation, just as you have done. You came into my house and married me under false pretenses, and then you fell to your back and spread your legs to make certain I was bound to you. I call that the worst kind of whore! At least with the wenches on the streets you *know* that they're expecting payment!"

Jacob lowered his voice and spoke through clenched teeth. "You stole my father's final wish, you stole my trust," he paused for a moment breathing raggedly and then quietly finished, "and you damn near stole my heart."

It was almost a whisper, but Jessica heard the words.

"Jacob, please! Listen to me! Ossie is—"

"I can't even look at you right now Jessica. I fear I may do something that I'll regret later; although I doubt I could regret anything more than ever setting eyes upon you. I had given up on trusting women until I met you. I can see now that my former notion had been the wiser."

"Jacob!" Jessica shouted as the door to the cottage slammed shut. "Jacob, please! You must hear the truth!"

Jessica gave in to the sobs that were wracking her body. She knew it was no use to try and stop him now. But somehow, some way she must make him listen!

Chapter 17

Jacob hurried out into the rain which had eased only a little. He quickly retrieved his horse from behind the house and led him around front.

From inside the dwelling he heard Jessica's sobs.

The heart-wrenching wails nearly pulled him back inside. Damn it! He wanted her to explain this away, he wanted her to belong to him in truth and honesty! Even the fact that he was her first and only lover couldn't ease the pain of her betrayal.

The idea that she had duped him and his father made him feel foolish for marrying her at all, and the fact that he'd begun to care so deeply, well, that just cut to the core.

His head was spinning. Who were Ossie's parents? What kind of people would allow their child, their *mute* child, to go off with a woman to lay a trap like this? Oh, she had to have offered them plenty of money to get them to accept this wild scheme.

And that Jacob couldn't accept. The possibility that she had been planning to steal from him was all too feasible.

He grabbed a handful of his roan's mane and swung up into the saddle. With a last look at the front door he shook his head. This was as close as he'd ever come to being in love; he knew that now from the pain that surrounded his heart.

With a boot to the roan's side Jacob took off for home. He knew if he remained any longer he would give in to his heart and go back to her, offering her a chance to explain. *A chance for another set of lies!* He leaned forward in his saddle and let his mount run at will.

He had to get away from here, from her!

Now!

More than ever he loathed the idea of being the main attraction at that damned Grand Ball. But the Marquis and Marchioness of Chesterly, Lord and Lady Winslow, had sent him word of the gala immediately upon hearing of his marriage. It was in Jacob's honor, to introduce his new bride to his aristocratic acquaintances.

Not only were Lord and Lady Winslow old and dear friends of his family, but they were very important people. A new duke, no matter how wealthy or powerful, simply did not refuse an invitation from the Marquis.

Jacob clenched his teeth against the frustration that threatened to burst forth in a howl. Not only must they attend the damned function, but they must pretend to be happy and well suited to one another. At this point he had no idea what the final outcome of their marriage would be, but he did not intend to give the rumor mills grain to grind by openly shunning his wife at their first public appearance.

I must get away from here, he thought again. *I need time to reason this out.*

It was only a short time later that the stables came into view. Jacob began to rein in the roan but even so they entered the rear of the stable at a fast trot.

Giles and a young stable hand looked up in surprise as Jacob nearly leapt from lathered horse before it came to a halt.

"What is it?" Giles asked.

Jacob threw the reins to the young man. "Walk this horse out, and take your time in doing so. He's to have no water until he's completely cool. Then rub him down well and blanket him."

"Yes, Yer Grace, right away, sir." The young man ducked under the horse's head and led the animal to the cooling arena.

When the lad was out of earshot, Giles asked again, "Jake, what the heck's the matter? You were ridin' like the devil itself was at yer heels."

"I believe she was," Jacob whispered. He looked at the bearded old Cockney and forced himself to calm his breathing. "I'm in a hurry, old friend. Have the other lad ready the black gelding. I'll be riding him to London. Put my heavier travel saddle on him. There are a few things I must take with me."

"London? Jake, in this weather?"

Jacob nodded solemnly.

The other stable hand appeared and Giles gave him Jacob's instructions.

The young man scurried off and Giles turned back to Jacob. "Now, would ye mind—"

"I'm in a hurry, Giles. I can't talk just now."

He turned to leave the stable. Jacob knew he didn't dare bring up the subject of what had him so agitated, for he feared he might well explode.

But Giles wouldn't be put off easily. "Jake, at least tell me if ye saw the Duchess out there." His words brought Jacob to a halt. He'd never lied to his friend, and couldn't bring himself to start now.

"Yes. I saw her." He answered tightly.

"Well, where is she? I'm a bit worried about her. She's been gone for hours."

"She's fine. Just fine. Jessica is at Father's cottage. I assume she'll be along shortly."

Giles noticed the set of Jacob's shoulders and the clip to his words. He was fairly certain he knew what had happened, but it wasn't his place to interfere—too much.

"Er, Jacob, perhaps now isn't the time to say so, but I think ye made a fine choice fer a wife."

Jacob whipped around and stared at Giles, his mouth hanging open. "What?"

Giles was unaffected by Jacob's thunderous glare. After all,

158

he'd helped raise Jacob and had seen many temper flares in his time.

"I said, ye picked a fine wife."

Jacob ran his fingers through his hair and ripped his wet cloak from his shoulders. "I did not pick her, Giles, nor would I have picked her given a choice—and all the facts." He tossed the garment carelessly on a pile of straw.

"Well, I can't pretend to guess what that means," Giles said without looking directly at Jacob, "but let me just say this: Ofttimes people must do things that, to others outside of their situation, may seem less than honest. And only when the whole truth comes out do we realized their reasons for doing so were justified."

Giles gave a quick glance to Jacob's untucked and misbuttoned shirt, and the trousers that were barely fastened. Yes, he was certain that Jacob and Jessica had spent some private time together, but apparently Jacob had only gotten half the story from Jessica before he stormed off.

"This one time, old boy, I must tell you that you are mistaken. I have not the time, or desire, to go into details just now. Suffice it to say, Jessica and the boy are not who we thought they were."

"I believe yer right about that, my boy. Righter than ye think." Giles turned and shuffled off toward the back of the stable.

Jacob stood there for a moment wondering at Giles' last words. More often than not, Giles, with his rather whimsical beliefs and odd mutterings, managed to get right to the core of things.

But not this time, Jacob thought as he hurried to the house.

It wasn't until two hours later that Jessica made her way back to the great house.

"Ah, lassie!" Giles greeted her. "I was beginning t' think we'd lost ye!" Knowing she'd been at the hunting cottage, Giles hadn't been worried enough to send riders out after her. He rightly surmised she'd need time without interruption.

"I'm sorry, Giles. I guess I just lost track of time."

Jessica had retraced her original route back to the stables. If she'd had the presence of mind to note which direction Jacob had taken, she would have found a trail that carried her home in about thirty minutes.

As it was, she was once again chilled to the bone and soaking wet.

It had been a miserable ride home, giving her far too much time to think about what had happened. Anger was what she wanted to feel. Anger that he hadn't listened to her; anger that he'd called her those awful names. But instead, all she could muster were feelings of self-recrimination and guilt, and an overwhelming sense of loss.

She knew now that she was in love with her husband; what had transpired between them, the tenderness, the understanding looks—before he found her maidenhead—could only have happened between two people who were in love. Jessica firmly believed that. But had Jacob sensed it, too?

Rage was expected, she'd told herself. It was natural that he would be upset. But he hadn't given her a chance to explain! And that's what she intended to do as soon as she was finished in the stable.

Her heart was near to breaking and her stomach felt as though a thousand demons were trying to break out. Jessica's knees were quaking, but not from the cold. She was scared to death that Jacob would not forgive her or try to understand her motives.

Added to her grief was the realization that when she did explain everything to Jacob, he still might not forgive her and may choose to keep Ossie from her after all.

Giles removed the saddle for her since Jessica's hands were once again fumbling and led Duchess to her stall. He glanced at Jessica, noting her tear-stained face and puffy eyes. "I take it yer outing didn't go quite as planned?"

Jessica leaned against her horse. "Actually when I left here, I didn't have a plan. A plan sort of found me."

Giles cleared his throat, wanting to comfort the young woman who looked so miserable. "Lass, I try not to interfere too much. Although anyone ye'd ask would likely tell ye I interfere more often than not." He got a tiny smile from Jessica for his honesty. "But judging from the looks of ye, I assume that Jake figured out at least part of yer dilemma."

Jessica's cheeks colored as she realized that Giles must have guessed what had occurred at the cottage.

He chuckled lightly. "Now, now. I don't mean to make ye uneasy. Private matters is yer own business, but an ol' coot like me has been around t' see plenty. Ye needn't be flustered wit' me. From the way Jake rode in—and out of here, I guess he hasn't figured out who the little boy really is. Just got through the first part of the mystery, eh?"

Jessica raised her eyes to meet the kind old gentleman's and shrugged off her embarrassment. "Let's just say he still doesn't know who Ossie is, but he does know that I did not give birth to him. Oh, Giles," she said as a sob overtook her, "I tried to explain but he just wouldn't listen."

"Give him time, lass. I believe things will work out."

Jessica leaned her forehead against the mare's hip and stared at the floor. "I don't see how…"

On the floor beneath the mare's foot was several spots of blood. Jessica knelt down on one knee. "Oh, Giles, Duchess has a cut on her ankle. It must have happened when we crossed the creek."

Giles bent and lifted the horse's leg. "It don't look too serious. I've got some salve and a wrap in the tack room. Why don't ye take her into her stall and we'll fix her up?"

Jessica led the mare into her assigned stall, grateful to be able to direct her attention to something else for a moment. She knelt once again to look at Duchess's foot.

From down the aisle Jessica could hear the two stable hands entering the building, laughing and joking loudly. "Blime! I ain't never seen 'is Grace in such a hurry!"

Jessica was about to stand, but their next words halted her in her hidden position.

"Yeah, 'e must've been in quite a hurry to get to 'is bit 'o tail in London. What's 'er name? Marga?"

The two laughed crudely. "Yeah, she's a looker too. Saw 'er last time I rode wit' Giles to take the coach to town. It's been a while since 'e's been to see her, from what I can gather. Guess it's become a matter of urgency!"

More guffaws passed between the two as Jessica felt her heart sink even further. "I'll bet! What I can't figger out though is why the Duke's keepin' that fluff in town when 'e's got 'is new bride out 'ere. She's one o' the tastiest morsels these eyes 'ave ever set on."

"Per'aps e's keepin' the one in town 'til he gets this one trained!"

"Yeah, an' then again, maybe 'e'll keep 'em both. I 'ear he's been quite the bed bounder."

"I 'eard the same 'bout 'is wench. Maybe 'at's why they're so well suited for each other."

"Aye! They'll keep the mattress-makers in business!"

Giles appeared around the corner in time to hear the last part of their conversation. "You bleedin' idiots get the hell out o' here!" he shouted as he hit each one over the head with his hat. As they turned in shock at the assault, they saw Jessica rising from within Duchess's stall.

"Oh, bloody rot!" the taller one whispered as the other one sucked in his breath. "I—we—we was just—"

"Be off wit' ye before I take a 'orse whip t' the both of ye!"

The two boys ran off in different directions, each certain that they'd been lucky to escape with their backsides in tact.

"Don't ye pay them no mind, Jessica. They're just a couple of ill-mannered curs."

Jessica turned slowly to Giles. "It just occurred to me that you said Jacob had ridden out again. Did he, then, really go to London to see Marga?"

Giles knelt to tend the horse's injury. He knew he was already too involved in this mess. "I don't claim to know exactly what he went to London for. But I can tell ye this: He was hurtin' worse than I ever seen him hurt before. And when someone is wounded that deeply, it can only mean that they care a great deal. Give him time to cool off, lass. Forgive anything he might do or say right now."

Jessica nodded and headed toward the house. Without his intending to, Giles' last words had confirmed her worst fears.

Chapter 18

The thought of Jacob seeking solace in another woman's arms was almost more than she could bear. Jessica stood before her window, staring out at the darkening evening, yet seeing nothing beyond her own reflection.

Mrs. Holmes knocked lightly on the door. "Are ye ready fer yer bath now, Yer Grace?"

Jessica slowly wandered to the door and opened it. "Yes," she said softly. Five servants entered, carrying two large buckets of steaming water each. They filled the enormous copper tub in the corner and then quickly turned to leave.

No one knew what had transpired between the new duke and duchess, but he'd left a path of destruction in his wake; and now she was sullen and weepy in intervals.

"Would ye like me to help ye with yer bath?" Mrs. Holmes asked.

Jessica remembered the blood stains on her thighs from her *moment* of passion and quickly refused the offer.

"Well then," the little housekeeper said with a worried frown, "I'll leave ye fer a while. If ye need anything, just call. I'll be down the hall in the play room with the children."

Jessica nodded and then began shaking her head after the door closed. Another paradox to try and understand about Jacob.

He could be so hateful at times. Yet he'd had an entire room furnished with dozens of toys where Ossie could romp with his two playmates. And just this morning she'd learned that Jacob had been instructing Ossie in horseback riding. The man was just too difficult to figure out.

She slipped into the steaming water after carefully stashing her stained trousers under the bed. Washing them herself in secrecy would be easier than having to explain anything to Mrs. Holmes.

Images of Jacob's body over hers, the way the firelight had danced in his eyes came unbidden into her mind. She slipped lower into the hot water, hoping that the steaming liquid would ease away the sensations she felt every time those thoughts crept in.

You fool! she chastised herself. *Why didn't you tell him? If you'd explained before he'd found out—well, you might well be in his arms again right now, feeling the heat of his kisses, the fire in his touch. Instead, he's likely bestowing that which is yours on that whore he keeps in London!*

The thought of the faceless Marga enjoying what should have been saved for her forced Jessica to sit up quickly, sending water sloshing over the sides of the tub.

She took a deep breath and tried to force the visions in her mind away. They wouldn't leave. Her heart was breaking over and over again.

Jessica took another deep breath and ducked completely under the water, trying to force the hopeless, lonely thoughts from her mind. She stayed there until her lungs were about to burst.

Water sloshed over the sides again as she broke the surface. She let the air out of her lungs in a rush. At last she'd found it! A small bit of anger was beginning to well up inside her. It grew little by little, and the bigger it grew, the smaller her pain seemed.

Selfish she was not. Jessica knew the core of this problem was hers. But Jacob was somewhat to blame too.

He should have listened.

He should have given her a chance to explain.

He should not have run to his mistress without a single word!

Anger was not an emotion that Jessica welcomed under normal circumstances, but just now it felt a lot better than the heart-breaking pain that had been plaguing her since this afternoon!

The guilt that threatened to override her anger was pushed aside. Strength of will was something that she and Jacob shared, and they were bound to have many disagreements because of it in the years ahead.

If they were to have any years ahead.

Stop! No more self-pity!

Is this how he would choose to react every time they argued? Would he run off and seek the company of another woman, one who would bow to his every wish or command?

Not if she could help it.

Jessica quickly got out of the tub and dried herself. If Jacob thought he could escape their confrontation—and the truth— this easily, then he was in for a great surprise.

A plan formed quickly in her mind. London would see her bright and early tomorrow morning, and if Giles or one of those mouthy stable hands wouldn't help her get there, well then she'd find him on her own!

In fact, maybe she should—

Her enthusiastic planning was cut short by a knock on the door.

"May I come in, Yer Grace?" Mrs. Holmes asked.

"Please do."

The little housekeeper entered the room. "I've come to inform ye that—"

Jessica waved her hand. "It'll have to wait, Mrs. Holmes. I need to pack some clothing and—well—you'll have to help me. I'm planning to ride to London tomorrow to find Jacob. He's going to listen to me if—"

"Beggin' yer pardon, Yer Grace, but His Grace has sent word—"

Jessica stopped her pacing. "He sent word? What about? Is he returning?" she asked hopefully.

"Well, no, but he's planning on you meeting him at his townhouse Friday."

"Friday? But that's three days from now. Why must I wait to see him?" Visions of Jacob with Marga threatened to cloud her thoughts once again. "I will not wait three days to—"

"But it'll take that long to get yer gown ready."

"My gown? What in the world are you talking about, Mrs. Holmes?"

Mrs. Holmes shook her head. "Men can be such oafs," she said under her breath. "Apparently His Grace forgot to tell ye that the two of ye are to attend a Grand Ball at the home of Lord and Lady Winslow?"

Jessica sat down heavily on the window seat. "Yes, he did forget to mention this little matter." She sat for a moment, stunned at what she'd just heard. How could he forget to tell her something like that? And did he truly expect her to just show up in London, primed and ready to be shown off, without any time to reconcile their differences? Well, she would just send word back with his messenger that—

"Mrs. Holmes, please summon the messenger. I will send word back to the Duke—"

"I'm afraid that won't be possible. Ye see, it wasn't a messenger who arrived. It was a private seamstress, Madame Conquille, with a coach full of fabric and two helpers. His Grace hired her in London and sent her here with the message. They've had a cold, wet go of it. I don't think they'll be wantin' to leave again too soon. Besides, His Grace gave them strict instructions to see—"

"Oh this is just fine!" Jessica stomped her foot in frustration and jumped to her feet. "Of all the—why I'm surprised he only sent the seamstress and two helpers! Obviously Jacob seems to think that his money can—"

"Er, that's not all he sent, Yer Grace," Mrs. Holmes said with an uneasy frown.

Jessica stopped her tirade and looked at the worried housekeeper. She reached out and touched Mrs. Holmes' arm. "I'm sorry dear, I know none of this is your doing. But when I get my hands on—"

She caught herself and took a deep breath. "Who else did our Lord and Master send to me?" she asked sarcastically.

"A tutor." Mrs. Holmes waited for the explosion.

"Did you say a tutor?"

"Yes, Yer Grace. A tutor."

Jessica sighed. She had no desire to vent her frustrations on an innocent woman. "Mrs. Holmes, don't worry. I know none of this is your fault. Now, please explain to me exactly what is going on."

"It seems the duke sent a tutor to help prepare ye for yer first public appearance."

The fact that Jacob had felt tutoring was necessary galled her no small amount. "Go on."

"While yer being fitted for yer ball gown and a few other dresses, Mr. Daley, 'e's the tutor, will be teaching ye the finer points of proper public behavior."

Jessica did her best to keep her temper. "How convenient that the tutor and the seamstress travel together to reform poor, mannerless creatures like me."

"Ah, Yer Grace. Yer anything but mannerless. And actually they don't travel together. Their arrival today at nearly the same time was purely coincidental. Mr. Daley knew nothing about the Grand Ball when he arrived. Evidently he'd been hired before His Grace even knew about the ball."

That made it even worse. Jessica sighed. "The ball. Tell me about that."

"All I know is that the Lord and Lady Winslow are hosting

the affair in your honor—yours and the duke's."

Jessica plopped back down on the bed. "So there's really no way of avoiding this, is there?"

"Not without a great deal of scandal. No one refuses such an invitation."

Jessica feared there may be enough scandal in her future to last a lifetime. She certainly didn't need to provoke any more.

But the fact that Jacob had hired the seamstress to deliver the message rather than telling her about the event himself didn't set well.

And this tutor! He had been assigned even before the ball! Apparently Jacob thought she needed help with her behavior even before the ball was an issue.

Well, she'd just let this tutor know right up front how she felt about that!

Chapter 19

It had been three days since the confrontation with Jacob.

Jessica looked down at the cheerful fabric of her travel dress and plucked absent-mindedly at the yellow flowers. It seemed as though donning the bright dress had nudged the rain into a temporary retreat.

As the coach bumped along on its way to London, Jessica couldn't tamp down the flutter of excitement that threatened to take full flight. Oh, she knew there was a veritable mountain of problems that she must overcome before life with her husband would be peaceful, but just now, it did not seem too insurmountable.

Outside, a variety of birds sang quick, chirpy songs and the plants and grasses sparkled with the remnants of raindrops in the early morning sun. Everything looked fresh and alive.

This is a good sign, she told herself. With even the slightest cooperation from Jacob, I can make this work!

She smiled at her own thoughts, for they were so different now than they'd been when Jacob had left. In the three days since his departure, Jessica had run the gamut of her emotions.

At first she'd been furious that Jacob hadn't bothered to tell her about the Grand Ball in their honor, and had instead left poor Mrs. Holmes to inform her. And then there was that tutor Jacob had commissioned!

Thinking on that particular subject threatened to ruin her

light mood. The realization that Jacob had surmised her so lacking in knowledge and social skills still did not sit well.

Mr. Daley had been a stiff, humorless bore. He'd actually seemed offended when she'd proven to him that her social skills were quite acceptable, and that her talent with reading and numbers was far more than adequate. Growing up away from high-bred snobs had not left her lacking quality, she'd assured him. Her father, though a common man, had manners and intelligence. And the etiquette that her mother had started teaching her had been carried on by her father after her mother's death.

Apparently Mr. Daley had been looking for a lump of coal he could fashion into a diamond and claim the successful transformation as his own. But Jessica showed him that she was already as strong as a diamond, and could shine like one when she needed to.

The only thing she was grateful to Mr. Daley for were the dance lessons. Dancing was something her father had known very little about, and something she'd rarely ever done. Mr. Daley was thrilled to finally have something to teach her.

Jessica caught on very quickly, and by the end of the second day, the tutor had taken his leave.

Taking a deep breath, Jessica was determined not to let the memory of Mr. Daley's forced presence foul her day.

She smoothed the fabric of her dress once again. It was by far the finest piece of clothing that she had ever owned. And this was perhaps the simplest of all her new gowns.

The seamstress that Jacob had retained was an expert with fabrics. Jessica had liked her immediately, and once the initial round of measuring, poking, and prodding was over, Jessica found that she enjoyed the process of choosing the fabrics and watching as the flat folds became elegant works of art.

Madame Conquille had been delightfully full of the latest gossip, all of which Jessica didn't understand, having never met the players. Most of the chatter drifted over Jessica's head until she heard her own—her new—family's name find its way into the conversation.

Jessica had been standing on a foot stool while Madame Conquille marked the hem on her ball gown.

She turned quickly at the mention of the former duchess's name, causing Madame Conquille to poke herself with a pin.

"Ah!"

"Oh, I'm sorry. But did you know the former duchess?"

"Know her?" Madame Conquille asked as she sucked on the small pin prick, "But of course. I may be getting on in years now, but I was, and still am, the most *magnifique* creator of fine clothing in all of London."

"Would you tell me about her?"

The seamstress's eyes brightened as she warmed to her topic.

"What would you like to know?"

"Everything. Why does everyone hate her? What did she do that was so evil? And what about Colin, my husband's younger brother? How did he die? No one here seems to be able—or willing—to answer my questions."

"Slow down, *cherie*, we have many hours of sewing left to do. I shall tell you everything I can."

Jessica stood in silence as Madame Conquille related the story of Anastasia Callaway, the former Duchess of Fairdale.

"You see, Anastasia tricked Austen into marrying her by pretending to be a woman of breeding, a woman who had supposedly fled France in fear for her life when her father had gone mad. Everything in her possession when she met Austen was stolen. Pah! She even stole the French accent.

Austen, such a kind and gentle man he was. Anastasia was many years younger than him and very beautiful, at least on the outside. He felt very protective toward her. It was the duke who needed protection. He should not have fallen prey to such a woman."

"Do you mean she lied about her upbringing and her family

in order to marry him?"

"*Oui.* The background meant nothing to him. If she had been an honest girl of no means, he would have loved her just the same. But she was not who she seemed. She lied about everything."

Jessica's head began to pound. No wonder Jacob had been so furious when he discovered her virginity. He must have thought history was repeating itself; the lies, the manipulations...

"Madame, how did she die? And Colin? There seems to be so much mystery surrounding their deaths."

"There was. A gruesome tale, *cherie.* Are you certain you wish to know?"

"Oh, yes. I must know. It's the only way I'll ever understand my husband's bitterness."

"Very well. It was well known that the duchess had a hearty appetite for young men. I believe that is what finally drove the duke to send her to London on a permanent basis. He bought her a house in town and gave her a very generous allowance. This I know because I still made all her gowns at that time.

But that was not enough for her. It is said that she still liked to, how you say, cuckold her husband. She would flaunt her young lovers in public and oh," Madame Conquille waved her hand, "she was a terrible woman."

"Why didn't he dissolve the marriage? Certainly he had enough reasons to denounce her."

"Divorce is not a common thing, my dear, nor is it easy to accomplish. And there has never been one in this family. Not even an annulment."

A small part of Jessica was thrilled to hear that. At least Jacob couldn't divest himself of her too easily—unless he decided to become the first Duke of Fairdale to set aside his wife. And that still left the question of Ossie—

Jessica bit her lip, afraid to ask her next question. "Did—did the duke have anything to do with her death?"

Madame Conquille sucked in her breath. "No, no, *cherie*. You must never think such a thing! As I said, he was kind to a fault. No, she caused her own death, and that of her son."

"But how?"

"Turn around, please, I must mark the other side." Jessica obeyed, afraid to do anything but comply until she had all of her answers.

The seamstress glanced at her two helpers across the room, finding them absorbed in their tasks and their own conversation. She lowered her voice further, making Jessica strain to hear her words. "I know all this because of Drucilla. She is the younger of the two women there; they are sisters, you see. Drucilla used to be employed by the duchess at the townhouse in London.

"Drucilla came to my house late one night, in a terrified state. You see, Anastasia had recently taken a secret lover, one that she did not flaunt in public. He would arrive at her home late at night, and leave very early, under the cover of darkness. Oh, the sounds that would come from that bedroom of hers!

"Well, one night Drucilla heard some horrible arguing from within the duchess's rooms. Not the normal sounds that came from the room, so she went to the door to be sure her lady was not in trouble.

"The arguing continued, loudly, and so she peeked in the key hole. All she could see was the man's naked back. She heard Anastasia call him *Jean Luc DuPont*, and then threaten to tell the authorities of his whereabouts.

"The man threatened back to her that she would be dead before she could do so. Anastasia, apparently quite drunk, said that she had already confided in her youngest son about their liaison and if anything happened to her, Colin would expose him.

"Poor Drucilla was so frightened that she left the house at once and came to find her sister. After hearing her tale, I insisted that she leave her position at once and come to live and work with us.

"The next morning we went to the duchess's house to collect Drucilla's belongings and to our shock and horror, we found the house burned beyond repair.

"I saw your husband there and went to speak with him, to see if he knew what had occurred. He was terribly upset, which seemed unusual since everyone knew he hated his mother so very much. When I questioned him, he told me that his brother had been found dead that morning in his home and that he knew the deaths were connected, but he didn't know how.

"Well, I brought Drucilla to him and told her she must tell Lord Callaway everything. She told him she'd seen only the man's back through the keyhole, that it had a long curving scar on the left side. She told him that the duchess had called him Jean Luc DuPont when they were arguing and that she had mentioned Colin's name as well."

Madame Conquille sat back for a moment and rubbed her forehead. "*Cherie*, you should have seen the look on his handsome face. Such anger, such frustration, such sadness. Me, I knew nothing of this Jean Luc. But apparently he was well known to the Crown and its supporters.

"Jean Luc is a notorious French deviant, one that had always eluded even the finest British soldiers. He is a cold-blooded killer and will let nothing stand in his way.

"It became clear that Anastasia had been toying with this man and when he grew tired of her, he simply killed her. He burned down her house while she was inside. And to be safe, he killed Colin as well, just in case she really had told the boy of his identity."

"Oh!" Jessica said in a whisper. "How awful! Did they ever find this Jean Luc?"

"No. To this day, no one knows who the man really is. It is said that he is back in London, but who knows? Jacob has sworn to kill him if he ever finds him, to avenge Colin's death, not his mother's."

The coach bumped over a pothole in the road, jolting Jessica back to the present.

After reflecting on Madame Conquille's story again, Jessica's light mood began to darken. Her worries and misgivings began to return and doubt about whether or not she could make Jacob understand — make him forgive her — were settling on her like a heavy weight.

Losing his beloved brother to circumstances which involved his mother, a woman he so despised, could easily have turned him into a world class misogynist. Jessica could now understand the fury he displayed when he'd caught her in her deceit.

She knew she had to make him understand.

Oh please, she prayed silently, let me make Jacob understand that I'm not a conniving whore like his mother; that I had reasons, good reasons for not telling him everything.

Chapter 20

A large, three-story town house loomed before the approaching coach. Although it was nothing compared to the mansion, the home was still breathtaking.

For a moment, Jessica felt as she had on the day they'd arrived at Fairdale, small and unsure of herself.

But a great deal had happened since then, she reminded herself. She drew on her inner strength and lifted her chin, trying desperately to feel the confidence she knew she would need for this forthcoming confrontation with her husband.

Giles opened the door and handed her down from the coach. "Remember, lass, the truth will give ye strength and make things right," he whispered as she took his hand.

Jessica paused for a moment letting Sara, the young maid who'd accompanied her, pass by and move out of hearing distance. "Oh, Giles, what if he won't listen? I can't say I would blame him after what he's been through." She glanced at the door to the house, then lowered her voice further. "Madame Conquille told me everything. Had I known about his mother and Colin I would never have strayed from the truth with him." She rubbed her forehead. "How did this get so muddled? I've never—"

"Now, lass. 'E's a stubborn one, 'e is. It's my guess that if ye'd 'ave told 'im right off, 'e wouldn't 'ave believed ye anyway. Imagine 'is surprise, thinkin' he's the last of the Callaways, only t' find 'e's got a wee brother. Take yer time, Jesse. That's my advice. Give 'im time to let the truth soak in rather than floodin' 'im with words 'e won't believe. I know yer achin' to run in there and make things right, but ease 'im into it. Give 'im time to realize that it 'appened just as you say. That yer not leadin' 'im down a merry path of lies."

Two strapping boys were just finishing unloading the luggage when Giles stopped one of them. "Mike, take down that chest from up front," he directed the lad, "and put it in the duke's bedroom."

"What is that?" Jessica asked. She hadn't noticed the box until now.

Giles grinned and winked. "It's a bit of help for th' comin' wars."

"What do you mean?"

"I took the liberty of packing the former duke's journals. Rarely missed a day's entry in those books, even towards the end. Often when I'd go t' visit wit' 'im e'd be scribblin' away in there. 'E once told me that he hoped the written words would serve as a lamp to guide his son should Jacob ever fall on dark times. I'd say a beacon might come in handy fer the young duke, and you, just now.

The journals should have some helpful proof for ye. I've never read them, of course, but Austen and I were close. 'E told me a great many secrets over the years, and my guess is that ye'll find those secrets and perhaps a few others in the journals."

"Thank you, Giles. But I wouldn't feel right about reading his private thoughts. I didn't know him that well."

"They're not for you, Jesse. They're for Jake. You don't *need* a good dose of the truth. He does. Perhaps Austen's words will make it easier for Jacob to accept your own words."

"Bless you, Giles."

"Now then, I've got to pick up some supplies for Mrs. Holmes and make my drive back to the estate. So if ye've no further need of me?"

"No. Have a safe journey. And please, give Ossie my love. I miss him already."

"I'll do that. Don't ye worry none about the lad. We'll keep 'm so busy 'e won't have time to miss ye."

Jessica waited until the familiar coach was out of sight before turning to enter the house.

John, the butler from Fairdale, had arrived a day ahead of her and was now waiting at the door.

"Welcome, Your Grace."

"Thank you, John."

Jessica looked around the entry hall. As was the case at Fairdale, there was a masculine feel to the decor of the house. Everything was bold and strong, right down to the ornately carved banister that lined the long, straight staircase.

Tapestries similar to the ones she'd seen at Fairdale created a colorful backdrop at the top of the stairs. Heavy wooden tables with unusual carvings and statues stood along the walls of both the lower and upper halls.

To her left a large parlor could be seen through a partially opened door, and to the right a sunny day room cheerfully beckoned. Neither room appeared to be occupied. Her pounding heart began to calm momentarily as she realized she'd have a few moments to collect herself.

Privacy was a must when she saw Jacob for the first time. She wanted no staff members present to force their behavior to be false; they must be alone so she could gauge his true feelings.

"I've sent Sara to your suite of rooms to begin unpacking. A bath has been ordered for you and it will be drawn as soon as you wish."

Jessica smiled. A hot bath did sound wonderful after the bumpy ride to town, and perhaps it would calm her nerves before she met with Jacob.

But no, there was no time for that. This matter had to be settled before they made their public appearance.

"That sounds lovely." She took a deep breath to brace

herself. "But before my bath, I would like to speak with my husband. I assume he knows we've arrived?"

"I regret to inform you that His Grace is not in at present."

The breath left her. What was that feeling that settled upon her? Disappointment? Relief?

Both.

And a bit of annoyance too.

Jacob had known she was going to arrive early this afternoon, and she'd been bolstering her confidence all morning to confront him.

Giles's words came back to her. *Take it slow....*

It would be better if she relaxed and planned her strategy rather than plowing into it head on as was her usual practice.

"Very well. Then if you would have the water taken up, I'll have my bath now."

Several hours later, Jessica was sitting before the mirror in her dressing room waiting for Sara to put the finishing touches on her upswept coiffure. She had to admit the look was very becoming on her, even though sitting through the styling was near to torture.

Every noise she heard in the hall caused her heart to resume its frantic beating. And as the noise would pass she would let her breath out, listening intently for the next sound.

There was very little time left before they had to leave for the ball, even assuming they were going to be fashionably late. How would she make it through this evening without settling this matter with Jacob beforehand?

As Sara finished with the last of the hooks on Jessica's ball gown, a knock sounded at the door nearly sending Jessica through the ceiling.

She cast a quick glance in the mirror. As Sara opened the door, Jessica positioned herself directly in front of it, hoping that if Jacob found her appealing it might help her cause.

Instead, John was at the door. But even the stuffy old butler had to take a breath before he could deliver his message. Having seen Jessica mostly attired in men's trousers until now, he was pleasantly shocked at her elegant appearance. "Your Grace, if I may be so bold, you are the picture of loveliness and elegance this evening."

John's stammered compliment took the edge off of Jessica's disappointment when she saw that it was not Jacob behind the door.

"Thank you, John. Has Jacob returned?"

"No, Your Grace, he has not. But Lord Malcom Sandeford is waiting for you in the downstairs parlor. May I tell him you will join him shortly?"

Jessica groaned inwardly. Malcom. He was a nice man, but he was not who she wanted to see.

Damn you, Jacob! Why are you torturing me so?

She took a deep breath. "Yes. Please tell Lord Sandeford that I will be down momentarily."

When the door closed, Jessica let loose with a small growl. "The nerve of that man!" She stopped herself before she said anything that could haunt her later. Sara seemed like a sweet girl, but as was to be expected, Jessica sensed that the girl's loyalties would lie with Jacob.

"Please fetch my cloak, Sara, and bring it to the parlor. I'll wait for my husband downstairs with Lord Sandeford."

Sara nodded scurried out of the room.

When Jessica entered the parlor it was to find Malcom helping himself to a snifter of brandy. She couldn't help but smile. He seemed to be so comfortable no matter where he was.

Leaning against the door, she waited for him to finish pouring. "It would seem that I find you filching liquor at our every meeting," she said with a smile.

Malcom turned abruptly, sloshing some of the amber liquid from his glass. A quick retort was on his lips, but when he caught sight of Jessica in the doorway, his mouth dropped open and the words refused to come.

His stare made Jessica uncomfortable and she straightened

from her relaxed stance. Her hands fussed with the waistline of the gown as she stood nervously before him. Did she look so out of place, then, in this finery?

After several moments of silence had passed she became annoyed and took a step forward, placing her hands on her hips. "Really, Malcom, if I look so ridiculous, just say so instead of standing there gawking!"

At last he found his voice and chuckled lightly. "Good lady, I was gawking, but you hardly look ridiculous. In fact I might say that you present the most beautiful sight I've ever laid eyes on. And, if I may be so crass, I have laid my eyes on many."

Jessica sighed in relief. That compliment was just what she needed to hear. The sincerity in his eyes and tone of voice told her that he was speaking the truth. "I don't doubt that you have, sir. I thank you for the compliment." Now if only her husband would see her in the same way.

Jacob. She felt the irritation returning. "Might I ask, Malcom, if you've happened to have seen my wayward husband today? I'm sure you know we're to attend this Grande Ball tonight, supposedly in our honor, and the cad has yet to even make an appearance here to see if I've arrived safely."

"Ah! So that bit of fire I thought you'd possessed was not merely a side effect of the liquor I'd imbibed on our last meeting. Glad to see it. As for your wayward cad of a husband, yes. I left him just a short time ago and he does know you're here. A messenger was dispatched to him the moment you arrived."

"Well then, where is he? I understand it is not 'the thing' to be early to a ball, but if he still has to come here and get dressed before we are to go, we might as well not go at all!"

"I'm quite certain that would be to his liking. However, he is already dressed for the ball."

"He—but how? Surely he didn't come here and dress without seeing me?"

"No, no. Actually, he has been in meetings most of the day. And as for his dressing, well he just had the final fitting for his suit today. His tailor was a bit slow.

But might I say, if he had come here and seen you, I find it hard to believe that you would have left the house at all."

For that Malcom was graced with an embarrassed but thankful smile. "You flatter too much, Malcom. And I find it admirable that you are trying to temper my frustration, but would you mind explaining to me just what is going on?"

Malcom could see that her gentle words were barely concealing her anger. "I'm sorry, my dear lady. I should not be toying with you. Jacob has been caught up in tedious matters all day." Malcom cursed himself for having to lie to her, but if she found out that Jacob had spent most of the day at Brooks', his favorite club, to avoid this meeting, he could well imagine her fury.

Malcom didn't know what had transpired between Jessica and Jacob, but he had never seen his friend in such a foul mood. "Jacob has asked me to escort you to the ball, and meet him there."

"What?! Are you telling me that I will be arriving at a ball in honor of my marriage with someone other than my husband?" She began pacing the room, clenching her hands at her side.

Malcom put his hand over his heart and feigned a look of pain. "Jessica, it hurts me to think that you are so offended at the thought of arriving with me."

Jessica stopped pacing. "It's not that, you buffoon. Imagine how you would feel if you were in my position!"

"Lady, if I were in your position, I fear I would have much greater worries on my mind than who I arrived at the ball with. I'm certain that Jacob and I would not enjoy life being married to one another."

His ridiculous words caught Jessica off guard and her laughter was Malcom's reward. He tossed back the rest of his brandy and went to the door to take her cloak from Sara. "Let's be on our way then, shall we?"

"Fine. But let me tell you this: Your humor relieves only you from my ire. Jacob will still have to deal with his."

Chapter 21

Jacob already regretted the fact that he'd let the Winslow's talk him into this, and the evening had hardly begun. He looked around the large ball room, trying not to make eye contact with anyone unless he had to.

The turnout was large. People were arriving in droves. Not that he had this many close friends, in fact he had very few. But all of the London aristocracy had turned out to see the woman who had finally snared the elusive Seventh Duke of Fairdale.

If Jacob hadn't still been so angry with Jessica for her lies, he might have felt sorry for her. He knew she would be mightily uncomfortable here. These people were not her kind. In truth, she was far better than any of them.

And the fact that she was going to be arriving with Malcom instead of him wasn't going to make things any easier for her. Already there were whispers circulating as to why Jacob had arrived without his new bride.

His first notion was to let the whispers go unchecked. But he knew Lady Winslow would not allow him to escape explanation.

Jacob was still plenty angry at Jessica, but during the past few days his rage had cooled a little. In fact, there were several times he actually found himself missing her again; a fact which didn't set well with him at all.

It was for that very reason that he had asked Malcom to

accompany her to the ball. His fickle emotions were not ready to deal with Jessica in private.

He knew her well enough to know that she would want to discuss the matter of her lies immediately. He also knew that he was not prepared for that yet. Privacy would allow her to look at him with those eyes that could pierce his soul and render him soft as butter in her hands. Lord knows she'd managed to manipulate him thus far!

"Jacob!" Lady Winslow's voice cut through his private thoughts. "Jacob, my dear, wherever is your duchess?"

Jacob turned to Lady Winslow and spoke loud enough for everyone near to hear. "She should be arriving shortly, Lady Winslow. I fear I was detained most of the day by business and so I've asked my good friend Lord Sandeford to escort her to your home."

Almost immediately the crowd around him turned to buzzing. He knew he had accomplished his feat. The explanation of his solo arrival was now being passed about the room.

"Trusting soul, aren't you?" Lady Winslow asked. "Lord Sandeford is quite a lady's man, as were you until recently."

Jacob forced a small laugh. "I trust Malcom with my life—*and* my wife."

It's my wife I can't trust, he finished to himself.

Just as he was about to be absorbed by more dark thoughts, the crowd began to buzz once again. When Jacob looked toward the door, it was his turn to feel his jaw drop.

Seeing his wife for the first time in four days, clothed in a splendid gown rather than her boy's attire or ill-fitting borrowed clothes, sent the air rushing from his lungs. No amount of forethought could have prepared Jacob for the sensations that assaulted his entire body when he looked at her, presenting a picture as close to perfection as was possible.

The shimmering dark green gown she wore flattered her to perfection. Dark gold braided silk and gold- dipped beads decorated the bodice and tastefully draped down each sleeve.

The color dramatized her hair and eyes, accentuating her natural glow.

As per his instructions, John had seen to it that Jessica had her choice of adornments from the family jewels, one of the few things his father had managed to hide from his mother.

She'd chosen the emerald necklace. It was perfect. And in her hair, several emeralds, each surrounded by gold-work, were strategically placed.

Jacob's eyes dropped to the plunging neckline that framed her softly rounded bosom, and it was with some effort that he tore his eyes away and rested them once again on her lovely face. He couldn't keep himself from glancing around the room and noticing the appreciative stares she was receiving from nearly every man in the room.

Suddenly he felt it quite necessary to be by her side and claim her as his own.

"My dear," Jacob said with a formal bow over her hand. He placed a gentle kiss on her fingertips, sending shock waves through Jessica's body.

He turned to Malcom. "I thank you for delivering my wife to me. I trust the task was not too distasteful," he said loud enough for only Malcom and Jessica to hear.

Malcom laughed and assured him it was not, but Jessica failed to see the humor in his statement.

When Jacob met her eyes again, it was to find a cold amber stare trained upon him.

He leaned close to her as he wrapped her hand around his arm. "I care not how you look upon me in private, Jessica, but tonight you will pretend to be a happy, devoted wife. That shouldn't be too difficult for you. I've found that you're very good at pretending."

Jessica kept her face a mask of complaisance as she sucked in her breath. "Apparently it's a good thing that I'm a master of pretense, for otherwise everyone would know how I truly feel about you." The smile on her face was so brittle she feared it would break.

Jacob offered her a smile of equal insincerity and then nodded to Malcom. "If you'll excuse us, I must introduce Jessica to our hosts."

Malcom nodded and left the two.

For all her poised appearance, Jessica felt as if she were dying inside. She had expected Jacob to be distant at first, even a bit angry yet. But this! This was an outright attack on her feelings. Oh, how would she ever make it through this night?

Her thoughts were interrupted as Jacob introduced her to Lord and Lady Winslow. Most of their words drifted past her, and Jessica hoped that she was making the correct responses.

It wasn't until Jessica heard a familiar name in the conversation and felt Jacob stiffen that she became fully aware of what Lady Winslow was saying.

"I'm sorry, Lady Winslow, but what did you just say?"

Lady Winslow chuckled. "Oh! I knew it would be a surprise for you! I said, I made certain that your grandparents were here to meet you!"

Lady Winslow leaned closer to Jessica. "I will admit, dear, that my husband and I haven't consorted with Lord and Lady Atterberry for many years, what with the various scandals and questionable behavior that has so often been associated with them. But now that their granddaughter has married a duke, the Duke of Fairdale no less, well, that rather changes things doesn't it?"

"I—I suppose it does," Jessica replied numbly, not truly knowing if it changed anything or not.

Lady Winslow prattled on. "Everyone knows the tragic story of how your father became *temporarily* estranged from the Atterberrys and how they've looked for you for years, wanting desperately to make amends with both you and your father."

"They did?" Jessica asked in surprise.

"Of course, darling." Lady Winslow continued. "Once you

get to know them, you'll see that they are really very kind."

Jacob felt his stomach turn. *They are not kind,* he thought to himself. *They are greedy, conniving, low-life scum who will stop at nothing to get what they want.*

Jacob was more than a little disappointed by the way Lord and Lady Winslow had seemed to forget all the negativity surrounding the Atterberrys and had instead chosen to focus on the fact that the Atterberrys now had a duchess for a granddaughter.

Ah, he reminded himself, *this is the ton. Who you know is everything.*

"But how did you know who my grandparents were?" Jessica asked. "I've met so few people since I arrived at Fairdale."

"Baroness Von Kraus told me, told everyone! You must understand, my dear, you have captured the heart of England's most eligible bachelor. Something like that cannot be kept a secret!"

Ha! Jessica nearly laughed out loud at the idea of capturing Jacob's heart. At this moment, she wasn't at all certain that he had a heart.

Jacob could have kicked himself for telling the baroness who Jessica's grandparents were. This was not the time or place for a family reunion. But there was little he could do about it now, except warn Jessica.

"Lady Winslow, if you wouldn't mind waiting for the reunion, I would like to dance with my wife."

Without waiting for an answer, Jacob swept Jessica out to the dance floor.

"What do you think you're doing? You can't just drag me about like—"

"I can do whatever I want. Now listen to me. You are not to cozy up to those grandparents of yours. You of all people should know what they're capable of after they ran your mother and father off."

"But you heard what Lady Winslow said. It was a horrible misunderstanding."

"Not very likely. They are evil people, Jessica. You will have nothing to do with them."

"You have no right to tell me what to do!" she whispered hotly.

"I have every right," he growled. It was a battle for each of them to keep their features pleasant. "After you meet them and exchange a few pleasantries, you are not to see them again. Not unless I'm with you. Is that clear?"

Jessica wanted to argue back, but she sensed that all eyes were upon them. It was becoming harder and harder to keep a civil look on her face and she knew if she continued arguing with him that it would become impossible.

"Whatever you wish, *Your Grace*," she said too sweetly.

Her complete turnaround told Jacob to be wary. But for now he didn't question her. He too was finding it difficult to keep up the congenial pretense.

All he really wanted to do was take her away and have it out with her; demand answers to his questions, make her convince him that there were good reasons for her lies, for the way she had hurt him.

"Damn!" he said aloud.

"Now what is it?" Jessica asked.

"Nothing." He paused, allowing silence to envelope them for several steps. Finding safer conversation was his only hope. "I must say I'm surprised by your talent for dancing. I would have thought you'd danced very little in your home."

Jessica's eyes narrowed as she remembered the hours of lessons with Mr. Daley. "Oh, don't play dense, Jacob. It doesn't suit you."

"And what is that supposed to mean?"

"You know very well that I learned to dance with Mr. Daley. I'm sure he gave you a full report."

"For God's sake, woman, what are you prattling on about

now? Who is Mr. Daley?"

"Please, Jacob, don't insult me. You know damn well—"

"Keep your voice down and refrain from swearing while we are in public."

Jessica lowered her voice. "You know who Mr. Daley is. That stuffy old tutor you ordered sent out to Fairdale. I'm sorry to say that he was greatly disappointed when he saw that I was not a simple idiot without any education. The only thing I had need of him for was the dance lesson."

"Jessica, for all that you think me to be, *I* am not a liar. I assure you I have no idea who this Mr. Daley is."

His stress on the fact that *he* was not a liar did not go unnoticed. She ground her teeth together to keep from shouting. "Mr. Daley said the duke had hired him to come to Fairdale and tutor me. Are you denying you did so? Are you calling that prim old man a liar?"

"I did no such thing, Jessica. I—" A thought came suddenly to him. "It must have been my father. He must have arranged for the man to come after I'd agreed to bring you to Fairdale. I assure you that my father would not have done such a thing to injure your pride, but only to help you. In truth, I know very little about your education and skills, but I would not have hired a tutor without consulting you first."

Jessica had to admit that made sense. She felt a bit foolish for having jumped to such conclusions, but not enough to stave off the anger that still boiled beneath the surface.

The dance ended and another was about to begin when Jacob felt a tap on his shoulder. He was surprised that anyone would approach him in that way now that he had his full titles. But when he turned, he saw that he should not have been surprised.

Jacob's initial gut reaction was to turn and leave Hayden Atterberry standing on the dance floor. But rather than cause a scene, he simply moved Jessica to one side and allowed Hayden to follow.

"My dear," Hayden said, light tears making his eyes glisten,

190

"you are the image of your mother."

Jessica looked to Jacob, but his jaw was set and he was looking beyond the older gentleman.

When Jacob made no introductions the gentleman said, "I am your grandfather, dear."

Jessica was speechless. Years of terrible stories swept into her mind as she recalled how horribly her father had been treated by this man and his wife. And now here he was before her, with tears in his eyes and a soft, pleading expression on his lightly lined face.

Could it all have been a mistake? The picture she'd painted in her mind of this man was nothing like the short, gentle person she saw before her. Oh, she wanted desperately to believe that it had been a misunderstanding. She felt so alone and wanted to have a family that she could call her own, someone to rely upon other than her infuriating husband.

"Hello. I—I don't know what to say. I never thought I'd actually meet—"

"You needn't say a word, my dear. It's just so wonderful to see you after all these years! Why, the last time I saw you was when you were a babe in lace. Come! You must meet your grandmother. She's waited for this moment for so many years."

Hayden placed his hand on her arm and began to steer her away, but Jacob halted her with a hand on her other arm. "Now is not the time, Hayden."

The little man turned to face Jacob, his expression now hidden from Jessica. His gentle visage of seconds ago was replaced by pure malice, but he kept his voice soft and kind. "Surely you wouldn't deny your wife a reunion with the only real family she has here in London, would you?"

"*I* am the only family Jessica needs to recognize now, Hayden. If you will excuse us?"

Jessica was appalled by Jacob's behavior. She gently but firmly removed her elbow from Jacob's grip. "No, Jacob. I wish to meet my grandmother, now."

Color rose in Jacob's face at her open disregard for his wishes. His eyes narrowed at Hayden, who sent Jacob a victorious look of triumph.

Rather than cause any more of a scene, Jacob acquiesced with a nod and walked away without another word.

He watched from near the entry hall as Hayden led Jessica across the crowded room. For nearly thirty minutes they kept her involved in conversation. From the trusting look on her face, Jacob could see that they were weaving a web of lies and laying a trap for her.

It would serve her right to tumble into their spiders' nest, he told himself. But even as those thoughts formed, he knew he would not let that happen.

"Lost your bride to interfering family ties already, Jake?" Malcom asked as he approached Jacob's side.

Jacob could not return the lighthearted jest. "Apparently." He turned his back on the room.

Malcom studied his friend. "Jake, would you care to discuss what has happened between you and Jessica?"

Jacob grunted but offered no immediate reply.

"The first time I saw you together you couldn't keep your hands off each other, and in fact, were well on your way to consummating your marriage right there on your father's desk." Malcom reminded him. "There's no way either of you could have pretended your way through what I burst in upon. But ever since then, you two have been at odds."

"We have. But not by my choice. She isn't who she seems to be, Malcom. I thought I could trust her. I thought since she was raised away from the games and the influences of the city and socialites, I could rely on the fact that she would be an honest and trustworthy woman. I was wrong." Jacob fished a small flask from his pocket and tossed back a healthy swallow of whiskey.

Malcom frowned, surprised by Jacob's actions and tone. "Come now, man. It can't be all that bad."

"Well, it is." He took another swig. "She's no different than any other woman I've ever met."

"Lord, I hope I never reach your level of cynicism, old man. I happen to enjoy women very much."

"As do I, my friend. But I've come to the conclusion that I must enjoy them without trusting them."

Malcom looked over Jacob's shoulder, a frown creasing his brow. "Speaking of enjoying, who is that fellow there with the Atterberrys? Whoever he is, he's certainly *enjoying* your wife."

Jacob whipped around to find a stranger verily leaning on Jessica. She was sitting on a small bench, leaning forward with her elbows on her knees listening intently to whatever her grandmother was saying.

Obviously, Jessica had never worn a gown so deeply cut, for she appeared to have no idea that she was exposing an enticing view of her bosom to any and all who cared to look; and several were looking.

So engrossed was she in her grandmother's words that she didn't even seem to notice the man who was standing at her shoulder and staring directly down the front of her dress. He was leaning familiarly close to her side, his hand resting on the back of the seat, as if he were staking a claim to her.

Rage rushed through Jacob's veins, surprising him as much as angering him. They may be at odds, by God, but she was still his wife!

Before Jacob could move, Malcom grabbed his arm. "Temper, temper old man. For your sake as well as Jessica's, handle this quietly. Regardless of your private differences, she is your wife, a duchess. If you show her any disrespect or snub her in any way you will open the door for others to do so. With her commonly reared background, Jessica will have a hard enough time fitting in with these snobs as it is. And might I add that I think that to be a distinct bonus."

Jacob yanked his arm from Malcom's grasp, but took the words to heart. When he reached Jessica, he bumped the stranger from her side with his shoulder and bent to her ear. "I wish to speak with you."

She began to protest but when he squeezed her elbow and said in a low growl, "Now!" she rose to accompany him.

"But Your Grace," Lady Atterberry said as she rose to her feet, a gleam in her eye, "we were just about to plan a visit to Fairdale so that we could all get to know one another better."

Jacob turned to Lady Atterberry. "I know all I need to know of you and your husband, my lady."

"Jacob!" Jessica breathed in a horrified whisper.

Jacob's eyes met with those of the unknown man at Lady Atterberry's side. The man's piercing blue eyes held the hint of a secret, but Jacob could not remember ever having looked upon his face before.

Still holding Jessica's arm in a vice grip he said coldly, "Though you appear to have met *my wife*, I don't believe you and I have ever met."

The man crossed his arms over his chest and smiled lazily, flipping his blonde hair behind his shoulder in a gesture that was just short of being haughty and disrespectful. Silence hung in the air for a brief moment.

Lady Atterberry hurried to introduce him, a sly smile on her face as well. "Your Grace, this is Viscount Percival Trent of Dovecliff. Percival, the Duke of Fairdale."

Another silence ensued, but finally the man nodded. "A pleasure, I'm sure. Although we've never met personally, I believe we've had some common—er—acquaintances in the past."

"Perhaps," Jacob said with a curt nod, wanting only to be away from these people. "Now if you'll all excuse us, I find that—"

"Oh come now, don't rush off with your lovely wife," Viscount Trent said suddenly with a slow step toward Jacob, his eyes trained on Jessica. "I find her well-rounded *wit* to be most enchanting." Percival dropped his eyes to Jessica's breasts and then back to Jacob's thunderous visage.

Jacob's eyes narrowed as he stared down the stranger. The man was nearly as tall as he, but without the width of shoulder that Jacob possessed and carried so well. Thrashing the man was foremost on Jacob's mind, but he could sense a goad when one was presented.

Viscount Trent was quietly challenging him but now was not the time nor the place to find out why.

"Yes. It was her well-rounded *wit* that drew me to her in the first place, and it is that and so much more, that will sustain me as her faithful protector and most possessive keeper—always."

Chapter 22

Without another word Jacob turned and guided Jessica back to the steps where Malcom was standing. Outwardly they appeared to be strolling quietly along, but the fury that was between them had them both vibrating.

Even Malcom was fooled until, when they reached the top of the steps just out of view of the main dance floor, he was unwantingly privy to their quiet war.

Jessica ripped her elbow from Jacob's grasp. "How dare you! You expect me to come here and perform like the happiest little wife in London, and then you humiliate me in front of my family and new friend!"

"Friend? *Friend*! Is that what you call that lecherous cur who was drooling down the front of your gown? Though I can't say as I blame him entirely since it was you who offered him such a spectacular view!"

"He was not! Percival was—"

"Oh, so already it's 'Percival', eh? My dear, you work faster than I had first imagined," he said sarcastically.

Malcom was trying to back away and let them hash it out in private, but found himself trapped by a large marble pillar.

"You—you bastard! Just because a man chose to be pleasant to me instead of accusing me of all sorts of horrible acts is no reason to—"

"To call the truth as it is? Good God, Jessica, don't try to pretend you didn't notice the man's subtle references to your 'well-rounded wit' when he was openly gawking at your—" he dropped his eyes to Jessica's breasts as Viscount Trent had done, "your well-displayed charms. You can't possibly be that thick!"

Jessica's cheeks burned scarlet. "If that's true then you are no better than he. And as for this dress, you ordered it made for me, so if you find fault with my display, you have only yourself to blame!"

That much was true, he admitted to himself. Jacob was still stunned by the jealous rage that was threatening to engulf him. Despite the fact that he didn't trust her and didn't *want* to want her, he could not tolerate the idea of anyone else having her. If they'd been secure in their relationship, the way he'd envisioned at one time, he would have been proud of Jessica's appearance. But with all the questions remaining between them, he could only feel uncertainty.

"You are to stay away from your new *friend*, Viscount Trent, and from the Atterberrys as well. Do I make myself clear?"

Jessica couldn't believe what she was hearing. Was he actually ordering her to stay away from the only blood relatives she had left?

"Ooh! You have no right—"

"I have every right! Regardless of the fact that I abhor this situation as much as you, I am your husband and you will do as I say! You are bound to me!"

"I am bound by honor only! My father's honor! Were it not for him and for the respect I felt for your father I would be long gone. And I will not do as you say! You took delight in reminding me quite often before we exchanged vows that you were offering me your name for protection purposes only. Well, fine! We shall be married in name only and therefore I will *not* meekly bow to your oppressive wishes!"

A cruel smile turned up the edges of his mouth. "Ah, but have you forgotten that we consummated this farce of a marriage? Could the act be so meaningless to you as to not warrant remembrance? Like it or not, Jessica, it is no longer a marriage in name only."

Jessica's rage was nearly blinding her. She wanted to hurt him, deeply, so she struck where a man was most vulnerable.

"Consummated? Ha! If what happened in that cottage is your idea of consummating a marriage then I'll not care to ever share it with *you* again!"

As soon as the words left her mouth she regretted them. Not only from the looks of shock and anger and—yes—hurt that crossed Jacob's features, but because it had been a lie. Up until the moment that Jacob had discovered her virginity, she had reveled in the passion they'd created together, wanting to lose herself in the spiraling ecstasy forever.

Jessica caught a glimpse of Malcom standing open-mouthed behind Jacob. Her regret increased ten-fold as she realized that she'd struck a damaging blow to Jacob's pride in front of his best friend.

A low rumble came from Jacob's chest, and without another word he grabbed Jessica by her upper arm and all but dragged her down the marbled corridor.

Fear enveloped her with every step but she refused to give in to the consuming realization of what she'd just done. It was a struggle to keep up with Jacob's long stride, but pride forced her to match his pace.

Jacob stopped at a door half-way down the hall and threw it open. Two young lovers were startled from their dimly lit rendezvous in the library by Jacob's ominous growl. "Get out!"

Without a question or a backwards glance the two fled the library with haste.

Jessica pulled her arm free from Jacob's hold, feeling the tender skin bruise as she did so. She backed several feet away as he kicked the door shut, rattling a small picture off its hook on the wall and sending it clattering to the floor.

Silence filled the room for a moment, and then the sound of the bolt sliding home to lock the door echoed in the darkened shadows.

Trapped.

She felt like a small, helpless animal being preyed upon by a skilled hunter. But she could not, would not let him see her fear!

Jacob slowly stalked toward Jessica. Jealousy had always been an unknown emotion to him, but at this moment it was near to choking him. His one wish was to strangle her, and so to avoid that end he forced his hands into balled fists at his side.

For all that he was furious about her behavior he realized with shocking clarity that his jealousy was true, that despite everything he still wanted her—desperately.

That revelation alone caused him to wince in light of her waspish comments about their lovemaking. True, she had nothing to compare it to, but she had seemed to enjoy it the last time, until the moment of truth. Perhaps he should give her another taste of the ecstasy he knew he could bring about. Just once, just to let her know what she would be giving up.

He let his shoulders relax a bit, regaining control of himself with several deep breaths.

Jessica stood her ground. The gleam that suddenly appeared in his eyes called for caution. She watched him warily as he moved slowly around her.

In a deceptively calm voice, he said, "I refuse to let you humiliate me in front of my peers ever again. Malcom is a good and honest friend. Although your vile words will make no difference in our friendship, you will never again treat me with such disrespect, either in public or in private. Do I make myself clear?" His words ended through clenched teeth.

Jessica held her head high, refusing to be talked down to like a naughty child. "You will not get that promise from me until I receive the same from you! You humiliated me in front of my family and *I* will not have *that*."

Warm breath brushed across the back of her neck as he moved in closer.

Jessica's knees were beginning to weaken, for try as she

might, she could not resist the pull of his nearness. With a bravado she didn't feel, she continued, "Furthermore, I do not need a protector, and I am not a possession, despite your flowery insinuations to Viscount Trent."

Ignoring her words, he took another step around her until he was facing her once again. He whispered dangerously, "Oh, but you are my possession, Jesse. Until death do us part, you are mine. That's part of the bargain you made the day you married me. As your husband, I have certain undeniable rights. I intend to exercise them."

Their faces were mere inches apart, his hands now clamping tightly on her shoulders.

Lord above, she was beautiful. Even in all her anger, her mesmerizing eyes held him tight.

Jessica could feel his nearness draining every ounce of strength from her body. If she didn't get away now, she never would.

"I will never be anyone's possession!" she said, her words trailing into a whisper. Even to her own ears the words sounded hollow, for she must surely be possessed to be feeling this moved by a man she so openly hated. Isn't that so?

Jacob could feel her anger waning and with it went his. Being this close to her, holding her in his arms, inhaling her scent, feeling her trembling was driving him mad with desire.

He bent his head and put his mouth to her ear, pulling her closer until her arms were trapped between them. "And as for your disappointment with the consummation of our marriage, I plead only that I was overcome by shock at finding you a maiden. This time, I promise you, will be more to your liking."

His intention was still punishment. He would show her what love could be like...and then deny her.

Oh, hell, he thought. *Give up.*

His lips were warm against her ear, his breath sending tingles of pleasure down her spine. Jacob slid one hand down her back, pressing her hips into his where his ready manhood made her gasp with surprise and longing. Heat shot from her core to the tips of her ears, melting all but desire in it's path.

"But—but there won't be a next time," she whispered unconvincingly, her eyes fluttering with the desire that was rapidly overtaking her.

"Yes, there will. I will possess you, Jesse," he whispered, "Have no doubt."

Jessica's half-hearted protest was cut short by his mouth as it covered hers in a searching kiss.

She pressed her palms against his chest, making a weak show at resistance. His racing heart beneath her hand told her that he was just as lost as she and that struck the final blow to her show of strength.

Her lips opened beneath his, her tongue challenging his, seeking out the sweet warmth of his mouth. Jessica slid her arms up around his neck, entwining her fingers in his dark hair, molding her body tightly against his.

Jacob groaned in surrender as he felt her resistance flee.

He tore his lips away from her only long enough to bend and lift her from the floor. Carrying her slowly toward the fireplace, he placed her on the large sofa that sat before the softly burning hearth.

Once again his lips sought hers and as he knelt beside her he allowed his hands to roam where they would: the throbbing pulse point at her throat, the long, graceful neck and determined chin, and then back down to those enchanting breasts that had so recently been a point of contention.

Jessica sucked in her breath as his hands trailed lightly across them. He bent his head, gently placing kisses on the rounded tops of each one, and then with something akin to wonder he slowly, slid the shoulders of her gown down, freeing first one soft mound and then the other.

Jacob buried his face between them, inhaling the sweet, warm scent he found there, and then gently took each taut nipple into his mouth in turn.

Jessica's head rolled back and forth. Nothing could have prepared her for the onslaught of pleasure that washed over her.

"Oh, oh, Jacob—please—I—" Her breath was coming in ragged gasps. "I *need you!*"

Need matched need and Jacob knew he could no longer wait to have her. Gently, he moved her over on the couch and sat next to her. He slid his hands under her full skirts, and as they deftly but impatiently worked the ties, he wondered if he would ever again let her out of her usual attire.

At last he found her silken thighs and all that lay between. Jessica gasped as he drew his fingers across the soft mound of curls hidden there and sat up quickly, no longer content with just teasing touches.

With a fierce intensity she peeled off his suit jacket and nearly popped the buttons off his shirt in her haste. Jacob helped her slide the shirt from his shoulders and as he did so Jessica's hands flew to his breeches.

Seconds later, she was rewarded when his proud staff sprang forward, eager to meet with her heated softness.

Jacob stood and kicked off his shoes, sliding his breeches to the floor. As Jessica began to fumble with the stays at the back of her dress, Jacob took her hands and leaned her back to the sofa once again.

"No," he whispered hoarsely, "I can't wait!"

Neither could she.

His lips found hers again as he worked the folds of her skirt up to her waist. Jacob pulled back and looked deeply into her eyes for a moment. Damn! He had wanted to take this slowly and introduce her to the sweet torture of waiting for ecstasy.

"Jessica, Jessica!" he whispered as he positioned himself between her thighs, lost to the passion he saw in her eyes. "I want to take this slow for you...."

He took care at first, knowing that she hadn't been fully initiated the last time. But soon, her answering thrusts were more than he could bear. Good lord! She fit him like a glove! Deeper and deeper he drove, her own rhythm making any thoughts of slow tenderness flee from his thoughts.

Jessica's surprise and wonder were overwhelming. She had enjoyed the brief tryst they'd had before, but nothing could have prepared her for the excruciating pleasure she was experiencing now.

On they drove, matching thrust for thrust, each relishing the wonder that was overtaking them. He gently bit her ear lobe, she raked her nails across his back.

Jacob felt her tense as her release was nearing. "Relax," he whispered, "let it take you over!"

Jessica heeded his words, arching her back, meeting his driving passion and in another moment the explosion that rocked her from within sent her spiraling through clouds of wonder. "Jacob! Oh, love...."

Her throbbing response was more than Jacob could stand. In a flash he too was consumed by an all-encompassing splendor as he spilled his seed into the warm embrace of her velvet softness. "Ahhh! Jesssss!" he cried out.

They rode the wave until pace finally slowed, each one reveling in the light dizziness that allowed them to float on a cloud of pleasure. For a moment neither could speak, nor did they want to.

Jacob finally dared a look at Jessica's face and was alarmed to see tears streaming down her cheeks.

"Jess! My God, did I hurt you, love?"

She chuckled softly and shook her head. "No, no. I've just never felt such—never known such—" she was at a loss for words.

"Ssh. I know." He kissed her on the forehead and then rested his chin there. "Neither have I." He shook his head again and dropped his forehead to hers, kissing her lips ever so lightly.

"Truly?" she asked, amazed that he would even say such a thing.

He raised his head again and looked into her eyes. "Truly. At the risk of sounding over-proud and rakish, I've had my share of women. But nothing, no one, ever came close to what I just shared with you."

Tears threatened to spill from her eyes again. Oh, she did love this man! The feelings had been no fluke. Even when they were fighting, her largest ache came from the fact the she didn't want to hate him; didn't want to hurt him. She only wanted to love him.

Could there be a chance for them? Only, she knew, if she told him everything. She had to risk telling him.

She took a deep breath as Jacob dropped his lips to her neck once again. "Jacob, I want everything to be right between us."

"Ssh. Enjoy the moment. Everything *is* right."

She laughed softly. "Believe me, I have—I *am* enjoying this. But I have to explain about my—my virginity, about my reasons for misleading you where Ossie is concerned. Oh, there is so much I need to tell you."

"Not here. Let's go home, that is, if you've had enough of this societal dung heap. I have no desire to spend the night on this uncomfortable sofa when I could be ravishing you in my bed."

Jessica smiled. "Ravishing me? But I recall you saying only minutes ago that you would like to go slowly."

He smiled back at her. "Did I say that? I must have been out of my mind." His smile softened and he brushed a lock of hair from her forehead. "In truth, I *was* out of my mind. But gloriously so."

He sat up quickly, knowing that if they didn't clothe themselves soon, he would be lost to her delicious temptations again.

As it was, it took several attempts and gentle admonishments from each of them before they were able to satisfactorily repair their appearances.

Chapter 23

Jessica and Jacob opened the door of the library to find Malcom tip-toeing half way down the hall. They both chuckled at his worried expression. "What's this, Malcom, were you intending to spy on us? Can't a man have a quiet moment with his wife?"

Malcom glanced at their entwined hands and then at Jessica's glowing cheeks. He grinned broadly, certain that the worst was over. "Of course. But you were in such a brawl when you left me that I feared for your life, Jacob. I had to make certain that this burly brute of a woman you married didn't hurt you."

Malcom glanced again at Jessica, thinking not for the first time that she was a definite prize. "But if I may be so bold, Your Grace," he said bowing to Jessica, "might I suggest you make use of yonder ladies' lounge to repair your hair? Why, it almost looks as if you've just had a romantic tryst."

Jessica put her hand to her slightly disheveled coiffure and blushed prettily. "Perhaps you're right. Will you gentlemen excuse me?"

At their nod, she rushed into a small salon that had been reserved for the ladies at the ball. Several long mirrors lined the wall of the red-carpeted room with chairs placed conveniently about. One look at her appearance in the mirrors brought Jessica's hand to her mouth. She giggled quietly behind it.

"Oh, you are a sight," she whispered, glad that she was alone in the room.

She chose a chair at the far end of the room and repaired her hair style as best she could. When she finished, the style was definitely different than when she had arrived, but passable nonetheless. Hopefully no one else would notice the change.

As Jessica put the final touches to her hair, the door to the salon opened. Glancing in the mirror, she made eye contact with Baroness Von Kraus.

Oh, wonderful, Jessica thought to herself, just what I need.

All she wanted to do was return to Jacob's side, but the baroness would not let her escape that easily.

"Well, well, well," the baroness said with a false smile. "If it isn't the Duchess of Fairdale. My, how different you look from the last time I saw you. I'd say that life as a duchess has settled quite comfortably with you."

Jessica no longer felt intimidated by this woman. "Oh, it has. I find being married to Jacob and sharing his life a true pleasure, in all ways." Jessica had not forgotten the way the baroness' eyes had hungrily followed Jacob around the room the day he'd announced their marriage. It wouldn't hurt to let the baroness know that they were more than satisfied in all aspects of their marriage, even if that had only become true a few minutes ago.

"Hmm. I'm sure." The baroness's smile faded, and then brightened again. "You must have a very strong faith in one another."

"We do," Jessica answered warily, not trusting the wicked smile she was receiving.

"I mean, you haven't been married all that long, and to trust him so completely, considering his past, well, I hope you're not disappointed."

"Why should I be disappointed by Jacob? He's a wonderful man."

"Yes. He is. I just meant that it's very big of you to allow him to keep company with his former mistress. Why my dear, I'm certain that *I* could not allow my husband such freedoms, especially with the scandalous circumstances."

Jessica felt the knot returning to her stomach even though she had no idea what the baroness was going on about. In the dream-like embrace of their passion, she'd forgotten all about Marga. But what did she mean by 'scandalous circumstances'? Rather than giving the baroness the pleasure of seeing her worry, Jessica raised her chin a notch and said, "I'm sure I don't know what you're talking about. Nor do I care, Baroness. If you'll excuse me, I wish to return to my husband."

The baroness chuckled evilly. "Of course, dear. You do that. I believe I saw him just outside."

Indeed, Jacob was just outside.

But what Jessica saw when she opened the door knocked the breath from her.

There, not ten feet away, was the most beautiful brunette woman she'd ever seen. And that woman had intimately draped her arms over Jacob's shoulders.

Jacob's back was to the salon door, and so he didn't see Jessica emerge. But Malcom did.

And so did Marga.

Smoldering brown eyes met glittering amber. Marga's lovely painted mouth curved up in a malicious smile and she tightened her grip on Jacob.

Without taking her eyes from Jessica, she said in a voice loud enough to carry across the hall, "But darling, we had so much unfinished business when you left me this afternoon. I just thought perhaps we could continue our—uh—discussion. Perhaps later, at my home?"

Jacob pried Marga's arms from around his neck. "Why didn't you tell me when I saw you this afternoon that you would be attending this ball? Surely Lady Winslow has more sense than to invite my *former* mistress to a ball honoring my recent marriage."

This afternoon? Jacob had been visiting Marga this afternoon and *that* was why he hadn't been at the townhouse to greet her?

Jessica felt sick. Surely she couldn't be this much of a fool.

Surely she couldn't have misread his words and actions so much. Had he played this cruel game with her just to get even for a wrong she could explain away?

Her hand went to the pillar beside her, balancing her when her knees began to go weak.

Only when Jacob finally removed Marga's arms from around his neck, did she begin to feel hope once again.

"Oh, I assure you Lady Winslow did see fit to over look my position as your lover and exclude me from her list," Marga said with a pout. "But my dear friends, the Atterberrys, insisted I join them here. Apparently they were unaware of our close relationship and how it might offend their granddaughter."

Jacob saw the expression that crossed Malcom's face and the way he rolled his eyes heavenward.

Without turning, he knew that Jessica was standing behind him. He could feel her.

"Come here, Jessica," he said, still glaring at Marga. When Jessica didn't move he turned to look at her. The look of confused hurt on her face tore at his heart.

She looked at Jacob's hands which were still grasping Marga's, but only to keep them from returning to his neck as they had twice before Jessica had joined them.

More gently, he said again, "Come here, Jessica."

She quickly glanced at Marga who was still smiling like a satisfied cat, and then at Malcom who stared intently at her and nodded his head slowly, urging her to do as Jacob asked.

Her feet felt like lead as she moved the short distance across the corridor. Behind her she heard the salon door open and knew that Baroness Von Kraus was now witnessing the scene also.

With as much dignity as she could muster, Jessica stopped before the trio.

Again her eyes met and clashed with Marga's.

"So," Marga said with a brittle smile, "this is the little duchess. I must admit, you're not at all what I expected."

"And just what did you expect, Marga?" Jacob asked as he dropped her hands and shoved her gently backwards. Jessica's hands were like ice as Jacob took hers in his and pulled her to his side.

Marga watched him with narrowed eyes. "Well, I didn't expect that you would chain yourself to such a frail, frightened child."

Jacob started to speak for Jessica but she took a step forward and answered for herself. "I assure you I am not frightened, I am not a child, and I daresay of the two of us you would be the only one who could be described as frail."

Jessica ran her eyes over the length of Marga's slim figure and then folded her arms beneath her breasts as she once again met Marga's eyes with a raised eyebrow.

Marga bristled and matched Jessica's stance. "Well, well. Apparently I was misinformed. You do have a backbone after all."

"I do."

"Good, for you are going to need it being married to your wonderfully lustful husband."

Jessica could not believe that this woman was so openly flaunting her past relationship with Jacob. Was this how all of the aristocracy spoke to each other, with no heed to privacy and intimate matters?

"I assure you I can handle my wonderfully lustful husband."

Jacob moved to stop the confrontation. He could just envision Jessica throwing Marga to the ground and having it out with her. He didn't care about Marga, but he didn't fancy his wife's reputation being so tarnished at this, their first public appearance.

Marga too ignored Jacob's attempt to interfere. Again she smiled. "Well, apparently your idea of handling him and mine are two different things, for if he were my husband, which he should have been," she said with a glare towards Jacob, "he would not have been visiting his mistress as he did with me today."

"Enough, Marga!" Jacob said with barely controlled anger. "I visited you today for one reason and one reason only."

"Yes, darling, I know that reason so very well," Marga said as she once again leaned toward him.

Jessica began to feel the flutter of doubt in her stomach again. God, no! Please don't let it be true. Her bravado of just moments before had cost her dearly. Jessica was afraid that if Jacob even remotely led her to believe that he had bedded Marga just hours before he'd made love to her, she would crumble right here and now.

"Marga," he growled lowly, "stop this. You know damn well why I visited you this afternoon."

She turned her eyes to Jacob at last. "Oh, yes. I know what you said. But I forgive you for the misguided assumption that I would be so easily set aside, even if only temporarily. I must admit that ten thousand pounds is a generous offer as a gift. I suppose it would keep many women satisfied for quite some time. I'm not one of those women, however. And even though I know you'll come back to me as you have time and again, I find now that I'm not satisfied with your attempt to pacify me. I find that I am in need of much more."

Ten thousand pounds! Jessica could not even imagine that much money, let alone imagine it as a gift to a paramour. She turned her eyes to Jacob. Could this woman really have meant that much to him? Did he offer her such a gift so that Marga *would* wait for him to tire of her? And just how long would that take?

She felt the muscles in her jaw begin to tighten as the full impact of what had transpired hit her.

Malcom stepped forward and took Marga's elbow tightly in his fingers, wanting to spare both Jessica and Jacob from any further embarrassment. "All right now, Marga. You've had your fun and made your scene. I believe Jacob has made his intentions clear. Now, how about we drop this and you grace me with a dance?"

Marga had seen Jessica's questioning look and jerked her arm from Malcom's grasp. Jessica was beginning to doubt her husband and Marga pounced on her chance.

"Thank you but no, Mally. I'm not nearly finished." She turned to gaze up at Jacob once again, a dangerously sweet smile caressing her lips. "You see, darling, I meant what I said. I am in need of much more. You and I both know that you should have married me. It was my right to be the Duchess of Fairdale. I've been with you for years; I know you better than you know yourself, just as I know that even though you lapsed into a fit of insanity and married this backwards wench, you will come back to my bed. I will be your wife, if not in name, then in your heart."

The color was rising in Jacob's face once again. He could feel Jessica slipping away from him, a coolness settling between them once again. Not that he could really blame her, for in truth she didn't know him that well, not nearly as well as Marga. But he'd be damned if he'd lose her now!

"Marga," he said through clenched teeth, "as I told you before, our association is over. Finished. I will have nothing more to do with you, ever!" If Jessica would just hold on until he could talk to her privately

But Marga's next words squelched all hopes of that. "Oh, but you will, my love. For you see, in six short months I will proudly bear you a child, hopefully a son. And although you've seen to it that he won't enjoy the true honors to which he's entitled, you will claim him as yours and see that we are both quite comfortable. And that includes your spending time with us, with both of us."

"What!" Jacob, Jessica and Malcom all sounded in unison.

"Oh, really, darling," Marga said with a smile, taking Jacob's hand and placing it on her belly. "Don't try to tell me you didn't know. Why, you are more familiar with my body than anyone. Surely you've noticed my changing figure."

In his shock, Jacob left his hand on Marga's belly for several moments too long. His head was swimming. It couldn't be! In truth he hadn't paid much attention—hell—any attention to any woman other than Jessica since the moment he'd met her. Any changes in Marga had gone unnoticed.

But now that he was forced to look at Marga, really look at her, he had to admit that although she was still slim, her stomach did appear just a bit plumper, and her breasts seemed to be fuller as well.

Lord, no. Not this. Not now. Not ever.

Jessica looked at Jacob, waiting, silently begging him to deny Marga's words, to say they couldn't possibly be true.

Jacob was desperately trying to think back, to figure if this could possibly be his child, for if it was he would definitely have to provide for it.

Jessica took his silence as confirmation. A ragged sob escaped her and that finally shook Jacob from his shocked reverie.

"Jessica, I—this can't be—" he couldn't think now. He needed time to sort this out. So much had happened in the space of a few months...he'd barely given Marga a second thought...it couldn't possibly be...could it?

Jessica took a shaky breath and glared at Jacob.

Just this afternoon, Marga had said.

Having Jacob's child, Marga had said.

Her right to be duchess, Marga had said.

She felt foolish, she felt betrayed, she felt sick.

Escape! It was her only hope of survival.

She began to back away and called on every remaining shred of pride and strength she had left. "I realized there's never been a divorce in the Callaways' history," she said shakily, "but I strongly urge you to consider being the first. After all, we wouldn't want another Callaway bastard roaming the streets of London, would we?"

Chapter 24

Jessica ran blindly down the corridor, past the great doors that led into the ball room. Tears that had filled her eyes were now streaming down her cheeks, and more were following.

Where was she? There, the front entry. If she could just get outside, away from probing eyes and...

"Oh!" she collided with a well-muscled chest and the two of them stumbled back against the wall. "Oh, I'm so—please excuse me, I—"

"Your Grace, what it is?"

Concern laced the voice of Viscount Percival Trent as he caught Jessica and helped her regain her balance. He grasped her gently by the shoulders and bent to look into her eyes, which were now red and swollen by her tears.

Again he tried. "Your Grace, if someone has so offended you that it's made you this upset, by God I'll see that—"

Jessica finally caught her breath, "N-no. Well, y-yes, but there's n-nothing I can do about it. P-please, just let me go, I must get out of here!"

Just then, Lady Atterberry appeared from around the corner. "My dear! What in heaven's name—"

"Lady Atterberry, your granddaughter is obviously very distraught. If I may borrow your coach I would escort her away from here and—"

"No!" Jessica sobbed. "P-please! I must be alone. Ggrandmother...." the word sounded foreign on her lips, but if it would help.... "Grandmother, please, may I just borrow your coach to go back to the townhouse? I'll have it returned immediately."

"Of course my dear, but are you quite certain that you wouldn't like someone to escort you? After all, it's—"

"No, I-I really must be alone. Please!"

At Lady Atterberry's nod and concerned touch to her arm, Jessica turned and fled from the Winslow's ball. She flew down the steps, stumbling a little in her unaccustomed heels, and then stopped short at the bottom.

Oh, no! Which one was her grandparents' coach? She looked left and right, and then turned to look up the steps. Lady Atterberry was there waiving to a plain, black conveyance. Immediately the driver brought it forward.

Skillful steering was the only thing that prevented a collision with Jacob's elaborately decorated coach, for the driver that had brought Jessica and Malcom to the ball had leapt into action as well when he saw Jessica running down the front steps.

She looked at Jacob's driver for a moment, wondering if perhaps she shouldn't go with him.

No! He would follow Jacob's orders only, and she doubted that he would leave here with out the Duke.

Without further hesitation she climbed inside the Atterberry's coach. Before she was seated it lurched forward, tossing her gently onto the rear cushions.

Jessica sat still for a moment. Her thoughts were swirling but relief settled over her as she realized she was at last alone, without the prying eyes of London's *ton*.

Once again the sobs overtook her. Jessica curled into a tight ball, pulling her knees to her chest and turning side ways on the seat. She'd left without her cloak and the night air was quickly finding its way through her gown. Pulling a fur blanket completely over the top of her, she closed her eyes and let her thoughts have free rein.

Oh, Jacob, Jacob, Jacob. How could you?

Just this afternoon...Marga...a baby!

Admittedly he'd seemed just as shocked as she and Malcom had been. But when he found out wasn't the issue. The fact remained that he was going to be a father - but not to my child! her mind screamed. To Marga's!

When at last she could cry no more tears, she took a few deep breaths and tried to calm herself. Several more minutes passed before her breathing returned to normal, only the occasional sob escaping from her constricted throat.

A plan.

She needed a plan.

Her first thoughts were to race back to Fairdale, gather up Ossie and her few belongings and then flee to her rustic cabin in the woods.

But no. Jacob could easily come after her. Besides, Ossie belonged with Jacob at Fairdale. Austen had insisted on it, and if nothing else was brought about by this sham she'd gotten herself into, then at least Ossie would claim his rightful place as Jacob's brother and she would make good on her word to Austen.

And the thought of leaving Ossie behind, well it would almost be as if she was leaving her own child.

No, she would have to stay, at least for a while.

But how could she face Jacob again? Or Marga?

How could she face any of the people she'd met this evening? For certainly by now the news of Marga's pregnancy would have spread through the crowd.

She shook her head. Stuck. Absolutely stuck. She could not leave without Ossie, yet she knew she couldn't take Ossie away. Not after she'd promised Austen they'd stay.

Picture that, she thought to herself. Me, living in one wing of the house while Marga and her newborn lived in the other. How ludicrous.

Not in a million years! I'll not share my husband with

anyone!

If he won't divorce me, then I'll leave anyway! But Ossie...

Again, the dilemma.

"I can't run away," she said out loud. "I must face this and demand that Jacob handle this matter expeditiously. He must divorce me and marry that - that - whore!" Having said it aloud, Jessica began to feel calmer, but the anger did little to ease her broken heart for she knew that whether she stayed or returned to her cabin, with or without Ossie, she would never recover from the tumultuous relationship she'd had with Jacob.

Her trust was gone.

Her faith in true love was gone.

Her hope for her own happy future was gone.

"Might as well get used to it," she said aloud.

"Michael!" Jacob yelled as he descended the steps with Malcom at his heels, "Michael, where the hell is she? Where's Jessica?"

The young man at the reins of Jacob's coach was trembling in his seat. He'd been so surprised when the Duchess had climbed into the other coach that he hadn't moved for the several minutes since the other coach pulled away. He knew the Duke wasn't going to like this. Somehow, he was certain he'd have to take the blame.

"I don't know, Yer Grace! I-I seen 'er come out an' before I could get t' 'er, another coach pulled up an' she jumped right in!"

"Whose coach was it?" Jacob demanded.

"Sorry, Yer Grace, but I don't know. There were no emblems or crests on it, I—"

"It was my coach," a voice said from behind Jacob.

216

Jacob whirled around to come face to face with Lord Atterberry and his wife.

"Then I ask you," Jacob said with a barely controlled growl, his hands fisted at his sides "where is my wife?"

"Your wife, my granddaughter, was very upset. I can only imagine why. Lady Atterberry and I offered her our coach so that she could leave and unburden herself of...whatever it was that had so upset her. However she chose to go off by herself."

"By herself?"

Jacob took another step towards Lord Atterberry, his hands raising from his sides.

The fear in Lord Atterberry's eyes diminished only slightly when Malcom stepped between them.

"Jake, don't do this. Strangling him, as I know is your fondest desire, won't help us locate your wife."

Still smoldering, Jacob took a step back. "Always the voice of reason, Malcom," he said, never taking his eyes from Lord Atterberry. "But if this milk-faced fop and his half-pence whore of a wife don't tell me where Jessica has gone, I shall be forced to ignore your voice of reason and throttle the man posthaste!"

Malcom raised his hands and turned back to Lord Atterberry, somewhat certain that Jacob had now regained some of his reason. "I've done as much as I can, Atterberry. I suggest you tell the man what he wants to know."

Lady Atterberry was still recovering from his insult but stepped forward to face Jacob herself. "My granddaughter had been horribly offended this evening—"

"She's your granddaughter only by an accident of birth."

"And she's your wife by another accident, I would presume. But none of that has aught to do with what happened here tonight. For you to flaunt your mistress in front of poor Jessica, and then lay claim to your child right here in front of everyone! Why, the poor girl had to have been devastated and humiliated beyond comprehension."

"I did not lay claim to any child. And it is my understanding that it was you who invited my former mistress here tonight. If anyone is to blame for this chaos it is you!" Jacob pointed his finger in Lady Atterberry's face.

Lady Atterberry smiled deviously, not backing down from Jacob's threatening demeanor. "Is that so? Why, I'm sure I didn't know until this evening that Marga was your mistress."

"Former mistress," Jacob interrupted.

"Former mistress," Lady Atterberry amended, and then added loud enough for all to hear, "And certainly I had no idea that she carried your child! Jessica tearfully revealed all as she ran from your brutal confession," Lady Atterberry lied.

"Oh!" the whispers and exclamations swept through the crowd like a tornado.

Jacob's thunderous look did nothing to stop Lady Atterberry's speech.

"Thank goodness we, along with Viscount Trent, were here to rescue the poor darling."

Jacob quickly scanned the crowd that had gathered at the foot of the stairs. All were eagerly watching the drama unfold.

Jacob's words of rebuttal were quickly forgotten as he realized that Viscount Trent was no where to be seen.

"And just where is Viscount Trent?" Jacob asked, his attention now focused on the whereabouts of the man who had been lasciviously doting on his wife just a short while before.

The man in question stood at the top of the stairs opposite Marga, the look on his face conveying that he was thoroughly enjoying the scene.

"I say old man, it appears that you've lost your wife. I shall assist you in locating her. I know many places where a distraught young wife might find solace." Viscount Trent smiled deviously and motioned for his own coach.

Malcom stepped forward and took Jacob by the arm. "I'm sure she just went home, Jacob. Where else would she go in this city? She knows nothing about it."

"That's what worries me...." his words trailed off at the

thought of Jessica gaining solace in Percival Trent's arms. The jealousy that ripped through him was like a physical blow. At that moment he came to know just how much Jessica meant to him.

Yes, there were still many things to work out between them but that aside he knew he had fallen deeply in love with his wife.

And there was no denying it any longer.

"Let's get out of here before the Atterberry's start charging fees to watch this spectacle they've created," Malcom said quietly.

Jacob turned back to the Atterberry's and then his eyes caught sight of Marga at the top of the stairs, leaning casually against a pillar with the smug smile she'd worn earlier still in place.

The look he sent her was caustic, but she retained the "I've won" attitude in spite of it.

"I'm not through with you," he said over the heads of the on-lookers. "Not by any measure!"

"You've made that quite clear," Lady Atterberry said loudly with narrowed eyes and a half-smile distorting her face. "Too clear, for Jessica's well-being. I feel I simply must intervene. I hold you responsible for ruining two womens' lives."

Lady Atterberry glanced pointedly at Marga who assumed a woeful expression on her face and then turned and placed her forehead on her raised arm for the sympathetic benefit of all who looked on.

Jacob grabbed Lady Atterberry's wrist in one hand and Lord Atterberry's in another. "Take heed," he said threateningly, "when I figure out your exact participation in this little scheme, or if anything happens to Jessica, to my wife, I will make your lives a living hell, more than I have already!"

Jessica sat upright in the seat and pulled the blanket down from over her head. She glanced out the window to her right and noticed that there were no houses along the street.

The street? No, it was a rutted roadway now. The cobbled stones of the city streets had been gone for quite some time, she now realized. For another mile or so she sat just staring out the window.

Trees. Now there was nothing but trees to be seen, in any direction.

She leaned forward and called out, "Driver! This is not the way to my house. Where are you going?"

There was a short silence, and finally he called back, "I'm takin' ye t' yer grandmum's."

"My—but no, there must be some mistake." Of course, how was the driver to know? She'd simply jumped in her grandmother's coach and he must have just assumed she wanted to go to the Atterberry's estate.

"Excuse me please, but would you turn around and take me back to King Street? That's where my - my husband's townhouse is." She nearly choked on the word.

"Sorry, m'lady. I 'ave orders t' take ye directly t' Lord Atterberry's."

"Orders? What orders? From whom did—"

Before she could finish her question, a loud crack split the night air. Jessica leaned further out the window and peered back into the darkness. Another loud bang! sounded, and this time she saw a flash that she knew was a gun discharging.

What in the—

"Get yerself inside! There's a group of thieves followin' us!" the driver shouted.

"A—what?" Jessica's questions were cut short by the sound of another shot. The horses lunged into a canter at the crack of the driver's whip.

Another shot. So far the shots appeared to have been fired into the air, at least none had struck the coach. But how long would that last?

"Heeyah!" the driver called out.

Jessica clutched the sides of the seat, her heart racing. She felt so helpless! Who could possibly want anything from her?

Of course! Whoever was following them must think her grandparents were inside. Perhaps they would let her go once they realized they'd made a mistake...

The shots were getting closer and Jessica began to feel panic overtaking her. How could this be happening? Where were they? Would anyone find them?

And the driver, why wasn't he going faster? He'd hardly quickened the pace since the first shot rang out.

Voices, shouts, more gunfire.

If only she had her own gun!

Two men bolted past the window where she was looking out and raced to the head of the team of horses pulling the coach. She could hear the driver shouting at the men, cracking the whip at the horses.

They were slowing down. Oh, God, the riders had taken hold of the horse's reins.

What could she do? Jessica couldn't bear the thought of what these cut-throats might do to her if they got her cornered. Fight she would, but to what avail?

Get out!

If she was going to escape it had to be now! Perhaps she could run and hide in the woods that surrounded them without being noticed by the two riders!

Before she had time to reconsider her decision, Jessica threw open the door to the coach and jumped as far as she could. She had counted on tucking herself into a ball and rolling off the side of the road.

What she hadn't counted on was a third rider still trailing behind the coach.

Just as her feet left the step, she saw from the corner of her eye the muscular chest of a tall white horse.

"What the—bloody hell!" the rider called out and yanked back on his mount's reins just as the horse's right shoulder connected with Jessica's.

"Ahh!"

She shrieked as she was trounced to the ground. Hooves flashed by her face, narrowly missing her. The wind was knocked from her as she rolled and rolled down a small hill.

At last she stopped, with a thud, as her head struck a partially buried rock. She'd landed in a shallow ditch. The icy cold water was a bitter contrast to the warm sticky blood she felt running down her forehead.

The pain in her head was blinding. Let go, let go! Relief swept over her as she surrendered herself to the soft, enveloping arms of unconsciousness.

Her last cognizant thought was that she hoped Jacob would take care of Ossie if she died.

Chapter 25

Jessica's head was pounding. The closer she came to full awareness, the more it hurt.

Sleep. She just needed more sleep.

But the throbbing at her temple wouldn't allow that. "Ohhh," she moaned softly. With a great effort she tried to lift her hand to her head, but it seemed so heavy...so very heavy.

Just a little more sleep...but before she could drift back into that pain-free atmosphere of unconsciousness, she heard footsteps scrambling and then a voice.

With dizzying speed, she was hurtling back to awareness. Who was talking to her? Jacob? Could it be Jacob?

He seemed so very far away. She tried to listen but didn't quite have the strength to focus on the words.

But damn if her mind would let her drift off again.

Jessica's eyes fluttered open. So bright! It hurt!

"Please!" she whispered desperately, "Please, Jacob, turn down the lamps! Too bright, too bright!"

"Now, now little miss. There ain't but two little lamps in 'ere. Ye jest shut yer eyes and relax. Awful glad ye came 'round though. Was beginnin' t' think that tap t' yer head was gettin' th' best of ye."

"Tap? What—who are you?"

Jessica's eyes were growing accustomed to the light now. She surveyed her surroundings from her position on an old straw mattress. She hadn't slept on a straw mattress since she'd left her cottage.

Something was not right.

Where was she?

Where was Jacob?

In a flash it all returned to her: the ball, Jacob making love to her, Marga, the humiliation...the bandits!

She bolted upright, the sudden action bringing a wave of nausea over her. After lowering herself back to the musty-smelling mattress, she looked up at the man who sat next to her.

He was an older gentleman with scruffy gray whiskers and a ruddy complexion. Two front teeth were missing from his crooked smile and a trail of tobacco spittle stained his chin.

Her eyes traveled slowly over his worn and tattered clothes. The smell of whiskey was faintly evident on his breath as well as his thin cotton shirt.

"Who are you?" she asked.

"Thems what bothers t' call me anything usually call me 'Orace," the old man said. "Not that it much matters. I answer t' jest 'bout anything."

"Who calls you Horace? Why am I here? Where am I?"

Horace chuckled. "So many questions. Can't say as I blame ye, though. Let's see now, my master calls me 'Orace, amongst other things—dependin' on 'is mood. As fer where ye are, ye'd be at my 'umble abode, ye would. Aye, everything ye sees 'ere is mine," he waved his hand proudly around the room as if it were a king's bedroom in a palace.

It was only a shack, really. The one window in the room was covered by a wooden shutter which hung precariously on crooked hinges. Beneath that stood a small, uneven table and two chairs, neither of which looked as if they could bear any weight. One small lamp burned on the table, the other was across the room on a shelf.

A small fireplace sufficiently warmed the room, even despite the cracks in the window shutter and the door.

Jessica looked back at the little man who was still grinning at her. He appeared kind enough, but she still had no idea where she was or why she was there. She leaned up on one elbow and her head began to throb again.

"Your—home seems quite comfortable," she said politely, putting her hand to the cut at her hairline. Then suddenly it made sense to her. "Oh, you—why you must have found me and rescued me after I leapt from the coach. I realized it was a foolish thing to do, but I was so frightened that I—"

She stopped talking when she realized Horace was sitting in his chair chuckling quietly.

"What's so funny?" she asked cautiously.

"Blimey! I didn't rescue ye! I was one of the men what stopped yer horses on the road."

Jessica sat up fully now, ignoring the pain and dizziness that threatened.

"What! But why? What could you possibly want from me? I have nothing—no money, or—"

"Aye that's true enough. But yer fine husband now, 'e's wealthier than a king!"

"My husband! But how did you know who I was? I didn't even leave in his coach."

"Ah, that made no difference. Th' master, 'e knows everything. Saw ye leavin' that grand party and well, the rest of it ye know."

"Who is this master that you keep referring to?" Jessica asked, her annoyance now turning to anger.

"Ye'll be meetin' 'im soon enough. In fact, I believe I 'ear 'im now."

Just then the small door to the cottage burst open, bringing with it a cold gust of wind that scattered the dirt from the floor into the air. When the cloud of dust settled, Jessica found herself staring at a black-clad figure whose very presence seemed to shrink the room even further.

"Well, I see our fair lady has decided to join us back in the land of the living," the man said in a very cultured French accent.

He moved closer to the bed and Jessica stared up into the coldest eyes she had ever seen. But that was all she could see.

The dark figure was wearing a full mask which covered his entire face, save for two slits for his eyes and a small slit for his mouth. His hair, too, was hidden beneath a snug, black hat.

Fear was attacking her from all sides, but she raised her chin and attempted to hold it at bay.

"Who are you?"

"I am, well, I am your savior!"

"My savior? I assume you are one of the men who attacked my coach, so how do you count yourself as my savior?"

"Why, madam, I was one of those men. However, had it not been for my skillful horsemanship, your pretty little skull would be lying in pieces on the ground."

A vision of four white legs and flashing hooves danced through Jessica's mind.

"True enough, you did avoid killing me, but it was your fault that the accident occurred in the first place!"

"Perhaps. But once started, I could hardly give up. No, no. In fact after I saw you this evening I knew that I would enjoy this endeavor very much."

"What endeavor? I demand to know what this is all about!"

The darkly clothed man threw his head back and laughed. "You demand? Oh, you are even more dazzling when you're angry." He bent closer to her and said softly, "I wonder, *cherie*, do you bring this brilliance, this passion to all that you do? To your lovemaking as well? But of course you do."

Jessica was caught completely off guard. "What! Oh! How dare you speak to me that way! Who *are* you?"

He laughed again. "Let's just say that I am a professional admirer and you are the object of my admiration, for now. When my appreciation for—an object—begins to diminish, I give them back to the original owners...for a price."

Jessica could feel her strength leaving her. She was scared. There was no way around that but she would not let him see her fear. "A professional admirer? Ha! More like a professional coward! Why else would you hide behind that silly black mask? Are you truly afraid of me? A simple woman?"

The man straightened and crossed his arms in front of him as Horace moved quickly to the far side of the room.

Perhaps she'd gone too far?

But then to her surprise, the masked man began to laugh once more. "A simple woman, ha! Do you know how long it's been since someone has insulted me thus and lived to tell about it? Horace, how long has it been?"

From his place in the corner, Horace simply answered, "A long time, master. Maybe never."

He turned back to Jessica. "Well, for now I find I simply must forgive that little indiscretion, for you are far more valuable to me alive."

"Valuable? In what way?"

"Why in the only way that truly matters. Monetarily. You see, I know who you are and I know who your husband is. And I'm certain he would pay a tidy sum to have you returned to him, untainted."

He moved to Jessica's other side and ran a leather-gloved finger along her jaw. "But then, perhaps I will return you just a little tainted and demand less money for you. Yes, I think it would definitely be worth it. Not only for *my* pleasure, but to let him know that we have something so precious in common." He took her chin in his fingers and forced her to look up at him. "We really do need to get you cleaned up, *cherie*. You were so much more presentable at the ball."

"The ball? You were at the ball?"

"Yes, of course. The one in your honor. That's where I first caught sight of you. Might I say, however, that a woman of your—considerable charms," he stared directly at her décolletage, "could have done better in finding herself a husband."

Jessica jerked her chin away, ignoring the flash of pain that action caused. "My husband is a fine man! He's a duke and he's—"

"And he's the father of Marga Desmond's child. Ah, yes, I was privy to all the whisperings. I make it a point to be informed of the latest mishaps."

Impressing this man with her husband's importance wasn't getting her anywhere. Jessica tried a different approach.

"Well, if you know all that, then you must realize that the Duke of Fairdale likely won't spare a shilling for me now that he has a child on the way with his former mistress."

The man laughed again. "Oh, very good. Not only beautiful and charming, but humble too. You put too low a value on yourself. Child or not, Marga Desmond doesn't stand a chance in replacing you. I know her *intimately*, you see, and although I've yet to taste your charms, I'd wager your own ransom that I will find you to be a sweeter dish. With each passing moment I begin to think I may take my own pleasurable time in returning you. Yes, the Duke would welcome you back even if you are a trifle—*used*."

"Well, you're wrong," she shot back, losing more of her nerve. "He wouldn't want me back if I'd been so sorely abused by you."

"Tsk, tsk. Sorely abused. Such a dreadful way to describe something that would be—*will* be so enjoyable. If you were a limp rag doll I could see where the enjoyment might be in question and then perhaps I would tamp down my *firm* desire," he said as he swept his cloak back and pointed, proudly displaying the bulge at his crotch.

Jessica glanced to where he'd pointed before she realized what he'd meant. She looked quickly away, her cheeks burning in fear and embarrassment.

Again he chuckled. "But you see, I know of your passion, your fire, your hunger for love. And I also know that your husband will pay dearly to have you back in his bed, used or not. A man doesn't wear that expression on his face after a bedding when he cares nothing for the woman he's with."

"What do you mean? How could you know—"

"Ah, my innocent little dove, you should learn that if you intend to fulfill your desires at public functions, you should be careful to choose a room that doesn't have a terrace leading to the garden."

Jessica's mind reeled, a sick feeling formed in the pit of her stomach. He couldn't have seen—no, he wouldn't have watched!

"How could you?" she asked, near hysteria.

"It was quite by accident that I stumbled upon you. I was taking some air, walking the back grounds, and when I passed the glass doors leading to the library I was held spellbound by what I saw. You have the most delectable derrier that I've seen in quite some time. And those luscious legs, firm and tight, able to hold a man right where you want him, hm?"

"You—you lecher! You perverted, voyeuristic deviant!"

"Oh, come now, my love. Don't say anything that you'll have to retract once you've seen how much better my lovemaking can be than Jacob Callaway's. If you enjoyed that pompous idiot's groping, you'll think you've gone to heaven when I'm finished with you. Truly, it will be a cruel thing I do when I return you to him."

Jessica could stand no more. She jumped up from her seat on the bed and threw herself at her tormentor, her fists pummeling his chest. "You beast! Don't you dare speak that way about my husband! About *me*!"

She tried to claw his mask from his face but he grabbed her wrists and forced them behind her back, pushing her against him. Jessica could feel his hardness against her thigh and that made her fight even harder. She had to get away from him!

"Continue that sensuous squirming and I may take you right here on the floor and allow Horace to witness what I saw earlier tonight," he said quietly.

Immediately she ceased her struggles. "It would be nothing like you witnessed earlier, you swine. What you so avidly watched was my husband and me making love. With you it would be rape, pure and simple."

"Alas, it wouldn't be the first time." He affected a sigh and shoved her back down on the bed. "But now is not the time. I have too many plans to make. First and foremost will be deciding how much money I should demand from your husband."

He turned and walked to the small table. "Horace, get out. Your nervousness is irritating me," he said as he slapped the old man alongside the head.

Without a word, Horace fled the small building.

Jessica stared silently at her captor. Was it true what he said? Would Jacob pay her ransom no matter the cost, no matter the circumstances?

What if he wouldn't?

What if—

She glanced at the door and then back at the stranger to find him staring at her. "Don't be foolish enough to try it, Jessica. You're still suffering from a blow to the head. I'm stronger, faster, and more determined than you."

"Stronger and faster mayhap, but doubtfully more determined."

The stranger shook his head. "I often find that the more beautiful the woman, the more stubborn. I'm glad to see you've not proven me wrong. But stubborn or not, you will be mine until I see fit to have it otherwise."

He reached inside his cloak and produced an odd looking pipe and a small pouch. With ultimate care, he filled the pipe and then lit it. An acrid-sweet smoke drifted in lazy swirls over his head as he placed the pipe in the small slit that opened over his mouth and inhaled. "Opium," he said simply. "Would you like some? It truly enhances your senses, makes lovemaking even more enjoyable, if that's possible."

Jessica looked away from him. "As I told you before, I have no intention of rutting with an animal like you, nor do I want any of *that*."

The man pulled his mask up just far enough to expose his lips. He took a long drink of Horace's whiskey.

"Of course you don't," he said, inhaling deeply a second time.

Smoke was filling the small room and the unusual odor was making her dizzy once again.

He laughed sharply. "You really can't escape it. Like it or not, you'll begin to feel wonderful. Then perhaps you can relax a bit."

"All I feel is sick," she said sharply.

He was silent for several minutes. When Jessica looked at him again, she noticed his eyes, what she could see of them, were glazed and had a faraway look in them.

"You damn Callaways. Always so righteous. Believing yourselves to be so good, so above the rest of us. Thinking you know what's right for all mankind."

As the drug claimed its hold on him, his words began to slur and his accent became deeper. "Well, you're not." He turned his glassy eyes back to Jessica. "No, no, Jessica. Just wait until you meet the ghosts in the Callaway closets. You'll see your upstanding family is no better than any common house of whores. Even the men. Of course you're finding that out already, aren't you? Poor little Jessica, her husband already running astray, filling the city with misbegotten brats."

"Shut up! You have no idea what you're talking about."

"Oh, but I do. Even Austen was a randy old bastard. Yes, he had a son from some little trollop in your own village, did you know that? Of course you do. You're bringing the boy up, aren't you?"

Jessica's mouth dropped open and her eyes widened in surprise. "How could you possibly know that?"

"Oh, I know all there is to know about the Callaways. I've made them my business."

"But why? What could they possibly mean to someone like *you*?"

He smiled crookedly and lifted the pipe to his exposed lips once again.

"Very influential family they are. Some of their ideas find their way into dangerous hands, hands that can be bought and sold for the right amount of money. Why they could — and have — helped finance battles that have naught to do with their own well-being." Again he fell silent for a moment. Then, "Why should they care about the slavery laws in France, eh?"

He slammed his fist down on the rickety table, causing it to wobble and spill the bottle of whiskey.

Jessica could see that the man's chain of thought was becoming random and abstract. If he would just fall asleep, or become too drugged to notice her....

"My father has owned slaves, and his father before him, and then you get people like your precious Callaways who fill the right coffers and whisper the right words and suddenly slavery is a bad thing. *Vive le France*! We don't need you English helping their cause! Just because you're wealthier, and have these ideas, and... and you're no better than that spoiled slut Marie Antionette that tries to rule from her diamond-encrusted bedroom...."

Jessica stood and took a tentative step towards the door while he continued to ramble on. "He probably supports that old mad-man George who pisses blue water from his throne, eh?" He laughed to himself, but then caught sight of Jessica as she made her way to escape.

"Oh no!" he said. With more speed than she would have guessed possible in his altered state, he leaped to stand between her and the door. Jessica found herself once again in the arms of her captor. He steered her back to the bed.

"You're a wily little thing. I must give you credit! Almost as wily as she was."

"Who?" Jessica asked as she struggled to get out of his grasp.

The man shook his head and took a deep breath. All too quickly, Jessica realized, he was regaining some of his senses.

"Who, you ask. I speak of the very woman who introduced me to the Callaway empire, the woman who first inspired my disgust for anyone bearing the Callaway name." He snorted to make his distaste even clearer before he continued.

"You, however, I forgive. For I know that you came to be a Callaway without knowing their true nature. You're really nothing like her, you know. I doubt you will be bent to my will so quickly."

"*Never*! And who the bloody hell is this woman you're talking about? There are no other Callaway women."

"Why, Anastasia, of course. Your husband's beloved mother."

Jessica felt all the strength leave her legs and her heart beat quicken. All color left her face and had she not been near the bed she would have fallen all the way to the floor.

He laughed again, evilly this time. "I see my reputation has preceded me." He swept low in a bow. "Jean Luc DuPont, at your service madam."

Chapter 26

Jacob stood from the chair behind his desk. He stretched the tired and aching muscles in his back and walked over to the window, pushing back the heavy green velvet curtains.

The sunlight that flooded through the windows did nothing to ease the pain in his head.

He dropped the curtain, leaving it open only enough to let a sliver light into the darkened room.

The whiskey bottle was on the table where he'd left it, nearly empty. He rubbed his eyes and picked up his jacket, making a mental note that no matter what future circumstances presented themselves, he would never again sleep in that straight-backed chair at his desk.

Several loud snorts came from the short couch next to the cold fireplace, followed by a loud *thud* and a curse.

Malcom sat up from his new position on the floor, rubbing his head and looking around the room in a moment of confusion.

"I take it you slept no better than I?" Jacob asked as he slowly crossed the office and slumped into a wing-backed chair.

Malcom hoisted himself back up onto the couch. "Did we sleep at all?"

"Apparently. The sky was just beginning to lighten when I looked out the window last, and now it's annoyingly bright."

"Do I need even ask if you've had any word from Jessica?"

The look on Jacob's face was all the answer he needed. After a moment, Jacob rose and ran his fingers through his hair.

"Damn that woman! Where the hell could she be?"

Malcom stood and stretched his arms over his head. "I don't know what to tell you, old boy. We covered every square inch of this city, three times! I still say the Atterberry's know where she is."

"So do I. But I checked there several times, and you know I had Michael posted there most of the night."

"I know, I know. But hell Jake, where could she *be*? Jessica only arrived here yesterday afternoon. She wouldn't know of anywhere else to go."

"As I see it, there are only two things that could have possibly happened. Either the Atterberry's directed her to some place other than their home and had their driver take her there...."

"Or?" Malcom asked.

"Or she told the driver to take her back to Fairdale."

"Fairdale? In the middle of the night?"

"Oh hell, Malcom. I don't know. I'm grasping for ideas." He walked to the window again and threw open the curtains. "She might have—"

"Jake, she would have had that poor driver going all night."

Jacob turned and glared at Malcom. "Well do you have any other ideas?"

Malcom held up his hands. "No. I don't. All I'm saying is don't get your hopes up. Have you sent anyone to Fairdale yet?"

"Yes, just after you dozed off." He turned again to look out at the street which was starting to fill with carriages and people. "Jesse, where are you?" he whispered.

Jacob leaned his head on the cool panes of glass. "Jesus, Malcom. She must feel so betrayed." He growled and turned back to the room, sitting on the window ledge. "Part of me doesn't blame her one bit for running and being angry. But the rest of me wants to shake her and scold her for leaving without giving me a chance to explain." He shook his head slowly. "However, I fear I am guilty of doing the same thing to her recently."

Malcom cleared his throat. "Uh, forgive me for asking, Jake, but how *will* you justify Marga's—er—condition to Jesse? Obviously it came to be before you even knew of Jessica's existence. But now...."

Jacob shifted on the ledge and crossed his legs at his ankles. "I thought about that near the bottom of that last bottle. In truth, I'm not too concerned."

Malcom's mouth dropped open. "Not too concerned? Might I remind you that your mistress—sorry—your former mistress just last night announced to half of London that she was carrying your child? Not that I have any concern for your reputation for I've no doubt that your name will not suffer for this. But what about Jessica? How will she be able to face her peers—your peers? There will be whispers and snorts and looks down those long, aristocratic noses every time she walks through a room. Jessica doesn't deserve that, Jake."

Jacob allowed himself a half-smile and tilted his head to one side, his left-eyebrow raised. "Well, well, haven't we become the fair lady's champion? Hmm? Pray, don't tell me I shall have to begin calling you Lancelot?"

Malcom felt the color rise to his cheeks momentarily and then found the wherewithal to smile back at Jacob.

"Nay, nay, good King Arthur. I'm not in love with your Guinevere," he teased. The smile faded. "But in truth, I have found that I like your wife very much. She's a beautiful and kind woman. She can laugh and give as good as she gets. And above all, I think she's good for you."

Jacob sent him a harmless glare. "Good for me, ha. She can be the most irritating, unpredictable, headstrong wench that I've ever met."

"Which is exactly why you've fallen in love with her."

Jacob sighed and leaned his head back against the window.

"Which is *exactly* why I've fallen in love with her." He closed his eyes and allowed a half-smile to settle upon his tired features. "I believe I fell in love with her the first time we met."

"Uh, I assume you mean *after* you discovered she was a woman, not before."

"Of course, you dolt. From the moment I 'discovered' her, she amused me, amazed me, and angered me over and over again until I didn't know if I wanted to make love to her or strangle her."

"Well," Malcom said lightly, "if it's any consolation, that's how they say you can recognize true love."

"Hmmf. I don't know about that. What I do know is that even when she made me so angry I couldn't think, even after our terrible row before I came to London, I still missed her. I wanted to be with her. Even if it meant more arguing, all I wanted to do was return to Fairdale and be with Jessica."

"Then why the hell *didn't* you?"

"Pride, I guess. I'll tell you Malcom, learning to swallow your pride just so you can spend time with a woman is not an easy task. But pride has a bitter taste when you're all alone and have no sweetness of love and desire to wash it down. Learn from my mistakes if you can. Don't let foolish pride keep you from whatever it is that you truly want."

Jacob sat looking down at his hands. Hands that less than twelve hours ago were caressing the woman who had become his wife, his love, his life.

"Dammit! I must find her!" Jacob slammed his fist down on the window sill and then got up and began pacing about the room.

"We'll find her. Just be glad that Jessica *does* have a great deal of common sense. It's evident in everything she says and does. Why, the only thing even remotely suggesting that she might be less than *perfect* is the fact that she has an illegitimate son."

Jacob looked up and smiled at Malcom. "That's where you're mistaken, where we were all mistaken."

"What do you mean?"

"She was—is—perfect. She doesn't have a son. Ossie isn't hers."

"But then whose son is he?"

"I don't know yet. She was going to tell me when we got home last night, but—"

"Then, then she is an innocent? And alone in this city."

Jacob paused, not really wanting to divulge his intimate moments with Jessica to Malcom. But hell, Malcom had been in the hall when they'd left the library.

"She was. Until last night. Well, not entirely—last night—oh, hell. I discovered her *lack of experience* on the afternoon I came to London. I wasn't exactly the epitome of a gentle lover opening virginal eyes to the wonders of passion. Admittedly, she caught me off guard. I'd thought—well, what I thought doesn't matter. Suffice it to say I accused her of some rather unsavory schemes. I was a complete idiot."

"And you hadn't spoken to her until last night?"

Jacob shook his head, almost laughing. "God, Malcom, I was actually a little afraid to see her. I wanted her so badly and yet I was so angry at her for having lied to me. And then angrier yet at myself, for I came to realized she had never actually said that Ossie was her son. I just assumed he was, and she never denied it. That conniving little wench had me at a complete loss."

"Then why were you so angry at the ball?"

"At first it was just bluster and bravado. I was buying myself some time to get used to her nearness lest I forget myself and become a cow-eyed school boy at her feet, forgiving everything without explanation."

Malcom laughed at the mental image that created. "You? I can hardly believe—"

"But then when I saw that lascivious Trent drooling over her and watched the Atterberrys drawing her into their web, well, in truth, I was furious."

"And so...to make up for that, you hauled her off to the

library and had a reconciliatory interlude."

"Something like that."

"And may I assume you were more...conscientious this time?"

Jacob nodded slowly, then ran his fingers through his hair again. "Conscientious as hell. But that was rendered void when we were accosted by Marga and her little announcement."

Now it was Malcom's turn to groan. "So in the wake of her first experience with true passion, she was dashed by the tidal wave of Marga's viciousness."

"Perhaps now you can understand why I'm so concerned for Jessica. Even if she is just venting her anger somewhere, she has to feel utterly betrayed and completely alone."

Malcom was silent for a few moments, letting the full weight of Jacob's words settle in. His mind began to wander backwards to that confrontation with Marga. And then he remembered his original question.

"By the way why did you say you're not too concerned with Marga's announcement? Don't you realize she'll make the most of this?"

"Ah, well, you see, I began thinking. Marga said she would present me with a child in six months, which would mean she's three months along in her pregnancy."

Malcom nodded. "Good, good. I'm glad to see your ability with numbers hasn't fled you along with your common sense."

"Very funny. What I'm getting at is that it has been over three months since Marga and I have actually slept together. Although I must admit there was very little *sleeping* taking place the last time we were together. But I was starting to feel that something was amiss. She was more demanding than usual and, I don't know. Just different. "

"Just over three months? Then what she says *could* be true. I don't see how you can remain so calm."

"I can because the next time I went to visit her, a couple of weeks later, we were unable to enjoy one another. She absolutely refused to let me be intimate with her whenever she had her—uh—woman's time. Any activity we had that particular weekend could have in no way gotten her pregnant. And I have not been with her since that time. I was growing tired of her and besides, my father was so very ill I rarely left the house for the past couple of months. There is no way the child she carries is mine."

"Well at least that's a bloody relief. But the important thing now is that we find Jessica. You can prove Marga is lying later. And, truly, her figure will tell in a couple of months if she's pregnant or not. Then you can have your revenge by just proving her a liar."

"Oh, I believe she is pregnant. But not three months along, and not with my child. Her comeuppance will be when the child's true father is revealed, whoever that poor bastard is." Jacob stood. "I believe I am going to pay another little visit to Lord and Lady Atterberry."

Michael had returned from Fairdale just before nightfall, but his sorry expression and news that Jessica was not at Fairdale were no longer needed. Jacob had somehow known that she wouldn't be there.

When Malcom arrived that evening, it was to find Jacob in the same condition, in the same room as he'd been that morning.

"Am I to assume we've heard nothing from your little duchess?"

"Mmm. Nothing. Michael returned empty handed but that was to be expected."

"Have you gone back to Lord Atterberry's?"

"Yes. Right after you left this morning."

"And?"

"And nothing. There were a handful of servants there who could, or would, tell me very little. They said only that Lady Atterberry had been extremely upset when she returned home last night, and they'd gone off to a country house early this morning."

"What country house? I thought they'd lost theirs with Hayden's last little run of bad luck at the tables?"

"They did. So they must be staying with friends somewhere. But no one at their house knew where they went. And no one admitted to seeing Jessica with them."

"So now what?" Malcom asked.

"Now, we just keep looking. She can't have just disappeared. Even if Jessica's met with foul play, somebody had to have seen something."

Chapter 27

While Jacob and Malcom spent the next four days looking for Jessica, Jessica was spending those days in fear for her life and her sanity.

DuPont had visited her daily, each time tormenting her with rude comments and suggestive remarks. And each time he visited he became a little bolder, letting his hands roam over her body as he wished.

After the second day, when Jessica had managed to connect her fist to his mask-covered cheek with a solid *thump*, he'd ordered Horace to tie her hands behind her back and keep her that way unless she was eating or seeing to her personal needs.

But now, on her fourth day of captivity, she sensed that something was happening. Horace was a little more skittish, nervously looking out the window every few minutes.

DuPont arrived, storming into the shack and ordering Horace to leave. Fear crept up Jessica's spine while watching DuPont's cat-like movements. He paced from corner to corner, as if the confines of the room were *his* boundaries, not hers.

Her nerves were strung taut. She could stand it no longer. "What! What is it?"

DuPont stopped and turned abruptly to face her. "What is what, *ma petite?*"

"What has you pacing around here like a caged animal? I'm the one who's caged. When are you going to let me go? Why haven't you demanded whatever it is you want for me?"

DuPont smiled and sat down, tugging gently on his black hat. For the moment he seemed to relax as considered her from behind his mask.

"I find, my sweet, that I enjoy having you here. Actually, not here. I would much prefer to have you somewhere clean and plush, somewhere with silk sheets and satin covered divans." He stopped and stared at her. "Somewhere with a bath. I will admit, you are becoming just a bit disheveled, my Jessica."

"I'm *not* your Jessica! And if you find my appearance so distasteful, why don't you just let me go?"

DuPont laughed. "I said disheveled, not distasteful. I simply meant, well never mind. For I think it is time to come to a decision about what I want for you."

Jessica glared coldly at him. "Well, it's about time. Please, just have this done with!"

DuPont stared at her as he leaned back in his chair and folded his arms across his chest. "Yes, it is about time. Time for me to decide if I should ask a full and hefty purse or if I should seek out my own pleasure with you and reduce the cost of return to your husband."

Jessica pressed back against the rough plank wall. Damn her stubborn tongue! Keep this up, she scolded herself, and you will find yourself flat on your back!

No sooner had she thought the words than DuPont was by her side. He placed a knee on either side of her and leaned close to her face.

With her hands tied behind her back and his knees on her tattered ball gown, Jessica could do nothing but turn her head from side to side to avoid his advance.

She half expected him to rip off his mask and kiss her, but no, he was too smart to reveal his features. Instead he stopped, just an inch from her.

This is it, she thought. *He is going to rape me.*

Oh, Jacob, please find me! Rescue me! Jessica closed her eyes and

243

let Jacob's face float into her vision. *I'm so sorry,* she cried silently, *so very sorry. If we could but have another chance I would never doubt you again. I don't care about Marga, I don't care about societal rules; I care about you! I love you! Please!*

She turned her prayers heavenward. Oh, God! Help me! As much as I want Jacob, I could never face him or let him touch me again if this beast violates me!

In the midst of her prayers, Jessica felt DuPont's hands on her breasts, slowly squeezing them and then pushing them up and out of the confines of her dress.

Jessica bit her lip to keep from crying out, but a little whimper escaped her. He toyed with her for a moment, and just when she was certain he was about to tear away the front of her bodice, he stood and stepped back several steps.

When she dared to open her eyes, she found him staring down at her from behind those narrow slits in his mask. And then, to her astonishment, he began laughing.

"You!" he said with an arrogant tone, "You are just as she was, your dead mother-in-law. She whimpered so prettily, pretending not to enjoy what I did to her at first, when in truth the old whore wanted as much as I could give her. She wanted it all, Anastasia did. Begged for it.

But I lost my taste for her. I wonder how long it will take me to lose my taste for you? How long until you will be groveling at my feet for just one more poke between the sheets, hmm?"

"If that's what she was like, then I'm not anything like her, for I truly do detest your very existence! You are naught but a rutting pig, a blight to all men good and decent!" Jessica said through clenched teeth, trying to keep a shred of dignity in the face of her frontal exposure.

"Oh, good and decent men like your husband, I suppose?"

"Yes! Like my husband!"

"He excites you, eh? This good and decent man of yours? If this feverish state is the result of mere thoughts of him, then I insist you think on him often. You are such a delicious sight, so feverish in your intensity. My loins warm just at the sight of you."

DuPont stepped closer until the rounded fullness of his crotch was but a foot from her face. "I assure you it won't be long until you think no more of him but only of me and the pleasures *I* can bring you."

He leaned down, his hot breath coming through the slit where his mouth was, burning across her bare breasts. "Ah, so excited you are, and such a tease! See? You *are* like her, like Anastasia. You sit there and deny your craving, yet you bounce your tantalizing breasts around with each heaving breath you take, seducing my eyes with their lovely, firm roundness. Why, they are begging me to reach out, to take, to fondle, to suckle until you cry out, 'more, Jean Luc, more!' And of course I shall indulge you, for a time."

He straightened and took several steps back.

Jessica struggled with the ties at her wrists, a primal scream poised in her throat, nearly choking her. But her wrists were tied tight, and she realized by the sound of his laughter that she was in fact indulging his sick visual pleasures by moving around so much.

"I do so enjoy you."

She would not cry. She would not! Burying her humiliation deep inside her, she challenged him. "Do you? Is this how you spend your time now, DuPont? You were correct when you assumed I'd heard of you. But I scarcely recognize you as the man called Jean Luc DuPont. I'd heard you were a quintessential spy, a lethal weapon for the French government."

Tension filled the room as he closed the distance between them once again. But Jessica was beyond caring for her own well-being by now. Degredation had in fact given her strength.

"And you would think different of me now? I assure you, I am still quite lethal," he said in a deep, growling voice.

"Oh, really?" She went on, heedless of the danger she was getting herself into. "Is that why you now spend your time as a voyeuristic fiend? Watching husbands and wives as they make love, kidnaping women and holding them captive until their husbands pay you off? Ha! That's some ending for the career of someone so lethal."

She could see his fists clenching and unclenching at his sides. A glimmer of worry eased its way into her mind. Had she pushed this mad man too far at last?

"My career is not at an end, I assure you!" He took a step forward, then halted and crossed one arm over his chest. With the other he wagged a finger at Jessica, shaking his head at the same time. "Ah, but you are ever so clever, *ma petite*. You almost made me angry. But, I am past that. Quite the opposite of what was your assumed intention, I find you even more captivating now. You've just caused me to drastically reconsider my next move. I may keep you with me for a bit longer after all. Horace!"

The door to the cottage flew open as Horace rushed inside. He stopped and stared, open-mouthed, at the picture Jessica presented: Arms tied behind her back, dress front pulled down, breasts exposed to all.

Her humiliation hit her full-force again at Horace's shocked expression. Turning her face away, she squeezed her eyes closed. This time she was helpless to stop the tears from falling.

"See to her," DuPont ordered as he strode out the door.

When the door slammed shut, Horace walked quickly to Jessica and untied the ropes at her wrists.

She righted the bodice of her gown and sat with her arms folded across her breasts, trying to erase the memory of DuPont's hands on them.

After a moment, she glanced up at Horace who was standing over her, wringing his hat in his hands and wearing a pitying look. "Are, are ye all right, m'lady?" he asked meekly.

The concern on the old gentleman's face was a comforting salve to her injured pride.

"I am," she sniffed. "But I don't know how much more of this I can take."

"W-would ye like some water er somethin'?"

Jessica managed a small laugh. "I believe I could use a dram of your whiskey."

When Horace jumped to retrieve it for her she stopped him. "No, no. I was only joking. I'll be fine. I think I'll just sleep for a while."

Truly, sleep was the furthest thing from her mind. But lying on the lumpy mattress with her face turned to the wall was a far cry better than trying to make small talk with Horace's sympathetic face staring down at her.

Jessica rubbed her chafed wrists, wincing at their tenderness. A flame of hope sparked within her when she realized that her wrists were still untied. For a moment she entertained the thought of escape.

But just as quickly, that hope was extinguished.

She had no idea where she was. Her clothes were in rags, poor protection from the wind she heard howling through the cracks in the walls. And still the biggest obstacle of all: Somewhere out there was the third man who had aided DuPont in her abduction.

Though she had yet to see him again, Horace had referred to him on occasion.

Horace. If she could just win him to her side!

With his help, she could escape.

Without it, she was doomed.

Somehow, she would have to find a way....

At last the strain of her confrontation with DuPont overtook her. Jessica drifted off into a light sleep, occasionally hearing Horace moving about the room from what seemed like a great distance.

Chapter 28

The door to the shack crashed open, bringing Jessica quickly out of her tormented dreams.

"What is it, Master? Didn' 'spect t' see ye 'ere agin t'night." Horace asked, clearly terrified.

DuPont slammed the door shut behind him and stalked over to Jessica, noticing her unbound hands. Without looking at Horace he said. "Apparently not. I see you've decided to let our little captive remain free. I thought you had better judgment than that, Horace."

From the corner of her eye, Jessica saw Horace nearly wilt with fear. "You said I could remain untied while I ate," she said, trying to relieve Horace of any blame. "I just finished dining on that stale bread that isn't fit for rats. I believe your faithful servant was about to bind my hands again."

DuPont glanced at Horace who was indeed holding the ropes in his hands, having grabbed them just as DuPont entered the room.

"I see." DuPont turned his stare back to Jessica.

Every muscle in his body seemed to be rigid, Jessica noted. Something had made him furious. "Well, what do you want from me now? More sick games? Are you—"

"Silence!" he shouted. He muttered a few words in French that she couldn't understand, but from the tone of his voice she felt sure that they were angry expletives.

"I have decided that I want nothing from you!"

Hope soared within her. He was going to set her free!

"Then I can go? Now?"

He laughed cruelly. "Go? Now? I think not."

"But you said you wanted nothing from me!"

"And I don't. I have decided that what I witnessed in that library must have been a good bit of acting on your husband's part. If he was that disappointed in your skills at lovemaking, then why should I bother?"

"Disappointed? What—what are you talking about?" she asked. Truthfully she was glad that he apparently no longer desired her, but now she was confused.

"I'm talking about your husband, the great Duke of Fairdale, Jacob Harwood Callaway."

"I'm well aware of who my husband is, you fool!" She ignored the dangerous way his hands began clenching at his sides. "Have you finally decided to go to him for payment? I certainly hope so, for I have no doubt that he will not only pay you but will see to your demise posthaste upon my return!"

DuPont folded his arms across his chest, a smug air settling across him.

"Oh, you have no doubts, do you? Well perhaps you'd better acquire some doubts, *cherie*, for I sent word to your husband as I said I would."

For some unexplainable reason, Jessica's heart filled with dread. DuPont was too cocky, too angry, too vengeful to have received good news.

She ignored her racing heart and asked confidently, "Then when will I be released? And where?"

"Released? No, no *ma petite*, you shall not be released. Not yet. Apparently, I must find another buyer for your luscious goods. Your husband won't pay."

What was this lunatic saying? "You've lost your mind, DuPont."

"No, Duchess, you've lost yours if you think that brief

encounter in the library would secure that bore of a duke to your side. You see, he doesn't want you."

"He—he what?"

"He doesn't want you."

"You lie! You're playing one of your sick, perverse games again."

DuPont sighed dramatically. "Oh, if only that were true. For a brief moment I thought perhaps you would be of no use to me whatsoever." He tapped a finger to his mask-covered temple. "But alas, clever man that I am, I have come up with another idea."

Jessica couldn't let go of DuPont's shocking words. "Jacob would never do this to me! I demand that you let me see him!"

"You demand? You have no grounds to demand anything. Besides, even if I were to agree to something so ridiculous, it would be impossible just now. You see, when my messenger arrived at the Callaway townhouse, they were just making ready to leave. I'm not sure where they were going, but apparently they were planning to be gone for quite some time, judging from all the trunks and valises that were piled in the entry."

"They? Who—"

"Oh, didn't I mention that? My messenger described a stunning, dark-haired woman who met him at the Duke's door. She said simply that they would be out of London until after the baby was born. I can only assume the woman was his long-time mistress. Unless you know of another dark-haired beauty who might be nurturing his seed?"

Jessica sat back, a tightness gripping her chest so hard that she could scarcely breathe.

This couldn't be true!

He wouldn't abandon her like this!

Oh, God, no! Please! Even if he discarded her as a wife, surely he wouldn't leave to her the likes of DuPont?

Jacob hated DuPont! She seized onto that thought.

"He wouldn't do this! But Jacob despises you! You killed his mother!"

"And he despised *her*. Perhaps he deemed that a favor."

"You killed his brother too! And Jacob loved his brother!"

"His brother? Oh, yes, so I did. But you see, I was saving my identity for a surprise for your wretched husband. He doesn't know that it is me, Jean Luc DuPont, who has his wife. So that was that."

"Well then tell him! Send your bloody messenger back or go and see him yourself. Surely you're not going to take Marga's word that Jacob won't pay my ransom. You could be missing out on a great deal of money."

"He went twice. The second time, the woman gave him a note in Callaway's own handwriting stating just what she had said earlier. And that he wouldn't pay a half-pence in ransom to get you back. He said he'd had his fun and was tired of you."

"I don't believe you! Let me see the note! Tell him who you are!"

DuPont exhaled as if conversation was irritating him. "Even if I wanted to tell him, which I don't, it would be too late. He's gone with that other woman to a destination unknown! As for the note, I fear I was a trifle upset after reading it and threw it into the fire. It would appear we are stuck with each other's company—for now!"

His voice rose once again as he glared at her from behind his mask. He took a step forward and pinched Jessica's chin between his thumb and forefinger. "And so once again your husband has—albeit unknowingly—beat me at my own game. Now, thanks to his blatant disregard, I'm stuck with an unwanted piece of baggage. You! I had such high hopes of returning you, spoiled and used and perhaps carrying my own seed to grow in your belly, with a hefty purse in return for my *gentle* care of you. Ha! What a coup that would have been! The blessed Duke of Fairdale, raising my child!"

He released her chin and shoved her back against the wall

251

behind the bed. "If my secondary plan doesn't work I shall have no choice but to kill you. Callaway likely will thank me. After all, with you out of the way, he could truly lay claim to his love child."

Jessica slumped over on the bed. She was sinking rapidly into shock. Whether it was from Jacob's callous disregard of her or DuPont's death threats, she wasn't sure. All she wanted was to slip in to blissful unconsciousness. And just now, that relief didn't seem too far away.

Her mind drifted as her eyes closed.

How could she have been so wrong about Jacob? Even at his worst temper, Jessica found it hard to believe that Jacob would abandon her like this. But if any of what DuPont said was true, then indeed he had.

Lord, if this was her true fate, then she hoped DuPont would kill her. She felt certain that sooner or later he would overcome his current apathy towards her and set upon her like the hungry animal he'd been those first few days of her captivity, letting his depraved sense of lust guide him to do unimaginable things.

Gratefully she surrendered to the warm embrace of unconsciousness, slipping further into the shock that had assaulted her mind, her body, her hope.

When she woke again several hours later it was to hear DuPont yelling for Horace once again. Horace jumped to his feet and ran outside, leaving Jessica alone for a moment.

But her solitude was short-lived. Slamming back against the wall, the door burst open. From somewhere in her groggy mind she wondered why he always had to slam into the room with such drama. Before she could grasp her thoughts fully, DuPont strode to the bed and picked her up by the shoulders.

"It would seem that you are not without some importance after all. Just knowing that has brought my interest back, with increased intensity."

Blood rushed to her cheeks as she curled her feet beneath her and rose on her knees, ignoring DuPont's insinuations. "Jacob!" she whispered. Confidence in herself and in Jacob were returning with lightening speed. "He agreed to—"

"No, not your wretched husband, you daft wench," he growled with annoyance, sending her faith spiraling down once again. "Your grandparents. Lord and Lady Atterberry. My messenger went to them, and they were more than eager to accommodate my wishes, and spend the tidy sum to have you returned to them. They, however, don't care what shape you're returned in just so long as you *are* returned."

The blow that Jacob still didn't want her made every fiber of her being ache, but with grateful clarity she realized that with or without Jacob she was going to be rescued. Her grandparents, people Jacob had done nothing but castigate, were coming to her aid and after only one meeting with her.

In that brief moment of realization, all her pain at Jacob's rejection turned to anger. A red haze settled before her eyes and she was gripped for the moment by the need for revenge.

DuPont chuckled as he followed her thoughts via the changing expressions on her face. Suppressing her anger for now, she focused on the situation at hand. Calmness and clarity were critical in dealing with DuPont to ensure her release without damage to her person.

"When shall I be released?"

"Soon.."

"The sooner the better, wouldn't you say? Since you have lost all desire for me," she suggested quietly.

"Oh, not all desire. And that was before I realized how important you were—to someone. No, the more I think on it, the more I believe that your husband's flagrant disregard for you and your bedroom activities must be based on the facts that he not only has a lovely and longstanding mistress by his side, but also that he has no true appreciation for the art of love."

DuPont stepped closer again. "I don't know what I was thinking to base the denial of my own carnal pleasures on a few words from a man that I consider to be a complete idiot. What I saw through the window that night was interesting to say the least. I believe under my dedicated tutelage you have a good chance to become an ardent lover."

Jessica's stomach turned. So they were back to that again. Just as she was about to protest his intentions, a shot rang out from in front of the building.

Jessica jumped and got to her feet, but DuPont pushed her back on the bed. "Stay there!"

In a flash he was out the door slamming it behind him.

Jessica ran to the small window, peering out into the darkness. She could hear voices; shouts coming from behind the makeshift barn. Another shot rang out.

Then a figure appeared, running towards the shack. From the manner of his uneven gait she knew it was Horace.

Heart racing, she pulled the door open and was nearly knocked over by the little man as he hurried inside and closed the door behind him.

"Horace! What is it?" Firmly she tamped down the brief thought that Jacob had rescued her after all.

No. He was not coming. Ever.

"Horace!" she shouted again when the old man just stared back and forth between her and the closed door.

"Get back from the door, m'lady, please! E's comin'!"

Jessica took several steps back toward the bed. "What's happening? Who's coming?"

Before Horace could say another word the door flew open, but it was not DuPont.

"Viscount Trent!" Jessica screamed in her surprise. The viscount glanced at her for a moment, but caught Horace's movement from the corner of his eye.

Without pause, he aimed his pistol at Horace and pulled the trigger.

"No!" Jessica screamed as the gun fired. "No! He was—"

"Your Grace, we have no time to waste!" Viscount Trent said quickly. "We must go!"

"You will not!"

Trent and Jessica both looked toward the door as the darkly robed figure of DuPont closed down upon them. He was holding his shoulder, blood oozing between his fingers.

"Leave her!" DuPont shouted in a strained tone, his voice heavy with pain.

DuPont leapt across the short distance between them and hit Viscount Trent with full force, knocking him to the dirt floor and sending Jessica stumbling back to the bed. Flying from the viscount's hand, the pistol landed somewhere behind the crates which were stacked in the corner.

The two men rolled about, fighting for the advantage. DuPont was on top, then Trent, then DuPont again. At last Trent was able to strike a blow to DuPont's chin, knocking him senseless for just a moment.

"Run, Jessica!" Viscount Trent ordered as he rose to his feet. But before he could take a step or Jessica could move, DuPont had cleared his head and made another grab for Trent's feet.

Again the viscount sprawled to the floor but not before he was able to produce a dagger from a sheath tied at his waist.

They rolled on the floor while Jessica watched in horror. Each took a turn in controlling the other, then back again.

DuPont seized the viscount's wrist and squeezed until the knife began to wobble in his hand. With a sideways thrust, DuPont slammed Trent's hand against one of the rickety chairs, splintering the chair and sending the knife flying from his hand.

Again they rolled, but this time DuPont landed a solid blow to Trent's gut, sending the wind rushing from him. He pounced on Trent once again, wrapping his fingers around the viscount's throat and squeezing with determined strength.

Trent clawed at DuPont's fingers, arching his back in an attempt to throw the mad man's balance off. But to no avail. DuPont seemed possessed, intent only on strangling the life from Viscount Trent.

The sound of Trent's ragged choking sent Jessica into action. Without another moment's hesitation, Jessica ran across the room, jumping over the struggling pair. She grabbed the knife with both hands and without pausing for thought, plunged the dagger into DuPont's back.

On impulse, without completely realizing what she was doing, she pulled the knife out and stabbed him again, this time leaving the dagger in the center of his back.

The first assault had brought DuPont's hands away from Viscount Trent's throat in shock and disbelief. The second made him fall back on his seat, trying in desperation to grasp the knife in his back.

Jessica covered her mouth with her bloodstained hands and turned away, retching uncontrollably in the corner of the shack. She wondered briefly if she would ever forget the sound created by that knife slicing into her tormentor's back, not once, but twice.

When she was able to turn around, she saw that Viscount Trent had risen to his knees and shoved a now dead DuPont over on his side. A look of astonishment crossed the viscount's features.

With no gentleness he stood and retrieved his ivory handled dagger from the man's back then with his foot he kicked DuPont to his back.

Viscount Trent looked at Jessica. "You saved my life, Your Grace. I am forever at your service."

Jessica stood, trembling violently and watched as the viscount bent and pulled DuPont's mask from his face. Her eyes widened in surprise, for he was nothing like she had pictured him.

Limp brown hair hung down past his shoulders and across his forehead, with a thinning spot on top of his head. His eyes, which were staring lifelessly at the ceiling, had deep lines etched at the corners and dark circles beneath them.

A long scar ran from his temple to the corner of his mouth, the tightness of it making it appear that he was smiling cynically even now.

This? This was the man that Anastasia Callaway had found so irresistible that she'd endangered her own son for him?

Indeed the rumors that Anastasia had become desperate for lovers in her last years must have been true.

Viscount Trent's voice invaded her perusal of her captor.

"Your Grace, Jessica. Come, let us get ourselves away from this place," he said with urgency. "We don't know how many others may be lurking in the shadows outside." He reached for her hand.

Jessica took his hand and stepped over DuPont's prone body, still shaking uncontrollably. Her eyes were still fixed on the man's haggard features. She couldn't stop looking at him, and so squeezed her eyes shut and began to follow Viscount Trent blindly.

Her foot brushed something. Looking down, she sucked in her breath. "Horace!" Jessica dropped to her knees, pulling her hand from Viscount Trent's. "You tried to warn me, tried to tell me something. What? What was it?"

"Jessica! We must go! He's dead. I'm sorry about the old man, but if you waste any more time all our efforts might be for naught!"

She stood wearily and choked on a last shuddering sob before stepping over Horace and running along behind Viscount Trent into the cold, crisp air of the moonlit night.

Chapter 29

Jessica could not recall how she came to be on Viscount Trent's horse or how long they'd been riding.

Wrapped inside his fur-lined cape, she suddenly realized she was being held tightly against his body. When her senses became her own again, she shifted slowly, trying to maintain her balance against the horse's smooth canter.

Viscount Trent looked down at her and smiled. "Welcome back."

"Did I—was I asleep?"

"No. But not quite awake either. I believe you are suffering from shock. But worry no more. You are quite safe now. Do you remember all that happened?"

Jessica was silent for a moment as the memories came rushing back to her.

Horace...dead.

DuPont...dead.

Jacob...as far as her life was now concerned, he too was dead.

She buried her face against Viscount Trent's shoulder as the cruel words DuPont had thrown at her echoed through her thoughts.

Giving way to wracking sobs, she surrendered to the hurt and humiliation she'd suffered this past week.

The viscount brought the horse down to a walk and then finally reined him toward a small group of trees.

"Ssh. Poor Jessica. You've been through so much! But you needn't worry anymore. I'll never let anything happen to you again."

Jessica sniffed and looked up at the man who was holding her so close. Despite the fact that he had just saved her from a fate unknown, she felt uncomfortable being held, cuddled, by this man she hardly knew.

"Viscount Trent, I—"

"Please, call me Percival, or Percy. I believe we've been through enough this evening to warrant a first name basis. Hmm? You saved my life and I saved yours. We're even. Let us call ourselves friends rather than just acquaintances."

Unease still filled her stomach, but she attributed it to the horrors she had suffered this night. He was right, of course. They had been through a great deal together.

Sitting up straighter she looked around the country side. "Where are we? How long have we been riding?"

"We're still several miles out of London. Don't you remember leaving that awful place?"

"Truthfully, no. I remember leaving poor Horace on the floor and following you out the door. After that I have no recollection until just minutes ago."

Percival looked at her and judged her to be telling the truth. "Tsk, tsk. You poor dear. Well, we've been riding for almost an hour, and at a pretty good pace."

"An hour? Dear God, where were we?"

"On the outskirts of hell, I believe. I was beginning to wonder where DuPont's messenger was leading me when he just kept riding and riding." Viscount Trent pulled his horse to a stop.

"DuPont's messenger? But how—"

"I'll explain everything," Percival said as he slid from the saddle and gently brought Jessica down with him.

Again she felt that he held her a little too close and a little longer than necessary. Guilt made her shrug the feelings off.

After all, Viscount Trent—Percy—had risked his own life to save her. Attributing her feelings to her experiences with DuPont and her raw nerves, Jessica tried to force herself to relax.

Percival led her to a fallen log beneath the shelter of another tree, leaving his horse to graze on tender grass nearby.

"In answer to your questions, I was at Lord and Lady Atterberry's when DuPont's messenger arrived. He'd asked to speak with them privately, so I waited in the library. When I heard Lady Atterberry shriek and Lord Atterberry curse, I hurried to see what had happened."

Percival settled his cape more securely around Jessica's shoulders. "When I reached your grandparents, they were pale and shaken, but I heard them agreeing to do whatever the man said, pay whatever price necessary. The messenger left and Lord Atterberry apprised me of the situation. I ran to my horse and discreetly followed DuPont's man back to that shack where you were being held."

"But I didn't see the messenger when you were fighting. Surely he would have come to DuPont's aid."

"No. That first shot that sounded outside was the one that took his life. The second one was aimed for DuPont. I thought I'd killed him, but apparently I only wounded him. I was ever so surprised to see him in the doorway."

Jessica shuddered at the memory of DuPont's image appearing at the door. "I keep expecting him to appear here."

"Not possible. Do you remember killing him?"

Jessica closed her eyes and nodded slowly. "Yes," she whispered. "I do."

"You were so brave, dear Jessica. So fearless."

Jessica snorted softly. "Fearless. Ha! I was scared to death."

"But what's important is that you didn't let it get the best of you. Are you ready to make the rest of the journey or do you need to rest a while longer?"

"No. I'm fine. But where are you taking me?"

"To Lord and Lady Atterberry's, of course. I do hope they'll forgive my impulsiveness in going after those scoundrels. When I heard you were in danger I acted on whim."

Jessica smiled weakly and took his extended hand. "I—I'm glad you did. If I haven't told you already, thank you."

Percy mounted his horse and reached down for Jessica.

She paused for a moment looking up into his face, searching for comfort and honesty. A good dose of both was needed for her peace of mind just now. "I can ride behind you, if that will make it easier. I—"

"Absolutely not. My dear, with all you've been through, it's entirely possible that you could faint again. And while living with those cretons for the past week may not have killed you, falling from this horse at a full gallop just might."

Swallowing any further protests, she nodded silently and let him help her up to sit in front of him again. His arm came around her waist and pulled her tightly against his body.

She scooted forward a few inches in the saddle, determined to stay fully awake and rigidly upright.

As the horse moved off, once again settling in to a smooth but fast gallop, Jessica tried to make sense of what DuPont had told her earlier. Despite the pain that tore through her heart, she still found it hard to believe that she could have been so wrong about Jacob.

Jacob was her husband. He was legally responsible for her. He had loved her! He had! How could he do this to her?

True, he'd never once *said* he'd loved her. But the way he kissed her, tenderly held her, the way he'd introduced her to the magic of making love...surely he couldn't have feigned that!

Maybe DuPont was lying! Maybe Jacob hadn't even been contacted!

Just as the joy of that hope was taking hold, reality swiftly stepped in to destroy it. Of course DuPont was telling the truth. How else would the messenger have known what Marga looked like? And above all, what would DuPont have to gain from such a tale? He would never be able to get as much money from her grandparents as he would from Jacob. They simply weren't as wealthy.

Anger crept back into her body like a slow heat. The warmer she got, the less her battered pride hurt.

Up ahead she was able to see several rows of lights.

"Is that London?"

"Yes. We'll be safe and secure at your grandparent's home in no time. They live just a few streets to the east of King Street, on Hampton Row."

King Street. Jacob's townhouse.

As they trotted through the city streets, there was very little activity due to the lateness of the hour. A few people scurried along the shadows, and from somewhere in the upper floors of a large hotel a woman's inebriated giggle rang through an open window and into the still night air.

Knots began to form in Jessica's stomach as they turned onto King Street. Closer and closer they came to Jacob's townhouse. With all her might she tried not to look at the front of that house where she'd spent so few hours.

Yet against her will her eyes became riveted on the front of the dwelling. She stared at the front door, and then slowly her eyes followed the huge white columns that stood at either side of the entry.

She hadn't expected to see any signs of life inside, for DuPont had told her that Jacob and his mistress had left town earlier that afternoon.

Yet when her eyes continued to travel upward, she saw a light in one of the upstairs bedrooms; in fact the glow of the lamp was coming from the bedroom that she had occupied!

A shadow moved in front of the window just then. It was distorted by the lamplight coming from behind, but obviously someone was there.

Jacob was there. It had to be him. And if he had that whore installed in *her* room, *ooh!* It would serve Jacob right if she barged in on them right now!

"Stop, Percival. There's someone at Jacob's townhouse, in *my* bedroom! I'll tell him just what I think of him and his whore! I—"

Percival glanced up at the top story window. Instead of coming to a stop, he kicked his horse into a canter.

"Stop! What are you doing? I must see him!"

Jessica felt Percival tighten his grip around her waist as they dodged around a late night hansom cab carrying two startled occupants.

"My dear, this is for your own good!" he said above the clamor.

Clattering hooves echoed through the night as they made their rapid departure from Jacob's house. Soon, they took a sharp turn to the left. Jessica was able to catch a glance at the street sign indicating they were now on Hampton Row.

"Why didn't you stop?" she yelled, turning to stare at Percival with narrowed eyes as he slowed his horse once again.

"As I said, it was for your own good!" he shouted back with an impatient tone.

All of the anger she'd built up during the past few days exploded from her lips in something near to a shriek. "My own good! I *owe* it to that beast to let him know what I think of him and his thoughtless dismissal! That bastard had no right to do what he did! Why didn't you let me confront him? And who are *you* to say what is best for me?"

Percival was silent for a few moments. Jessica saw his eyes wander to her heaving bosom which was all but exposed by her tattered ball gown. Quickly she grabbed the neck of the cape and pulled it close, fighting the familiar feeling of revulsion she'd known when DuPont had all but wrecked her bodice.

At last he brought his horse to a stop. In a very calm voice he said, "Who am I to say what's best for you? I am the man who saved you from death or a fate far worse with that maniac. I'm not denying that you deserve the right to confront that wretch Callaway, but if you could see yourself as I see you right now you would understand my meaning."

His eyes scanned her again, this time without appreciation. "Your gown is stained and in shreds, your hair is matted and dirty. You smell like an old, moldy blanket, and your face is bruised and smudged with dried mud. On top of all that, the hate-induced delirium in your eyes would give anyone who saw you the opinion that you are quite mad and should most definitely be locked away in an asylum!

"Now, my dear Jessica, if that bastard you have the misfortune to call your husband had half a wit about him, which I sometimes doubt, he could call out the authorities and have them haul you away, claiming that you've gone insane. No one would doubt the Duke of Fairdale's word. In fact, one look at you just now would confirm it.

"What a tidy way to rid himself of you—forever. Other than me and your grandparents, who as I'm sure you know are not in the best standing with Callaway, you would have no one to testify for you. And as much as it galls me to admit it, we are no match for his money and power. And beyond your own well-being, if he has you put away, who would take care of that boy of yours? You have a choice to make: Trust me to keep you safe, or trust the man who has already set you aside and endangered your life."

She started to protest. Jacob wouldn't do that to her; have her committed to an asylum? No!

Her shoulders slouched and she shook her head slowly. Of course until a few hours ago, she hadn't believed he would hand her over to the likes of DuPont either. As she felt the fight go out of her, she glanced back into Percival's eyes and a question struck her.

"How do you know about Ossie? About—my boy?"

Viscount Trent bent his head towards her. "My dear, when something as newsworthy as a new duchess with an illegitimate child hits the town, it doesn't take long for the word to circulate. Add to that the announcement that the duke had fathered his own bastard and well, my lovely, try as you might, the true story may never be told. The embellished versions are far more interesting."

Jessica sighed. "I am so weary."

"Jessica."

She turned in the saddle once again.

"Illegitimate child or not, you have found a place in my heart. Nothing matters to me but your safety and happiness. I shall do all I can as your friend and champion to see that you are protected; from everyone."

Oh, how could she have said those things to him? He *did* rescue her; he *was* taking her to a safe haven.

Mist filled her eyes and Percival's face wavered before her. "I'm so sorry," she whispered. "You're right. About everything. Please forgive the cruel things I said."

Percival took her chin gently in his hand. "Ssh! There's nothing to forgive. You are so overwhelmed and distraught. Think nothing of it."

Before Jessica could move away, he leaned forward and brushed a kiss across her trembling lips. A firm rebuke worked its way to her mouth, but she bit her lip to stop it from coming out.

It was just a friendly kiss, to comfort and console her.

Jessica knew she should be so very grateful to him. She should not bristle from one little kiss, no matter how inappropriate.

A friendly kiss. Comfort and consolation.

She kept repeating those words over and over in her mind as Percival held her tightly pressed to his chest for the remainder of the short ride to Lord Atterberry's house.

Chapter 30

Jessica awoke the next morning to a bird's song, floating in on a soft spring breeze through an open window.

She sat up with a start, clutching the silk bed sheet to her breast. Nothing seemed familiar in this sparse but delicately appointed room.

Think! Think! You are—

A knock on the door interrupted her thoughts.

"My dear, are you awake?"

"Lady Atterberry! Oh, thank heavens! I was beginning to think last night's rescue and all this—this loveliness," she waved her arms around the room, "were part of a dream."

Lady Atterberry laughed. "No, no. I assure you we are quite real." She approached the bed and sat down next to Jessica's curled up feet. A smile turned up the corners of Lady Atterberry's mouth, but it didn't reach her slate-blue eyes. "Darling, I insist you call me 'grandmother'. If you feel up to it, we really should get you a bath and wash your hair." Lady Atterberry barely refrained from sniffing.

Self consciously, Jessica reached up to her matted hair. "Oh, yes. Please! We didn't do that last night, did we?"

"No. After you arrived, your grandfather practically poured two hefty brandies down you. He believes a good brandy will cure anything," Lady Atterberry said with a wink. "I'll admit it did calm you down considerably, but it also put you to sleep just after you recounted your terrifying experiences. Percival carried you up here and saw you settled in the bed."

"He—he—" Jessica looked down and blushed profusely. She wore only her chemise. "But—"

"Please, don't fret, my sweet. Don't you remember any of it?"

At Jessica's blank look, Lady Atterberry continued. "I enlisted Percival's help, you see. We'd given all the servants the evening off in the hopes that you would be returned last night. We had no idea what condition you'd be in, so we thought it best to have as few people here as possible. Your grandfather was unable to carry you up the stairs, so Percival offered to do it for him."

Jessica sat in silence, trying not to recall the uneasy feelings that had filled her when Percival had lightly kissed her the previous night.

"Now, don't you worry, Jessica. Lord Trent has seen many a young lady, in various states of dishabille, I daresay. It didn't bother him in the least. He's been known as quite a lady's man, but of late he's begun to consider settling down."

"It was my own modesty I was concerned about," Jessica said, mildly surprised that her grandmother seemed so nonchalant about the matter.

"Oh, well, I apologize for that. When he carried you up here I went to get some biscuits and tea for Percival. The poor dear had had quite a night! By the time I arrived in your room he had made you comfortable and was tucking the sheets around you. Really, darling. There's nothing to be ashamed of. He did it all purely out of concern for your well-being. By the way, I'm afraid your gown was a total loss."

Jessica buried her embarrassment and wished dearly that she could feel as nonchalant about Percival attending to her undressing as her grandmother did.

"I was certain that the gown was ruined. But what shall I wear? All of my clothes are at my—at Jacob's home."

Lady Atterberry rose from the bed. "Once again, Viscount Trent has come to the rescue! Apparently he has a few day gowns left from one of his most recent—uh—lady friends. He felt certain they would fit you perfectly."

Another knock sounded at the door.

If that was Percival—

Instead, a maid entered the room bearing soft, white towels and what appeared to be several scented soaps. She was followed by several young boys carrying steaming water.

"Bring the large copper bath from my rooms," Lady Atterberry directed the boys. "Then fill the tub and leave my granddaughter to her leisure."

"Will you need assistance with your bath, m'lady?" the young girl asked.

"My granddaughter is a duchess! You will refer to her properly."

The little maid bobbed a curtsy. "I beg your pardon, Your Grace. I was unaware."

Jessica smiled at the girl. "That's quite all right. I tend to forget that fact myself now and again." Would that I had never become a duchess, she thought silently. "I won't require any help. Thank you."

The maid oversaw the filling of the tub and then scurried the boys from the room.

Lady Atterberry moved to the door. "If you need anything my dear, please just ask. Milly will be at the end of the hall."

"I'm sure I'll be fine. But what shall I wear until Viscount Trent arrives with the dresses?"

"Oh, I'm certain he'll be here before you're finished bathing. He was so very concerned. I believe he's quite taken with you, my dear."

And you let him undress me? Jessica wondered silently.

"I'll bring the garments up as soon as he arrives. Just relax here until I return."

As if I could relax, Jessica thought glumly.

But to the contrary, as she slipped into the tub of gardenia scented water, a sense of relief washed over her.

Don't think, she told herself. Just enjoy.

She managed to do that for a little while. But soon, unbidden thoughts crept into her mind.

Whatever would she do now? Now that Jacob had obviously abandoned her.

Her grandparents had been so very kind, and Viscount Trent as well. She knew she could never fully repay them for their kindness and bravery.

Opening her eyes, she watched the steam curl up from the large tub. It rose and rose until it reached the ceiling and spread out.

That's what I must do! she decided. Rise above this.

Thoughts began to rush at her as soon as she decided to take affirmative action.

I don't need Jacob! I don't have to rely on him for shelter or food or clothing! I certainly don't want his argumentative company!

What am I so worried about?

I have my cottage, I have Ossie, I have my *life*! That's more than I was certain of just twenty-four hours ago, she thought with determination.

And as for her promise to Austen, well, obviously he didn't know his son all that well, either. Certainly he would forgive her for removing Ossie from Jacob's distorted influence.

Just what, Jessica wondered, had Jacob intended to do with Ossie now that he'd dismissed her? She was certain he wouldn't harm the boy; even after all Jacob had done to her, she couldn't imagine him being so cruel to Ossie as to turn him out. Especially if he ever took the time to read his father's journals and discovered Ossie's true parentage.

Jessica lifted her chin further out of the water. I have everything I need! I don't need this fancy lifestyle in big, cavernous mansions. I don't need frilly dresses and exotic foods.

I don't need the passion that only Jacob can arouse in me.

Now where did that thought come from?

She slumped a little further into the tub again.

I can't let him win. I will fight; not for money or material items, but for my pride.

True to his word, Viscount Trent delivered half a dozen gowns before Jessica had even finished her bath.

Relief swam over Jessica when Milly brought the gowns up rather than Percival himself.

She tried on three of them before finding one that was suitable for daytime.

"Good heavens," Jessica said to Milly. "Lady Atterberry had said these would be day gowns. I feel half naked in these dresses!"

Milly giggled behind her hand.

Jessica met the maid's eyes in the mirror and smiled. "What do you find so amusing, Milly?"

"I was just thinking, Your Grace, that more 'n likely that was the intent when the gowns were made. T' be half naked, I mean. I recall Viscount Trent saying they belonged to his latest mistress."

"Oh dear, I hope she won't mind if I'm borrowing them."

"I doubt it. I heard tell that Viscount Trent turned her out just last week. 'E gave her a rather hefty parting gift, if you know what I mean."

Jessica did. Her thoughts flew back to the conversation between Jacob and Marga and without warning, tears sprang to her eyes. If Percival was even half as generous as Jacob, his mistress would not miss a few gowns.

"Oh, I'm sorry, Yer Grace! Forgive me gossipy ways! I didn't mean to offend you! I'm not used to addressing such a foin lady!"

"Oh, Milly, no. You didn't offend me. It was a personal matter that upset me. Don't fret. Please."

Turning quickly from the mirror, Jessica wiped the tears

from her eyes before they could fall. She took a deep breath and put a hand to her hair, simply braided and coiled around the back of her head.

Realizing she needed some diversion lest she be swept away by painful thoughts, Jessica turned and headed for the door. "Thank you, Milly. I will join my grandmother downstairs now."

As she approached the doors to the library, Jessica heard the now familiar voice of Percival Trent. She tried to ignore the knot in her stomach, feeling guilty for having these dread thoughts about the man who'd saved her life.

A brilliant smile adorned her lips as she made her way through the doors, though she felt none of the warmth her face portrayed.

"There you are, my dear," Lady Atterberry said, rising and holding out her hand. "Come sit with us."

This room, although large and bright, was also sparsely appointed. Few paintings hung on the wall. Four straight-backed chairs and a desk were the only furniture in the room.

Although rows of books lined the wall near the fireplace, dozens of other wall shelves remained empty and dust-lined. The carpet had some areas that were less faded, attesting to the fact that at one time, this room had been full of other furniture.

Jessica now remembered hearing Jacob say that the Atterberrys were having financial difficulties, and although he thought they deserved the hardship, Jessica felt nothing but compassion. And to think these dear people would have used what money they had left to pay her ransom.

She looked again towards her grandparents and felt an overwhelming sense of fondness descend upon her. Bless them. She would do whatever they asked. It was the least she could to repay their kindness.

Both Lord Atterberry and Viscount Trent rose to greet her.

Lord Atterberry moved forward, taking Jessica's hands and kissing her cheeks in a very grandfatherly way. "Looks like my cure of brandy did you a world of good. Works every time! You appear to have slept soundly!"

"I did, thank you. Why, I wasn't even aware that I'd been— put to bed." Jessica glanced at Percival who ignored the questioning look she sent him.

Percival came forward and took her hands from her grandfather, kissing each one while keeping his eyes locked on her breasts.

"Ah, worth every hint of danger! You look lovely, Jessica."

He finally lifted his eyes. As he straightened and pulled her forward, he slid a possessive arm about her waist and guided her to the chair next to Lady Atterberry's.

It took every ounce of tolerance Jessica possessed not to push him away. She was still angry with him for having undressed her; something that, no matter what the circumstances were, could have waited until he was gone. After all, she'd spent the last four days in those grubby clothes; a few more hours wouldn't have mattered.

"Sit with us, dear," Lady Atterberry said as she reclaimed her own seat. "We've all had our breakfast, but I've ordered cook to bring you some sweet rolls and tea."

"Thank you," she said uneasily. "I haven't eaten much these past few days."

Relax! she told herself. *This is your family. These people, not Jacob! They are the ones who care for you!*

Her mind took off again on another journey through her likely options. She nodded at her grandparents' small talk and hoped she was making the appropriate responses. All the while she could feel the viscount's eyes upon her.

After what seemed to be a great while, Viscount Trent rose and made excuses for his leaving, claiming a great deal of business that he needed to attend to.

He turned to Jessica as they all rose. "I shall be honored if you will be my escort this evening at the Savoy. They serve the most delectable lobster, and I would so like to share it with you."

Jessica was taken aback. She rose to her feet. No, she was not ready for—

"Really, Percival!" Lady Atterberry scolded. "The poor dear has just returned from the fires of hell! She'll need at least a day or two to recover. Isn't that right, my dear?"

Jessica nodded gratefully at her grandmother. "Yes. At the very least, a week I think. Thank you so much for the offer. After all you've done for me I really couldn't impose on your kindness and generosity any further."

"Impose?" Percival said, taking a step towards Jessica.

The chair she'd been sitting in was at her back. She could go no where without making a too-obvious avoidance.

"I assure you, fair lady, that the only imposition on me will be if you force me to dine alone when I would so enjoy your company. However, your grandmother may be correct. I shall leave you to your recuperating—for a day or two."

He bowed with mock gallantry and then made for the door. "I shall call on you again, soon. Good day."

When Jessica heard the front door close she sank to her seat with a sigh. Looking up, she met her grandmother's eyes which held questions, and—annoyance?

"I—I'm sorry. I'm just not ready to be courted, especially not in public. After all, despite Jacob's unforgivable treatment, I am still a married woman. And although I don't care a whit for *his* reputation, I certainly don't want to damage mine any further."

"Of course not, dear." The questioning look in Lady Atterberry's eyes faded. "May I just point out, however, that Percival is a very gentle person. He may seem overwhelming at times, but that's just his nature. He's a true admirer of all things beautiful, whether it be art or music or women.

I'm sure he seems over-eager to you after the appalling way your husband ignored you. You'll get used to Percival's ways. I have a feeling the two of you will be spending a fair amount of time together. And if I were you," she said in an advisory tone, "I would not push him too far away. He may be just what you need in the coming months."

Before Jessica could question Lady Atterberry's remark, her grandmother continued. "As for that scoundrel of a husband of yours, we must do something right away. You must let him know that you are alive, well, and ready to fight for what is yours."

"But—but I don't want anything from him. I just want to go back to my cottage and live there with Ossie. Back to the life I never should have left!" she finished angrily, staring out the window.

"Oh no! You can't possibly do that!"

Was that panic she heard in the older woman's voice?

Jessica looked up in surprise at Lady Atterberry. "Why not?"

"Be—because, my child, I so want you to remain here with us. We lost your mother, and as you know, we were estranged from your father from all those years. Such a horrible misunderstanding, the worst part being that we were denied access to you. We did search everywhere, but your father was a clever man. Our searches did nothing but drain our resources."

Again Jessica felt the guilt seeping in. "I'm so sorry, Grandmother. If only my father could have known—"

"But he couldn't possibly have known...out there in that small village you told us about. Portraying you as a boy and he with a false name even! He was a clever man," she said again, her voice laced with bitterness.

Lady Atterberry drifted away for a moment, then shook her head as if to clear her thoughts. "And then we find you again, and married to a Duke no less. My, my. Such a wonderful opportunity for you. Still, the Duke of Fairdale is the last person I would have chosen for a husband for you."

"Why is there such ill will between you and my—you and Jacob?"

Lady Atterberry's eyes narrowed again and she opened her mouth to speak.

But before she could say a word, Lord Atterberry cleared his throat. "Let's just say we have a great many political differences, and Fairdale, with his money and political pull, was able to have me drummed out of Parliament in great shame and with little hope of political recovery. I'd had a seat in Parliament for years."

"Why?" Jessica breathed? "Why would he do that?"

Lord and Lady Atterberry exchanged glances; his apologetic and embarrassed, hers demanding and silencing.

"As your grandfather said, it was political differences. But enough about that. I insist that you remain here with us and give us another chance to make—uh—to get to know you."

"But I can't. I have Ossie to think about."

"Oh, yes. That boy you're raising. I'm guessing he's not yours, Jessica, and for the life of me, I can't understand why you'd pass him off as yours and tarnish your reputation with—"

At Lady Atterberry's snide tone, Jessica rose to her feet. Grandmother or not, no one would ever speak disparagingly about Ossie. Aside from the fact that he was a wonderful child, he was the only hold she had on the remnants of her life as she knew it.

Lady Atterberry saw the spark flare in Jessica's eyes and quickly amended. "But the child can't be blamed for that. It's admirable that you care so much for the boy. Of course you will bring him here to live with us! It will be so lovely to have a little one around the house again! Don't you agree, Hayden?"

"I—I can?" Jessica's surprise was real. She truly hadn't thought Lord and Lady Atterberry would consent to her bringing Ossie here, despite what Percival had said last night. This just wasn't a house that seemed as if it would welcome children.

"Of course! Anything you want, Jessica. Just please, don't leave us again."

Jessica smiled, feeling hope for the first time in a great while. With Ossie here, things might not be so bad. And once Percival saw her devotion to Ossie, perhaps he would be less interested as well. Not many men would have the patience to tolerate someone else's child for great lengths of time.

She hated the thought of using Ossie for such a purpose as getting rid of an unwanted suitor, but it would be best for both of them.

"Thank you. Thank you so much. You'll love him, I just know it! I'll send for him immediately. If I may have some paper to write a message?"

Lord Atterberry roused himself from his chair and went to his desk. "Here's all that you need, my dear." He left the room then, seemingly lost in his own world of thoughts once again.

Jessica went to sit at the desk, but before she could begin writing, Lady Atterberry stopped her.

"Jessica, why don't you let me help you compose your messages?"

"I'm very capable—"

"I'm sure you are my dear. But let's look at this realistically. Jacob doesn't even know you've been rescued. If you simply send a messenger to Fairdale to retrieve your belongings and the boy, he may intercept them and not allow the boy to leave. We must send word to him first. Today."

"That's not possible. He and his *mistress* left town yesterday afternoon."

"Who told you that?"

"DuPont. His messenger said they had their baggage ready to be loaded and—"

Lady Atterberry waived her hand dismissively. "Oh, yes, yes. But Percival told me that you saw someone at Jacob's house last night on your way here. He checked this morning and apparently the duke decided not to leave. We need to write him first and make your demands."

"But Lady Atterberry, Grandmother, I *have* no demands other than that he keep his distance from me." *And that demand will be the hardest to make*, she continued silently.

"Of course you have demands. You must free yourself of

him, and as soon as possible."

"I don't understand the urgency. I never want to see him again. As far as I'm concerned, he can believe that I'm dead for a while."

"But you're not dead. And sooner or later, you will want to go out in public and perhaps even marry again."

"Marry? I doubt that I'll ever marry again. But even if I wanted to, it would be impossible. He won't divorce me. No one has ever been divorced in the Callaway family line."

"Well, there's a first time for everything. Do you want him to retain control over your life? Do you want him to make you answer to him for everything you do?" Lady Atterberry nearly shouted.

Jessica was taken aback by the viciousness in Lady Atterberry's tone. Her brow furrowed as she answered, "No, of course not. But—"

"Well he could, you know! There's one very sure way for him to control your life."

"I don't see how."

Lady Atterberry threw up her arms, looking at Jessica as if she were a dim witted child. "Are you telling me there's no chance you could be carrying his child? That the marriage was never consummated?"

Jessica's face burned at the memory of the heated passion she'd shared with Jacob less than a week ago. She looked down at her hands, hating the fluttering that sprang to life in her stomach and worked its way between her legs merely from thinking on those precious moments. "No. It was consummated."

"Then don't you see, girl? If you are by any chance carrying his child, he will have another hold over you. For at least nine months. After that, he could take the child from you and raise it without you, perhaps even with his mistress and *their* bastard."

Jessica's gaze flew to Lady Atterberry's. Oh God, what if I am pregnant? What if he took my baby and then somehow managed to get Ossie too? "Over my dead body! No! I would never let him! He can't...."

She closed her eyes for a moment.

Wait, wait. This is going too fast. She looked up at Lady Atterberry who seemed about to explode. Why was she so intent on securing this divorce?

"Well? Do you want to lose your child?"

"Of course not, but I may not even be pregnant. And if I was, it would be blatantly obvious whose child it was. I shall simply have to deal with that if the situation arises."

Lady Atterberry smiled. "Not if you marry someone else and we send you away for a year or so. When you return, you and your new husband will have a happy little baby. Some may suspect, but no one will know the child's true origins. Are you willing to take a chance with your unborn child?"

Jessica just shook her head. She didn't feel pregnant. Hadn't even considered the possibility until just now.

Jacob wouldn't—or would he? Knowing him for as short a time as she had, she couldn't be sure of anything. Especially after his heartless abandonment.

Lady Atterberry appeared to calm down. "Now, my dear. I have it all planned out."

Yes, so it appeared she did. How could the woman have made so many plans in the space of a few hours?

Lady Atterberry pulled a chair up next to Jessica's. "It must be in your own handwriting—"

"Of course, but I'll simply tell him that due to his obvious disregard for my safety and the fact that he wouldn't post ransom I feel that—"

"No! You must not mention that. You need to press the issue of his upcoming illegitimate child."

"But why?"

Lady Atterberry rolled her eyes. "Because if you want to press for an annulment or divorce, you'll want to use the unborn child as grounds for the request. If you simply whine about the fact that he didn't pay the ransom, Jacob could just as easily say he was calling the kidnaper's bluff, waiting him out. No, no. You must go for the angle of the poor woman who's carrying his child and— "

"Poor woman?"

"Never mind, dear. Just do as you're told. This is what you must say."

Chapter 31

Jacob stood in the entry hall of his elaborate town house. He scanned the brief letter over and over again. This couldn't be. She wouldn't just....

But she had.

He crumpled the letter in a ball and threw it on the marble floor. Raising his clenched fists above him he threw his head back and let loose with a primal yell.

Maids and housemen alike ran for cover as Jacob picked up one piece of furniture after another and threw it across the entry way. When he could find nothing else to destroy, he went into the front parlor and began disassembling that room.

For thirty minutes the sound of breaking glass and splintering furniture could be heard throughout the house.

When Malcom finally arrived, he had to duck quickly to avoid being hit by a crystal vase which shattered just above his head.

Jacob's eyes focused on Malcom at last, and he stood in the middle of his wrecked parlor, his breathing heavy and strained. "What the hell are you doing here?" he growled, throwing a last porcelain statue to the ground with shattering force.

Malcom looked around the room which was growing dark with the fading afternoon sun and leaned against the splintered doorway. "I'd heard you were looking for a new decorator, so I thought I'd apply for the job. But apparently I'm too late. I must say, Jake, I love what you've done with the place."

The look Jacob sent Malcom would have sent most men running for cover. The fact that Jacob had another crystal missile in his hand didn't help matters any. But Malcom stood his ground, trusting his friend not to do *too* much bodily damage to him, should it actually come to that.

Jacob dropped the figurine and crunched through the broken glass to a small marble table where two bottles of whiskey stood, miraculously untouched.

"Actually, you scared the very life out of poor young Michael. He thought you'd finally lost your mind and although I assured him that you'd lost that some time ago, he beseeched me to come and try to calm you."

"I'm not in the mood for your wit, or lack thereof, Malcom. I think it would be best if you left. Now."

Undaunted, Malcom entered the room and picked his way to a chair, which had sustained damage such that it's back was torn off. He brushed a few shards of glass from the seat and sat down, reaching for one of the bottles of whiskey on the table.

"I assume this has something to do with this crumpled note I found in the entry, just preceding the war zone?"

Jacob nodded, still breathing heavily. He stared out the window, seeing nothing but amber eyes and waves of auburn hair floating in the sunset's reflection.

"Perhaps you would care to share with me the cause of all—this?" Malcom waived his hand in a half-circle.

"Read it yourself," Jacob said, taking a hefty swallow of whiskey.

Malcom smoothed open the paper. It was growing too dark to read, so he rose and lit the large candelabra that sat, albeit crooked now, near the window ledge.

He glanced at Jacob once before reading the missive and found him still staring out the window.

20 April

Jacob:

I will never forgive you for what you've done to me. The humiliation and degradation your careless actions have brought upon me will forever cause me pain.

I am writing to you now only because there are a few matters which must be seen to.

First, I have sent for Ossie and my belongings to be brought from Fairdale to my grandparent's house. Lord and Lady Atterberry have been kind enough to offer Ossie and me a place to live, considering the fact that I can under no circumstances ever reside with you again.

Second, I request that you never seek out my company, nor attempt to speak to me should we happen to meet in public. I have no wish to be linked to you in any way.

Which brings me to my final demand: I want to be free from this farce of a marriage. I realize there has never been a divorce in your family, so I am willing to accept an annulment. Despite the fact that we regrettably consummated our marriage, I'm certain that fact can be overlooked when it's pointed out that you had promised marriage to your mistress and gotten her with child shortly before you married me, and that your marriage to me was done purely as fulfillment of a request by your father. With your influential connections, and the respect your father held, you should have no problem securing my freedom.

Should you have any questions, please direct them to my loving grandfather, Lord Hayden Atterberry.

Regretfully yours,
Jessica.

Even to Malcom, a party uninjured by the words, the letter seemed unbelievably cruel—and utterly ridiculous.

Malcom read the note over twice, unable to believe his eyes the first time through.

When he finished he looked up to find Jacob's eyes on him.

"So, this is the place our fine little Jessica has brought us to. Do you still believe she's the perfect wife for me?"

Jacob swallowed another dose of whiskey then drew his hand across his lips.

"In league with the Atterberrys. You know, the thought crossed my mind once before, but I dismissed it."

"What thought is that?" Malcom asked, setting the note on the table.

"When I discovered that she was a virgin, that Ossie couldn't possibly be her child, I accused her of being in league with someone else. At the time, however, I accused her of having some financial arrangement with Ossie's true parents, whoever they might be. But now it becomes very clear."

He paused and took another swig of liquor. "Hayden Atterberry. He's behind all of this. He and that cow of a wife he has."

Jacob laughed sardonically and rubbed his temples with his thumb and middle finger. "I thought those old weasels had given up the game, stopped fighting a war with me they couldn't win. When I had him toppled from Parliament, shortly after exposing him as a cheat at Brooks', I truly thought he'd not be a bother any more. But the old man was sharper than I thought, or at least more vengeful."

Malcom stood. "I'm afraid I don't quite follow you, Jake."

"Don't you see? The letter from James Patrick that started all of this, the sad tale about raising Ossie all alone...she convinced my father and she convinced me that she was a genuine innocent, in need of help."

He smiled a vacant, humorless smile. "God, she put on a good show. Almost too good. The thought crossed my mind to leave her there in that bloody cottage of her father's to live alone with the boy.

I should have suspected something like this when she so suddenly agreed to come with me. But I'm sure that was all a part of Hayden's plan. They must have schemed for months! What a calculated plot! I would never have thought that old bastard could come up with something like this. And now, now that I'm securely married to their granddaughter, they think they'll be able to leech off me."

"If that was their intention, why would she demand a divorce?"

"It's a ploy. Jessica knows I would never give her a divorce. Or an annulment for that matter. Somehow they think to make me their financial champion. Think about it. If I were to beg for Jessica to come back, one of her conditions could be that her family be attended to. They must all be daft if they think that a tumble or two with that wily creature would be enough to render me senseless and gullible."

He grew silent for a moment, wishing to God that he *didn't* want her as desperately as he still did. The pain that she had betrayed him, that she had used him, was far worse than any he'd ever known.

"And what timing! This whole mess with Marga just played right into their hands. I wonder how long they would have waited to find another means to their...." Jacob's voice trailed off. "Unless Marga is in on this as well." He ran his fingers through his hair as that cold thought struck him.

"God, Malcom. Could I have truly been that blind of a fool? Me, the renowned lady's man, sucked into a trap by my ex-mistress and my young chit of a wife?"

"Go easy on yourself old man. We don't know that this was all a carefully laid plan. It could be sadly coincidental. Though I'll admit that it all appears to fall a bit too neatly into place."

Malcom walked through the littered floor and stood next to Jacob looking out at the darkening sky. He placed his hand on

Jacob's shoulder. "What do you intend to do now?"

Jacob took a deep breath and slowly turned his head to look at Malcom. "Sit and wait. I'm far too angry to do anything rational. If I saw Jessica right now I'd likely break her lying little neck. She's right about one thing. I won't give her a divorce. But time is on my side just now. The longer I sit and wait, the worse it will be for them. Sooner or later, one of them will either make a mistake or redefine their demands.

After a time, I'll let it be known that my wife has abandoned me. That shouldn't come as any great surprise since that seems to be the plotted course for Dukes of Fairdale," Jacob said bitterly. "And just as was the case with my mother, Jessica and her cohorts will find themselves without much support and with fewer friends as each week passes. She can have her precious belongings and the boy."

Jacob thought about Ossie for a moment and felt a pang of sadness. He'd grown very fond of the lad in a short period of time. There was something about Ossie's quiet sweetness that had endeared the boy to Jacob.

"Ossie," he said aloud. "Now there's the one question that still bothers me."

"What's that?"

"Who are Ossie's parents, and how is he involved in all this?"

Chapter 32

Three weeks had passed since Jessica's demanding letter had been sent and there was still no word from Jacob.

Every time someone arrived at the door, her heart started pounding and she felt the blood rush to her face.

And each time after the caller had left, she retired to her rooms, trying to sort out if she felt relief or regret.

Ossie had arrived just four days after the letter was sent to Fairdale. She'd been brief in her instructions to Mrs. Holmes, stating only that she and Jacob had come to irreconcilable differences, and that while she didn't know what the future would hold for their marriage, she wanted to have Ossie sent to her.

The little boy had arrived full of smiles and hugs and kisses for Jessica, quickly dispersing her depression. A note was tucked in his pocket from Mrs. Holmes, offering her sympathy and support if she should need help with Ossie in the future.

Jessica had celebrated Ossie's birthday with a private picnic, just the two of them, behind the potter's shed in the overgrown back gardens. There was so much wild growth that they felt they were in a jungle far away. Finally knowing some peace and true relaxation there in the warm spring sun, she made an attempt to leave the house with Ossie on a daily basis and visit their secret place.

Although it was raining this day, Jessica would not be put off from spending some quiet time alone with Ossie.

He pointed to the clouds that covered the sun and shrugged, trying to hide his disappointment.

Jessica smiled down at him. "Well," she whispered, "since we can't go outside today, what do you say we explore this old house?"

At Ossie's eager nod, she took his hand and started up the stairs.

When they were halfway up the steps, Lady Atterberry's voice halted them. "And where are you two going? It's such a shame that your daily outing has been curtailed by this rain."

Jessica tried to ignore the tension that crept into her shoulders at her grandmother's voice. She turned, with a polite smile on her face, and said, "We were just going upstairs for a while. I'm going to try and find something to occupy Ossie's time."

Jessica didn't want to tell Lady Atterberry that they were going exploring, not only because she was afraid her grandmother wouldn't want them on the third floor, but also because she just wanted to be alone with Ossie.

"Hmm. Yes. Well, whatever you find to do, be ready to receive your gentleman caller in an hour."

"My caller? Who might that be?"

Her grandmother gave her a look that said she thought Jessica was slow. "Why Percival, of course. It's been two days since you've received him, and he's nearly desperate with longing to share your company. And while you're about it, I insist you put on a presentable dress. You know how I loathe those oversized trousers, and I'm quite certain Percival prefers to see you properly dressed."

"I'll bet," Jessica said under her breath.

"What was that, my dear?"

"Nothing. I'll come down when he arrives."

"Do that. And leave the boy with one of the maids. You and Percival need some time alone."

It was on the tip of Jessica's tongue to argue, but she could tell from her grandmother's stance that she would hear none of it.

"As you wish, Grandmother."

When Lady Atterberry disappeared, Jessica felt Ossie's hand loosen it's hold on her own. She brushed the hair back from his forehead.

The poor little dear. He was so nervous whenever her grandmother was in the same room.

Lord Atterberry rarely said a word to Ossie, so Ossie pretty much ignored him too. And although Percy tried desperately to win Ossie's friendship, Ossie was distant and distrustful of him.

Not unlike my own feelings towards the man, Jessica thought dismally.

Jessica and Ossie made their way down a long hallway. The further they went, the more untended the house became. Dust and cobwebs were plentiful, and by the time they reached end of the hall where the door to the third floor was found, Jessica noticed that the wall paper was peeling and the carpets were worn and faded.

This was the first time she'd been in this section of the house. Glancing back down the hall, she wondered at the shabby conditions they'd found.

She shrugged and assumed that with just the two of them there, Lord and Lady Atterberry had found it unnecessary—and expensive—to keep up the rest of the house.

Ossie reached up and tried the knob on the door. It turned freely, but the door wouldn't open. Jessica was about to give up, thinking that the door was somehow bolted on the inside. But the thought of spending the remainder of her morning with Viscount Trent made her desperate for a little solitude now. She put one foot against the wall and gave a strong *heave*.

The door flew open, the draft from the sudden breeze sending dust flying into the air. Both Jessica and Ossie sneezed several times before the dust settled enough to see up the stairway.

"Are you ready?" she whispered to Ossie.

At his grinning nod she took him by the hand and led him up the stairs.

Each step creaked and groaned beneath the dust laden carpet. She knew that no one down stairs could hear them, but the noise seemed very loud in the surrounding stillness.

Once at the top, Ossie let go of Jessica's hand and walked to one of the windows. The view was nothing short of spectacular. Rows of houses could be seen, most of them even larger than this one.

From here, one could see that Hampton Row had, over time, become one of the less fashionable streets to live on. Though Hampton Row was just three streets east of King Street, where Jacob's house was, it was obvious by the size and style of the houses to the west that it was slowly but surely being relegated to the less desirable list of places to live.

Despite her efforts to the contrary, Jessica's eyes searched, found and locked onto the tall brick walls that marked Jacob's townhouse. She stood there for several minutes, staring at the strong, enduring structure—*so like Jacob*—and once again fought with the fact that she still missed him greatly, in spite of everything.

At last she tore her eyes from the view and ushered Ossie away from the window.

The third floor of the Atterberry's house was large and remarkably open compared to the two lower floors. Huge windows lined the entire length of one wall. A large open room stood in the middle, with a few slightly smaller rooms separated at the far end.

Ossie sucked in his breath and jumped up and down, pointing at something against the far wall.

A rocking horse! He looked up at Jessica and waited for her nod before running to the old, beautifully carved toy. A sheet, which had at one time covered the entire horse, now covered only the body and legs. Ossie carefully lifted the cover off and then used his hand and sleeve to wipe the dust from the horse's neck and head.

The years of sitting with its neck and head exposed had faded the once-bright colors. But the lower part was still in perfect condition.

Jessica pulled it a few feet out from the wall and helped Ossie climb on the wooden steed's back. He grinned and began rocking immediately.

Jacob had purchased a rocking horse for Ossie at Fairdale. It was newer and the colors were brighter, but this was a very acceptable replacement.

The thought of Jacob's kind gesture towards Ossie brought the all too familiar knot to her stomach. She turned away quickly before Ossie could see the tears that sprang to her eyes and walked to the far end of the big room.

Why did thoughts of him still make her an emotional wreck? More than once she had regretted sending that letter to him with her demands; demands which were actually based on her grandmother's wishes. Oh, how she had wanted to go to Jacob and force him to tell her the truth; why he'd denied her ransom, why he'd chosen Marga over her.

But the letter had been sent and there was no taking it back. The fact that he'd seen fit not to respond only made the wounds ache more deeply.

Jessica ground her teeth together and willed herself to stop crying. She moved towards a pile of stacked boxes and some other items that were hidden under sheets.

Curiosity and her need for a diversion pulled her to the boxes on the floor.

She carefully opened one box and reached inside. There were several school books in the box along with some old and yellowed papers with writing on them.

Jessica carefully leafed through the papers until she found one where the ink had not faded. She dropped to her knees, mouth hanging open, as she realized that she was holding some lessons that her own mother had completed.

"Oh," she whispered, "Mama!"

Quickly she shuffled through some more of the papers, finding an essay on one of Shakespeare's sonnets and a test on her ciphering abilities.

Jessica smiled and shook her head as she spotted a mistake that apparently the tutor had overlooked.

When she'd finished with the first box, she glanced back at Ossie, finding him sitting on the floor looking at the pictures in a faded children's book.

Feeling as though she'd just found a treasure trove, Jessica carefully removed some of the sheets covering the rest of the items in the corner.

An old trunk yielded several beautiful gowns, many of them suitable for formal occasions. She stood and pressed one of the gowns to her front. Her mother had been a few inches shorter than Jessica, which was obvious by the length of the gown. "But it looks as if it would fit everywhere else," Jessica whispered with a smile.

She returned the dress to the trunk and moved on, uncovering several small desks in varying sizes and a chair.

Yet another box held two porcelain dolls. Their dresses were faded and one had a black smudge on her face, but they were obviously dolls of some expense.

Shaking her head, Jessica wondered how her grandparents came to be in such a sorry financial state as they were now. At one time they must have been quite affluent, for the dresses in the trunk, though outdated, were of superior quality and materials. Even the few toys scattered about the room were well made.

When she finished returning the dolls to their box, she noticed a large flat shape in the corner, again covered with sheets. A portrait? Her hands shook as she carefully peeled the sheets from the painting. Indeed, it was a large portrait of her mother.

Jessica recognized Elizabeth from the miniature that James had given her after her mother died and also from the fact that, aside from the color of her hair, the painting looked so much like Jessica herself.

She knelt down and reverently touched the well-preserved painting. "You're so young and beautiful," Jessica whispered. Taking a guess, Jessica gauged that her mother had been about seventeen when the portrait was done.

Her dark brown hair was swept back into a cascade of curls falling softly across her shoulders. Amber eyes, the same color as Jessica's, were framed by thick lashes.

Jessica put her hands to her own cheeks and decided that her own prominent cheekbones had come from her mother's side.

But one thing bothered her about the portrait: the look on her mother's face. It wasn't quite sad, yet it could not be called happy or content either.

More like concerned, or hopeless. Yes, that was it. Her mother looked as if she had no hope.

She recognized that look as one she'd been wearing herself of late, in fact every time she'd looked in the mirror she'd seen that very expression. Jessica looked away for a moment, feeling an uneasiness creep over her.

Until now she hadn't allowed herself to carefully examine her feelings. Keeping them locked away and ignoring them had been easier than allowing them to sweep over her.

But now, in this moment of discovery, she realized that she, too, was feeling hopeless. Control of her life seemed to have been handed over to her grandparents, more accurately her grandmother, since the moment she'd set foot in this house.

They'd used guilt and a sense of duty to force her to write that letter to Jacob and remain here when she would have rather returned to her own home in Wilfordshire. They made it seem as if she *owed* it to them, for some reason, to stay here.

If she'd owed them money for her rescue, she could understand...but no money had been exchanged. Only the loss of the lives of DuPont and his men. She was, actually, free to leave now that she had Ossie with her.

It suddenly became clear to Jessica why she was constantly nervous and unsure of herself. None of the decisions made since her rescue had been her own. Everything had been set in motion before she'd even fully recovered from her kidnaping. For a young woman used to depending only on herself, having her freedom taken away was like a physical malady.

At Fairdale, some of her freedoms had been curtailed, but not to this extent.

Another thought struck her. If her grandparents were so sorely misunderstood, if they had truly wanted her mother to come back to them with no conditions, as they claimed, then why were all of her mother's belongings stuffed up here in this deserted school room? Come to think of it, there was no sign of her mother anywhere in this house other than under these sheets. It was as if her mother had never been a part of their lives.

She looked back at her mother's image. Amber eyes implored amber eyes.

Follow your heart. The words came as a whisper, from out of no where.

Jessica turned her head, almost expecting to see her mother standing in the room. But there was only Ossie, still occupied with the book, sitting in the middle of the floor.

There had to be a reason she'd found this portrait today. "You're trying to tell me something, aren't you?" she whispered as she looked back. "I just pray I have the common sense to understand and act accordingly."

Chapter 33

Ossie came running for Jessica, nearly knocking her over. In her absorption with her mother's portrait, she hadn't heard the footsteps coming up the stairs.

Jessica held Ossie and turned to look just as Milly appeared at the top of the stairs. Relief flooded over her at the sight of the maid and she put her hand to her chest.

"Milly! You gave us a start!"

"Oh, no, Your Grace! Ye mustn't be up here!"

Sighing with relief that it wasn't her grandmother, Jessica asked. "Why not? There are a host of wonderful treasures up here."

Milly made her way forward, wringing her hands. "No one is allowed up here. It's off limits."

"Then why are you here?"

"I saw the door open as I freshened your rooms. I figured it was you up here. *They* haven't been up here since the day they stored away your mother's things."

"Milly, how long have you been employed here?"

"Only a few years, Your Grace, but my own mother and my aunt worked here for thirty years before that. In fact, my aunt was your mum's personal maid." Milly stepped close and looked at the portrait. "She was a lovely thing. So sad they had such a fallin' out."

"What do you know about it?" Jessica asked hopefully.

"Not much, really. Just that they considered her dead long

before she actually was."

"But I thought my grandparents tried to reconcile with my parents."

Milly shook her head slowly. "Not the way I heard tell, but I'm not in a position to say for sure. I hear a lot around here, more than I want to hear. But I don't recall them ever discussin' any regrets over the way things turned out."

Jessica was about to ask the maid more, but Milly began wringing her hands again. "Please, Your Grace, go back down stairs. If they catch us up here, we'll all have to pay for it. I'll straighten these covers and put things away. You'd better go and get dressed. I heard milady say that Viscount Trent would be here soon."

Ossie's shoulders dropped and he kicked at the floor at those words. Jessica smiled and squeezed his hand. "I feel the same way, sweetling. But don't worry, you won't have to see him. You can stay up in my room and I'm sure Milly will find something entertaining for you." She looked to the maid for confirmation and received it. "Come on. We'd better go."

Just before they reached the top of the stairs, Milly called out to Jessica. "Your Grace, if I may be so bold, remember what I said about hearing too much?"

Jessica nodded.

"Well, sometimes that's a good thing. If ye keep yer ears open, ye may just hear something worth listening to." Milly turned back to her work. "In fact, the lady that's visiting Lady Atterberry right now might be a good place for ye t'start."

Jessica realized that the maid was trying to tell her something without jeopardizing her place in the household.

Taking the warning to heart, Jessica hurried down the stairs and into her bedroom. She handed Ossie over to Milly's younger sister who thoroughly enjoyed the time she spent with him. Then she quickly donned one of her simplest day gowns that had arrived in the trunks that accompanied Ossie.

Not only was it an easy garment to dress herself in but she

knew it was not overly flattering which was a good thing considering that Viscount Trent would soon be here.

Jessica quickly descended the stairs, stopping at the bottom when she heard a vaguely familiar voice. It couldn't be…

She ignored the warning bells in her head and strode to the closed library door. Throwing it open, she barged in to the room uninvited and without warning. Jessica could see only the back of the visitor's head.

"But what am I supposed to do? Time is—"

"Jessica!" Lady Atterberry stood quickly, cutting off the other woman. "What are you doing in here?"

"I heard someone arrive and thought it might be my gentleman caller, Viscount Trent," she lied.

"Viscount Trent!" the visitor said, standing and turning to face Jessica.

It *was* her! It was Marga!

Even assuming who Lady Atterberry's visitor was in no way prepared Jessica for the blow she felt when Marga turned and looked at her with those malicious, cold eyes.

"Marga!" Lady Atterberry shouted.

"What do you mean Viscount Trent is your gentleman caller?"

Again Lady Atterberry raised her voice. "Marga!"

When Marga turned to look at her Lady Atterberry continued. "What difference does it make to you with whom my granddaughter keeps company? You have made your claim to your man!"

Jessica noted the strained look her grandmother sent Marga, but was too angry to consider it just now.

"What in the bloody hell are you doing here, you wretched slut!" Jessica shouted. All the anger and betrayal she'd felt towards Jacob and this woman was purging itself from her soul.

"Me? A wretched slut? You are the married woman who is receiving gentleman callers only three weeks after abandoning your husband."

"Abandoning? Abandoning! I was the one who was abandoned," Jessica growled taking two steps toward Marga. "And you are the one is having a married man's child! I'd say that pretty much qualifies you as a slut!"

"I was pregnant with this child before he even knew of you!" Marga shrieked.

"Ladies, ladies!" Lady Atterberry cried out.

"Ladies? Ha!" Jessica spat. "If she is considered to be a lady, then I have no desire to be one!" She turned back to Marga. "Nor should my grandmother have to be defiled by your presence. Get out of this house, you whore!" Jessica pointed to the door.

She knew she was assuming a position she didn't really hold by ordering Marga to leave, but Jessica could not bear to have Jacob's mistress in her presence.

"I'll not leave until Lady Atterberry requests it. After all, she invited me here!"

Jessica turned her eyes to her grandmother, a betrayed look settling upon her face. "Invited her?" she said in little more than a whisper. "You invited this woman here?"

Lady Atterberry cleared her throat and sent Marga another warning look. "Yes. I did. But only to tell her that she was never speak to me again or seek my help or advice on any matter. I had no idea that the man she was seeing was your own husband, dearest. Not until the night of the ball. I was astonished!"

Jessica looked back at Marga whose mouth was drawn in a grim, tight line. Her breathing was heavy as if she were desperately trying to hold herself back.

"I see," Marga said, her voice brittle and strained. "Then by all means, I shall abide by your wishes." Marga turned a wicked smile upon Jessica. "I won't even bother bringing the baby over when he's born. The ambience of this place would be completely unsatisfactory for my child, for *Jacob's* child. Of course, I'm sure we'll be back at Fairdale by then anyway. Jacob does so want the baby to be raised there."

It should be *my* child, Jessica cried silently. Mine and Jacob's.

The painful reminder was too much. Jessica could stand no more. With a last questioning look at Lady Atterberry, she turned and fled the room.

Once outside she stepped behind the door, not having the strength to go further. She wrapped one arm about her middle, her hand clenching at her waist. The other she brought to her mouth to quiet the scream that was so close.

Why, why?

The clatter of horse's hooves drew Jessica's attention to the front windows. Viscount Trent's coach was just pulling up. Oh, God, what else will I have to endure today?

Jessica lifted her skirts and ran up the stairs, taking two at a time. She knew she would never make it across the landing without being seen, so instead she ducked around the corner to wait until Percival had left the entryway.

Her position behind the velvet drapes that hung there allowed her to see the entry way clearly, without being seen herself.

Percival handed his cloak to the old butler and then turned, having heard voices from the library.

Marga backed out of the library, hissing something back to Lady Atterberry and slamming the door. When she turned, she stumbled right into Viscount Trent's arms.

"Ooh! And you!" Marga said with narrowed eyes. "So you are a gentleman caller now? I swear I'll not have this, Percival. I—"

Before she could make her threat, Percival grabbed Marga's wrists, one in each hand, and raised them over her head while shoving her back against the wall. He stared at her for a brief moment and then knocked her head back against the wall with his brutal kiss.

Marga squirmed and fought for a moment, then began to weaken and surrender. Before long, Jessica could hear little mewling moans coming from the woman.

Percival released her hands which she quickly wove through

his blonde hair. His own hands slid intimately over her breasts and then down to her buttocks, grinding her hips into his pelvis.

He finally pulled back from his attack and wound his fingers in the short hair at the nape of her neck, forcing her head back. "You'll have what ever I tell you to have, Marga. And you'll not give me a moment's grief over it. Is that clear?"

Jessica felt she was going to be sick. Oh God, what was happening here? Percival and Marga? What about Jacob?

Without a care for being seen, she ran across the landing and down the hall.

She'd gone unnoticed, for no one called out to her.

Once in her bedroom, she locked the door, thankful for once that Ossie wasn't there. She slid to the floor and tried to make sense of everything that had just happened.

But try as she might, nothing seemed to fit together.

Marga—and Percival?

But Percival had pursued her so ardently these past weeks. He acted the sad, unappreciated hero at some times, while other times he was blatantly lustful, with hungry glances and raking stares.

And then there was Marga—pregnant with Jacob's child and supposedly back in his life, crawling all over Percival like a bitch in season. And Viscount Trent certainly did not act the misunderstood gallant with Marga!

What she'd witnessed between the two of them was as near to violent passion as she could imagine and in no way could it be construed as a casual acquaintance.

Nothing made sense. What had Marga been saying when she walked into the library, something about time running out? What did that mean?

Even with Lady Atterberry's show of siding with Jessica, she knew that her grandmother was somehow much more involved with Marga than she let on.

All that on top of the mysteries surrounding her mother and the Atterberry's apparent dismissal of their only daughter left

Jessica swimming in a pool of confusion.

Jessica sat on the bed, her mind spinning.

A knock sounded at her door. "Your Grace?" Milly called out. "Viscount Trent is here to see you. He's in the library with Lady Atterberry."

When no answer came, Milly called out again.

This time Jessica answered. "Tell them I'll be down in a moment, Milly."

She turned and looked in the full length mirror. Her mother's eyes stared back at her, giving her strength.

Jessica lifted her chin. "I will leave this place, Mother. No matter what it seems they've done *for* me, I have a feeling it will be greatly overshadowed by what they intend to do *to* me."

She recalled her father's words, telling her about the terrible atrocities that were commonplace in aristocratic circles. Never truly doubting him at the time, yet feeling his opinions were perhaps a bit skewed by his pain, Jessica now knew he was very likely correct.

Save for the few moments of happiness she'd snatched here and there with Jacob, her life had been miserable since she'd left her cottage near Wilfordshire.

Making her decision, Jessica left her room. She would go down and tell her grandmother that she intended to leave. And as soon as was humanly possible.

Chapter 34

Jacob wandered into Jessica's room again. It was a habit he'd gotten into since the night of her disappearance. Even in his blinding rage, he'd made his way to this room and sat upon the bed. A small measure of sanity had kept him from destroying her room as he had several downstairs.

He inhaled of her scent, thinking how strange it was that even though she'd only been here for a few hours that one day, her scent seemed to linger like a ghost. It haunted him every time he walked by the door.

Three times he'd tried to leave, to go back to Fairdale and regain some order to his life.

But each time he'd found an excuse not to go, the last one being that he had to oversee the repair work to the rooms he'd damaged in his tirade.

Finally he just gave up even trying to leave. Until this matter with Jessica was further resolved, he knew he would not leave London.

But just how would it be resolved?

True to his word, he'd not answered her demanding missive. Giles had arrived several days later, informing Jacob that Ossie and Jessica's trunks had been delivered to the Atterberry's home.

Jacob had known that would happen, so why did it send his gut to roiling again when Giles had told him?

Sitting on her bed was only making matters worse. Though

she'd not slept in it, Jacob could almost feel her presence when he sat there. He picked up a silk stocking that had been tossed on the bed in her haste to dress for the ball.

With a bitter growl, he threw the stocking on the bed and stormed out of the room. As he slammed out of the room, he vowed not to go in there again. But the vow was a weak one, he knew.

The bright May sunshine did nothing to ease his mood as he wandered into his own rooms. He pulled the curtains shut, and then opened them again.

Perhaps he should get out for a while, maybe go to Brooks' for a card game or for a ride through Hyde Park.

Before he could change his mind, he shouted for Michael to have his stallion saddled and hurried through the garden entry to the back of the house.

Hyde Park was busy as usual on such a fine spring day. Most of the visitors were ladies, taking their daily dose of fresh air and catching up on the latest gossip from their circle of friends.

Jacob stopped his horse to the side of the path and found himself staring at several small birds that were hopping and fluttering about.

Even the warm sun and fresh air could not alter his foul mood. Every where he looked, something reminded him of Jessica. What kind of sorceress was she that she could put such a spell on him?

She'd lied, she'd coerced, and she'd laid a pretty trap for him. So why, *why* couldn't he feel the hate for her that he so desperately needed to purge his soul of this ache?

"I say, Your Grace, this is the first I've seen you about in weeks. Have you been...*ill?*"

Jacob slowly turned as he recognized that grating voice. "No, Baroness Von Kraus, I've not been ill."

The baroness leaned out of her stylish landau. "Oh. Well, simply *everyone* has been asking after you."

"Have they?" Jacob said with as little caring as he could

muster.

"Oh, yes, yes. I tell you, you've created quite a buzz."

Jacob snorted and looked back towards the center of the park.

Baroness Von Kraus continued, undaunted by his apparent dismissal. "Why, here you are—were—the most eligible bachelor in all of London for so many years, and now suddenly you have not one, but *two* ladies of consequence in your life: a wife and a pregnant mistress. I say, you are a busy man."

Jacob barely felt the need to answer the nosy wench, but did so anyway. "Yes. I suppose I do have a wife, and an allegedly pregnant ex-mistress."

"Allegedly? Surely you don't doubt Marga's word?" the baroness asked wide-eyed.

"I'm not certain if I believe her about the pregnancy or not. Either way, it matters little to me, Lillian."

"What? But how can you say that?" the baroness asked, aghast.

Jacob finally looked at her again and gave a derisive chuckle. "Very easily, since I'm not the child's father."

Baroness Von Kraus sucked in her breath. "But—but of course you are! Why, we share all of our intimate secrets. I have utter faith in my dear friend."

"Then you, madam, are an utter fool. And if you are so close to all of Marga's intimate secrets, then you should be able to see that she is lying. As I did." Once again he turned his attention to the parade of coaches rolling past.

Baroness Von Kraus was silent for a moment then smiled wickedly. "Oh, really. You're just nervous about being a father. You'll get used to the idea. Your wife did."

Jacob's head jerked back to the baroness. "And just what is that supposed to mean?"

"Simply that she has apparently accepted the lot she's been dealt. Why I daresay when I saw her last, she was positively glowing. She was the picture of happiness, as was her escort. I saw them leaving the theatre just two nights ago. It was—"

Jacob felt the ever present knot begin to tighten in his stomach. "And please tell, since I'm sure you are dying to, who was her escort?"

"Oh, didn't I mention that?" Baroness Von Kraus asked with feigned innocence. "Why it was Viscount Trent. I believe they met at the Winslow's ball. From what I hear, they've been inseparable ever since." It was a complete lie, but the look on Jacob's face told the baroness she'd hit her mark.

Jacob didn't trust himself to speak. The muscles in his jaw were cramping and twitching from being held so tightly.

At last he said. "You hear a great deal, Baroness. The next time you see my wife and her escort, please give them my regards. I do so hope she's getting on well." He touched his fingers to his temple. "Good day."

He booted his stallion to a gallop, leaving Baroness Von Kraus with her mouth agape.

"Giles!" When Jacob returned to his town house he shouted for Giles who had taken it upon himself to come to London after hearing no word from Jacob for so many weeks.

Giles took his time making his way to Jacob's rooms, knowing by the timbre of Jacob's voice that he was in a foul mood.

"Aye, Yer Grace," the old stable master answered. "What can I do for ye?"

"Giles, get the coach ready. I am leaving for Fairdale immediately."

Giles looked at the tortured man standing before him, a man who was now a duke. But he'd been close to that duke since he was a little boy and he was counting on the fact that Jacob loved him like an uncle to keep his face in one piece with what he was about to do.

"No."

Jacob stopped pacing the room and looked at Giles. He threw the coat he'd had in his hands to the bed. "*No?* Did I hear you correctly?"

"Aye."

"And to what do I owe this sudden mutiny?"

"Ye owe it t' the fact that yer actin' like the south end of a northbound horse!"

Jacob's astonishment was apparent on his face. He braced his legs and folded his arms across his middle. "Oh, am I really? And perhaps you would like to explain that statement before I relieve you of your position in my household?" Jacob threatened without sincerity.

"With pleasure." Giles walked over to a wing-backed chair near the fire place and sat down. He stretched his stubby legs out before him and leaned back, lacing his fingers together across his portly belly. "I've tried to stay out of this, hoping that you'd come to your senses about yer lady, Jessica."

Jacob rolled his eyes. "Oh wonderful. Another admirer of the poorly maligned duchess. And what fair insight do you have to shed on this situation?" he asked sarcastically.

"Just that ye'd better check yerself, and all the facts, before ye go runnin' and hidin' back at Fairdale."

Jacob's mouth hung open for a moment. Then he said, "Running and hiding? Perhaps you've not noticed that my so-called wife has left here, supposedly over a misunderstanding about an ex-mistress and a baby that isn't even mine! And on top of that, she's thrown in with the Attterberrys, knowing full and well that they are my enemies. It has become obvious to me that this was all a carefully laid plan by those leeches to suck my coffers dry.

To ice the cake, I find out today that she's being escorted

around town by a licentious viscount of questionable heritage. Now suppose you tell me one good reason why I should stay here and give fodder to those gossip-mongers when I could return to Fairdale and let the scandal die a natural death?"

"Since when have you ever cared what the gossip-mongers had to say?"

In a barely controlled voice Jacob said, "Never. But I am sick and tired of this whole affair. I should never have acquiesced to my father's wishes. But of course, that's hindsight. She deceived him, and then she deceived me. If I were to see Jessica right now, I'd be hard-pressed not to strangle her with by bare hands. Now that would be grist for the rumor mill, wouldn't it?"

Giles stood and held out his hands. "Jakey, I can see that you're in no mood to let me talk you out of this hatred you have for Jessica. I don't honestly know what's going on between your wife and those Atterberrys, but I do know that there's a lot more to Jessica than you've discovered."

"Ha! After what I've discovered, I'm not sure I want to know anymore."

Giles let out a heavy sigh, sounding irritated with him for the first time that Jacob could ever remember. He pointed a finger at Jacob. "Boy!" Jacob raised his eyebrows, but Giles continued. "I've not worked as a loyal servant and friend to this family for nigh on forty years and not been privy to some matters of which you have yet to learn. Now, if ye want some insight into yer wife's character, I'll tell ye how to go about it.

"As fer the rest of this mess, well ye'll have to work that out with her. I don't know why she left you without explanation. Or why she fled based on faulty assumptions. I don't know why she's supposedly been seen out and about with that Trent fellow. But I do know that she has a good and charitable heart. She's taken more upon herself in her young life than you'd suspect, and she deserves chance to explain herself—if she still has any desire to do so."

Jacob was growing weary of people extolling Jessica's

virtues and had it been anyone other than Giles doing so just now he probably would have throttled the person.

Hell, he had nothing better to do. Running his fingers through his hair, he stared at his old friend across the room. "If you will cease referring to me as 'boy', then I will submit to your attempts to alter my opinion of my wife."

Giles gave him a lop-sided grin. "Now that's the first sensible thing I've seen ye do in ages. However, it's not my lessons ye'll be studying."

With one booted foot he slid a box out from in front of one of the chairs.

"What's in there?" Jacob asked.

"Your father's journals."

"Now how the hell did they get here, and how the hell are they supposed to help me understand Jessica? He only spoke with her for a few minutes before he died."

"Aye, but believe me, your father knew her well. They shared something in those few moments that allowed his soul to rest in peace. As for how they got here, I brought them in when I delivered Jessica from Fairdale. I put them up here thinking that you'd find them and read through them. Guess ye been a little too busy wallowing around in yer own doldrums."

Jacob bent and opened the box, running his hand over the worn leather spines of the journals. He looked up just as Giles was about to exit the room.

"Giles, why can't you just tell me what's in here."

Giles studied him for a moment. "Two reasons. First, it'll mean more to ye if ye read it in yer father's own hand writing. Second, I'm still bound to secrecy by yer father, rest his soul. I won't discuss anything with you that you don't discover in those journals." He moved to leave and then stopped again. "Unless of course yer too thick to catch on to what he's telling ye."

Jacob actually smiled for the first time in what felt like ages.

He pulled one of the large chairs over near the window and

sat down to read.

Several hours passed and he was still no nearer to understanding Giles's insistence that he read his father's journals.

Most of the entries were business-related. A few scathing pages made references to his mother, and yet another page brought tears to his eyes as he read an eloquent passage that was a heartfelt goodbye to his younger brother.

Beyond that were two full volumes of nothing but business ventures and ideas he'd had for remodeling the west wing of Fairdale.

Jacob put the heavy book down and stood, arching his back and stretching his legs. He moved to the table in the corner where the remainder of the volumes were stacked.

The light in the room was dimming, so he lit a lamp and moved his reading chair next to the table.

He sat back in the chair and looked at the volumes he had left to peruse. "What's the point?" he said dispiritedly to the quiet room.

Giles had to be wrong about this one. So far there had been nothing in his father's writings that would make any difference in his feelings toward Jessica.

He had to admit he was hopeful when he'd started reading that he would find some shred of evidence to enforce Giles's words. Oh how he wanted an explanation that would put this all to the right.

He glanced up at the clock. Six o'clock. He'd give it another hour and then he'd leave off. And then he'd give Giles a good piece of his mind.

Jacob reached for the next in the series of volumes, but as his hand reached over the nearest stack, it bumped one of the leather-bound chronicles off the table and sent it to the floor with a thud.

At first he thought to ignore it, but on a second glance he noticed that there were several loose pieces of paper that had been jarred out of their places between the pages.

Curiosity got the better of him.

He reached down and pulled the volume into his lap.

His eyes began to open wide and his reading became faster as he scanned the pages of what could only be described as love letters.

His father had had a lover for several years! Austen had met her on one of his visits to Wilfordshire to see James Patrick.

How could he have not known? Jacob wondered.

He scanned the first letter again.

Lizette. Her name was Lizette.

That explained the last sounds his father had made upon his deathbed; and the peaceful look on his face. He had died with his love's name on his lips.

He read the rest of the letters, too astounded to feel any guilt over reading the flowery protestations of the woman in love with his father.

There were three more letters. The first one was full of sadness, claiming her undying love but refusing to marry Austen nonetheless, claiming only their vastly different social classes as her reason for denial.

Marry him? The old man had offered marriage and been denied? No woman in her right mind, especially one from the poor village of Wilfordshire, should have turned down a marriage proposal from his father.

He read on in bewilderment.

A horse? Austen had sent Lizette a horse as a gift. So that explains why one of the prime mares had turned up missing. His father never had satisfactorily explained that.

The next letter sent waves of shock through Jacob that forced him to stop and pour himself a brandy.

A baby. A boy. Christ! I have a brother somewhere in that Godforsaken village! Jacob's mind was reeling, the woman's words turning over and over in his mind.

She still wouldn't marry Austen. Lizette was afraid that

upon Austen's death that *he*, Jacob, would try and take her child.

Jacob shook his head. He would never have done that. But in Lizette's defense, she couldn't have possibly known that about him.

The final letter was full of sorrow at his father's worsening condition, and a final plea that he not speak of the child to anyone who might be able to use the knowledge against either of them.

There were no more letters.

Jacob returned the letters to the table and picked up the final journal.

Every once in a while there were references to Lizette, but for the most part, the words were merely reflections upon Austen's own life. Jacob thumbed through the pages until he came upon the last written page. It was dated the day his father had died. The handwriting was so weak and jittery that parts of it were hard to read.

But it was not just a journal entry, it was a letter.

My son,

I write this as quickly as I can in what I'm certain are my last moments. If you've read these journals, then you know of my darling Lizette, and of the brother you have.

Lizette has passed on, but I find great comfort in the fact that I will soon be with her again. She was the one true love of my life. My only regret is that I wasn't more forceful in trying to bring her to Fairdale as my wife.

Be wise, son, when it comes to your own heart. I will once again urge you to marry Jessica, for she is the very essence of all that is good. Ignore her stubbornness, laugh at her temper, and above all, love her faithfully.

Fate has a way of bringing people together who

truly belong together. It was such for my Lizette and me, and it is such for you and Jessica Patrick.

Trust in her. She will be a good mother to your children, Jacob. I know this, for I have seen how she is with both of my sons. By that I mean that I've seen how she is with you, and I've seen how she is with Ossie.

Yes, Jacob, little Ossie is my son, your half-brother. Due to an incredible twist of fate, Jessica has been raising him since Lizette's death. I don't know if I'll have time to tell you this in person, so I'm telling you now. I love you, son. Follow your heart.

Jacob sat back, letting the journal fall from his lap to the floor. His mouth was dry; his heart was pounding. God, could this be true?

His thoughts flew back to that hunting cottage in the rainstorm when he'd discovered her virginity. The things he'd said, the things he'd accused her of!

Could it be? Ah...God, if it was all true...what he'd done to her....

Jacob stood and began pacing the room. He put his hands to his head. *Hold on, old boy.* This was all too much to take in.

He needed something, something real to hold onto just now. Jacob looked around his room, not at all certain that this wasn't some strange dream.

Giles. Giles could verify all of this.

He bolted out the door, shouting for Giles as he went.

"He—he's in the stable, Your Grace," a frightened little maid said.

Running at full speed, he reached the stables in a matter of seconds. "Giles, I need..." He stopped, unsure just exactly what he needed.

Jacob ran his fingers through his hair, and then his eyes settled upon the horse in the nearest stall.

He pointed at the mare as she nickered at him. Giles answered Jacob's unasked question. "Yes. That's Jessica's horse, Duchess. I believe she acquired it from a friend of hers. One who passed on and left the raisin' of her boy to Jessica. Got a familiar mark on her underbelly, she does."

Jacob opened the stall and gently ran his hand down the mare's leg as he dropped to his knees. There it was; the upside down heart, the birthmark that marked all of their prime mares as one of Titan's daughters.

This was the horse that his father had given Lizette. And in turn, she had given it to Jessica before she died.

Jacob sat back in the straw, a dumbfounded look on his face.

Finally, Giles spoke again. "I brought the horse with me for two reasons. First, I was hopin' that by the time I'd arrived, you and the duchess would have reconciled your differences. Second, if that hadn't happened, I figured you might need something flesh and blood to hold onto in order to make sense of all this."

Jacob rose and brushed the straw from his trousers. "Well, you're right about that."

Duchess nickered and nuzzled his palm while Jacob took another moment to absorb all that he'd just learned.

"Well?" Giles asked. "What are ye goin' t' do about it?"

Jacob narrowed his eyes and stared at Giles. "Well, I can tell you what I *won't* do! I won't let my young brother remain for one more minute than necessary at those cretins' house. Jessica will still have a great deal of explaining to do, and she can take her time doing it. But Ossie will not spend another night under Hayden Atterberry's roof. Hitch the coach and be quick about it. I'm going to fetch my brother. And possibly my wife."

Chapter 35

Jessica bolstered her courage and was ready to make her demands to her grandparents. But when she'd reached the library she found only Viscount Trent waiting for her.

"Your grandparents left on an overnight visit," he informed her. "Didn't they tell you?"

"No. They didn't." Her irritation was rising.

"Ah, well perhaps that's partly my fault. I'm afraid I chatted away, occupying their time until they finally had to rush to be out of here just before dark."

Jessica didn't answer. She was now well aware that the gallant gentleman before her was a complete façade. The behavior that she'd witnessed between Viscount Trent and Marga confirmed her earlier doubts that Viscount Trent was anything *but* the polite hero he was now portraying.

Her disappointment was somewhat softened by the realization that without the careful watch of Lady Atterberry, Jessica had no reason to be polite or patient with Viscount Trent.

"Well, then, I'm sure you'll want to be on your way."

"Oh, not at all. I'm actually looking forward to spending the evening with *you.*"

"I don't think that would be appropriate now that my grandparents have left. So if you'll—"

"My dear, certainly if your grandparents had thought it to be inappropriate, they would not have left me here, alone with you." He smiled, though it didn't reach his eyes.

Jessica fought to retain her calm. "Viscount Trent, apparently there are a great many things that my grandparents find appropriate that I do not. So, again, I would ask you to leave."

"But—"

"Now."

She sat in the formal parlor now, several hours after Viscount Trent's departure. The parlor was the only room left in the house which seemed to hold on to some of its formerly lush appointments; a room reserved just for entertaining important guests.

Jessica found a small pleasure in breaking one of her grandmother's rules and occupying the parlor on this, what she hoped was her last night here. The sooner she was away from her grandparents, who had turned out to be everything both Jacob and her father had said, the better.

Jessica shivered when she recalled the look of rage that had crossed Percival's face when she'd told him to leave. She put the book she'd been reading down on the sofa next to her.

I find it hard to believe that you would treat me this way, after all, I saved your life! You owe me! Viscount Trent's words echoed through her mind again.

Worry tugged at the back of her mind. She was alone here, save for the few servants and Ossie. Come to think of it, she hadn't seen any of the staff except for Milly since her grandparents had left.

Horse's hooves announced that someone was driving by on the street outside. But when they stopped in front of the house, she got up to look out the front windows.

On her way to the entry hall, she saw Ossie playing with his wooden soldiers. He'd 'set up camp' behind a group of potted plants in the corner of the parlor. Jessica smiled at the boy, then continued to the entry way.

Before she could reach the window the door slammed open, swinging back on its hinges and breaking out one of the windows.

She stood with her mouth open, staring at the intruder.

"Viscount Trent, what is the meaning of this? You should not be here!"

"Tsk, tsk. I assure you, my presence here would be greatly welcomed by your doting grandparents."

With great force he swung the door shut behind him, causing the remaining glass in the broken window to shatter on the floor.

"Oooh, I see you're ready to entertain me in the fancy parlor this evening. To what do I owe the pleasure?"

"To nothing! Get out of this house!"

Viscount Trent laughed evilly. "I don't think so, *ma petite*."

He grabbed her by the arm and shoved her into the parlor.

Jessica caught Ossie's eye and made a "sh" shape with her lips, imploring the child to stay hidden.

She turned to face Percival, surprise hitting her full force. "What did you just call me?"

Percival had removed his cloak and was unbuttoning his shirt as he answered. "I called you *ma petite*. It's a French sweet-name used for special loved ones." Viscount Trent's speech was thicker, and his fine British accent was all but gone.

"I know what it is, but I can't for the life of me see why you would use it on me. I have no desire to be your loved one. And just what the bloody hell do you think you're doing?"

He laughed and flung his shirt at Jessica's head, shoving her backwards until she lost her balance and fell to the couch.

"I am getting comfortable, *ma petite*," he said, stressing the last words, "and preparing to make you a loved one indeed."

Jessica pulled his shirt from over her head and in doing so noticed a sickly sweet odor. It was one she'd smelled before…

When she looked up at Percival again, ready to fire a string of fiery expletives, she stopped and choked on her own breath.

Percival was standing with his back to her, doing something on the table that she couldn't see. But that wasn't what had shocked her into immobility.

His back! He had a long curving scar down the left side of his back. The dressmaker's words came flooding back to her: *"through the key hole she could only see the man's back. There was a long curving scar on the left side...."*

Thoughts came rushing at her from all sides: that odor — she'd smelled it in the shack when DuPont had smoked that strange pipe. That scar. The pure revulsion that swept over her whenever Percival had fawned over her! That alone should have warned her, she thought with a mental kick to her backside.

She put the shirt down and stood slowly, not trusting her wobbly knees to take a step.

Quietly she whispered. "Jean — Luc — DuPont."

The man before her stiffened, his shoulders going rigid. Then slowly he turned to her, the odd pipe in his hand once again.

"Ah, so you've finally figured it out, *cherie*. I was wondering if you would," he said, dropping all traces of his phony British accent.

"But — but you're dead! I killed you!" Jessica choked out, not wanting to believe the truth that was being presented to her.

He chuckled cruelly, *"Non, non, cherie,* you killed poor Mully. I had him dress in my disguise so that I could fool you into believing that I, the magnificent Viscount Percival Trent had come to your rescue. The fact that you killed Mully during our staged fight truly did surprise me. Poor bastard. First I shot him in the shoulder to make it look authentic and then you proceed to stab him in the back. Rather ironic, really. I'm sorry to disappoint you. Many people would like to have the honor of taking my life. And such a triumph that would be for a little woman such as yourself!"

Her knees buckled and she sank to the sofa once again. "But you let me *kill* him, thinking it was you. And Horace, *you* killed Horace."

"Alas, Horace had served his purpose. He was growing soft,

too. I think if he'd had another day or two under your charms he would have helped you escape. So, I killed him. *C'est le vie!*"

DuPont lit the pipe and stood before her, inhaling the acrid smoke.

Jessica could see his eyes glaze over almost immediately.

DuPont caught her staring at the pipe. "Would you like some, Jessica? It truly enhances your senses."

"No! I would like you to leave."

Instead, DuPont joined her on the couch, draping one of his heavy legs across hers before she could move.

"But I don't want to leave. Now where was I? Oh yes, I was telling you how I intend to make you my loved one. Really, Jessica, you shouldn't fight it. It's so much more enjoyable if you don't. But alas, I intend to have you either way." He inhaled deeply from the pipe again.

Oh, God. He fully intended to rape her, and with Ossie right here in the room!

Suddenly she remembered how his mind had wandered the last time she'd seen him like this.

She leaned back on the couch, pretending to relax. "So tell me, Percival— "

"Please, don't burden me with that silly name. I am Jean Luc."

"Fine. Jean Luc. Just how deeply are my grandparents involved with you?"

"Oh, *beaucoup, cheri*. Very much so. You know, I've been acquainted with them for years. Your grandfather used to have the most wickedly sensuous gatherings. People, men *and* women, would come from far and wide to indulge in the sex games he would sponsor."

Jessica shook her head in disbelief. "That simply can't be. He's just a quiet old man, usually lost in his own thoughts."

Jean Luc paused, the pipe half way to his lips, and chuckled. "A quiet old man? Yes, I suppose he is… *now*. He used to have a rather voracious sexual appetite with a penchant for the bizarre. But a bit too much of this," he raised the pipe, "and a fondness for his brandy eventually caused him to, eh— how to put this? lose his fervor. After a few embarrassing episodes in which he was unable to rise to the occasion, he stopped hosting the parties to avoid further ridicule. A ruthless bunch, we were, turning on our host even as a pack of dogs would turn on its own leader if it was injured."

Jessica tried to ease Jean Luc's leg from her lap but he tensed and grabbed both of her hands in one of his large, strong ones. Doing her best to remain calm, she knew she had to keep him talking. Perhaps he would smoke himself into oblivion.

She turned her head to take a deep breath; the smoke from Jean Luc's pipe was making her just a little dizzy. "Surely my grandmother didn't allow this."

"Surely, your grandmother did. Your *grand-mere* came from very humble beginnings and didn't dare do anything that would anger your grandfather. He didn't force her to participate, and she never willingly did, either. But she was well aware of what went on in the west wing of this house every Saturday evening. The women coming and going, the men loud and boisterous. Ah, those were good days." Jean Luc drifted away for a moment. "It was there, you know, that I met Anastasia. Your deceased mother-in-law."

"My— she attended these— these gatherings?"

"Attended? Darling, she was usually the main attraction! Why on earth do you think that your grandmother hated the Callaways so? Anastasia made no secret about her affair with Hayden, much to the old duke's chagrin. And with a beauty such as hers, Hayden made no secret of the affair either, flaunted Anastasia right in front of your grandmother. Until, that is, Hayden became unable to perform. Then, fickle beauty that she was, Anastasia sought other forms of entertainment. Namely, me.

When Hayden lost his edge, there was a definite shift of power. Lady Atterberry vowed revenge on anyone bearing the

Callaway name, for she felt certain the partying had lasted as long as it did because of Anastasia. And Anastasia was the only paramour that Hayden had boldly displayed in public. Lady Atterberry, she took control everything. Alas, no more parties, no more fun. Everyone drifted apart, except for Anastasia and *moi..*"

Jean Luc lifted his pipe and pointed to the large portrait of Lord and Lady Atterberry. "Those poor fools. Whether it was the extravagant parties, the gaming tables or supporting ridiculous, radical politicians, they've managed to divest themselves of nearly all their money."

Jessica looked directly at Jean Luc. "And why would they stay in contact with you? What do you have to offer them?"

"Me? Well, everything, really. Actually, it was I who stayed in contact with them. I needed a desperate, aging man of title who would be willing to introduce me into society as Viscount Trent, a mysterious and wealthy man. I needed the position to get the information I sought and to be close to the men who are in positions to be of aid to me, unknowingly, of course."

"And my grandparents were just the people to do that?"

"*Oui.* In return, I give them enough money to live on, to keep this house operational."

Jessica felt her heart sinking. How could she have been so wrong about these people?

"So where do I fit into this sordid scheme? What could you possibly want from me?"

DuPont set the pipe on a table at the end of the couch. "Isn't it obvious what I want from you, my pet?" He drew his knuckles across her breasts and chuckled at the look of loathing she sent him as she slapped his hand away. "But besides that, I felt we could use you to get to your husband. Although I'll admit, you were not our first plan of action. No, you caught us all quite by surprise."

"And what was your first plan?" She just had to keep him talking!

"Why, Marga of course. She is a greedy bitch if ever I saw one. When your husband ended their relationship, she made such a fuss that Lady Atterberry saw a way to get back at Jacob. With very little persuasion, Marga decided to join us. We would all be winners. By making her out to be pregnant with your husband's child, she would get the duke, and we would get a direct line to his money via Marga."

Jessica's heart leapt. "So, she's not really pregnant?"

DuPont laughed. "Oh, she is very much pregnant. But with my child, not the Duke of Fairdale's. I must say though, that little mission was one of the most delightful I've had in a while. Until she started getting possessive." His mind wandered for a moment, but then he shook his head and continued.

"And then you came along. Threw our plans a bit askew at first. With the duke married before Marga could set her little trap, we were nearly defeated. But then we found out *who* he married. What a marvelous coincidence! Lord and Lady Atterberry's long-lost granddaughter. I thought it was time for a loving reunion."

"Then everything at the ball was a set-up. My grandparents' attentions, Marga's announcement. All of it."

"Correct."

Jessica's heart pounded as she asked the next question. "Then did Jacob really refuse to pay my ransom?"

DuPont sat in silence, enjoying the tension that was evident in Jessica's entire being. "Oh, hell. I suppose it doesn't matter now. No, he didn't refuse. How could he? I never demanded it. You see, if we made you think he didn't want you, we knew you'd come willingly to your grandparents. And if we let him think you'd come *here* willingly, well his rather large ego would eventually have to try and get you back. And that, of course, would only be accomplished with large sums of money settled upon your grandparents. You see, I'm growing bored with supporting your grandparents and to be honest, my own reserves are beginning to feel the strain."

She let her breath out, relief coursing through her body. Jacob hadn't abandoned her!

Dupont moved closer to her on the couch, settling on Jessica's skirt so that she was unable to move away. He reached under her legs and and tried to pull her into his lap.

She pressed her hands against his chest. "One more question."

DuPont sigh, bored now with the small talk. "What?"

"Why didn't you just ask him for the ransom?"

"Two reasons, really. First, a ransom is a one-time payment. After that, I'd have to kidnap you all over again to get any more," he said with a humorless smile. "And that would be dangerous. The second reason is that I truly had no idea how much or even *if* he would pay for you. From all appearances at the ball, you two were not on the best of terms. It wasn't until I saw the two of you in the library that I realized he had some emotion for you; even if it was only lust. Having you here with your grandparents gave me more time to plot my next moves. But enough talk. I find that reminiscing about that scene I witnessed in the library has brought my own desire to a fevered pitch. Come, Jessica. You are mine!"

DuPont leaned over to pull her into his lap, but as he did so Jessica gathered all her strength and pushed off of him. She rolled off his lap and to the floor scrambling to get up.

"Run, Ossie! Get out of here! Hide!"

Jessica saw Ossie run to the front door and heard it open before DuPont landed on her with full force.

With all her might, she fought him, kicking and scratching and screaming with every ounce of strength she had.

But it was no use. DuPont was not only unaffected by her, but was laughing at her futile struggles.

He bent his head towards her, seeking to capture her mouth.

"*Nooooo!*" she screamed.

On the front steps, Ossie heard his Jessica cry out. He turned and ran down the front steps as fast as his little feet would carry him. For the first time in nearly a year, a cry escaped the little boy's mouth.

Jacob was staring out the window of the coach, trying to figure out just what he'd say to Jessica when he saw her.

His thoughts were interrupted by the cry of a child. "Giles! Stop!" Without waiting for the coach to come to a complete stop, Jacob leapt out and ran for the sidewalk.

Ossie saw him and recognized him immediately. The little boy ran as fast as he could to Jacob's outstretched arms.

"Ossie! Ossie! What is it?" Jacob asked, forgetting for the moment that the child didn't speak.

But suddenly Ossie opened his mouth and squeaked out, "Pease! Help my Jesse! The bad man hurts her! John Luke!"

"What?" Jacob asked. He set the boy on the ground.

Ossie pointed to the Atterberry's house and repeate the name just as Jessica had, "John-Luc-DuPont! He hurts my Jesse!"

"Giles, take the boy with you and bring the authorities back here!"

He handed Ossie over to Giles and ran to the house, now hearing Jessica's screams from inside. He crashed through the front door and followed her cries into the parlor.

"DuPont!" Jacob yelled, "Let go of my wife!"

"Jacob!" Jessica cried out through her tears.

DuPont looked up from where he had Jessica pinned on her back, his hand at her bodice about to rip it open.

In DuPont's altered state of mind, he was having trouble assimilating the fact that his object of prey, the Duke of Fairdale, was standing at the door.

Jacob didn't wait for DuPont to comply. He ran forward and kicked DuPont squarely in the chin, sending him arching up and backwards off of Jessica.

Jessica rolled and scrambled to her feet, watching in disbelief as Jacob picked DuPont completely off the floor and threw him across the room where he landed very nearly in the fireplace.

To their disbelief, DuPont rose, and when he did he grabbed the fireplace poker from its stand. He wiped blood from the corner of his mouth and looked at the stain it made on his hand.

"So we meet at last, Jacob, with no false names as a pretense. It's too bad you interrupted us, for I was just about to enjoy yet another female member of your family. I had high hopes that she would outperform your mother." The smile left his face as he continued. "And I will finish my enjoyment of her after I kill you."

He lunged at Jacob with the sharp poker.

Jacob jumped back and leapt to one side. Again DuPont swung at Jacob, this time barely connecting with Jacob's ribs.

Jessica screamed as DuPont went on the attack again.

This time Jacob side-stepped him and threw his elbow into DuPont's back. When DuPont sprawled on the floor, Jacob jumped on his back and slipped his arm around DuPont's throat.

"I'll kill you for what you did to my brother, and my wife!"

DuPont was gasping for air, but managed to grab a small statue from the floor in front of him. He swung it backwards at Jacob's head.

Jacob ducked in time to miss it, but it released his hold enough on DuPont that DuPont was able to get to his feet. He lunged at Jacob who was still rising and caught him around the waist.

Both men went crashing onto the sofa which tipped over and toppled the men to the floor. Jacob managed to land on top and straddled DuPont, his hands finding DuPont's throat and closing tightly around them.

A red haze floated before Jacob's eyes as he strangled the life from DuPont. So many years of hate and vengeance were finally being released.

"Jacob! Jacob! Wait, man! Don't kill him!" From somewhere far away he heard his name being called, felt a strong hand on his shoulder.

Of a sudden, his vision cleared and he became aware that the room was full of men.

A royal soldier pulled Jacob to his feet and moved him away from DuPont. He looked around the room, several more soldiers, the Prime Minister, and three fellow members of Parliament were in the room, including Malcom.

Malcom stepped forward and took Jacob by the shoulders. "Are you all right, Jacob?"

"Yes, yes." He looked back at DuPont who had recovered only slightly. He was being hoisted to his feet, surrounded by soldiers on all sides.

The Prime Minister stepped forward. "We owe you a world of thanks, Jacob. As you know, we've been after this bastard for a long time."

"I'm sure no one will like to see justice done more than you."

When the Prime Minister turned to leave, Jacob turned quickly to Malcom. "Where's Jessica?"

"I—I'm here," she sobbed, curled up in the corner by the plants.

In three quick strides he was by her side, lifting her into his arms.

She threw her arms around his neck and held on to him as if she'd never let go. With a start, she looked up. "Ossie! We've got to find Ossie!"

"I assure you, he's safe. He's with Giles in the coach outside. He was the one who warned me that you were in trouble. He *told* me."

Jessica's brown wrinkled in confusion. "He—he told you? But he can't—"

"Yes, he can talk. I guess it just took a matter of urgency, and a little encouragement from his big brother to bring it out of him."

"His—his brother? Then you know everything?"

Jacob walked to the only chair in the room that was still upright. "I know almost everything. Jessica, why did you leave me? I didn't give you a chance to explain yourself about Ossie, but knowing how much trouble that caused, why didn't you at least let me try to explain about Marga?"

Jessica managed a small smile through her tears. "I intended to do just that, eventually. After I'd calmed down and had come up with a few choice names for you. But after I left the ball, my coach was attacked by DuPont."

The rest of the story tumbled from her lips and Jacob tensed each time she mentioned DuPont.

He hated to ask, he shouldn't ask, not that it made any difference, but...."Jesse, did he ever...."

Jessica looked deeply into his eyes. "No, he didn't. But if you hadn't come in right when you did, he would have."

The sound of little footsteps sounded in the hall as Ossie, flanked by Giles and Malcom, entered the room.

"My Jesse!" he shouted as he ran and climbed up Jacob's legs settling himself on Jessica's lap. "Can we go home now, with Jake? Pease, Jesse. I like being with Jake."

Jessica smiled up at Jacob. "I guess that's up to him. Well, Jake?" she teased, using Ossie's version of his name.

Without taking his eyes from Jessica, he nodded. "Of course. And I'll be damned if I'll ever let either of you out of my sight again!"

Epilogue

Jessica looked up from her cross-stitch work and set the fabric in her lap. A warmth spread over her, which was not caused by the warm August sun, as she gazed upon her husband playing with their son on a large blanket on the grass.

Harwood James Callaway, called Jamie by the family, had been born two months earlier, yet even now, Jessica felt a sense of wonder when she looked upon him.

Jessica closed her eyes and lifted her face to the sun. At times she had to remind herself that this wasn't just a dream, that she and Jacob and Ossie and Jamie really lived in this wonderful, peaceful world at Fairdale.

Wandering slowly through her memories, Jessica shivered as she recalled the date.

"What is it, Jess?" Jacob asked when he saw her peaceful expression change to a frown.

Jessica looked over at him and smiled to ease his worry. "I was just thinking of the date today. It's been one year today since DuPont was hanged."

Jacob's face clouded for a moment as well. "A year. It doesn't seem long enough since we last saw that bastard. I'm glad he's finally gone, but I still can't believe how long it took to convict him."

"Well, it wasn't just our circumstance that had to be dealt with. It was bound to take time to investigate the numerous charges brought against him. At least you were able to speak out for Colin's death. You must feel some ease knowing that he was found guilty for that and for your mother's death as well."

"I suppose you're right," Jacob said.

Mrs. Holmes approached them with a smile on her face. "Oh, I just love it when it's Jamie's nap time. It means I get to hold him again!"

Jacob and Jessica both smiled as the little housekeeper took their son and went into the house.

Jessica laid down on the blanket, reaching up to cup Jacob's face in her hand.

"What do you suppose ever happened to my grandparents?"

Jacob grimaced. "I don't know and I don't care."

"I really don't either," Jessica said. "But still, it's odd that no one has heard from them since the day you rescued me. Do you think DuPont had ordered them killed?"

"Perhaps. Or he may have just threatened them. Hayden didn't have enough backbone to stand up to his own wife, let alone a madman like DuPont."

"I suppose we'll never know."

"With any luck," Jacob said.

"Jesse! Jakey!"

Jessica and Jacob waved to Ossie who sat proudly upon his new pony. Milly, the maid they'd rescued from the Atterberrys, stood by nervously, wringing her hands and watching her little charge.

"Blime, Master Ossie! Ye better hold on with both hands!" Milly cried out.

Jessica looked back to Jacob. "Did you ever imagine yourself being a part of such a boring, normal family?" she teased.

Jacob chuckled. "Normal, perhaps. But boring? I've yet to have a boring moment since I met you and Ossie."

Jacob leaned forward and kissed her deeply. He was amazed at how Jessica could still make the blood rush through his veins, still bring desire flooding over him with a simple touch.

When at last their lips parted, Jessica looked down at the top button on his shirt and toyed with it absently. Without meeting his eyes she asked, "Jacob, do you ever have any regrets about us? About the way we came to be together? Your life is so very different now."

Jacob took her chin in his fingers, forcing her to look up at him.

"Jessica, I bless the day my father bade me to uphold his honor and keep his word to James Patrick. You and Ossie and Jamie have made my life complete. With no regrets, I am bound to you for life. Bound by honor, bound by love."

——The End——

Printed in the United States
35891LVS00005B/46-357

9 781413 759105